P9-BWY-901

More praise for Dewey Lambdin and his hero, Alan Lewrie

"I am such an enormous fan of the informed, superbly paced, witty adventures of Dewey Lambdin's Alan Lewrie, who is no better than he should be, that I found myself at a bookstore trying to plunk down cash for the next in the series six months before it was to be published."
—GREGORY MCDONALD
Author of *Fletch*

"We get a great taste of British naval life and some marvelous combat on the high seas. . . . Alan Lewrie [is] a raunchy hero who always fights the great fight and escapes death to swashbuckle another day. . . . No doubt he is on his way to an admiralship in future books, but it is enough to take them one at a time and follow this boy's career. Hornblower he ain't, and thank goodness for that."
—*Lincoln Journal-Star*

"Fascinating . . . A salty, bawdy sea story that will delight fans of the historical action novel."
—*Library Journal*

By Dewey Lambdin:

THE
KING'S
COMMISSION

*The Naval Adventures of
Alan Lewrie*

Dewey Lambdin

BALLANTINE BOOKS • NEW YORK

A Fawcett Book
Published by The Random House Publishing Group
Copyright © 1991 by Dewey Lambdin

Published in the United States by Fawcett Books, an imprint of The Random House Publishing Group, a division of Random House, Inc., New York, and distributed in Canada by Random House of Canada Limited, Toronto.

FAWCETT is a registered trademark and the Fawcett colophon is a trademark of Random House, Inc.

ISBN 978-0-449-22452-6

This edition published by arrangement with Donald I. Fine, Inc.

Printed in the United States of America

First Ballantine Books Edition: March 1996

OPM 15 14 13 12 11 10 9 8

This One's For
Marrin & Mary Delle Fleet in Memphis

We shot our way through Memphis for years when we were all in television production, and sailed our way into more "white-knuckle" experiences than I can shake a stick at. By now they must feel like part-owners in *Wind Dancer*, one long splice at a time.

And to both my ex-wives;
Don't flatter yourselves—neither one of you is in this.

"He rises fastest who knows not whither he is going."
—attributed to
Oliver Cromwell

Foreword

Before diving right into Alan Lewrie's latest naval adventure (if one may do so without besmirching one's own fine sense of honor by exposing it to such a rogue), it might be a good idea to discover just exactly who in the hell this Alan Lewrie character was.

Of course, for those of you with a taste for stirring action and some salacious wenching, you may plunge right on to Chapter One and elide this brief *curriculum vitae*. But for the more inquisitive reader unfamiliar with the previous accounts about our nautical hero, a reader not entirely taken in by splashy dust jackets and titillating blurb copy, believe me, this chronicler understands your plight. You have found this tome, and it sounded as though it might contain scads of blood and thunder, shivering tops'ls and timbers (as in shiver *me* timbers, mate), lots of derring-do, and some naughty bits tucked into the odd corner, but it's a wrench trying to pick up on the middle release of a whole series of nautical adventure in mid-tack, as our protagonist has learned to say at this stage of his career.

So allow me to condense this young Corinthian's past for you before getting into all the sex, swords and sailing ships (not necessarily in that order). I look upon it as a public duty. After all, did C. S. Forester do this for you? No, you had to wait for *The Hornblower Companion*. Did Sherlock Holmes ever have a biography, or did you have to search for clues in the works themselves?

Alan Lewrie was born on Epiphany, 1763, in St. Martin's In The Fields Parish, London. His mother Elizabeth Lewrie passed away soon after this "blessed event" and he began life a bastard in the parish poor-house (quite appropriately, since the sobriquet of "you little bastard" was said about him by quite a few people in his life).

1766—Rescued from the orphanage and poor-house, ending a promising career of oakum-picking and flax-pounding, for no apparent good reason by his true father, Sir Hugo St. George Willoughby of St. James Parish, St. James Square (unfortunately not the good side), Knight of the Garter, ex-captain 4th Regiment of Foot (The King's Own), member White's, Almack's, Hell-Fire Club and the Society for the Diminution of the Spread of Venereal Diseases.

There is a long biographical gulf between 1766 and 1776 for lack of information, but since most childhoods are wretchedly uninteresting, who bloody cares?

1776—The American Colonies rebel. Alan Lewrie discovers what a goose-girl will do for a shilling, and chamber-maids and mop-squeezers may do for free if one can only run fast enough to catch them.

1777—Entered into Westminster School, obviously to get him out of the neighborhood, instead of being tutored at home with his half-sister Belinda and half-brother Gerald. Expelled same year for licentious behavior, though he did post some decent marks.

1778—Entered Eton, expelled Eton, see above.

1779—Entered Harrow, expelled Harrow. As above, but with the codicil that he was implicated in a plot to blow up the Governor's coach house in youthful admiration for the Gunpowder Plot. There was no mention in the school records of licentious behavior this time, so we must assume that such goings-on were not taken as seriously at Harrow as at other places in those days.

1780—Nabbed *in flagrante delicto* with his aforementioned half-sister Belinda Willoughby. For once, this incident was not his fault (well, not totally, anyway). Booted from the bosom (so to speak) of his family with one hundred guineas a year and told never to show his face in Society or the family digs again. Turned over to an officer of the Navy Impress Service and entered the Royal Navy as a midshipman, in Portsmouth.

January 10, 1780, signed aboard HMS *Ariadne*, 3rd Rate, sixty-four guns, Capt. Ezekiel Bales. Seven months Atlantic convoy duties. During this time, he became, believe it or not, a passably competent midshipman, which says volumes for the return of corporal punishment in schools and flogging as a spur to proper naval discipline.

July 1780—*Ariadne* fights a bloody battle with a disguised

Spanish two-decked ship, and upon arrival at Antigua in the Leeward Islands is adjudged too damaged to repair. Her captain and
first officer are court-martialed for her loss, the third officer for
cowardice. None of this was Alan Lewrie's fault, either. In fact,
he acquitted himself well under fire on the lower gun deck and
won some small fame for his coolness in action (though readers
of *The King's Coat* remember his behavior differently, especially
his wish to go below and hide among the rum casks).

August 1780—Appointed midshipman into HM Sloop *Parrot*,
Lt. James Kenyon master and commander. There followed five
months of enjoyable duties wenching and swilling all over the
Caribbean and Atlantic coast.

January 1781—A new personal best of two older ladies in
Kingston, Jamaica, in two days, but, during a week on passage
for Antigua, he (1) became second officer when almost everyone
senior went down with Yellow Fever; (2) saved the ship from a
French privateer brig, burning her to the waterline in the process; (3) saved a titled Royal Commissioner and his lady who
were their passengers; (4) almost had the leg over the lady; and
(5) came down with Yellow Fever himself (a damned trying
week, in all).

February–March 1781—Recovering on Antigua, then staff-
serf to Rear Adm. Sir Onsley Matthews. Met, wooed and fell in
thrall with the admiral's niece, Miss Lucy Beauman. Fought a
duel for her honor (her family was *awfully* rich), killed his op-
ponent, and was posted to sea before he could say "Jack-Ketch."

April 1781 to present—Midshipman into HM Frigate *Desperate*, 6th Rate, twenty guns, Comdr. Tobias Treghues (one of
God's own cuckoos). Several successful raiding cruises, raid on
the Danish Virgin Islands, many prizes taken. Battle of The
Chesapeake, Siege of Yorktown (from which he escaped, or we
wouldn't be following his career any longer, would we?). Evac-
uation of Wilmington, North Carolina, November 1781 (see *The
French Admiral*). Made acting master's mate, confirmed in December 1781.

One might just mention in passing a smallish theft from a
captured French prize, a trifling sum, really, of, oh, some two
thousand guineas, more *ren contres* with young ladies of the
willing or commercial persuasion just to keep his hand (so to
speak) in, and one surprisingly chaste bout of amour with a pen-
niless young Loyalist, a Miss Caroline Chiswick. Chaste perhaps
because he had served ashore with her two Tory soldier-brothers
and knew what he could expect if he ever ran into them in a

dark alley; chaste perhaps because there's damned few places to put the leg over even the most obliging female aboard a man o' war; or chaste perhaps because he had seen The Light, become a better person for his service in the Navy, and really did like her and through her found a new respect for Womankind and—but no, we have deduced a pattern here, and a man's usually true to his nature when the blood's up, damme if he ain't.

One more annoyingly minor matter of biographical *minutia* before we proceed to the flashy stuff (and I promise broadsides before *you* can say "Jack-Ketch"). The alleged rape of his half-sister was discovered to be a theatric staged by his father Sir Hugo to gain unlimited access to a positive shower of guineas from the Lewrie side of the family, but Sir Hugo was diddled in return by Alan's grandmother who obstinately refused to go toes-up at the proper moment, and Alan Lewrie ended up smelling like Hungary Water with two hundred pounds per annum remittance. Since this last involves so much stupendously boresome legal mustification, we hope the reader will appreciate the chronicler cutting that short, as he goes bleary pondering the matter himself.

Acknowledgments

It would be impossible for me to begin an Alan Lewrie adventure without the assistance of the U.S. Naval Institute and its reference books—such as John Harland's *Seamanship in the Age of Sail*, to mention one of many—and the staff of the History Department of the U.S. Naval Academy. To them, my many thanks.

For details about Turk's Island and Horatio Nelson I am grateful to Mr. Iain MacKenzie of the National Maritime Museum in Greenwich, England, who was kind enough to dig up lieutenants' journals and material from contemporary accounts, such as *Schomberg's Naval Chronology* and *Beatson's Naval and Military Memoirs*.

I would also like to thank Derek Rooke of Memphis, Tennessee, who culled a lot of material for me. I had to repay him by being his only crew when he wanted to race his thirty-three foot sloop, which is the sort of long, painful and humiliating tale I'd rather not go into, ever, even if we did come in seventh in a class of twenty-eight boats.

Clenell Wilkinson's biography, *Nelson*, provided good insight into the famous admiral's personality. Thanks also to Mr. Herbert Sadler of Grand Turk Island, The Turks and Caicos, who serves as historian to the islands.

John Richard Alden's *The South in the Revolution* and Gloria Jahoda's *Florida, A History* provided details on the role of the Southeastern Indian tribes in the Revolution. A debt must be expressed as well to Charles Hudson's excellent one-volume treatise, *The Southeastern Indians*, for the wealth of information on the social life, customs and language of the Creek and Seminole tribes.

I

"It is confessed by all that from his youth he was of a vehement and impetuous nature, of a quick apprehension, and of a strong and aspiring bent for action and for great affairs."

Life of Themistocles
—Plutarch

Chapter 1

The French fleet made a brave sight to leeward, twenty-nine massive ships of the line bearing up toward the smaller British fleet on a bow and quarter line, their gunports gaping and filled with hard iron maws, the white-and-gold battle flags of Bourbon France streaming in the moderate winds, and their halyards bedecked with signal bunting.

"If this is going to be anything like the Chesapeake battle, we're about to get our arses knackered," master's mate and midshipman Alan Lewrie observed sourly, comparing the twenty-two English vessels against that bellicose spectacle to the west.

"Frogs like ta fight ta loo'ard," said Mr. Monk, the sailing master, shrugging as he worked on a bite of half-shriveled apple. "But we got 'em this time. Cain't work ta windward of us ta double."

Monk waved a stray hand at the shore close aboard to the east past which they barely scraped. Nevis Island ghosted by, crowding the disengaged-side frigates such as *Desperate* up close to the battle line.

"Un you'll note, young Lewrie, the wind's a prodigy ta loo'ard of an island," Monk went on. "Got a kink in the Trades here that'll bear us along on a nice quarter wind. Too close into shore yonder an' we'd be winded by the hills o' Nevis. Too far out as well, but winds come slidin' down the hills and touch water out here where we are. See how yon French are luffin' and fillin' ta keep station further out? Too far out for this little river o' wind we're ridin'. Second lee."

"If the battle line crowds us much more, we'll be winded, sir," Alan observed, noting the strip of azure waters that was shoaling and shallows close aboard to starboard. "Even if we don't run her aground we'll end up in the island's lee under

3

those bluffs. Last in line of the repeating frigates. Last in line for pretty much everything since Yorktown, too."

"Can't go spoilin' the admiral's dinner with our stink, Lewrie," Monk spat—literally and figuratively, for he wandered over to the binnacle to fire a dollop of tobacco juice at the spit kid. How the man could eat and swallow fruit, and reserve his quid in the other cheek, almost made Alan ill just contemplating the feat.

"Wasn't our fault we escaped, Mister Monk," Alan said, going to the wheel to join him and peer into the compass bowl.

"Lord Cornwallis give us verbal orders we could try sailin' outa York River, nothin' in writin', see, Mister Lewrie?" Monk smiled with a weary expression. "Whole army goes inta the sack, titled *gentlemen* imprisoned'r on their parole for the duration. America lost, and us come out with a whole skin. A damn fine feat o' seamanship gettin' down river an' outa the Chesapeake under Cape Charles, even on a fine day'd be cause fer praise, if you'll allow me t'boast a mite. Night as black as a boot, a whole gale blowin', it'd get most young captains a bloody knighthood. But them dominee-do-littles up in New York sat on their hands an' swore what a damn shame it was losin' the army an' all our other ships, well . . . it'll take a piece o' time, er somethin' ta rub the shite off'n our boots fer their likes."

"For what we are about to receive, may the Good Lord make us grateful," Comdr. Tobias Treghues, *Desperate*'s master and commander said as the French fleet began to open fire at long range. With the wind carrying the sound of cannonading to leeward, it sounded no more dangerous than the thumping of pillows, and the sour grey-tan wall of smoke climbed above the bulwarks and lower masts of the enemy ships, to be ragged away to the west. Admiral Hood's ships began to return fire, and their view of the proceedings was obscured as great billows of expended powder blotted out the sky.

"Now we'll give those French, and this de Grasse, a proper English quilting," Treghues prophecied with a tight, superior grin.

Not bloody likely, Alan thought. They had been at the Battle of The Chesapeake, where this self-same Admiral de Grasse had snatched victory from a budding disaster, and the British admirals, including Hood who now commanded their fleet, had stood about in stupefaction until there was nothing left to do but call if off. Hood had kept back the strongest division of the com-

bined Leeward Islands and North American fleets, never even
fired a ranging shot all day, and *Desperate* had been trapped in
Chesapeake Bay at the siege of Yorktown, and Alan nearly lost
his life ashore; had stood with the Army expecting the Navy to
return and break the siege and save the men before they had
been forced to surrender. It need hardly be said that Alan Lewrie
had a low opinion of Admiral Hood's reputed fighting qualities.
In point of fact, he also had a rather low opinion of a naval career, since it wasn't his choice in the first place, but everyone
knew that by now, which took the bite out of any carping he
might have done in the privacy of his midshipmen's mess.

They had had a hard dash south under a full press of sail for
Barbados to carry word to Hood that the island of St. Kitts had
been invaded by de Grasse and the French on the eleventh of
January. Hood had sailed for Antigua to pick up seven hundred
or so troops, all that could be spared, and then made a fast passage to round the southern shore of Nevis, the twin island to St.
Kitts, to confront the French, dragging *Desperate* in the fleet's
train like a barely tolerated relative.

Yesterday had been thought to be the day of decision, but all
they had accomplished by their presence was to draw this massive Frog fleet out of its anchorage out to sea off Basse Terre.
Rumor had it that Hood had wanted to sail right in and fire into
the anchored ships, as they should have at The Chesapeake, but
that had been postponed.

Once more, this de Grasse had been given a heaven-sent
chance to escape the massacre of his fleet. The last time, he had
destroyed any last chance to recover the Colonies. Would his
luck hold, and would they begin to lose the fabulously wealthy
Sugar Islands now?

"They's a gap!" Monk pointed out with alarm in his voice.

"Oh my dear Lord," Treghues whispered, more a short prayer
than a curse, for he was a fanatic when it came to quelling the
English sailor's easy penchant for blasphemy. "*Prudent*'s never
been a fast sailer."

Prudent, a seventy-four-gunned 3rd Rate, fourth from the rear
of the British line, had not been able to keep up to the speed of
her consorts, and the ships behind her were backing and filling
to avoid running her down and tangling their yards in collision.
Part of the French line, led by the massive three-decker flagship
Ville de Paris, de Grasse's own ship, bore up to close in and
penetrate. It would be the beginning of a disaster.

Alan couldn't watch—he'd been there before—and made his

way to the starboard side to stand by midshipmen Avery and Burney, who had been relegated by duty to a poor view of the proceedings.

"Mister Lewrie," Avery said coolly, echoed a second later by the startlingly beautiful Burney.

"Avery, Burney," Lewrie replied, touching a finger to the brim of his cocked hat to return their salutes. Avery had been his best and nearly only friend in the Navy, especially on *Desperate*, until Alan had returned from the debacle at The Chesapeake and had been appointed an acting master's mate. They had caterwauled together, schemed together and shared almost all of their innermost thoughts, but now they were separated by the gulf between a junior warrant officer and a midshipman, though Alan knew that if he well and truly fucked up in his new posting, he could end up swinging a hammock in the cockpit with David Avery and Burney in the blink of an eye.

"Goddamn my eyes, I hope they brought a good lunch," Alan spat as he looked shoreward. At the last and most westward point of land above Fort Charles on Nevis, quite a crowd had gathered, treating the naval battle like a spectator sport and an excuse for a feast.

"Civilians, sir," Avery agreed with a properly naval scowl of displeasure.

"May they get an eyeful, sir!" Burney said with some heat.

Alan didn't know quite what to make of Burney; he was sixteen, had a good kit and was obviously from money, but he was so keen, nautical and unfailingly of good cheer that Alan felt his skin crawl every time he was around him. Little get's got a fiddle, he thought suspiciously, as was Lewrie's usual wont. Besides, Burney was so beautiful in a manly, gentlemanly way, his features so clear and well-formed, that Alan felt like throwing shoes at him. Where were the usual boils, the pimples of a teenaged midshipman—God help, he didn't even half stink like most people. It was uncanny.

"At 'em *Canada*!" Treghues enthused. "Would that Lord Cornwallis had shown half the bottom of his brother Captain Cornwallis yonder!"

The next ship ahead of *Prudent* had shivered her tops'ls and lost way to seal the gap against the French probe, and the two ships ahead of the gallant *Canada*—*Resolution* and *Bedford*—had also slowed down to form a solid wall of oak and iron to frustrate their foes.

"Foiled, aha!" Treghues laughed, another sign of incipient

madness to Alan's lights. Comdr. The Hon. Tobias Treghues had been a straight-laced prig of the worst blue-stocking sort at first, but between a head injury the year before, a "slight" trephination by the ship's surgeon, and a course of medication consisting of a rare South American weed that Dr. Dorne referred to as *Nicotiana Glauca* (taken in wine and smoked), he was as fickle now as some young miss. He had made Alan's life a living hell, then half a joy, then again a hell as his moods shifted. Now he seemed favorably disposed to Lewrie, but one never knew, and Alan missed the security of knowing that he was either a hopelessly lost cause or some nautical paragon to be praised and lauded to the skies; and to the Admiralty, which was more useful for a career.

Sensing that Treghues was safe enough to approach this day without fear of being bitten, Alan wandered back past the wheel and the binnacle to the larboard side, after pausing to check the quartermasters on the wheel, the compass bearing, and the set of the sails.

"Bosun, we're nigh past the last of Nevis. Be prepared at the braces to take the wind abeam," Alan cautioned.

"Aye, Mister Lewrie," Coke grumbled, disliking to be told his duties by a jumped-up younker, but forbearing philosophically.

"Wonder if they left anything in the anchorage?" Lieutenant Railsford asked, plying a telescope northward toward the western-most point of land below St. Kitts' main-town, Basse Terre, and the anchorage in Frigate Bay.

"If they did, they'd best shift 'em afore ya kin say 'Jack-Puddin',' " Monk opined, "er we'll be among 'em a'sharin' out some solid-shot grief. We're head-reachin' the devils, damned if we ain't."

Desperate leaned a bit as the wind shifted, bringing their collective attention inboard, away from the engagement before them.

"Hands to the braces, Mister Coke!" Lieutenant Railsford ordered. "By God, this'll put a bone in our teeth!"

With the fresher airs playing between St. Kitts and Nevis down the narrow mile and a half channel, their small frigate began to fly, as did the larger ships of the line, leaving the leeward vessels in the French line behind, still caught in a pocket of stiller air to Nevis' lee. Even *Prudent* was catching up handily now.

"Now what's de Grasse done wrong here today?" Treghues demanded of his officers, once the ship was fully under control

and the braces had been belayed by the waisters along the gangways above the guns. "Avery?"

"Abandoned his anchorage, sir," Avery said brightly.

"Burney?"

"He doesn't seem too eager to close us, sir, and fight at close
pistol-shot," Burney piped up, the eager student. "And he
stranded himself out in the second lee of the island before making his approach."

"Lewrie, you're the student of that fellow named Clerk, what
do you say?" Treghues asked, and Alan flinched recalling the
last time he had dared to open his mouth back in September
about Clerk's tactics book.

"If he wanted to fight, sir, he could have defended his anchorage, or backed and filled during the night much closer towards
St. Kitts, sir," Alan surmised. "Starting that far to the suth'rd
and out to sea from us, he practically gave it away. And he
could have pushed through the gap *Prudent* made if he'd tried."

"Has Admiral Hood made any mistakes yet?" Treghues went
on, loving his role of experienced teacher to his neophyte officers.

"He almost abandoned the last four or five ships, sir," Burney
ventured. "But it was more important to get on north to St.
Kitts."

"Very good, sirs, very good." Treghues nodded with a pleasant smile and strolled away with his hands clasped in the small
of his back.

Hood had indeed head-reached on the suddenly baffled
French, and as they watched, and the afternoon of January 25
wore on, Hood's line-of-battle ships gained the anchorage,
swung east and anchored in line-ahead from almost the reefs of
Frigate Bay stretching back west to seaward, blocking the
French from entry into their former anchorage. *Desperate* had to
snake her way between the heavier 3rd Rates as they rounded up
to anchor, passing to the disengaged side through the battle line,
which was the proper station for frigates to find safety once
more inside the screen of larger ships.

"Find us good holding ground to leeward, Mister Monk,"
Treghues said. "We shall anchor west and north of the last ships
in the line of battle."

"Charts show thirty fathom there'bouts, sir," Monk replied after a long squint at one of his heavily creased and much
doodled-upon charts. "Soft sand un mud, though, not good
holdin' ground. Hard coral 'bout a mile closer ta shore, though."

"We could fetch to, sir," Lieutenant Railsford suggested. "If there is a threat, we'd be caught putting put a kedge anchor from the stern and not have the springs ready."

"Anybody ta loo'ard o' us'd take the devil's own time beatin' up ta windward ta get at us, though," Monk chuckled. "We *might* have time ta put out the kedge un bower, un get springs on the cables."

"Or get caught anchored by a 3rd Rate, sir," Alan stuck in to try the waters. It was not *Desperate*'s place, or function in life, to become an immobile target for a larger ship that could blow holes in her.

"Hard to get a bower up out of soft sand and mud," Treghues speculated audibly. "Very well, bring her to, Mister Railsford. Back the mizzen tops'l and shift the head sheets."

With the foresails cocked up to produce forward motion, and the square-sails laid aback or furled to the yards to retard her, *Desperate* "fetched-to," her helm hard over as though she were trying to tack and had been caught in irons by a capricious shift of wind, drifting slowly and making barely discernible sternway, to all intents at a dead stop.

"Stand the hands down from Quarters, Mister Railsford," Treghues ordered as eight bells chimed from the belfry at the break of the fo'c'sle, ending the afternoon watch and beginning the first dog-watch at 4 P.M.

"Cooks to light the galley fires, sir?" Railsford asked. It took time to develop enough heat under the steep-tubs so the rations could be boiled up, and the first dog was the usual time to start cooking.

"Not yet, not until we are sure we shall not be called upon to engage should a foe break the leeward end of the line," the captain said, frowning. "I'll not risk fire aboard until dusk. There's still daylight enough to do something glorious."

Freed of the tedium of duty, Alan betook himself below after one last lungful of fresh, clean Trade-Wind air. Below decks in the cockpit it would be a close and humid fog of humanity's reeks. The day had been pleasantly warm, and the wind bracing, and his nostrils pinched at the aromas of a ship when he reached his tiny dog-box of a cabin. Pea soup farts, armpits, unwashed bodies and rancid clothing, the garbage-midden stink of the bilges and holds where cheeses, bread-bags, dried beans and peas slowly rotted, where kegs of salt meat slowly fermented in brine.

"Got you, you bastard!" he exulted as he managed to mash a

large roach with his shoe at the foot of the accommodation ladder. At least half a dozen more scurried from sight.

He tossed his cocked hat onto the peg above his cot, peeled off his tail-coat, and almost tore the stock from his throat to open his collar, oblivious to the continual booming and thudding of artillery that still roared between the two opposing fleets.

"Freeling, fetch a bucket of seawater," Alan demanded past the flimsy lath and canvas door to his cabin. Indeed, the whole dog-box afforded nothing more than the semblance of privacy, framed out in light deal and canvas that could be struck down before battle.

"Coomin' zurr," the mournful Freeling intoned joylessly, sounding even more put-upon than normal. Alan had finally gotten the man's measure, and was no longer in thrall to the cockpit servant's truculent behavior, as he had been when still merely a midshipman.

Once the water arrived, Alan took down a mildewed rag, sniffed at it and thought it could do for a few more days, then soaked it in the seawater and stripped to scrub himself down. Aboard a ship of war, the water was rationed at a gallon a day per man and officer, but not much of that went for washing or drinking; most of it was used in the steep-tubs to boil food. Personal consumption for cleanliness or shaving was limited to a pint a man, and most people found drinking the small-beer or wine more palatable than ship's water after it had been in cask for a few weeks, for it usually turned whiskey-brown, stained by the oak casks or the animalcules that grew in it. It was best when used to dilute rum or wine, which killed the brackish taste. Certainly, seawater made you itch all over, and one developed rashes and boils from constant exposure, but that was a sailor's lot. Besides, everybody itched and scratched constantly, even ashore. At least ships were free (for the most part, anyway) of lice, fleas and ticks.

"Ah, that feels good," Alan whispered, working up a slight lather from a stub of soap cake he had purchased in Wilmington. He would be sorry when it was finally gone, for in his lengthy shore service with the Army at Yorktown during the siege, one of his few pleasures was a soak in a creek or a hot half-barrel of clean water with some soap at least once or twice a week. Most of the hands, who came from poorer circumstances, thought him "tetched" for his obsession with hot water.

He rinsed down and shook out his clothing. Now that he was a junior warrant, his clothes did not take half the abuse of a midshipman's uniform. The tar and linseed oil stains were almost gone from the days and weeks he had lived in the rigging aloft and had turned positively grimy from the running rigging, standing rigging, and the spars. Sure he could pass muster, he flapped his breeches and shirt to air the last of the sweat from them and put them back on. He'd save his clean clothing for Sunday Divisions. No sense getting potty about things.

"Bloody Frogs!" Burney was crowing from the cockpit outside his flimsy door as they rumbled down to their berth from the gun deck. "What a jape on those bastards!"

"Freeling, trot out some Black Strap," Avery called.

"An't been no eesue, zurr," Freeling mooed mournfully.

"Then break out a bottle of our personal stores, and be quick about it, man," Avery insisted. "We'll drink confusion to our foes, damme if we shan't."

Putting his stock back on, Alan came out from his dog-box and took a seat at the scarred mess table with the midshipmen, which put a chill on their cock-a-hoop airs.

"I take it the Frogs have indeed been confused?" Alan asked.

"They sailed right up to us in column and had to sheer away as our line took them under fire," Burney said proudly. "Then they loped off to seaward, to the sou'west."

"Trying to think of something to do about us holding the harbor." Alan smiled. "Probably try something tomorrow at first light. Are we to anchor?"

"The captain still hasn't said, Mister Lewrie," Avery replied in his best professional manner, unable to look Alan in the eyes. Freeling arrived with some chipped glassware and a bottle of fairly decent Bordeaux, part of a lot the mess had gone shares on in New York after Yorktown, when *Desperate* was still refitting from the pummeling she had taken before her daring escape.

"Only two glasses?" Alan pointed out. "I mind I went shares on that case of bottles, too. Freeling, fetch me a glass."

"Oh," Freeling groaned. "Aye, *zurr*."

"If you do not mind me joining your celebrations?" Alan put the dig in with a sly smile.

"Not at all, Mister Lewrie," Burney chirped.

"Honored, sir," Avery added.

They were into their first glass of wine when Railsford, Cheatham the purser, Dr. Dorne and the Marine lieutenant Peck came aft through their quarters for the airier and more spacious accommodations of the wardroom dead aft of them in the stern.

Burney put down his second glass, then was caught short and stumbled off for the beakhead up forward to make water, leaving Avery and Lewrie alone in the midshipmen's mess.

"I don't think this Frog de Grasse is half as smart as we've been thinking, sir," Avery said shyly. "We diddled him pretty well today."

"Aye, that we did. He was badly placed to get to grips with us, too far to leeward and he waited too long to come about from south to north and take us under fire."

"Might have been better for him if he had reversed course and order as soon as he saw us and waited closer to St. Kitts, yes." David grinned. "Gotten to windward inshore of Nevis himself."

"Frogs like to fight to leeward, though, David," Alan stated. "Makes sense if you're a two-decker and can keep your heaviest artillery on the lower deck in action. If you take the windward, your guns are slanting down and even with the quoins all the way out, you don't have the range an upward slanting deck could give you."

"And they like to fight at long range, too, and shoot for the rigging 'stead of closing for a clean shot."

"Probably top their whores at arm's length, too," Alan laughed.

"Won't get to grips like a good Englishman," Avery added, getting more comfortably into the conversation.

"Like that buttock shop we went to in Charleston on your birthday?" Lewrie reminisced. "What was it, Maude's?"

"Lady Jane's," David hooted. "I still owe you for that."

"Well, it was only a crown apiece. Or are you thinking of the brawl we got into after we left?" Alan shrugged and made free with the bottle to top up both their glasses.

"I owe you for that one, too. They'd have split my skull in that street if you hadn't been there, sir," David shot back.

"Sir, is it?" Alan asked. "Damnit all, David . . ."

"Well, you are a master's mate now."

"That's only because we're short-handed. I'm still the same as you, just another midshipman. I could be chucked out of my dog-box and back in a hammock next week. You've been acting like I've been made post. The Navy and its discipline be damned!"

"It's not just what the Navy expects." David sobered. "It's the way you came back aboard after Yorktown. Maybe even before then, when we went inshore. Before we were equals . . . fellow sufferers in this nautical misery, eh?" David essayed a small laugh. "But you changed, became a hard man. Like you'd aged ten years and I was still seventeen, d'ya see?"

"So you're afraid of me?" Alan gaped. "In *awe* of my new grandeur?"

"Nothing like that," David replied with a sarcastic expression. "And your grandeur be damned, 'cause you still break the vilest wind of any human I've ever seen. You're miles ahead of me now . . . Alan."

"I suddenly became your older brother?" Lewrie chid him.

"Something like that." David nodded seriously. "More like you'd come back aboard a commission officer with years of authority about you. You'll make your commission before me, maybe make post before me."

"If I stay in the Navy after this war is over," Alan scoffed. "Damme, I'm sorry you feel that way, David."

"I am, too," Avery grimaced, "but there it is. I still count you my dearest friend, but friendship is based on equality, and we're no longer equal, not as long as we wear uniform. Sorry if I've been acting standoff-ish, but it comes with the Service. If we joshed each other as we were used, then I'd get a caning and you'd get a tongue-lashing. As long as we're aboard ship, at least. Perhaps on a run ashore, things might be different. I hope so, anyway."

"Then we shall have one, soon," Alan promised.

Burney came back from his trip to the heads, and Alan stood up to finish dressing in waist-coat, coat and cocked hat. He went on deck to leave the two midshipmen to their fledgling friendship.

Damme, how did this come about? he asked himself. I'm not two full years older than David, and he's looking up to me like a distant uncle. Maybe if we both make an equal rank, he'll feel different.

But no, he realized. There was a gulf greater than rank between them now, some perception on David's part that saw him as some older and more competent man. He didn't *feel* old. He was barely nineteen. Looking back on his life, he wasn't sure if he had ever been young and innocent, but by God he didn't feel as old and competent as David implied. He was still groping for his own way in the Navy, and in life, still making stupid mistakes, floundering about in Society like a drowning man clutching at a floating spar, even if his finances and family background had finally been ascertained.

Neither, he gathered with a smirk, was he the same incredibly callow seventeen-year-old that had crawled through *Ariadne*'s entry port soaking wet from a dunk in the Solent because he had no idea how to manage scaling man-ropes and battens up a ship's side. He admitted to himself that he had made progress in skill and knowledge in the Navy, and had gotten a few glimmerings about Life, but was he not the same shameless Corinthian brothel-dandy and buck of the first head who could roister through London streets like a rutting ram-cat with no thought for the morrow except a vague wonderment about where he was going to awaken, and with whom?

"Jesus, this fucking Navy is making a doddering fossil out of me!" he grumbled. "Let's beat this damned de Grasse and have done with the whole humbug before—my God—before *I* start taking me seriously!"

The bosun's pipes began to cheep then to break his irreverent reveries. "All hands! All hands on deck! Prepare to anchor!"

"Mister Lewrie, do ya take charge o' the fo'c'sle!" Monk bellowed in a quarterdeck rasp that could have cut through a whole gale. "Clear hawse bucklers, seize up ta the best bower with the two-cable line, un prepare ta let go!"

The next morning, de Grasse had at them again. During the night, Hood had ordered his ships to shift their anchorages, so that an unbroken line stood from the point below Frigate Bay. The van ship was about four miles sou'east of Basse Terre, so close inshore not even a sloop could have clawed inshore of her; she was also inside the point and shoal as further cover. Twelve more ships lay astern of her to the west-nor'west, a mile-and-a-quarter to a mile-and-a-half of line-of-battle ships with their artillery ready. The remaining six liners bent about to curve the last of the line to the north, with Admiral Hood's 2nd Rate *Barfleur* at the apex of the bend. All ships had springs rigged on their anchor cables so they could shift their fire right or left as needed to take on a foe at extreme range as she approached, and swing with her to pour more deadly broadsides into her as long as she sailed past them.

Desperate had upped her own anchors and gotten underway shortly after breakfast, and was now prowling behind the battle line like a caged wildcat, waiting for something to maul should she be given a chance, ready to pass messages, or bear down upon a crippled British vessel to render her assistance.

The Trades were blowing well out of the sou'east, so an attempt to get round behind the line would involve hours of tacking close-hauled, and the ships drawn up *en potence* guarded that vital flank from the attempt. The French were presented with one hell of a quandary, and the English waited to see what brilliant maneuver the wily de Grasse would pull out of his gold-laced cocked hat.

"Here they come, damn their blood," Lieutenant Railsford finally spat, after a hail from the lookout at the main-mast crosstrees.

The French fleet was strung out in a perfect order in single line-ahead, a cable's length between ships, aimed like a spear at the head of Hood's line. With implacable menace, they bore down as if they would crash through the anchored ships and smash them in the process. But the lead vessel drifted west, unable to bear close enough to the wind, and now aimed at the third ship in line. When within range, she turned west.

Immediately, Hood's ships returned fire upon her.

"Bless my soul, will you look at that, now!" Treghues rejoiced, slapping his thighs. "Can you mark her, Mister Railsford?"

"*Pluton*, looks like, sir, 3rd Rate, seventy-four guns."

Alan had access to a spare telescope and was standing on the bulwarks with an arm and a leg hooked through the mizzen shrouds for a better view. The French ship staggered as if she had just run aground, surrounded by a thin pall of dust and smoke as she was savaged by the fire of at least four British ships that had swung on their springs to direct their gunfire into her together.

"I can see scantlings flying from her *far* side, sir!" Alan said. "They're blowing her to flinders!"

Pluton, if that was her as they surmised, passed down that long mile-and-a-half line, being taken under fire in order. And a cable behind her came a second ship, and a third, and a fourth, all taking the same terrible drubbing. Like sheep to the slaughter, the entire French line-of-battle followed that dreadful course, shooting high as was their usual practice, but doing little damage to ships at anchor, who couldn't have cared less whether their rigging was cut up. The British followed their usual practice as well, aiming 'twixt wind and water to punch star-shaped holes into the hulls and gun decks, to kill men and make the wood splinters fly, scything down crews and dismounting guns.

Desperate's crew was jeering as the lead French man o'war turned away and staggered back toward the south, her masts sprung and rolling, and her hull ripped apart by high velocity iron.

"Now damme," Alan relished over the din, "this is more like it!"

Desperate went about and worked her way to leeward, past the bend of the British line, for a better view of the proceedings, loafing along under reduced sail, away from the predictable thumping that the rest of the French fleet was suffering, to see what would transpire as they bore away. Which was nothing threatening, as they could see after half an hour. The French were making no more attempt to do anything offensive.

"What do you think of Admiral Hood now, Mister Lewrie?" Railsford asked him, cocking one eyebrow in mirth.

"Well, sir, after The Chesapeake, I thought he was the biggest poltroon in uniform, but he's showing well today," Alan answered.

"If he'd been in charge then, we'd have never swung away. We'd have been in that anchorage among the Frogs, and cut them to pieces. Or we'd have winkled them out of their anchorage as we did yesterday, and put up such a wall of gunfire de Grasse would have shattered his fleet trying to reenter."

"And gobbled up *their* damned army, 'stead of them gobbling up ours, sir," Alan concluded with a wolfish expression.

"Not that we could have really won against the Americans, even after such a victory."

"Indeed, sir?" he said politely, thinking, Mine arse on a bandbox!

"Too few men, too big a country, too much hatred by then. Even if we could have bagged Washington and Rochambeau on the march down from New York, there'd be another Washington come out of the backwoods with another army." Railsford shrugged. "But, we still come out of this Rebellion with Canada. And the important thing now is to beat the Frogs and Dagoes until they scream for mercy, so we'll not have any more of these coalition wars for the rest of the century, if we do it proper."

"De Grasse isn't as good as we touted him to be, is he, Mister Railsford?" Alan asked, feeling as though there had been an exorcism.

"We *gave* him victory in The Chesapeake. He couldn't help but show well there. To my mind, he's an over-rated clown when up against the sort of admiral we have here today," Railsford opined. "Lord North's cousin, Graves, was a clown, appointed by petticoat influence. Hood is not, and, pray God we get him back in the Leewards, neither is Rodney."

"The captain once told me something similar, sir, about getting Hood and Rodney together, and sweeping the seas."

"I'd love to see that. Would you?"

"Aye, sir, I would," Alan said, realizing that it was so, half-pleased by the prospect, and half-startled that he cared anything more for the Navy than getting out of it with a whole skin.

"Well now, if you were this de Grasse bugger, what would you be thinking of about this time?" Railsford asked by way of instruction.

"Well, sir, I'm French, so I'd go below and have me a good sulk. Maybe boot hell out of my servants for starters." Alan chuckled. "Some good fortifying brandy. Then, I'd come back up and split my fleet. Half to attack the ships *en potence*, half to beat up past our line as far as Brimstone Hill. It'd take hours, but one could make east-nor'east. Then tack and fall back down on the anchorage. Hood would have to shift the van ships closest the shore to counter. If he did, I'd fight both halves of my fleet for a cross-fire, with us in the center."

Lieutenant Railsford studied him closely for a long moment, lips parted as though about to sneer, and Alan felt a total fool. Railsford had been an ally in the early days after he had come aboard *Desperate*, an ally even after Treghues had turned on him. From Railsford he had learned much more than he ever had from Treghues' teaching sessions, for Treghues was more fond of his own voice and opinions than in imparting anything worthwhile to his charges. What improvements in his behavior and in his nautical lore he had learned *for* Railsford's sake, and now he had most likely revealed himself a complete, incompetent idiot. Alan blushed and looked away with a shy grimace to show that he was not to be taken totally seriously.

"God be thanked you wear *our* King's coat and not that of *their* slack-jawed monarch," Railsford finally commented. "Should this bastard try that, he'd have the Leeward Islands Squadron on a plate."

Fuck me, Alan exulted to himself, have I said something clever?

"Indeed, sir?" he asked with as much false humility as he could muster at short notice.

"I shall say some serious prayers for anyone foolish enough to cross your hawse should you ever hoist your broad pendant,

Lewrie," Lieutenant Railsford went on. "You think on a grand scale."

"For such a lowly, sir," Alan stuck in, the humility now in full ooze. When called upon, and if given warning enough to be on his best behavior, he knew he could toady and suck up with the best.

"That won't last, not if you watch your helm," Railsford told him with a grin. "Are you considering continuing your naval career?"

"Well, sir, it may not be up to me." Alan sighed. "If we beat de Grasse bad enough today, the war may be over soon. There was talk about a Peace Commission to parley with the Rebels, some guff about a meeting with all the belligerents to call it off soon. And what use is one more lowly midshipman out of thousands, when nine-tenths of the Navy would be laid up in-ordinary?"

There, I said that right well. Not my bloody fault if they dump me, is it? he thought. Why just blurt out I'd rather be whoring around Seven Dials than put up with another day of this misery and deprivation? Come to think on it, either one's just as dangerous.

"What's left, Mister Lewrie?" Railsford asked with a wry expression. "Trade? Not exactly the *ton* for a young man raised as a gentleman like yourself. Clerking for someone? You're too honest for Parliament and too much a rogue for holy orders. Stick with what you do best, and believe it or not, young sir, what you do best is the Navy."

"Well, thankee kindly, Mister Railsford, sir," Alan replied, glad to be complimented, and blushing a bit, genuinely this time.

"Enough praise for the devil today." Railsford sobered. "Else I shall expect your head to swell and burst."

"Aye aye, sir."

"Deck thar," came a leather-lunged shout from the lookout aloft. "They'm be comin' h'agin!"

"Now we shall see if de Grasse has discovered something new to try on us," Railsford snapped, turning back to the rail. "And I hope he does not commune with the same creative muse as you, Mister Lewrie."

Once more, after reeling off to the sou'west in a long curve, the French came back, their alignment and spacing in line-ahead perfect as they could make it.

"Headed directly for us," Treghues commented nearby as everyone crowded the larboard bulwarks of the quarterdeck. "Their turn-away took them down to leeward and beating back to try the line again did not work. They shall assay their luck against the ships *en potence* this time."

"What if they could get a slant of wind around the rear of this shorter line, sir?" Railsford asked. "The Trades are still out of the sou'east. Three points more would flank our dispositions."

"Mister Railsford, I would much admire if you do lay *Desperate* as close to the wind as you may and bring her to on the opposite tack," Treghues said, standing slim, elegant and foursquare with his ornate personal telescope to his eye.

"A 6th Rate to impede the path of a 2nd or 3rd Rate, sir?" Railsford asked, aghast that anyone could even countenance such an idea.

"Not to match broadsides, no," Treghues said, laughing easily, still intent on the sight of the enemy fleet. "But we should be able to deflect them. They cannot sail closer to the wind to avoid us or they'd be in irons and get shot to ribbons by the ships *en potence*. To bear away to avoid us would deny them precious minutes. It is an acceptable risk."

"Aye aye, sir," Railsford nodded in the hush that had fallen on the quarterdeck. A captain's decisions could not be argued, and any unwillingness expressed volubly enough to try and counter a captain's tactics could be construed as direct violations of several of the merciless Articles of War; cowardice in not being courageous enough to fight; insubordination; not doing everything in one's power to ready a ship for a fight. They were all court-martial offenses and usually resulted in the offender being strung up from a yard-arm by the neck.

I knew I should have gotten off when I had the chance, Alan thought shakily. I could be languishing in a Rebel prison right now, training rats close-order drill or something, on parole at the easiest. Maybe it would have been better to have been captured with the Army at Yorktown than to put up with this tripe-skulled clown!

"Bosun, ready to wear ship!" Railsford bellowed. "Quartermaster, we shall put the helm up and bring her to on the starboard tack."

By the time they had finished their evolution, and *Desperate* rode cocked up into the wind once more, the French fleet was sliding up on them with the wind on their quarter. *Pluton* was no longer the van ship, having been pounded half to matchwood in the first attempt, and a new vessel presented herself as a target.

Barfleur, the ninety-gunned 2nd Rate, opened fire first at the apex of the line, swinging about on her spring-lines to get off several hot broadsides at the same target, and the other ships *en potence* joined in as the French came within range. Clouds of smoke soared into the tropic skies, and artillery belched and thundered, spitting long red tongues of flame and sparks from burning wads into the smoke clouds. The view was blotted out once more; it might have been a gunnery exercise, as far as the men in *Desperate* could see. Even the masts of the French vessels disappeared, and the sun was eclipsed into dusk.

"There, sir!" Railsford gasped, pointing out the shape emerging to the west of the worst powder smoke. A French 3rd Rate broke free from the pall, and everyone breathed out in relief to note she was not pointing her jib-boom at them any longer, but was hauling her wind to leeward to break away west, her best attempt rejected.

"Hmmph," Treghues snorted contemptuously. "Is that the best de Grasse can do, then? Not much heart put into this sally, was there?"

"Signal, sir!" One of the new thirteen-year-old midshipmen piped from aft in a reedy voice. "Our number! From the flag! 'Well done,' sir!"

"Ah," Treghues preened. "Is it?" With little risk to themselves, they had finally done something to expunge part of that silent, faceless and therefore uncounterable cloud of disapproval. If Hood could take a moment to be magnanimous, perhaps even their squadron commander, Comdr. Sir George Sinclair could forgive them for losing him his nephew, one of their midshipmen who had not escaped with her that stormy night in the Chesapeake. It was all Treghues could do to not begin leaping about the deck and breaking into a horn-pipe of glee at that most welcome signal.

"If that's all the excitement for the day, gentlemen, we may haul our wind and come about on the larboard tack once more. Course due west. Make easy sail."

"Aye aye, sir," Lieutenant Railsford agreed.

"We made 'em look pretty stupid, hey?" Mr. Monk chortled. "This de Grasse ain't nothin' like the ogre we made him out ta be."

"I want you all to witness that we have done something glorious in the last two days," Treghues said, handing his sword to his servant Judkin before going below for a late dinner. "We bedazzled them out of their anchorage, and just shot the heart right out of them. Give us another week of steady breezes out of the sou'east and their troops ashore will be running low on rations. There's no foraging here on an island as small as St. Kitts. There may be six thousand men in their army. A loss so large would be as disastrous to them as Saratoga or Yorktown was to us. Pray God, all of you, that this may come to pass, and our Merciful Savior shall vouchsafe English arms with a victory so grand we shall speak of it as Henry V did of St. Crispin's Day!"

The hands cheered to his ringing speech, but since Treghues' patriotic fervor did not extend to "splicing the mainbrace" and trotting out a celebratory tot of rum, and he did not mention Agincourt by name, most of the unlettered could only scratch their heads and wonder what the fuss was about, except that Sam Hood had laid into the Frogs and given them a walloping.

But barely had the ship been put about, the hands stood down from Quarters and the galley fires been lit than the lookouts summoned Treghues back to the deck.

"Where away?" he asked.

"There, sir." Railsford pointed with his telescope held like a small-sword in his hand. "A despatch boat of some kind, fore'n'aft rigged, coming on close to the wind. And there's a frigate out to leeward to support her. Mayhap a message from de Grasse to his troops ashore, sir?"

"Aye, today would take some explaining," Treghues sniffed. "Get sail on her, Mister Railsford. We shall drive her back out to sea, or take her and read her despatches ourselves."

"Dinner, sir?" Railsford prompted.

"My dear Railsford, your concern with victuals is commendable." Treghues laughed. "Biscuit and cheese, and serve out small-beer. We may be beating to Quarters within the hour. Tell the cooks to put out their fires."

Chapter 2

Among the many things Alan Lewrie hated about the Navy was the need for cold dinners. The biscuit was thick and unleavened, hard as a deck plank, and could only be eaten after being soaked in beverage; that is, as soon as one had rapped it on the mess table enough to startle the weevils out of it. The cheese purchased by the Navy was Suffolk, hard and crumbly and the very devil to choke down. There had been no time to get Freeling to dig into their personal stores for a more chewable Cheddar picked up at Wilmington, and the sudden call to Quarters had brought them boiling back onto the upper decks, while the ship echoed with the sounds of expected combat. Doors and partitions slammed as they were struck down and carried to the hold so they would not form splinters that made most of the injuries in battle. Chests and personal gear went below as well. A towed boat was brought up alongside and the captain's furniture and the livestock were tossed into it, the sheep bleating and the hens in their crates squawking; a thin-shanked bullock was simply tossed over the side to sink or swim as God and the tropical sharks willed. Hundreds of horny bare feet slapped as men ran to their guns, the gangways, to the clew lines ready to reduce the main course and brail it up to the yard to reduce the risk of fire. Chain slings were rigged aloft to prevent spars from breaking loose and falling onto the packed mass of men who would be serving the guns. Boarding netting was slung over the decks and draped in unseamanly bights to protect against a surge of men over the rails should they lay close-aboard an enemy, and to form a screen against blocks and tackles (and bodies) falling from aloft.

"Two-masted schooner," Railsford said, studying the despatch boat with a telescope. "I believe we have the reach on her, sir. She'll not get past us, even as weatherly as she is."

"That frigate is closing as well, though." Treghues nodded, lost in thought. "I make her a twenty-eight. Do you concur?"

"Aye, sir," Railsford agreed, swinging his glass to eye the other vessel, which was coming on in the schooner's wake in her support, a little wider off the wind since she was a square-rigged ship and could not beat as close-hauled as a fore-and-aft rigged ship. They were on a general course far north of the British fleet anchorage, almost on a bearing for the northern limb of Frigate Bay, where the French Army had landed two weeks before.

"One point harder up," Treghues said. "Lay her full and by as close to the wind as we may. I shall want the wind gauge even should she turn away and run down back to her protector."

"Aye, sir."

Alan turned to the starboard rails and looked back towards the fleet anchorage. There was another British frigate back there to the south trying to close up with them, but she was nearly two miles off, and could not be up with them for some time.

Laid close to the wind, *Desperate* put up a brave picture, her battle flags streaming from every mast, her bow slamming into the bright tropical waters and flinging spray as high as the bow sprit, wetting the foresails with an atomized cloud of salt water, and the quarter wave hissed down her side and spread out like a bride's train of white foam.

Alan leaned over the bulwarks to see how the suction of the wave on her quarter exposed the weeded quick-work of her bottom that rarely saw daylight, heeled over as she was against the wind. Spray flew about in buckets, splashing as high as the quarterdeck and showering him with cooling droplets now and again.

Damme, this can be exciting on a pretty day like this. Alan beamed. This is a glory. Makes up for all the humbug.

"Ahem!" Monk coughed, drawing Alan's attention back inboard, and he walked back down to the wheel and binnacle with some difficulty on the slant of the deck, his shoes slipping on fresh-sanded planking, getting traction from the hot tar that had been pounded between the planks.

"I hopes the hull meets yer satisfaction, Mister Lewrie," Monk said. "The captain ain't payin' much attention now, but juniors don't go ta windward if the captain's on deck—that's his by right."

"A cod's-head's mistake, Mister Monk, I admit," Alan realized. "But you'll be happy to know the coppering is fairly clean."

"Aye, I'm *sure* the bosun un the carpenter'll be pleased," Monk drawled pointedly. "Now stay down ta loo'ard, iffen ya don't object."

"Aye aye, sir."

Alan joined Sedge, the other master's mate. He was older, in his very early twenties, a Loyalist who had joined the Royal Navy years earlier, and who was thirsting for revenge against the Rebels who had ruined his family. He was a thatch-haired and ungainly fellow with a hard hatchet face, and so far had been no more friendly than he had to be to get along in the mess, or on duty.

"Think we'll get a chance to fight 'em?" Alan asked.

"Na, this schooner'll run to momma, an' momma'll drive us off," Sedge opined gloomily. "She's a twenty-eight. You kin mark her, if you've a mind now. Long nines for chase guns on her fo'c'sle, ten carriage guns abeam—twelve-pounders most like—and six-pounders on her quarterdeck."

"Only one more gun than us per broadside."

"Aye, but twelves, not our nine-pounders," Sedge said as though Alan had uttered some lunacy worthy of Bedlam. "An' two of our nines aft're short brass pieces just as like ta blow up in our faces sure as damnit."

"Wish we still had the 'Smashers,' " Alan shrugged, giving up on making pleasant conversation with a man who looked more at home tumbling out of a hay-wagon than on a quarterdeck. "Then we'd give 'em the fear of God and British artillery."

"Aye, but ya left 'em at Yorktown, didn' ya?" Sedge sneered. "I told ya. There she goes, haulin' her wind, runnin' for safety."

Alan thought the comment was grossly unfair. The "Smashers," the short-ranged carronade guns that threw such heavy shot had been commandeered by the Army. *They* had lost them, not anyone in *Desperate*, and now two older long-barreled six-pounders graced the frigate's fo'c'sle as chase guns. But then, he realized, Sedge was ever the graceless lout.

The despatch schooner had indeed fallen off the wind to wear to the west-nor'west to take the Trades on her larboard quarter, running off to leeward and the protection of the French frigate.

"Ease your helm, hands wear ship! Due north, quartermaster!"

The waisters and idlers sprang to the braces to ease them out to larboard, angling the yards to allow *Desperate* to take the wind on her starboard quarter, so they could interpose between the schooner, frigate, and the shore, maintaining the wind gauge advantage. The French ship eased her helm as well by at least a point, screening her weaker consort. The two warships were now on two sides of a triangle; one headed north and the other nor'east. If allowed to continue, they would meet about two miles west of the port of Basse Terre.

The schooner passed close ahead of her escort, then gybed to the opposite tack and began to reach sou'west away from the anchorage with the wind abeam. Moments later, the French man o'war came about as well, but instead of wearing down-wind, she threw herself up into the wind's eye for a tack. Since it slowed her down so much to do so, *Desperate* began to close her more rapidly.

"Helm up a point, quartermaster. Hands to the braces!" Treghues bawled. *Desperate* turned a bit more westerly of due north, taking the Trades more directly up the stern, a "landsman's breeze."

"She'll pass astern o' us; mebbe a mile, mile un a half off," Monk speculated, calculating speed and approach angles in his head after the Frenchman steadied on a course sou'sou'west to provide a mobile bulwark for the schooner.

"About two miles off now," Treghues commented, rubbing his chin thoughtfully. "Once astern, they could come about and try again, with us north of them and to leeward. They'd get into Basse Terre before we could beat south to interpose again."

He paced about at the windward rail, from the nettings overlooking the waist to the wheel and back, his fingers drumming on his ornately engraved and inlaid sword hilt.

"Hands wear ship, Mister Railsford! Gybe her and lay her on the same tack as yonder Frog. If we shall not have her information, I do not mean to allow her to pass that same information ashore for lack of effort on our part."

"Aye, sir!" Railsford shouted. "Stations for wearing ship! Main clewgarnets and buntlines, there, bosun!"

"Spanker brails, weather main cro'jack and lee cro'jack braces!" Alan cried at the afterguard men. "Haul taut!"

"Up mains'l and spanker!" Railsford went on with a brass speaking trumpet to his lips. "Clear away after bowlines, brace in the afteryards! Up helm!"

Desperate fell off the wind more, her stern crossing the eye of the wind slowly, for she was no longer generating her own apparent wind but sailing no faster than the Trades could blow.

"Clear away head bowlines! Lay the headyards square!" Railsford directed as the wind came directly astern, gauging the proper moment at which the foresails would no longer be blanketed by the courses and tops'ls. "Headsheets to starboard!"

"Main tack and sheet. Clear away, there. Spanker outhaul and clear away the brails," Alan added as the wind drew forward on the larboard quarter.

Within a breathless few minutes, *Desperate* was squared away on a new point of sail, paralleling the Frenchman to the sou'sou'west, and just slightly ahead of her by a quarter-mile.

"Smartly done, Mister Railsford." Treghues nodded in satisfaction at how professionally *Desperate*'s crew did their sail drill.

"Thankee, sir." Railsford beamed. "Steady out bowlines! Haul taut weather trusses, braces and lifts! Clear away on deck!"

"He's shivering his mizzen tops'l, sir!" Alan pointed out as the French frigate tried to slow down, possibly so she could pass astern of *Desperate* and still get up to windward for Basse Terre.

"He's a game little cock, isn't he, Mister Railsford?" Treghues chuckled. "Once he gets an idea into his pate he won't give it up. Back the mizzen tops'l and haul in on the weather braces. Get the way off her."

Realizing that he could not dodge about *Desperate*, the Frenchman came up close to the wind and began to put on speed once more close-hauled, closing the range slightly. Oddly, Treghues let her approach to within three-quarters of a mile; just about the range of random shot, before ordering *Desperate* to haul in once more and maintain the distance.

"Pretty thing," Alan commented to Monk after a quick sharing of a telescope with the sailing master. The frigate had a dark brown oak hull, with a jaunty royal blue gunwale stripe picked out in yellow top and bottom, with much gilt trim about her bulwarks scroll-work and taffrail carvings of cherubs and dolphins and saints. Her figurehead could almost be discerned, a sword and shield wielding maiden surmounted by a gilt *fleur de lis* crown.

"She's hard on the wind to close us, sir," Alan noted.

"Aye, but we'll draw ahead if she stays so," Monk growled.

There was a sudden puff of smoke from the Frenchman that blossomed on her far bow, then was blown away to a mist by the Trades. Seconds later, the sound of a shot could be heard, a thin thumping noise. She had fired one gun to leeward, the traditional challenge to combat. Evidently the French captain was so angered at being stymied by *Desperate*'s maneuverings that he wanted to vent some round-shot spleen upon her.

Alan looked back at Treghues and saw the glint in his eyes. It would be galling to refuse combat, especially for a ship and captain under a cloud for previous actions, no matter how unfair the accusation was, and Alan could see Treghues' jaws working below the tan flesh of that narrow, patrician face.

No, he can't be thinking of it! Alan quailed. We can't fight a twenty-eight. We've done enough to clear our hawse already!

"Mister Gwynn, fire the leeward chase gun," Treghues said. "Brail up the main course, Mister Railsford. I think this stubborn Frog needs a lesson in manners. Mr. Peck, would you be so good as to assemble the band and have them give us something stirring?"

The starboard six-pounder banged, and the ship's boys with the drums and fifes met in the waist just below the quarterdeck rails and began a tinny rendition of "Heart of Oak," as the waisters and topmen took in the large main course and brailed it aloft on the main yard. The Marine complement paraded back and forth on the lee gangway by the bulwark and the hammock stowage, which would be their breast-works in the battle to come. A few of them who were better shots than others went aloft into the tops with their muskets and their swivel guns.

The Frenchman was closing fast, close enough to make out her open gunports. Alan groaned to himself when he saw that there were eleven of them. Two bow chase guns, six-pounders like Sedge thought, but only four quarterdeck guns, and *eleven* bloody twelve-pounders in each broadside battery, not ten! he noted with a sick feeling.

He wished he could squat down below the bulwarks of their own quarterdeck, for with her angle of heel, *Desperate*'s decks were bared just enough to make everyone aft a prime target.

The French ship fired, a solid broadside as all her guns lit off together, and his flesh quivered as the shot moaned in at them at twelve hundred feet per second. The range was just about five cables, half a nautical mile. Black shot droned overhead, slapping a hole in the spanker over where Lewrie stood. Fired on the up-roll, upward from a slanting deck, the lee ship had the advantage of range over *Desperate*. Alan's passion was artillery of all the skills he had been forced to learn in the Navy, and he knew *Desperate*'s nine-pounders could not be elevated high enough to reach as long as she was close-hauled and heeled over.

"Finish that verse and then get below," Treghues told his band, and the ship's boys scattered after a final tootle, to stow away their instruments and revert to their roles as powder monkeys who would fetch up the wooden or leather cylinders that held pre-measured charges from the magazines, or to assist the surgeon in the cockpit once the wounded worth saving were hauled below by older men.

"Ease her helm a point free, Mister Railsford, get the heel off her and we'll try our eye," Treghues snapped. "Stand by, Mister Gwynn!"

"Aye aye, sir!" the master gunner said in reply from the waist.

Desperate came more upright by a few feet, the bulwarks seeming to rise up like stage machinery, with the French frigate just slightly aft of abeam, and the range dropping to four cables.

"Quoins half-out!" Gwynn instructed his gun-captains. "Point yer guns! Ready!"

"I leave it to you, Mister Gwynn," Treghues said cheerfully.

"As you bear . . . fire!"

First the reloaded starboard chase gun, then the first of the long nine-pounders began to bark, the firing rippling down the ship's side one at a time as steady as a fired salute, with Gwynn pacing aft at the same pace as the ignitions. Shot erupted from the black iron muzzles in a rush of flame and sparks and thick clouds of spent powder, and bright beautiful feathers of spray leapt up close-aboard the enemy frigate's side as iron shot ricocheted to thud home below her gunports.

"Lovely shooting, Mister Gwynn!" Treghues commented. "Load with double-shot and hull him this time!"

Alan's legs were quivering with excitement, almost too tremulous to keep him erect as he stood by the wheel with the sailing master. In previous actions, he had been a midshipman on the gun deck, too busy supervising the loading, firing and running out, too intent on gunnery to think much about being afraid, about being maimed or killed, lost in the heat of the moment. But as a master's mate, his main role was to act as a sitting duck of no mean seniority on the bare quarterdeck, which would be the prime target of the French after they got within musket-shot.

Another broadside from the French, a positive avalanche of iron, and *Desperate* shrieked in oaken agony as things let go aloft. The mizzen royal and t'gallant yards were smashed by bar-shot or chain-shot, and the pieces rained down into the overhead nettings. A Marine and a top-man from the mizzen tops'l thumped onto the nettings like bloody steers, the Marine minus both legs at the crotch and spraying a scarlet shower on the deck.

"Firing high as usual," Treghues noted with a frown of disapproval. "When shall they learn?"

Desperate's guns were thundering once more, slamming four-inch, nine-pounder iron balls into the French ship, this time concentrated 'twixt wind and water, right into her hull. Planks were shattered and nibbles were taken out of her upper-works bulwarks, scattering the enemy Marines who had been gathered for a musket volley or two. But, being bigger and heavier enough to handle 22 twelve-pounder guns, it would take a lot of nibbling to do her damage, for her scantlings were thicker, her beams and cross-pieces were heavier and stronger.

"You've made your point, you damned fool," Alan grumbled aloud under the sound of the cannonading. "Now get a way on and get us out of here. Honor is redeemed and all that shit!"

But Treghues was in nautical Paradise, pacing back and forth in a maniacal joy, oblivious to the blood trails on the quarter-deck, or the hurt *Desperate* had suffered aloft.

"For what we're 'bout ta receive . . ." Monk whispered the old saw as the Frenchman's side lit up like red signal fuses seen through a thick fog, a fog of powder smoke that rolled down from *Desperate* to the foe. The smoke seemed to glow, and then the world was hammered into matchwood.

The starboard bulwark by the ladder leading below to the waist was flung into ruin, and a cloud of oak splinters flicked through the air like startled sparrows. Men were screaming like frightened horses, and *Desperate* staggered as heavy shot burst through her sides. The deck below Lewrie's feet jumped, almost throwing him to his knees.

"Eighteens if they's a pound!" Monk managed to say, grabbing onto the binnacle and traverse board table to stay erect.

"No more than twelve-pounders, surely, Mister Monk," Alan said in a shaky voice, trying to maintain that maddening *sang froid* demanded of a professional Sea Officer.

"Felt like eighteens, anyway," Monk spat.

As the smoke began to rag away, Alan could see that the enemy was now on a parallel course, just two cables off. She would not get closer; but then he realized, she didn't have to, for she could lay out there a fifth of a nautical mile away and shoot *Desperate* to lace unless they did something soon.

"Helm up, quartermaster!" Treghues yelled through the din as the guns belched fire again. "Bear down on her!"

Two loblolly boys stirred the savaged body of a petty officer by the torn-up starboard gangway. They shrugged and rolled the body to the hole in the bulwarks and tipped the corpse over the side.

"That was Mister Weems!" Alan burst out in shock.

"Aye, poor bastard," Monk agreed. "There'll be an openin' fer a new bosun's mate tamorra."

A screaming waister was picked up on a carrying board and taken below to the cockpit surgery as they watched. There was nothing to be done with the dead or the hopelessly wounded but to get them out of sight and out from under foot. Words could be said later from the prayer book.

More shot screamed in, and *Desperate* reeled with its impact. More screams from the waist, a puff of smoke from the nettings that set hammocks writhing like a box of worms as a round-shot scattered them. A Marine keened and fell from the gangway clutching his belly. Dull flames licked around the torn canvas from a small explosion, and men from the larboard side rushed to pour water on the fire before it could take hold and eat their ship.

One cable's range now; two hundred yards. Alan went forward to the quarterdeck rail to look down into the waist. A larboard gun had been overturned and its crew decimated. As he watched, the loblolly boys dragged another screaming unfortunate to the midships hatch, a man as quilled with jagged wood splinters as a hedge-hog. The dead Marine was being passed out a larboard gunport and someone was retching bile as he used a powder scoop to shovel up the man's spilled intestines. The gun crews labored away with their scarves around their ears to save their hearing, intent on their artillery. Burney, up by the fo'c'sle, and Avery in the waist, were pacing among their men, shoving them to their places and speeding them along. Then the guns were barking and recoiling back against their breeching ropes, hot enough now to leap from the deck instead of rolling backwards on their small trucks.

Another broadside from the French, and this one felt like an earthquake. Alan clung to the hammock-nettings as the ship felt as if she had been slammed to a halt. Something whined past his head, and the hammocks before him punched him in the crotch. He looked down as he was bent over by the pain and saw a chunk of the bulwark, nearly three inches across and a foot long, sticking from the far side of the barrier.

"Bloody Christ!" he yelped, feeling his crotch in fear he had been de-bollocked, and was relieved to feel that his "wedding-tackle" was still there. The deck continued to tremble with each strike and there was a lot of screaming from back aft as he winced with his pain.

"Lewrie, stir yourself!" Treghues bellowed, pointing behind him to the wheel, where men lay torn and bleeding.

Alan limped aft, bent over. Mr. Monk was propped up by the binnacle with Sedge bending down over him. The rotund sailing master had been struck in the leg with a grape-shot ball, a full ounce of lead that had almost ripped his limb off above the knee, and was now hanging by a few tattered sinews. Sedge was seizing a piece of small-stuff about the upper thigh to staunch the copious spurting of blood, and Lewrie knelt to aid him.

"Sedge, ya've more experience, do ya take charge," Monk gasped from a pasty white face sheened with shock-sweat.

"Aye, I shall, Mister Monk," Sedge promised as the surgeon's assistants rushed to his side with a carrying board.

"At least Dorne won't have ta saw much to take this bugger," Monk tried to jest, too freshly wounded to feel much pain yet. The loblolly boys rolled him onto the board, strapped him down, and made off with him by the larboard ladder, and Monk began to moan as the pain hit him. "Hurry me below, damn yer blood!" he cried out.

"Spare quartermaster to the wheel," Sedge barked. "Hot work, ain't it, Lewrie?"

"God's teeth, yes!" Alan concurred.

Sedge laughed and strode away to assist Toliver the bosun's mate in ordering the afterguard into shape once more, leaving Lewrie by the wheel with two new white-eyed quartermasters who flinched every time something whined nearby, their feet slipping in the blood trails of their predecessors.

"Watch your helm," Alan told them, being careful to station himself to windward, using them and the wheel drum as a shield.

The guns were now firing as fast as the frightened and weary crews could load and run out, all order lost in the maelstrom of battle. Every few seconds there was discharge, followed by one from their foe. Lieutenant Peck and his Marines were now firing by squads from the rail, and the masts of the French frigate were towering alongside, nearly as high as *Desperate*'s own; less than half a cable off, perhaps sixty yards and adequate musket-shot. To confirm it, a volley of balls hit the quarterdeck, one warbling off the rim of the compass bowl, another raising a large splinter from the deck before Alan's feet.

Desperate reeled again like a gut-punched boxer.

"Mister Lewrie, come here!" Railsford yelled through a speaking trumpet. "Go forrud into the waist and take charge!"

"Aye, sir?" Alan said, dashing to his side.

"Gwynn is down!" Railsford snarled, shoving him to the larboard ladder. "Go, no time to chat about it! Keep the guns firing!"

Alan hammered down the ladder to the waist. The master gunner Mr. Gwynn was stretched out on the deck to larboard, his shirt and waist-coat sodden with blood, and flecks of bloody spume on his lips as he tried to breathe.

"God save me!" Alan whispered, then mastered himself. "Avery?"

"Aye, sir?" a white-faced David Avery asked, trotting aft.

"I'll take charge. Go aft and tend the gunners there. Is Burney still alive?"

"Aye, sir."

"Good. Quarter-gunners!" Alan bawled, glad to have something concrete to do. "Pace your damned gun-captains! Ordered firing!"

Alan watched as the senior quarter-gunners passed among their charges and stilled their individual efforts, making them work in unison once more, loading and touching off together. He bent down to peer out a gunport at the enemy.

"Direct these guns at the same aiming point, here! Base of the main-mast is your target. Punch a hole clean through her! Burney, do you aim at the base of their foremast!"

"Wait for it, ya stupid get!"

"Prime your guns . . . point your guns . . . on the up-roll . . . fire!"

Three at a time, the guns barked and leaped backwards, first Burney's charges, then Alan's, then the guns below the quarter-deck in the cabins aft.

"Better," Alan snapped. He strode aft to look at the hands as they swabbed out and began to load. Gwynn gave a mournful groan as one of the men did him the merciful favor of smacking him on the head with a heavy mallet to knock him unconscious. He was too badly hurt to live, and the surgeons could do nothing with such a savage chest wound. Out cold and knowing nothing of the indignity, he was passed out through a larboard gunport where he splashed into the sea to drown quickly.

More French iron hammered into them, and Alan fell to the deck as a rammer man staggered into him. A covey of splinters took flight like passing quail over his head, and his head rang with the shock wave of a concussion somewhere. The rammer man was sprawled across his lap with his back flayed open to the spine, and Alan gave it a long thought before shoving him off and getting back to his feet. Damned if it had not felt rather safe flat on his back, out of the line of fire.

"Spare man from the larboard battery here," Alan directed, and a rabbity man darted forward to scoop up the discarded rammer and take his place in the starboard battery.

One of the new midshipmen, the youngest and stupidest, tugged at his coat tails, and he turned to look down at the child.

"Mister Railsford says prepare the larboard battery as we're . . . we're . . ." The boy fumbled, his teeth chattering in fear.

"We're ready to what, damn your thin blood!" Alan barked like an exasperated commission officer. It felt damned good to yell at the boy instead of musing on his own quaking.

"We're to come about and rake her, sir," the boy finished.

"Larboard quarter-gunners, to me!" When they had gathered round he told them to ready their pieces, double-shotted with grape for good measure.

"We'm short, sir," a grizzled older man told him.

"Then fetch the hands from the starboard chase gun," Alan told him. "That six-pounder is only making them sneeze. Run out as you are ready and get those ports open now. Starboard battery, load and stand by for broadsides!"

" 'Ware below!"

"Oh, Jesus!" Someone cringed as the repaired main yard came down with a crash across the cross-deck beams where the boats usually nestled.

"So much fer fixin' that fucker," a quarter-gunner spat, drooling tobacco juice from a massive wad in his cheek.

With a loud creak, the mizzen tops'l was thrown aback to slow their ship down. Alan bent down to peer out a gunport and saw that the Frogs were drawing ahead rapidly.

"On the up-roll . . . fire!"

At such close range, even their light nine-pounder shot could do harm to a frigate with heavier scantlings, and the broadside brought a groan of racked timber from the French ship as she was struck hard. Nettings and bulwarks flew, and screams sounded from French throats this time. Alan could feel when *Desperate*'s helm was put hard up to windward, even without looking at the waisters on the riddled gangways as they flung themselves on the braces to wear ship.

"Take your time and reload the starboard guns! Sponge out

your guns! Overhaul that tackle there, or you'll get mashed like a pasty," Alan called. "Mister Burney, do you take charge of readying the battery. Larboard guns, stand by."

The ship swayed like a drunkard as she wore down-wind, and the yards and masts of the French ship swung across the bow, with the tip of *Desperate*'s bow-sprit barely clearing her mizzen shrouds and taffrail lanterns.

"We may only get one chance at this, so make your shots count," Alan warned his larboard gunners. "Don't aim too high and blow holes in her quarterdeck. Let's put round-shot and grape down the full length of her gun deck, just like a good game of bowls. Tear her stern out, shake her mizzen to shreds."

Willing or not, Alan had to climb up onto the larboard gangway to judge the best moment, his hanger tangling between his shins. They would pass the Frenchman's stern at close pistol-shot.

Damme if we might win this yet! Alan thought as he drew his lovely gift hanger and let the pristine blade flash silver in the sun.

"Ready . . . as you bear . . . Fire!"

The larboard chase gun went off and its load of double-shot and grape gouged the taffrail open, shattering the carved cherubs, dolphins and saints into gilt tatters, strewing six French naval infantry down like corn-stalks. Then the nine-pounders began to discharge, and the stern windows, the larboard quarter-gallery and the transom were riddled in a flurry of broken planking. The rudder twitched back and forth and the mizzen mast shivered as it was struck. Screams from the French ship could be heard as her gun crews were mown down by the shot passing down the length of her decks.

"That's the way, Desperates!" Alan howled in triumph, waving his sword over his head in derision at the French he could see on the poop and quarterdeck. Swivels barked from the tops and the Marine sharpshooters let fly. Peck and his squads formed up to larboard and began to volley into her. "Sponge out! Overhaul your tackle! Charge guns!"

Desperate put her helm down and began to swing back onto the wind to rake the Frenchman's stern with the other battery, but the frigate, bearing the name *Capricieuse* on her torn gilt stern-placque tried to bear up as well, blocking their way.

"Avast!" Railsford screamed. "Helm hard up! Lewrie, ready to rake her again with the larboard battery!"

Quicker to return to her original course, *Desperate* wavered, then got herself under control. *Capricieuse* tried to sag down off the wind with her, but *Desperate* was already to leeward. The angle was acute, but it would be a stern rake, right up through the shattered wood, at least into her after batteries.

"Wait for the transom, wait for the transom!" Alan screamed in glee as he capered up and down the gangway, looking down on his gun crews. Sweating men hauled on tackles to heave the heavy guns up the slightly canted deck. Priming quills were inserted. Crows and levers were shouldered and muscles strained near to rupture to shift the aim of the barrels. Fists were raised in the air as gun-captains signaled their readiness. A few shots were fired by the French from their own larboard side before *Desperate* passed out of their gun-arcs.

"As you bear . . . fire!"

One at a time, the guns roared out their challenge, and spat their tongues of flame through the smoke. Wood on the larboard quarter was chewed up. The rudder twitched again as a ball smacked into the transom post. The mizzen swayed and jerked, and Alan could see one ball carom off an interior beam with a puff of smoke and dust and paint to go ricocheting down the length of the gun deck. The after guns belched fire, then *Desperate* was staggered once more as though she had just been struck hard herself, but Alan could not see one French gun that could bear to do that damage.

Capricieuse sagged down off the wind, fully presenting her stern to *Desperate*, trying to bring her unused starboard battery into action, and there was no movement from aft to shift their ship's course. Alan scrambled back down to the gun deck off the gangway, where it would be safer to suffer what they were about to get in retribution.

"Got a gun burst aft, sir!" a runner told him. "One o' them brass nines. Blew a hole right up through the deckhead!"

"Tell Avery to deal with it." Alan shrugged, intent on his men. "Load with double-shot! Run out!"

"Tha's just it, sir, Mister Avery's bad hurt, an' the quarter-gunner's dead," the man told him.

"Oh, shit. Hogan, leave the chase gun and go aft. You're a quarter-gunner now!" Alan chilled. He grabbed Hogan as he trotted by and held him close for a moment. "Avery's been hurt. Get word to me on how he is."

"Aye, I'll do that, sir."

"Ports is openin'!" someone warned.

"Gun crews, lay down!" Alan yelped. If they were struck

while the men were still on their feet, it would be a slaughter. A second later, the broadside from the fresh battery struck them, and wood and iron howled in agony and the deck shuddered beneath them. Alan stuck his head up and looked around, coughing on smoke and engrained dust.

"Up and at 'em, Desperates, come on, larboard!" he called, rising. "Prime your guns! Point! On the up-roll ... fire!"

A ragged cheer arose as the tortured mizzen-mast of the French frigate gave a final shudder and toppled forward, chopped to flinders below the deck by those stern rakes. It fell into component pieces, top-mast dropping straight down as the lower mast fell forward, and the t'gallant and royal masts and spars spiraled about to drape themselves over the main topmast, dragging it sideways in a tangle of rope and canvas.

"Damme, will you look at that!" Alan hooted. "Just bloody beautiful! Keep it up, lads, and we'll *have* the bastard!"

The aged carpenter came scrambling up from below decks past the parade of powder monkeys, shoving them out of the way in his haste to get to the quarterdeck, and Alan noted that "Chips" was soaking wet from mid-thigh down, which made him suddenly wonder if *Desperate* would stay afloat long enough to actually "have the bastard," or whether the bastard, damaged as the French frigate was, would end up having them!

The youngest midshipman was back suddenly, tugging on Alan's coat once more, his face streaked with soot and powder stains, the tracks of tears carved into the grime.

"Please, Mister Lewrie, sir, the captain presents his respects, and requests could you spare half a dozen hands to assist the carpenter."

"Hulled and leaking, are we?" Alan asked close, so the hands would not hear.

"Sinking, sir!" The boy quailed, but soft enough for discretion.

"God's balls," Alan breathed. "What next, I wonder? Maple?"

"Aye, sir," the fo'c'sle gunner answered, breaking free of the larboard battery.

"Select five hands who aren't doing us much good at the moment and assist the ship's carpenter, if you would be so kind," Alan directed, trying to remain calm, but it didn't fool Maple, who rolled his eyes in alarm and glanced upward at the cross-deck beams where the boats most definitely *weren't* any longer. Other than flotsam from a wreck, the boats were the only life-saving devices available.

"Oh, shit, Mister Lewrie, sir!" Maple sighed, dashing off.

If I'd stayed in London, I'd have become a wealthy pimp by now, Alan speculated sourly. I can't even bloody swim!

There was a volley of musketry of such volume and intensity that only a company of infantry could have made it. A larboard waister came tumbling down from the forebraces to sprawl across the breech of a gun, his face shot away and his brains oozing and sizzling on the hot metal.

Alan ducked to look out a gunport once more. *Capricieuse* was close-aboard, not fifty yards off, her bulwarks lined with men as though her last chance was to board *Desperate* and take her in a hot hand-to-hand action.

"Quoins out!" Alan yelled to his gunners. "Load grape and canister atop ball! Cease fire and stand by for a broadside!"

"Double-shotted, zurr!" a gun-captain called back.

"Worm 'em out of there and reduce your powder charges! I'll not have another burst barrel!"

"Got grape, but no canister!" another shouted.

"Fuck it! Shoot out your loads!" Alan thundered, at the same time grabbing the nearest powder monkey on his way below with an empty leather cylinder. "Tell Mister Tulley in the magazine I need grape and canister and reduced charges. I'm going to triple-shot the guns!"

That brought Tulley up from below in a rush, his ginger hair sticking up in all directions and his sun-burned complexion glowing at the danger to his precious artillery.

"Damme, sir, you'll burst my barrels! Where's the master gunner? I'll see him and . . ."

"He's dead and gone, Mister Tulley," Alan said brutally. "Now we have a Frog frigate at pistol-shot and I want round-shot, grape and canister with reduced charges or we're boarded and taken. So what are you going to do to help me?"

"Excess loaders from the starboard battery, fetch canister!" the burly gunner's mate said, his face paling with shock at hearing of his senior's demise, and the straits they were in. "Boys, tell the Yeoman of the Powder Room to issue reduced charges! My God, Mister Lewrie, my merciful God!"

The sound of cannon fire had ceased. Either the French had stripped their gun deck of men for a boarding party, or they were also loading a massive broadside and were waiting for the proper time to fire it into *Desperate* to shatter resistance just before they came surging over the rails.

"Let's go, let's go!" Alan prodded as the case-shot and grape bags came up, along with the half-size saluting charges. With so much iron-mongery crammed into the muzzles, a larger powder measure would truly burst the barrels, and at such close range, a smaller amount of powder would be preferable anyway. Low velocity shot did not shoot through scantlings clean, but bulged and ravaged them, producing more splinters that ripped men apart, creating more havoc.

The midshipman was back, this time not so polite.

"The captain wants to know what the deuce you're playing at, Mister Lewrie, sir?" the boy wailed. "They are close aboard and Mister Railsford demands you fire into them before they grapple to us!"

"Triple-shotted broadside, go tell them!" Alan growled, pacing past the boy as if he wasn't there. "Go, get aft, you minnikin!"

"Charge yer guns . . . shot yer guns, round-shot, then grape, then case-shot . . ." Tulley was directing with the voice of a bawling steer, his face its usual red flush once more.

"Mister Lewrie!" the second young midshipman yelled, dashing to his side.

"Holy hell, will you stop pestering me?"

"Mister Railsford orders you prepare to repel boarders!"

"Run out!" Tulley screeched, and the hands tailed on the tackles to draw their pieces across the deck with the rumble of a cattle stampede as the small wooden wheels of the trucks squealed and drummed.

"Gun-captains to remain, tackle-men and loaders take arms and prepare to repel boarders!" Alan cried. "Tulley, give 'em the broadside and then bring your hands to join me. Let's go, men!"

"Prick yer cartridges . . . prime yer guns . . ." Tulley droned on, as the excess hands dug into the weapons tubs for cutlasses and boarding axes, stripped the pikes from the beckets around the bases of the masts, and flung open the arms chests for heavy (and usually inaccurate) pistols. Once more Alan was at a disadvantage, for he did not have any of his pistols with him. He took a tomahawk-sized boarding axe for his off-hand and stuck it into his breeches, unwilling to try his luck with a Sea Pattern pistol again.

"Up to the gangway, quickly now!"

"Take yer aim . . . stand by . . ." Tulley called as they scrambled up to the larboard bulwark behind the Marines, who were still volleying into the foe. Sedge dashed past him on his way forward to join the youthful Burney to protect the fo'c'sle. Alan looked back to see Railsford bringing all the afterguard and mizzen mast crew to the break of the quarterdeck to defend the after portion of the ship. Musket bayonets glinted dully from those hands who had gotten a chance to break out the long-arms. Pike heads bristled like medieval infantry ranks, and cutlasses fanned the air as men loosened their arms for the bloody work to come. The French lined their own rails, striped-jerseyed sailors and men in check shirts much like British seamen, naval infantry in blue coats with red facings, with here and there an officer in blue coat edged with gold oak-leaf lace and epaulettes, with red waist-coats.

"Fire!" Tulley finally shouted, and everyone ducked below the bulwarks and nettings as the guns erupted so loudly, avoiding the rush of hot gases and the clouds of smoke, and the whining, ricocheting bits of grape-shot and canisters of musket balls as each piece was turned into a scatter-gun.

Alan stood back up just in time to see Railsford leaping onto the after bulwarks and waving his small-sword in the air. "Boarders!" he screamed. "Away boarders!"

With a lusty roar, Desperate's crew went up onto the bulwarks themselves. Grapnels had been thrown by the French, and British implements flew across to complete lashing the hulls together. Nettings came down as they surged across, leaping the churning mill-race of white water between the ships.

There wasn't much opposition. That final broadside fired at the highest angle of a naval carriage gun had shattered the upper-works of Capricieuse, ripping the rails to knee height and scything boarders into mangled meat. Alan landed atop the torso of a French marine who had lost belly and intestines, his feet slipping in entrails and excrement as he staggered to the inner side of the riddled gangway and fetched up on the rope railing overlooking the waist of the gun deck.

A weak volley of bullets fanned the air and he jerked his head back quickly. There was resistance forward, but Sedge and Lieutenant Peck of the Marines were dealing with that. There was a large party of Marines on the frigate's quarterdeck, but nothing much between, the waist having been stripped of men, and those men mostly were now dead or dying, the few still on their feet tossing down their weapons and raising their hands in surrender, too shocked by the sudden carnage and boarding to wish to continue fighting.

"Take the larboard gangway!" Alan shouted, pointing with his hanger at a knot of men still armed on the other side of the ship.

He dashed out onto one of the wide cross-deck beams that spanned the waist and reached the far side. A man confronted him with a cutlass, but before he could engage, a hole sprang up in his chest and he tumbled to the deck. Alan whirled to engage a second, but a boarding axe sprouted from that man's shoulder, thrown by one of his men, and that foe fell down as well, screaming in agony. The rest threw up their hands quickly and congregated into a submissive knot by the main chains.

"Stap me, that wuz easy," a Marine corporal said at Alan's side. "Jus' 'bout wot ye'd expect from Frogs, ah reckon, sir."

"Disarm the buggers before they get their wits back, corporal," Alan shrugged, sheathing his still unbloodied sword. "Herd 'em up forward with that other lot and don't forget to pat 'em down for knives and such." The corporal's eyes lit up at that order, for it would be a good excuse to loot the prisoners of what little value they carried on their persons, regulations be damned.

"Ah 'spects ye're right, sir, ah'll atten' ta that direckly."

Alan strode aft to the quarterdeck where Railsford seemed to be in complete charge. The first lieutenant had a bloody gash on his head from which gore still oozed, but his blade was properly slimed with the life's blood of a foe, and his face was split open in a magnificent and triumphant grin. There were French dead laying about like rabbits underfoot all over the quarterdeck, over which he paced unconcernedly.

"I give you joy of this day, Mister Lewrie!" he shouted.

"And to you, sir," Alan replied, studiously trying to avoid the sight of so many men reduced to bloody offal.

"God, what a victory!" Railsford went on. "An old tub such as *Desperate* taking a 5th Rate with twenty-eight guns. How's your French?"

"Bloody awful, sir," Alan told him, beginning to realize just what an improbable thing they had just pulled off.

"Who'd a thought such a thing possible?" Railsford enthused at some length. "Of course, yon thirty-two helped them make up their mind to strike. But ours is the principal effort, and there's glory enough to share."

Alan noted a British frigate of thirty-two guns falling downwind to them rapidly from the main anchorage, possibly the ship he had spotted before fire had been exchanged. Lashed as she was to *Desperate*, *Capricieuse* would have been made a prize even if she had emerged victorious over their puny efforts.

"Here, I can't make out a word this queer-nabs is trying to say, not half of it, anyway," Railsford said, gesturing casually with his sword to a knot of French officers, and a suitably senior man jumped back with a start as the tip of that bloody blade got within scratching distance of his nose. "I thought you might help interpret."

"Pardon a mois, monsieurs, parle vous l'Anglais?" he asked hopefully, doffing his hat to the startled senior officer who seemed to be in command, but that worthy merely pinched his nostrils and went into a positive flood of rapid Frog, and stepped back, snapping his fingers to summon a junior officer.

"Monsieurs, permittez-vous, ici l'troisième lieutenant de Marine Royale . . . 'ow you say, three officeur? I 'ave en peu English," the junior officer volunteered.

"Bloody good," Railsford beamed.

"Charles Auguste Baron de Crillart, à votre servis. Notre capitaine la frégate *Capricieuse*, Jules Marquis de Rosset." The Frenchman handled the introductions with all of them bowing in *congé* and doffing their cocked hats. "My capitaine 'e say 'e is 'ave très honneur to be striking to you, monsieurs."

In sign of their victory, a Blue Ensign was hoisted on a mainmast signal halyard, with the white and gold Bourbon banner displayed below it, and the crews of both British ships raised a great cheer. The French captain screwed his face up into a grimace worthy of a half-frozen mastiff and unclipped his smallsword from his belt frog to hand it over with a polished gesture.

With de Crillart translating as best he could, arrangements were made for quartering of prisoners, the care of the many French wounded, and the Christian disposal of the dead. Railsford had to protest that their captain should not have to surrender his sword, since he had put up such a spirited resistance, and after more florid speeches, this privilege was extended to the surviving commission officers as well. De Rosset then bowed his way to the ladders leading to his quarters as though leaving the presence of royalty where one never gave the monarch the sight of a human back, and went below, probably to see what he had been looted of while honor was being satisfied.

"Thank God that's over," Railsford said softly as they turned to go back aboard *Desperate*. "The prize isn't that damaged, but our poor ship was knocked about pretty badly. Get me a report from the carpenter, and then see who's left in charge of the various departments."

"Aye, aye, sir."

Desperate had indeed been knocked about; she looked as though she had been eaten at by giant rats, her bulwarks jagged and her decks ruptured and sprung. Nettings, rigging and sails hung about her like a funeral shroud, and those spars and sails still aloft had been shot through so completely a brisk breeze would have brought them down in a total ruin. The sound of chain-pumps clanking made a mournful tempo as streams of flood-water gushed from her. Men picked about her decks to find the wounded or the dead, and the sailmaker and his crew were already at work on the quarterdeck sewing up shrouds for burials.

A quick trip below into the holds assured Alan that their ship would not sink, though the repairs and patches had not stopped the leaks but had only slowed them to a manageable in-flow.

"We'll be at the pumps all the way ta Antigua, sir, but we've got a chance, iffen we could fother a patch er two," "Chips" told him.

That seemed good encouragement, which lasted only until Lewrie got to the surgery on the lower decks, and Dorne gave him the bad news.

"Mister Monk has passed over," Dorne began, in between suffering seamen as the leather cover over the midshipmen's chests was sluiced clean of blood and torn flesh with a bucket of seawater. "The loss of blood was too great, I'm afraid. And our captain was struck down in his moment of greatest triumph as well."

"Dead?" Alan asked, ready to spew at the sights and smells and sounds of the surgery. Could we be lucky enough to be rid of him? he thought.

"No, praise a merciful God, merely splintered, and if suppuration does not set in, he stands a fair chance for recovery. Hoist him up here," Dorne directed as a moaning body was laid out on the table. "That arm shall have to come off. Who is he, one of ours?"

"A French seaman, I believe," Cheatham the youngish purser informed him after looking at the pile of clothing on the deck that had been cut off the unfortunate. Cheatham took a swig of rum from a cup, to steady his own nerves, then offered it to the Frenchman's lips for him to suck on as an anodyne.

"Wondered where he was," Alan muttered, shivering with chill at the sight of the man's rivened arm, and the instruments that Dorne was removing from a bucket of bloody water for re-use.

"Who?"

"Treghues," Alan said.

"Non, non, mon dieu, non!" the Frenchman screamed as the weary loblolly boys took hold of him to keep him still, and Dorne lifted up that arm and quickly flensed the flesh away above the major wounds, not five inches below the shoulder. Cauterizing irons sizzled to stop the flow of blood from opened arteries and veins, and the air was putrid with the reek of scorched flesh, and the savage rasp of a bone saw.

"Oh, Jesus," Alan said, turning away, ready to faint, ready to "cast his accounts" on the slimy deck.

"Fifteen seconds, I make it," Dorne grunted, pleased with himself as the amputated limb dropped to the deck. "It is a point of pleasure to my professional skills that I never cause undue suffering by taking long, once a course of action has been found. Sutures, quickly now, while he is unconscious. Hogan, more cotton bast for this."

Alan staggered away from the table, almost tripping on the legs of the many wounded who groaned and cried out in agony.

"We win, sor?" someone asked.

"Aye, yes we did," Alan nodded, almost unable to speak.

" 'Tis Judkin, sir, is the captain arright?" the captain's servant asked, his face almost muffled with bast and bandages, with only part of his mouth free.

"I am told he shall live, Judkin."

" 'At's right good, sir, 'e's a good master ta me. 'Ere, Mister Lewrie, 'tis Mister Avery over here," Judkin piped, full of good cheer. "Mister Avery, sir, Mister Lewrie's come a'callin' on ya."

Avery had been stripped bare and covered with a scrap of sail, and what flesh was exposed had been scorched by the explosion of that burst gun, cooked the color of a well-done steak, oozing red.

"Oh, Jesus," Alan reiterated, kneeling down by his friend as David Avery gasped air through his open mouth. "David? Hear me?"

Avery seemed to be trying to whisper; his lips moved, but no words could be made out. His eyes opened for a moment, bloodshot as cherries floating in coal sludge, staring blankly at the deckhead.

"David, 'tis Alan," Lewrie said louder, bending down near the young man's ear. Avery only closed his eyes and gave no sign of awareness, but continued to breathe as though each one would be his last. His body was shivering as though the touch of air on that overheated flesh was excruciating. "Do you want anything, David? Water?"

There was no response, just the uneven heaving of that charred chest. Alan stood back up, almost cracking his head on a deck beam in his haste to flee the compartment, tears flowing down his face.

Too many people he had come to like had just died, too many of the warrants and mates he had dealt with on a daily basis for nearly a year in *Desperate*, so that it felt much like the grief a sole survivor would feel of a Red Indian massacre.

"Ah, Lewrie!" Sedge called out as he spotted him on deck. "I was wondering where you'd got to. Mister Coke needs help with jury-rigging the mizzen mast. Well, get with it! We've not time to moon about!"

Chapter 3

Peaceful night in Frigate Bay, with a light breeze flowing over the decks, bringing cooling relief to crowded mess areas through wind-scoops and ventilators. Lanterns burned at the taffrail, binnacle and fo'c'sle belfry, and work-lanterns glowed as the last of the major hurts to *Desperate* were repaired. Saws rasped, hammers and mallets thudded now and again as something was tamped home in the torn deck or bulwarks.

Commander Treghues was propped up by a mound of pillows in his bed-box hung from the overhead below his repeating compass. His midriff was banded about snugly with white gauze and bast, as was his left arm and shoulder. Beyond the hinged-open stern windows in the transom the riding lights of the fleet could be seen, and close-aboard, the lights of their prize, the twenty-eight-gunned 5th Rate *Capricieuse*.

Freeling had been borrowed from the midshipmen's mess to tend to the captain's needs, serving him a cup of wine laced with his favorite medication, and to serve glasses of wine to the assembled officers and senior warrants.

Alan nodded over his glass, wishing he could lay his head down on the fine mahogany desk and go to sleep on the spot, as Lieutenant Railsford droned on through a list of repairs still necessary to both their own ship and the captured frigate.

"Admiral Hood's flag-captain has assured me he shall be taking charge of those prisoners able-bodied enough to cause mischief to us, sir," Railsford concluded. "Doctor Dorne has replenished his medical supplies well enough to tend to the wounded, both ours and theirs, and a surgeon's assistant shall be coming inboard at first light to aid."

"Very good," Treghues said softly, too sore to take a deep breath or reply with his usual force. "Doctor Dorne, how many of our men show a fair chance for recovery?"

"About eighteen, sir. There are nine that I can do little for, limited as we are. Should we get them to hospital, one or two may yet be saved," Dorne replied heavily, looking as exhausted as a man could and still draw breath himself.

"Our casualties, Mister Railsford," Treghues asked.

"Mister Monk, sir," Railsford said, referring to a quick tally of the dead and badly wounded. "Mister Weems, the master gunner Mister Gwynn, midshipman Avery, Murray the after quarter-gunner, Sergeant McGregor of the Marines, Corporal Smart, Tate the senior quartermaster, . . ." Railsford intoned, going through the long list. Altogether, they had lost eleven dead and twenty-seven wounded, with many of the dead from the senior warrants and department heads.

Damned near a quarter of the crew and Marines, Alan sighed to himself, tipping back his glass of celebratory claret without tasting it. He held out the glass for Freeling to refill, and the lugubrious lout sprang to do his bidding, now that he had a chance to strike as servant to a victorious captain instead of a jumped-up midshipman.

David had died just about an hour after Alan had gone back on deck, never regaining consciousness, which Dr. Dorne assured him was a blessing, for they could not salve his worst burns without bringing away bits of charred flesh on the bandages.

"Mister Sedge is more senior, I believe?" Treghues asked. "He was appointed acting sailing master by poor Mister Monk himself, I recall?"

"Aye, sir," Railsford agreed, and Sedge sat up more erect to preen as his name was mentioned.

"Then we shall honor Mister Monk's dying request. Mister Sedge, you are acting sailing master of *Desperate*."

"Thankee kindly, sir." Sedge beamed.

"Mister Tully to be advanced to take Gwynn's place, and the Yeoman of the Powder Room advanced to gunner's mate," Treghues went on, his mind wonderfully clear for all the claret he had put aboard, and his eyes shrunk to pinpoints by the drug. "A deserving quarter-gunner for Yeoman of the Powder Room?"

"Hogan, fo'c'sle chase-gunner, sir," Alan heard himself suggest. "I sent him aft to clear away the raffle after that brass gun burst, and he did good service."

"Aye, a good report. Make it so, Mister Railsford."

"Aye, sir," Railsford assented, borrowing quill and ink to make corrections in his quarter-bills.

"Promote whom you think best into the other positions and give me their names for my report to Admiral Hood," Treghues said, "along with those Discharged, Dead. How many men shall we need for the prize?"

"A dozen hands, sir," Railsford reckoned, "and I'd suggest a file of Marines under a corporal to keep an eye on the senior Frogs and the wounded who may try to retake her once she's away from under *Barfleur*'s guns."

"Make it eighteen hands and I shall be grateful to you, Mister Peck, if you could supply ten Marines under a corporal into her."

"Aye, sir," Peck agreed, favoring his splinted and wrapped arm.

"Bless me, but we're a damaged lot this evening," Treghues said with an attempt at good cheer. "Prize-master?"

"Well, I could go into her, sir," Railsford replied shyly. If he were to take *Capricieuse* into port, he could parley the fame and the glory into a promotion to commander himself, yet badly as he wanted it, he had to act modest, and shrug off his own suggestion.

"No, I shall need you here in temporary command, unless Dorne is playing the fool about my hurts."

"You should not attempt to rise from that bunk for at least a week, sir," Dorne warned him, "until we know there is no lasting harm from the splinters I withdrew."

Treghues winced at the remembrance of how he had been quilled with wood, and the agony of their extraction, some of them acting like barbed arrow-heads that had torn more flesh as they came out.

"Then I shall rest on my laurels until allowed to rise," the captain said with a small grin. Laurels indeed: he had taken a more powerful ship in bloody combat, with a casualty list sufficiently impressive to awe the Admiralty and the Mob at home. Men had been knighted for less. Captain Pearson of *Serapis* had been knighted for *losing* to the Rebel John Paul Jones after a splendid three-against-one defense.

"Mister Lewrie," Treghues said, turning his head to gaze upon him. "In Lieutenant Railsford's stead, I shall appoint you into the prize. And I think the post of acting lieutenant would not be out of order after today's gallantry."

"Ah." Alan could only gawp in surprise and weariness. Damme, but don't he shower his favorites with blessings, he thought.

Treghues positively glowed at him. "You did good service today with the guns, and in carrying the boarding of our prize. And I mind you've been prize-master before, after that fight off St. Croix? See, you shall have those paroled French officers aboard, and I doubt they would stand for being guarded by a master's mate. That captain of theirs probably would be insulted with anything less than an earl for his gaoler."

Everyone chuckled appreciatively at Treghues' wit, and he had a small laugh himself, before a cough interrupted him and forced him to sit still until it had passed.

"You shall take a care not to lose my prize, though, young sir," Treghues cautioned with only a hint of humor, and Alan knew if he did, he would be hung from a yard-arm in tar and chains until his bones fell apart.

They sailed on the last day of January 1782, passing north-about St. Kitts and to windward of the prowling but ineffective French fleet, *Desperate* repaired enough to accompany them as escort and surety that *Capricieuse* would make Antigua without mischief.

The weather was balmy and the Trades steady, and a carpenter's mate could have commanded the prize, Alan sneered to himself. With the quarterdeck people and the Marines armed to the teeth, and *Desperate*'s guns not half a mile off at any time, the French gave them no trouble.

Captain de Rosset sulked in the officer's wardroom along with this surviving officers and senior warrants, and Alan made free with the captain's quarters as prize-master, lolling on fine cotton sheets and tippling the best wines and brandies he had tasted since he had left London two years before. De Crillart proved a cheerful companion once he had given his parole—he was only a year older than Alan but a droll wit, not given to too much sobriety about life in general, and unimpressed by life in the French Royal Navy as well. His family did not have connections good enough to gain him a commission in a good cavalry regiment, so the Navy was for him, though most people in France looked down on that Service as second to its magnificent Army. Minor nobility or not, the de Crillarts were a genteelly impoverished lot, and his purse had not run to the fineries of his marquis-captain, which while on passage he savored as much as Alan did, as his gaoler's guest.

One rather sodden night in the privacy of the cabins, Alan and de Crillart dined together, with Lewrie's hammockman, Cony, serving as waiter.

"To 'is Brittaneec Majesty, George the t'ird!" de Crillart proposed, raising his glass on high, which pronunciation of "third" sent Lewrie reeling with mirth.

" 'E ees votre roy. What ees so foony?" de Crillart asked.

"Turd, you said," Alan explained between titters. "Nombre trois, in English, is third, not turd. Turd is merde. Dog merde, merde d'chien, merde d'chat, merde d'homme."

"Oh, pardon!" de Crillart gasped as it hit him. "Mon dieu!"

"We call him Farmer George, anyway," Alan went on. "Wants to be thought of as a country squire, when he can't even speak bloody English himself half the time. Vot, Gott in Himmel, eh vot?"

"To 'is Britanneec Majesty, George the . . . th . . . third!" the Frenchman managed this time. They drained their glasses, seated. "The King!" Alan echoed. "And to your king. To his Most Catholic Majesty . . ."

"Dat ees the Espagnole, Lewrie."

"Well, to Louis what's his number, then."

Then de Crillart had to propose a toast to Treghues, whose name he didn't even attempt to butcher, and Alan countered with one to his own captain, Marquis de Rosset, which drew a flash of anger from his supper guest before the young man drained his glass in a gulp.

"Not too fond of him, are you?" Alan surmised.

" 'E ees the buffoon, eh?" de Crillart grimaced. "A fool."

"So is ours," Alan confided, leaning over the table.

Alan explained how Treghues had been addled by a rammer, cut at to relieve pressure on his brain, and what odd medicine he was taking. He also told of the escape from Yorktown, and what the rest of the Navy had thought of that.

"You were in Chesapeake?" de Crillart gasped happily. "Moi, aussi! Une frégate in York Reever? Formidable! *Capricieuse* aussi, le potence to keep you in, n'est-ce pas?"

"Sonofabitch! Really?" Alan barked. "Cony, he was there!"

"Oh, notre capitaine very anger you escape. After 'e swear no one get out. And how tres ironique, we fight at last. Capitaine de Rosset 'e . . . 'e 'ave great anger to pass you. I z'ink 'e 'ave need to be victorieuse, after York Reever." De Crillart shrugged.

"Ours, too," Alan agreed. "My God, Charles, look here. If we had had a different captain, we'd never have needed to have fought you, just kept you from getting into Basse Terre with that schooner. Treghues needed a victory to regain his bloody reputation!"

"And de Rosset need le combat to avenge ees criteecs! Merde, eef any ozzer capitaine 'ave *Capricieuse*, we sail avec no challenge!" de Crillart realized. "So many bon hommes are le mort for zees . . ."

"Touchy bastards," Alan supplied.

"Oui, toochy bastards."

After that mutual admission, their friendship grew firm, until by the time *Desperate* and her prize were under the guns of the hill forts in the outer roads of English Harbor, he was sorry to see the fellow have to go.

They parted with many cries of *"bonne chance"* and promises to keep in touch, and then the world settled down to a long string of boredom once more. Alan stayed aboard *Capricieuse* for weeks as prize-master. Sir George Sinclair was out with some of his Inshore Squadron, so only Prize Court officials and the Dockyard Superintendent were available to upset their lives. Some more repairs were made, with little help with spares from the dockyard unless heavy bribes were offered, but there were too few hands from shore to take over charge of her as she was laid up in-ordinary awaiting her fate. *Desperate* swung at her anchors, too, repaired as well as could be managed under the circumstances, her burst gun replaced, but with no orders to either join Sir George their commodore, or return to St. Kitts.

Alan was loafing under the quarterdeck awnings, tasting the last of his morning tea, when a frigate came in from St. Kitts noisily saluting the flag and the forts.

"Hold up on inspection for a moment," Alan ordered. "Tell the corporal to let his men stand easy while I read her hoists."

Laboriously, in the limited code flags, the arriving frigate spelled out the baleful news that the fort on Brimstone Hill had fallen, and the French now owned the island. Hood and the fleet would be arriving late in the afternoon, after abandoning the anchorage during the preceding night and getting clean away, leaving de Grasse befuddled.

"So that's all we get, sir?" the senior quartermaster asked him as Alan put the glass away into the binnacle rack. "No more ships took?"

"If there were, we weren't in sight to share the prize-money."

Any allied ship within spy-glass distance, even if all the view she had was tops'ls above the horizon, could claim shares in any action that resulted in prize-money, so taking *Capricieuse* within sight of all the line-of-battle ships in Hood's fleet wouldn't provide enough silver per survivor to make a decent meal in a three-penny ordinary, even counting the head money bonus per man in the crew of the prize.

"Might get a plug o' baccy at best, sir," the quartermaster spat in disgust, and Alan knew it was going to be a grueling inspection that the quartermaster was about to visit on his small crew.

"We may only hope for advancement from this," Alan comforted, hoping there was indeed advancement. He had gotten used to having that large frigate under his sole control, of being an acting lieutenant even for so short a period.

"Politics," Alan griped, once more a master's mate back in the dreary misery of the midshipmen's mess in the cockpit. "Petticoat influence. Family connections."

"Don't take it so hard, Lewrie," Sedge told him. Sedge could talk, since he had been confirmed as sailing master in *Desperate*. "We get a new captain out of it, and you should be glad for Mister Railsford."

Hood had conferred with the Prize Court and instructed them to purchase *Capricieuse* into the Royal Navy. Treghues had been made post-captain into the prize, and Railsford, as the senior lieutenant of such a magnificent seizure, had been promoted to Commander into *Desperate*.

This also allowed Hood and his flag-captain to do favors for some of their patrons' protégés, or promote some of their own. Two young men had gone into *Capricieuse* as lieutenants of a coveted frigate instead of loafing as very junior officers in a

line-of-battle ship. More midshipmen had to be appointed into
both ships, more junior and senior warrants transferred, giving
promotion to them and their replacements aboard their old ships,
more master's mates made of promising midshipmen.

"There's always an examining board," Sedge yawned as he
told his family now in New York of his luck, by letter. "You've
had over two years as midshipman or master's mate. Ask of
Railsford and he'll recommend your name if they seat a board
soon."

Alan doubted that possibility very much, for there was also
the niggling requirement that one had to have been entered in
ship's books for six years of sea duty. And from what he had
learned from others who had gone for oral examination before a
panel of captains, it was more fun to be flayed raw, with the
chances of promotion by that route about as sure as the proverbial camel passing through a needle's eye.

Altogether, Alan was getting very fed up with Sedge. He had
started out as a graceless lout, and he was rapidly turning into
an insolently superior and graceless lout.

"Well, I shall shift my dunnage aft. Good luck to you, Mister
Lewrie," Sedge drawled in his nasal Jonathon twang, which
sound was also a rasp on Alan's soul.

"And you too, sir," Alan was forced to say to his new sailing
master. "May you have joy of your promotion and the pleasures
of the wardroom." Damn his blood! Alan added to himself with
some heat.

The new master's mate and new midshipman off *Barfleur*
were in the process of unpacking and stirring around the cockpit,
so Alan took himself on deck to get away from them.

With all the ships back in harbor, it was a damned busy place
with rowing boats working like a plague of water-bugs at all
hours and a constant stream of flag signals from shore or the
flagship.

"Mister Lewrie, one o' them boats is fer us, looks like," Cony
told him, pointing off to larboard.

"Right. Mister Toliver, gather up your side-party. It looks as
if the new first lieutenant may be coming aboard at last. Cony,
run aft and inform Commander Railsford."

"Aye, aye, sir."

Once within hailing distance, Toliver the bosun's mate leaned
over the entry port and cupped his hands around his mouth.

"Ahoy, there!"

"Aye aye!" the bowman in the boat shouted back, putting up

two fingers in the air to show that a commission officer was aboard and was for them.

"Sergeant, muster Marine party and side-men fer a lieutenant!"

Alan paced back to the quarterdeck nettings overlooking the waist while Marines and seamen formed up to welcome their new first officer, and Alan hoped that he was as equitable a man as Railsford had been in that position. He had seen just a glimpse past the oarsmen to an officer in the stern-sheets, a tanned face under a cocked hat with a dog's vane and buttoned loop of gold lace, a slightly shabby coat bespeaking an officer of lengthy sea duty, and probably bags of experience, a real tarpaulin man.

Pipes trilled as the new officer's hat appeared level with the lip of the entry port, and he finished scrambling up the manropes and battens to stand on the gangway, doffing his hat to the side-party. The duty watch and the working parties stopped their labors to doff their own flat, tarred hats in return or touch forelocks.

"Oh, stap me," Alan muttered. God, he thought sadly, we need to have a little chat someday about frightening the very devil out of me like this. Fashionably a Deist, he was still imbued with the myths of many a governess, who had crooned or beaten a more personal and vengeful God into him from his breeching on, and he spent a futile few seconds trying to discover just what was so bad that he had done, the last few months at least, to deserve such a fate.

Their new first lieutenant, the man who could make or break any warrant or hand, was none other than Alan's former master and commander from the *Parrot* sloop, Lt. James Kenyon! There was possibly no other officer in the entire Navy, much less the Leewards, who had a lower opinion of Alan Lewrie's honor and morals.

The cruelly ironic thing about it was that it was Alan who had saved the man's command from capture, but had he acted the slightest bit grateful for that act? Hell, no.

Kenyon had been flat on his back with Yellow Jack, lost in his delirium, when they were accosted by a French privateer brig just days from port and safety. *Parrot* had already struck her colors, her mate at a total loss, and if Alan had not disobeyed him and opened fire into the enemy ship, setting her afire and scything away her jeering boarding party, Kenyon would now be languishing in some prison hulk on Martinique, if not dead as mutton.

But when Alan had emerged from the throes of Yellow Jack himself in Adm. Sir Onsley Matthews' shore establishment on Antigua, he found a galling letter from Lieutenant Kenyon, accusing him of everything low and base that the officer could think of. Kenyon had put out one hundred guineas at least to gift Alan with the lovely sterling-silver trimmed hanger he now wore on his left hip, a parting gift intended for Alan to use to defend what little honor he had left, the next time it was called to question, as Kenyon was sure it would be. The memory of those phrases still rankled; "firing into an admirable foe after striking the colors," "violation of a sanctified usage of the sea," disobedience, insubordination, "eternal shame," and much more in the same vein. Kenyon had sworn on paper that he could no longer stomach having Lewrie anywhere near him, and were it in his power, he would toss him out of the Navy before he befouled it with a loathsome stench.

Kenyon finished taking the salute and began shaking hands with the senior warrants whose lives he would control from that instant, and made his way aft towards the quarterdeck to report to Commander Railsford. Alan doffed his hat to him as respectfully as he could and gauged Lieutenant Kenyon's reaction as he recognized him.

Just a little help here, God? Alan prayed silently as Kenyon squinted hard and turned down the corners of his mouth in distaste.

"You, is it?" he said, mouth working as though sucking on some acid fruit-rind. He tossed off a brief salute in return, which allowed Alan to lower his arm. "I heard you'd been posted into *Desperate* last year. Matter of fact, I was hoping you would still be here."

"Thank you, sir," Alan replied evenly.

"No no, don't thank me, Lewrie." Kenyon laughed curtly. "There was always the chance I would not catch up with you, if you had been behaving to your normal standards, and had been dismissed from the Service for licentiousness or another act of disobedience."

"Still prospering, sir," Alan told him, knowing exactly where he stood now, and determined to ride it out with as much dumb civility as the lowest ordinary seaman.

"The Devil's spawn usually do, I fear," Kenyon said. "I see you still have the hanger I gave you. Cut anybody lately?"

"Just that one duel, sir, and that over a young lady."

"What right have you to wear it 'stead of a midshipman's dirk?"

"I am a master's mate, sir, confirmed back in December."

"Indeed?" Kenyon pondered that for a time. "Yes, I'd heard some talk of you being brave and efficient. But we know better about you, do we not, Mister Lewrie? What sort of a sham whip-jack you really are."

"Excuse me, sir, far be it from me to advise my seniors, but the captain is probably expecting you to see him," Alan suggested softly.

"Oh, how droll, how politic of you," Kenyon sneered. "And how unlike you to find this sudden modesty about advising, or disobeying your seniors, as you put it. You were quick enough to disobey Mister Claghorne, weren't you."

"Damme, sir, I saved our ship!" Alan insisted.

"But at what price, Mister Lewrie?" Kenyon hissed. "Claghorne's authority, my honor, the honor of the Royal Navy? I shall attend our captain, but then I'll be wanting to talk with you further on this matter. Don't leave the quarterdeck."

"Aye aye, sir."

"Claghorne is dead, you know," Kenyon said over his shoulder.

So bloody what? Alan thought as Kenyon left.

"Old friend, Mister Lewrie?" Sedge asked after the first officer had gone aft to present himself.

"Ah, he was master and commander of *Parrot*, my previous ship," Alan replied, feeling weak in the knees. "And second officer of *Ariadne* back in '80, sir."

"What, that old receiving hulk in the inner harbor?" Sedge said. "You were in her when she was condemned?"

"My first ship, sir," Alan informed him.

"Well, what sort is he, then?"

"Kenyon's a taut hand, very professional," Alan went on, putting on a grin and an air of old comradeship that he most definitely did not feel. "You'll find him a fair man, sir."

Unless he hates the fucking sight of you, Alan qualified to himself. Then he'll be a raving bastard.

"Was he much of a flogger?"

"No, sir, and neither was our old Captain Bales."

"All's right, then," Sedge sniffed in his Jonathon twang and paced away to his own concerns, satisfied that *Desperate* would be getting a first lieutenant much like her new captain in spirit, and that there would be no unreasonableness to upset his new rating.

Fuck it is, Alan thought, and wondered why these things had to happen to him so continually. First Kenyon's animosity after *Parrot*, then that bloody duel with that sneering fop of an Army lieutenant. In *Desperate* he could do nothing right in Treghues' eyes, but had almost won the man over when up pops Sir George Sinclair and his flag-captain who was the same man from the Impress Service that had carted him off to Portsmouth to sling him into Navy uniform. Treghues had turned on him meanly, and probably would still despise him if it had not been for that blessed French gunner and his damned rammer. Erratic insanity could sometimes be a blessing. He had settled the smut on his name back home, found a family he didn't even know he had and a remittance anyone would kill for. A small measure of fame in the Fleet, promotion to master's mate—and now this. Every time he had things in hand, some perverse twist of fate brought him crashing down in ruin, until he did not imagine he would have any chance of security in anything this side of the grave.

"Better people than you have tried to ruin me, damn your blood," Alan cursed softly as he pondered what Kenyon had in mind for him. And he grinned suddenly as he realized that it was true. His father had laid a plot almost inescapable, and look who still could trot his phyz out in public without being snatched into debtor's prison! If Kenyon would use his power as first lieutenant to bring Lewrie down, then he would be forced to fire off his own broadside in reply. Kenyon was not invulnerable, for all his rank and position and talk of honor. The man was a secret Molly, a butt-fucker of the windward passage, wasn't he? Alan had been told that odd goings-on between Kenyon and their host in Kingston had occurred in the wee hours. Alan had seen the men bussing like practiced lovers in the dark coach outside The Grapes the last night in port; Kenyon and Sir Richard Slade, rekindling a boyish passion for each other when their paths crossed once again. Hadn't Lieutenant Kenyon hinted once that he had not wanted to go to sea any more than Alan had, but there had been . . . reasons?

You'll not have me, Jemmy, Alan swore to himself. If you try, I'll have you! Railsford'll never abide a sodomite in his ship, not with the Navy trying so hard to stamp it out on long cruises. We're not in Cambridge.

Kenyon came back on deck once more, and made his way

towards the taffrail, out of ear-shot of the other people in the harbor watch or the working parties. He crooked a finger to draw Lewrie to follow him.

"I am sorry to hear that Mister Claghorne passed over, sir," Alan said, trying to mollify the man.

"He shot himself, Lewrie."

"Ah, too bad." Alan frowned. Claghorne had been an idiot, but there never had been anything in his life that Alan knew of that would force him to that. "Gambling debts, sir?"

"You, you little bastard," Kenyon snarled. "Admiral Matthews gave him a commission after *Parrot* made port. He got her as his command, and the shame was too much for him."

"But why in hell would they do that, sir?" Alan marveled. "He's the one struck her colors. Moody the bosun called him a coward to his face!"

"Ah, but remember, Lewrie, our passenger Lord Cantner and his lady, who thought you were so bloody marvelous that you'd saved their lives and their profits from the sale of his Jamaican properties, all the gold they'd brought aboard with them." Kenyon sneered. "They went to Matthews and bade him make sure you were written up a hero, and that meant there could be no mention of the colors being struck—not quite the honorable usage of the white flag—and they didn't want it getting round that a British ship had done such a thing. Fortunately, there were no survivors from that privateer brig, you made sure of that."

"Claghorne wouldn't allow us near her as long as she was afire, sir, and I was down with the Yellow Jack myself before we could do anything, so that is grossly unfair, sir," Alan shot back.

"Keep a civil tongue in your head, boy," Kenyon ordered. "So poor Claghorne is a new commission officer, senior in a victory over a more powerful foe, and what's the reward for a faithful first?"

"Promotion and command, sir," Alan stated, in control again of his emotions.

"Yes. And would they transfer him into another ship?"

"If they had half a brain, sir, given the circumstances."

"Aye, they would, but old Onsley is not blessed with brains, is he, Lewrie? More tripe and trullibubs upstairs to match the suet down below. What sort of chance do you think Claghorne had in command of a crew that knew him for a man who once was forced to strike? Whether or not there was a chance to fight that privateer, he was in command, and his decision was correct, simply because he was a senior officer, do you comprehend that, Lewrie? You disobeyed him!"

"So you'd rather be dead or in chains, sir?" Alan demanded.

"Damn you to hell, sir!" Kenyon spat. "Have you learned no shame, no sense of guilt for what you have done? You cost a good man his life."

"I saved yours, and every man-jack aboard, sir," Alan retorted. "Besides, Claghorne was ready to strike as soon as he saw that brig, and nothing you or anyone else could have said would have changed his mind, and not doing everything in one's power to prepare a ship to fight, or offering no resistance when there's a chance to do so is cowardice, at least a court-martial offense on one charge, sir. But we did offer resistance, and I proved that resistance was possible, so Claghorne should have been strung up, or cashiered. Now it's not my fault Sir Onsley gave that fatuous clown *Parrot*, sir. Had he given it a little thought, he would have known it was a death sentence, and . . ."

"God, I knew you were base, but I had no idea you were such a cold-blooded, dissembling hound, Lewrie!" Kenyon marveled. "Had the colors still been flying, your resistance would have resulted in every man-jack, as you put it, slaughtered with cold steel. And to smear a good man's name, to call him a clown, a fatuous clown . . . I once thought highly of you, Lewrie. I asked for you in *Parrot*. I took you under my aegis when I saw how you were floundering about those first weeks in *Ariadne*. I'd like to think that what little you have learned about the Navy was partly my doing."

"It is, sir, believe me."

"I gave you my trust," Kenyon went on, his heart almost breaking as the enormity of Alan's perceived sins overwhelmed his anger. "I brought you up from a seasick younker, taught you, gave you room to grow as a seaman, gave you responsibility, and I thought you were growing into a fine young man. But then you let me down so badly."

"I am sorry you see things that way, sir." Alan calmed, knowing he would not be able to get through Kenyon's screen of bile with any logic. "But I was technically second in command of *Parrot* at the time, and had a responsibility to do everything I could to prevent us being taken. Lord Cantner's knowledge of government secrets, their persons, the ship's people . . ."

"Don't cloak your actions in any false sense of duty," Kenyon snapped, back in rancor again. "I told you in my letter I'd not abide you in my presence, nor in my Navy, and I meant it.

There's a vile streak to you that belongs in the gutter, not strutting about a quarterdeck as a junior warrant. Now I'm first officer into this ship, I shall make sure you serve her, and the Fleet, no longer than necessary."

"And satisfactory performance at my duties could not alter your resolve, sir," Alan sighed, steeling himself to use his ammunition.

"Not a whit, Lewrie. I mean to see you cashiered, or broken to ordinary seaman and sent forward in pusser's slops."

"That's devilish unfair, sir."

"Not to my lights it ain't."

"There are other officers who think highly of me in this ship, sir," Alan countered. "Your intent will look like persecution."

"I've been in the Navy ten years longer than you, Lewrie, I can find a way, believe me," Kenyon promised with a lupine grin that lit his countenance for a bleak moment. "And when you are broken, I'll shed a martyr's tears over your lost potential. No one shall portray sadness more than I."

"Ah, but you *are* good at acting, sir," Alan let slip out as the threat loosened his last cautions. "By the way, sir, have you seen Sir Richard Slade in Kingston lately?"

"What do you mean, sir?" Kenyon asked, suddenly on his guard.

"I was just wondering if he was still buggering his little black link-boys, and the odd house-guest?" Alan replied. In for the penny, in for the bloody pound, he thought grimly.

"You think that I . . ." Kenyon spluttered, but Alan was delighted to note that the man had blanched a fresh, book-paper white under his deep tropical tan, and his eyes almost bulged out of his head.

"I was in 'The Grapes' when you and Sir Richard came up in his coach, sir," Alan went on. "I saw the crest on the door, recognized the man, *and* the naval lieutenant in the coach with him, sir."

"I never suspected until now just how *filthy* you are, Lewrie," Kenyon muttered, still floundering after that broadside to his hull. "All the more reason to break you and toss you back into the sinks and stews you came from!"

"But do I malign you, sir?" Alan asked, fighting a grin of triumph. "Or is your manhood just another sham?"

"You'll pay for this," Kenyon said, once he had regained control over himself. He smiled wickedly, which smile made Lewrie wonder if he was half the sly-boots he had thought himself just a second before. But he knew what he had seen, didn't he?

"A beslimed little get like you'll not hope to threaten me with a blackguard's tale, Lewrie," Kenyon swore. "I promised I'd break you, and I shall. And I tell you this. For trying to blackmail me into leniency, I swear I'll see you at the gratings, getting striped by the cat. You'll leave the Navy wearing the 'checkered shirt' that I'll put on you. I'll see you flayed raw and half-killed, and you know I can find a way to do it, don't you. Don't you? Answer me, you Goddamned rogue!"

"Aye, sir," Alan was forced to admit, for the sin of not answering could be construed as a charge of dumb insolence, enough to get him dis-rated from master's mate, if Railsford was of mind.

"I assure you you'll pay," Kenyon promised, with almost a lover's sweetness. "You'll not enjoy a moment's peace from this day on. And I also assure you, you'll not enjoy what's coming to you. Now get out of my sight!"

"Aye aye, sir," Alan said, saluting and turning away. As he made his way blindly forward, he suffered a cold, shivering fit at what a cock-up he had made of things with his defiant remarks. There was a sheen of sweat on his body and he was like to faint from the encounter.

Damme, how could I have been so abysmally bloody stupid! he thought. If it was just Claghorne and *Parrot*, I could have found some way to prove my worth to the dirty bastard. Why did I have to say that? In for the penny, in for the pound, indeed! Why, why do I have to think I'm so bloody clever, when I just dig my grave deeper every time I do so?

He fetched up somewhere on the fo'c'sle and pretended to study the angle of the anchor cable and the chafe-gear on the hawse, as he found his breath and tried to still the rising panic in his heart. Where was salvation? Should he go to Railsford immediately and tell him what he had seen? There was a good chance Railsford would not believe him, or Kenyon would have a good excuse for his actions in that coach. He and Sir Richard had been childhood friends, and what was more natural than a goodbye kiss between old friends? It could be painted a lot more innocent than what Alan had seen. And he *was* sure of that, wasn't he?

Should he parley his new fame into a transfer? He would have to state reasons, and would be back to the same contretemps. Should he simply cash out and escape? Damned if he would!

You and your mouth, Lewrie! he castigated himself. You and your bloody, stupid temper! I've tossed the dice this time, damme if I haven't!

Chapter 4

Desperate spent another week swinging at her anchorage in the inner harbor, as Hood's presence forced the dockyard officials to pay attention to her final repairs, and Alan Lewrie spent that week staying as far forward or aft of the first lieutenant as one could in so restricted a world as a 6th Rate frigate. When forced by duty into immediate vicinity he sweated buckets trying to shrink into his coat and hat to be as anonymous as possible. Oddly, once Kenyon had gone through the ship with a fine-tooth-comb with the warrants and department heads, he had ducked aft into the wardroom as officers did in harbor and stood no watches. And when forced to converse with him, Kenyon showed absolutely no malice or any signs that they had ever had a cross word with each other, which possibly made Lewrie even more nervous than anything else Kenyon could have done.

He'll wait till we're at sea where he can really bugger me, Alan concluded to himself, almost writhing in dread anticipation of how many ways he could be caught out at his duties by an alert and vengeful first officer. With grudge enough, the bloody wooden figurehead could be found derelict and flogged, he realized.

"Passin' the word fer Mister Sedge an' Mister Lewrie!"

Alan was torn from his frightful imaginings and summoned aft to Railsford's quarters, which brought even more dread to his already tortured soul. He could not remember one good thing ever happening in the great cabins, even if Treghues was no longer there as their occupant.

Railsford had seemed to expand since his promotion to command. He lolled in a leather-padded dining chair behind a new desk in the day cabin. The furnishings were not as fine as Treghues' had been, much of the dining table and chairs bought used from a shore chandlery, or put together by the carpenter's crew out of such limited selection of lumber as could be found in English Harbor or across the island at St. John's.

Railsford seemed merry enough as they removed their hats and tucked them under their arms. He had one leg flung across a chair arm, his shirt open and his stock removed to savor the balmy breeze that blew in through the transom windows and the open skylight and ventilator chute.

"Admiral Hood informs us he's to seat an examining board day after tomorrow," Railsford began, stuffing tobacco into a clay church-warden, while Freeling puttered about striking flint and tinder to get a light for him. "I thought you two might be interested in it. Mister Sedge, what say you?"

"Beggin' yer pardon, sir, but I'd not be interested."

"The devil you say!" Railsford gawked. "You'd pass easy."

"Aye, sir, I might," Sedge agreed with a small smile. "I've been at sea since I was nine on family ships, sir. But I intend a career in merchant service 'stead of the Navy."

"But still—" Railsford shrugged, his pipe now lit.

"The Navy don't pay, sir, and my family needs money to get back on their feet after what the Rebels looted from us," Sedge concluded in a sigh. "The Navy's only been temp'rary. Sailin' master's high enough for me, and more suited to my future employment, sir."

"Hmm, if you are sure, I don't suppose anything I say could convince you," Railsford acquiesced. "I wish you joy of your career. But after the war, there'll be a glut of qualified officers once the Fleet's been reduced. Passing may give you the leg up."

"Aye, sir, but my uncle and my dad still have two ships, and I'd be at least a mate come hell'r high water," Sedge told him smugly.

"Thank you, Mister Sedge, that'll be all, then. Well, Mister Lewrie, what about you?" Railsford asked as Sedge left.

"Yes, sir!" Alan answered with alacrity, sensing escape from his problems. "But only ... I don't have six years on ship's books, sir."

"Oh, the devil with that, there's a war on, and no one gives a tinker's damn about piddling details, not on a foreign station."

"Really, sir?" Alan brightened, wondering if he could stand on firmer ground as a passed midshipman, if he wasn't immediately made a lieutenant. Please, dear God, I promise I'll keep my mouth shut! Please!

"If your records are in order, and you may answer their questions sensibly, they'd have no reason to refuse you, Mister Lewrie," Railsford told him, now puffing a wreath of smoke around his head.

"Then I would like to try, sir," Alan agreed quickly.

"You're fortunate that I can give you a good report, as well as Captain Treghues over in *Capricieuse*, all in harbor at the same time. And the former second officer and your old commander in your first two ships as well, just in case you didn't keep your professional *bona fides* in order," Railsford maundered on lazily.

"Ah, the first lieutenant, sir." Alan turned a touch gloomy at the thought of Lieutenant Kenyon, and the very idea of having to depend on him to put in a good word for him now.

"I'll ask of him for you," Railsford offered. "Now, there's not much time to study, so you'd best be about it. Dine with me this evening and I shall fill you in on procedure and what the likely questions are to be. Go through your *Falconer*'s and especially your navigation texts. Mister Sedge would be a good tutor."

"Aye, sir," Alan nodded. God, what if I'm passed for lieutenant? he speculated once on deck again. There *must* be openings for dozens of officers in all these ships, else they'd never seat the bloody board! Well, maybe a dozen in all. And how many midshipmen to examine? A hundred? In one day, two days? They can't spend more than half an hour on any of them, could they? Maybe even a quarter hour. I'm not stupid, and I *have* learned a lot. And there must be plenty of idiots who'll stand no chance before a board. I could be one of those dozen who pass and receive a posting into a new ship. Even if I don't get an immediate posting, I could become prize-master the next time we take a foe, and be away from Kenyon again, free as the birds. Or, he concluded grimly, God help me, I could fail and be stuck here.

"Well turned out, I see," Railsford commented on Lewrie's uniform as he was announced into the after cabins. "I trust you're saving your best for the board."

"Aye, sir," Alan replied, feeling on tenter-hooks at the sight of Lieutenant Kenyon seated aft on the transom settee with a glass of wine in his hand.

"Take a seat, Mister Lewrie," Railsford directed, meaning to put him at his ease. "Address yourself to that decanter of claret in front of you. Just in from home on the packet, though I fear it did not travel at all well. Still . . ."

"Thankee, sir," Alan replied, clawing a stemmed glass from the towel and pouring it almost full.

"I must tell you that when I informed Captain Treghues of your intent to attend the examining board, he was delighted at the idea," Railsford related, seating himself at the dining table. "Mister Kenyon, do come join us for a companionable drink before supper is served."

"Aye, sir," Kenyon said. When he sat down, Alan was pleased to note that, though the night was relatively cool, the first officer wore a sheen of sweat on his brow and his upper lip, and beads of moisture trickled down his cheeks.

"Little did you realize, Mister Kenyon, that our prodigy here would be presenting himself for the chance at a commission in your lifetime, hey?" Railsford began with a small jest.

"Indeed not, sir," Kenyon chuckled with a superior little drawl, like a gambler whose hole-cards will take the game as soon as he shows them. "I'd have expected more like another year or two of seasoning. Spent five years a younker before I stood a board."

"The full six for me," Railsford reminisced.

"Two years and a bit, though." Kenyon frowned, warming to his theme. "Well, that's cutting it a bit fine, even in wartime."

"But we were callow little cullies of twelve or thirteen." The captain laughed, which made Alan dart a thankful glance at him. "Mister Lewrie was more mature when he first put on King's coat, and a cut above the average midshipman in intelligence to begin with."

"Seasick in Portsmouth, and adrift in old *Ariadne*. In harbor," Kenyon added with relish. "Took an hour to report to our first officer after he stepped below."

"Still, he learned quickly," Railsford said, chuckling at the image of Lewrie "casting his accounts" over the side of a ship safely moored in Portsmouth. "Some learn faster than others. I've no qualms about his prospects, if you don't."

"Did I not learn, sir?" Alan interrupted, directing his gaze to Kenyon. "So many things. About the Navy. And *people*."

Damned if he was going to sit there being discussed like a *thing*, and damned if he was going to let Kenyon lay doubts about him. Kenyon almost choked on a sip of wine at the last comment.

"Enough to stand before a board, I'll warrant," Railsford went on, oblivious to Alan's little verbal shot. "Captain Treghues sent me a packet for you, Lewrie. Letter of recommendation, and a list of some questions you'll likely be challenged with. Ah, here's the one about outfitting a ship from truck to keel. And some other posers he's heard about over his years."

"I'm most grateful for any aid from him, sir."

"Didn't exactly love you when you first joined *Desperate*, did he?" Railsford shrugged. "Our late captain did not hold with dueling, and our Alan here had just put some Army bastard's lights out."

"Yes, I heard about that," Kenyon said. "Even if the girl was your admiral's niece, I'd not have approved, either."

"Well, I can say it now he's got his new command and is gone from us," Railsford stated. "Captain Treghues played the most devilish favorites, sometimes for the worst people. It was feast or famine for everyone, and no sense to it, no way of knowing how one may have offended."

"His cater-cousin, Midshipman Forrester, sir." Alan grimaced.

"Thank God we left the surly turd at Yorktown," Railsford said with a laugh. "Yet, prejudiced as he was in the beginning, he came 'round to appreciate Mister Lewrie, so his praise is doubly blessed."

"To everything there is a season, so to speak, sir," Kenyon replied. "Approbation or shame. But did your captain shun the worthy and praise the unworthy by seasons, sir? Then perhaps . . . well, if he had learned of young Alan's past, and if he was, as I've heard, a perfect Tartar on religion and proper behavior, who's to know why Captain Treghues would recommend him now so highly. Or is it more of the same?"

"You speak of Mister Lewrie's antecedents, sir?" Railsford bristled a little at his first officer. "Our purser's brother straightened that out for him. There's no shame in having a shady past, or a Corinthian brothel-dandy for a father, if one may rise above it, sir. Excuse me, Mister Lewrie, if I portray your father in that light."

"One might add forgerer, thief, bigamist, false witness and bugger, sir," Alan ticked off cheerfully. "I'm told he only sticks his head out o' Sundays when he can't be taken for debts."

"There's no family so blameless the light of day wouldn't turn up a rogue or two, Mister Kenyon. All the more reason to wish Lewrie well with the examining board, since he's risen so far above his own. A captain must not become too familiar with his officers and crew, so I will most definitely *not* mention the rumors of smuggling and ship-wrecking spoken about the Railsford's in the past back in Weymouth." He gave them a look in conclusion that indicated they should laugh.

"I must confess I was not bound for the sea from the time I was breeched, sir, as you were," Alan said to Railsford. "But, once I did get to sea, and I found my legs, as it were, I must own to an ambition to become a commission officer and serve as best I can."

Oh God, Alan thought, if I heard another shit-sack like me spout such things, I believe I'd box his ears first and then spew in his lap. Damn Kenyon! First poison about my abilities, now these slurs on Treghues' opinion, and my past. Surely Railsford can see the bastard's prejudiced against me! I'll most likely fail the board and then he'll have me triced up and ruined if I don't put him in his place now!

"One would think you harbored some grievance against Lewrie yourself, Mister Kenyon," Railsford chid his first officer.

"I wish him fortune with the board, sir, though I doubt he's seasoned enough to be a commission officer yet," Kenyon countered with a beatific grin that belied his motives. He did look a little desperate, though, as he realized that he had overstepped the bounds of subtlety. He had his own place to earn with Railsford in this new ship.

"Perhaps, sir," Alan said to Railsford, "Mister Kenyon remembers my first days aboard old *Ariadne*, when I as much confessed to him that I did not wish to make the sea my calling. But, Mister Kenyon, I remember as well, you once told me that you were not enamored of going to sea when you first joined, but that certain reasons made it necessary. Would your own personal history be reflected upon mine? Ordinarily I would not presume to inquire, but this seems such an informal occasion. Perhaps your beginning might make a merry tale."

Squirm your way out of that, you whoreson! Alan thought happily.

"Yes, Mister Kenyon. How did you get your ha'porth of tar?" Railsford asked, pouring them another glassful as the salad arrived.

Kenyon had not expected such a frontal attack, and he turned queasy as a land-lubber in a full gale. But, over the years, he had invented a plausible past, and had polished it with retelling, so whatever unnatural act he had committed that forced him to sea "to make a man of him" had been submerged. It should have tripped from his lips without effort, usually. And he began it, but didn't quite gain that casual, bluff and hearty, tarry-handed air he usually affected.

"Well, sir, boys will be wild animals, you know . . ." he started with a shaky laugh, taking time to glare evilly at Lewrie in warning.

That carried them through soup and salad. Commander Railsford in his turn related his own entry into the Navy after that, and through most of the main course, unbending from the stiffness, aloofness and anonymity expected of a captain who held the lives and careers of his dining companions in his hands for good or ill.

At least, Alan noted, Kenyon dropped his dirge about Alan being so unready for the attempt at a commission, and watched him with a chary eye for the rest of the dinner, never knowing at what moment he might pop up with another question, or a veiled comment that would expose him.

The man sipped from the same glass of wine all through dinner, and sweated as though he had been forced to stoke the fires of Hell, which gave Alan a great deal of pleasure to witness.

Chapter 5

Feeling nervous as a kit-fox who has just heard the hunter's horn, Alan Lewrie climbed through the entry port into *Barfleur* on the morning appointed for his ordeal. The waters in English Harbor had been swarming with boats trying to ply oars as midshipmen from all the vessels currently present had assembled to the summoning flag pendants, bearing their hopeful occupants.

He clutched his canvas-wrapped documents to his breast after he had saluted the side-party and the quarterdeck, feeling an urge to read through them once more to assure his twanging nerves that they were still all there, and that they still sang his praises as nicely as they had when he had first received them.

Treghues had penned a fulsome letter from his new command in *Capricieuse*. His aptly named capriciousness of mood had indeed turned full circle, and now Midshipman Lewrie had been one of his best junior warrants right from the start, more mature and quicker of mind than any young man he had ever met, etc.

Railsford had penned a neat little recommendation, not so laudatory as to stir disbelief; taut and nautical like the man himself. And, Alan still marveled, Kenyon had added recommendations of his own, with no mention of nagging worries that Lewrie might be a little wet behind the ears. Beyond the bare recitation of the deeds in which Alan had taken part and distinguished himself by his conduct and bravery, or his developing knowledge of sea lore, there was little *real* praise, but it did leave the impression that he was at least somewhat worthy of examination.

Lukewarm Kenyon's approval might be, but at least he did not disapprove, and Alan thought that Railsford had something to do with that. He might have had to press Kenyon for a favorable letter, but what could Kenyon do, Alan asked himself in a moment of smugness, refuse to recommend his new captain's favorite? Show displeasure with such a well thought of young fellow with so much promise?

There was also the possibility that Kenyon was hedging his bets, laying groundwork of his own so that when Alan failed the board and came back aboard with his tail between his legs, he could tell Railsford that he had told him so. And if Alan failed, would he lose enough of Railsford's approval that Kenyon could then begin to lay a stink upon him, carp at failures and bring him down until he caught him out and then proceeded to break him?

"There must be an hundred of us, I swear to God," a gangly midshipman commented at Alan's elbow. "And more coming all the time. Every fool with white collar tabs must think he has a chance, this board."

The speaker was in his twenties, and while all the others that Alan had seen were turned out in their best kit, this one was wearing a somewhat shabby coat, and his waist-coat and breeches were dingy. Was he poor as a traveling tinker, or did he just not care? Alan wondered.

"Let us hope most of them are abominably stupid," Alan said to be pleasant, still praying, as most of them did, that he would pass.

"This is my third board," the older midshipman confided with a breezy air. "But I'll pass this time. Think you I look salty enough?"

"Aye, salty's the word for you," Alan said with a raised eyebrow.

"They'll have a host of little angels in there today, all alike as two peas in a pod, scrubbed up so their own mothers wouldn't know 'em," the older lad reasoned. "But when they see a real tarry-handed younker, they'll just assume they've a prime candidate on their hands and go easy on me."

Alan wished the fellow would go away. He was trembling with anxiety, and all the guidance, set questions and trick posers he had been coached in had flown out of his head. He was sure if he did not have space to think for a while before they started examining people, his brains would leave him utterly. But he had to respond.

"I should think they would dig down for the most arcane stuff if you show too knowledgeable as soon as you enter the room," Alan said.

"God, don't say that," the young man snapped, losing a little of his swagger. "Besides, I know my stuff, you see if I don't."

"Then the best of luck to you." Alan bowed, wanting to be alone. The quarterdeck was swarming with midshipmen, all furrowing their brows as they re-read their texts once more, casting their hopeful faces skyward, reciting silently the hard questions they had drilled on as though at heartfelt prayer.

"Right, you lot," an officer shouted above the low din. "Now, who'll be first below?"

Not a soul moved, shocked by the suggestion of being the first sacrificial lamb to the slaughter.

"What a pack of cod's-heads," the officer grunted with a sour expression. "You lads to starboard, then. Lead off. You, the ginger-haired one, you're the bell-wether, whether you like it or not. They've had their breakfasts already, so they might be pleasant."

That started a parade toward the ladders into the captain's quarters on the upper gun deck, where clerks met them and took down their names and ships. All the furnishings from the outer cabins had been cleared, so they were forced to stand. Alan was about twentieth on the list; he had reasoned that the closer the examining board got to their mid-day meal, the less time they would want to spend asking damn-fool questions of damn-fool midshipmen, and might throw him two or three posers and then make up their minds quickly, allowing him a better chance to show well without being grilled like a steak.

Like a patient waiting for the surgeon to attend him, he took a place against an interior partition and forced himself to think of something pleasant. It was already too crowded and warm in the cabins, and there was almost no elbow room to dig into his snowy-white breeches for a pocket handkerchief to mop the slight sheen of sweat from his face.

"Git off my fuckin' shoes, damn yer blood."

"Who's on the board, then?"

"Captain of the Fleet, Napier off *Resolution*, Captain Cornwallis of *Canada* . . ."

"Oh, fuck me, he's a Tartar!"

"Box-hauling? What the hell do I know about box-hauling?" Hands flurried to open texts at that strangled wail of despair.

Alan had considered bringing his own books with him, but after two days of cramming in every spare moment, he realized that he would either know the answers or he would not, and anything he read at the last second would melt away before he could recall it. So he did not have the diversion of reading to pass the time as the others did.

The first young aspirant, the ginger-haired boy of about seventeen who had been first below, went into the examining room, and everyone hushed and leaned closer to see if they could hear the proceedings through the deal partitions. Close as he was, Alan could only hear a dull rumble now and then. The boy was out in five minutes, shaking like a whipped puppy and soaked in sweat.

"It's box-hauling," he stammered, tearing at his stock as though he was strangling. "Fourteen steps of gun-drill, d . . . d . . . dis-masting in a whole gale . . . Lord, I don't know what else! They *love* lee shores!"

The next hopeful was in there for *ten* minutes, and he came out fanning himself with his hat, but wearing a smug expression, as though he had been informed that he had been passed. To their eager questions as to what had been required of him, he had another terrifying list of stumpers, which made all of them dive back into their texts, and Alan suddenly didn't feel so very confident any longer. He could cheerfully have killed one of the others for a book to review.

The board also upset his hopes; they went through a dozen young men in the first hour-and-a-quarter, and not two of them looked at all sanguine about their prospects when they emerged. Most were told they had failed, and to try again in another six months or so.

The older midshipman in the shabby coat went in, and he was out in *three* minutes, his eyes moist with humiliation at the quick drubbing he had received. Please God! Alan thought as a litany, Please!

"Midshipman Lewrie?" the clerk called from the open door at last. "Midshipman Alan Lewrie."

"Here," Alan heard himself manage to say through a suddenly dry throat.

"Then get in . . . *here*," the clerk simpered at his own jest.

Alan tugged down his waist-coat and shot his cuffs, played with his neck-stock and then strode to the open door as if he were walking on pillows in some fever-dream. He stepped through the door and past the partitions, and the door was closed behind him. He beheld a long dining table set athwartships, behind which were seated at least a dozen post-captains in their gold-laced coats, and every one of them looked grumpy as ill-fed badgers. There was a single chair before the table as though it was a court-martial, and Alan almost stumbled over it as he took a stance before it.

"Well?" one of the captains snapped.

"Midshipman Alan Lewrie, sir, of the *Desperate* frigate," he managed to say, clutching his packet of letters to his side and almost crushing his cocked hat into a furball under the other arm.

"*Desperate*, hey?" one of the others said, beaming almost pleasantly. "Saw your fight with *Capricieuse*. Damned fine stuff. Your Captain Treghues has a lot of bottom, what?"

"Aye, sir."

"Well, don't stand there like death's head on a mop-stick, give me your packet."

Alan handed over his letters and *bona fides*, and the flag-captain in the center of the board looked over them, reading aloud salient points to the other members.

"Joined January of '80, *Ariadne*, 3rd Rate of sixty-four guns. Only the two years of service?"

"Aye, sir."

"Mentioned honorably. Took charge of the lower gun deck after both officers were killed, credited with getting the guns back in action and thus saving the ship. My, my, we have been busy, have we not?" The flag-captain chuckled. "I remember you, I believe. You were the lad escaped Yorktown with some soldiers. Turned a brace of river barges into sailing craft. Fought your way out too, as I remember."

This ain't so bad after all! Alan thought with relief. Was there some "interest" on his behalf of which he was unaware working in his favor—was it from Admiral Hood, or his flag-captain here? "Aye, sir, we did. But as for the boats," he informed them, "I had two fine petty-officers who did most of the creative work. Mister Feather and Mister Queener. Both dead now, unfortunately."

He congratulated himself as he saw the tacit approval of his comments on the captains' faces; it never hurt to share out the credit and sound a little modest, while still implying you were a genius anyway.

So they went through his records from *Parrot*, his staff work for Rear Adm. Sir Onsley Matthews, with Alan dropping the blandest sort of hint that he and that worthy, who was now in London controlling these captains, were still in affectionate correspondence. Then his service in *Desperate* and all her heroic exploits in which he had taken part, including being a prizemaster; the raid on the Danish Virgin Islands, Battle of The Chesapeake, Yorktown, his promotion to master's mate, the fight with *Capricieuse* and his service as acting lieutenant. By the time they reached the present, he was damned near swaggering. It was going splendidly, and he could see by one board member's large watch that they had spent over ten minutes just being pleasant and approving.

I could walk out of here without one question, if they have that herd out there to examine today, he speculated. And most of those sluggards haven't done a tenth of my service.

"Sit or stand, Mister Lewrie?"

"Sir?"

"Do you prefer to sit or stand for the examination?"

"Um, I'll stand, sir," he replied, all the cock-swagger knocked out of him, knowing he would not get off scot-free.

"Think better on your feet, hey?" Captain Cornwallis chuckled. "Mister Lewrie, you're first officer into a seventy-four-gunned 3rd Rate at present laid up in-ordinary. Your captain orders you to prepare her to be put back into commission. What steps are necessary, and what orders would you give?"

That's one of the questions Treghues sent me, to the letter, Alan realized, striving to dredge up the proper answer, or even get his brain to function. But he took a deep breath to steady his nerves, and launched into the long, involved reply. He was only half-way through it, though, when he was interrupted by one of the captains.

"Good on that. Now, this same seventy-four is on a lee shore under plain sail, wind out of the west and you are on the larboard tack as close-hauled as may be. Shoals under your lee, eight cables off, almost embayed by a peninsula to the north'rd, extending nor'west. Do you have that in mind so far?"

"Aye, sir."

"The wind veers ahead suddenly by six points, and freshens to half a gale. What action would you take, sir?"

"Excuse me, sir," Alan asked, stalling for thinking time. "How far off is that peninsula you mentioned?"

"Makes no difference," one grumbled impatiently. "Half a league?" Another shrugged, and the rest seemed it as good a predicament as any.

"I would endeavor to tack immediately, sirs," Alan began. "I would shift the head sheets and the spanker with the duty watch, at the same time summoning all-hands, as I would be laid aback and in irons. Get her head about, even if the square-sails would be flung aback. I would lose all headway until I could free the braces and shiver the yards, but I would be on a safer tack."

Do you want more? he wondered, as they sat there staring at him. He no longer felt any confidence at all.

"Ah, hmm, your cooks were preparing dinner during this emergency, and the galley fire has been scattered by your sudden evolution," Captain Cornwallis demanded. "What do you do to combat this fire below decks, and how many hands may you spare, as you are still attempting to tack your ship and square away your yards?"

Jesus, are these buggers serious? he quailed. Barely had he gotten a fire party together, rigged out a foredeck wash-deck pump as a fire engine, than another captain added the complication of jammed brace-blocks aloft on the main yards, and a sprung main top-mast that threatened to come crashing down from the wind pressure on those laid aback tops'ls. Alan decided to send two men aloft and cut the upper weather brace so the yard could swing a'cock-bill to save the mast.

One hypothesis came at him after another, mercilessly swift and demanding, and his answers showed no signs of mollifying anyone. They all frowned and leaned forward, savoring his roasting, much like Grand Inquisitors from Spain watching a particularly enjoyable *auto-da-fé* and wanting to hear the bleats of the torched victim better.

His shirt was clinging to him, his breeches felt clammy, as if he had just been dunked over the side into the sea, and his face streamed so much perspiration it was all he could do not to reach up and try to mop himself dry, before it all ran down into his eyes and made him blink and squint. He had the distinct impression that he had begun to babble like a two-year-old, instead of sounding like a young man with the prospects to be made a lieutenant!

Am I making any sense anymore? he wondered. Jesus, just a little good fortune here, please!

"Hmm, alright, Mister Lewrie," the flag-captain said finally, which brought a pent-up sigh of relief to Alan's lips before he could control himself. "You'd probably have lost that top-mast eventually, but the ship might have been spared being wrecked on a lee shore. As for that fire, you forgot about it, but I'm sure someone would have come and told you if it got out of control. Gentlemen?"

"Fair enough," Captain Cornwallis said, shrugging affably.

"Agreed, then?" The flag-captain peered down the table for a consensus. "Passed for lieutenancy, then. That'll be all."

"God!" Alan blurted in total stupefaction.

"Well, if you'd rather not be . . ." a post-captain laughed.

"Oh, nossir, thank you, sirs. I mean, yes sirs!"

"Hush. Take your records and go before we change our minds!"

"Aye aye, sir," Alan agreed, stumbling over the chair again on his way out. He stepped into the breathless hush of the cabin full of nervous aspirants who still had to endure their own ordeals.

"My God, you were in there near twenty minutes!" one gawped.

"What did they ask?" another demanded.

"It was . . ." Alan began, and then began to cackle in hysterical relief. "I can't bloody *remember*! Dis-masting, and a fire . . . I think."

"Fire," someone said, opening his *Falconer*'s to see if there was an approved fire-drill.

"On a lee shore, mind you." Alan grinned, unable to stop shaking with laughter and relief such as a felon must feel pardoned at the foot of the gibbet. "Bloody daft on 'em, they are!"

"Well, did you pass?"

"Passed!" Alan beamed at them, drawing a deep breath. "Yes!"

"Bloody Christ, not one in five," came a sorrowful moan.

"Best of luck to you all," Alan said, meaning every word of it. He pulled out his watch and consulted it, trying to calm down. "Ah, what good timing. I shall be back aboard just in time for dinner."

"Bastard," someone whispered loud enough to hear, but Lewrie was too used to hearing it spoken of him to care, and too proud and pleased, for the world was suddenly a much sunnier place.

"That's *passed* bastard!" he chirped on his way to the upper deck. "And I'll thank you to remember it!"

Chapter 6

The letter came aboard the morning before *Desperate* was to put to sea. After returning to his ship, Alan had time to reflect that passing the examination had not improved his chances much. There was no extra pay with the honor, since no one paid midshipmen anyway, and it gave him no more perquisites that he didn't already have as a master's mate. And after the glow of achievement had cooled, there was still Lieutenant Kenyon to deal with; once at sea the first officer could slowly crucify him, one spike at a time, destroying whatever good he had gained from his incredible fortune before that dour captains' board.

Last-minute stores were being stowed, so Alan was busy in the holds supervising so that the fore and aft balance was preserved, and nothing would shift to either beam once they were under way.

Cony, his new hammockman who had been ashore with him at Yorktown, came below to fetch him.

"They's a boat come, Mister Lewrie, an' they brung a letter for ya, from the flag, I thinks," he said quickly, eyeing him with almost a religious reverence all of a sudden.

"Pray God," Alan said. Of one hundred and fifty midshipmen that had faced the board, thirty had been passed, but rumor had only promoted ten into immediate commissions. Part of that was based on favoritism, whose son needed a place, who had the better connections or more experience. Was it possible, though? Could he have shown well enough to be one of the lucky ones? God knows the Navy was full of passed midshipmen who didn't have the luck or the "interest" to be lifted out of their penury, and he had almost thought himself ready to join their embittered ranks. With *Desperate* out at sea on her own once more, there would be no access to places that came open unless they took a suitably big prize. Was he one of the suddenly anointed ones, and was he about to find his escape from the certain, implacable wrath of Lieutenant Kenyon?

He charged up the ladders from the holds to the upper deck and the starboard gangway, where an impeccably dressed midshipman of about fourteen was waiting with a sealed letter.

"I'm Lewrie," he said, wiping his damp palms on his working rig slop trousers as though the folded and waxed parchment was a holy relic.

"For you, sir, from the flag."

"Thank you," Alan said, turning it over. He sucked in his breath in surprise. It was addressed to *Lieutenant* Alan Lewrie, Royal Navy.

"Yes, by God!" he shouted, thrusting that missive at the sky in triumph. It was salvation from Kenyon's wrath, a certain posting into another vessel. It was vindication for all the misery and danger he had faced, willing or not, since being forced most unwillingly into the Navy two years before. It was also, he reflected in his victory, the keys to Lucy Beauman and her father's money as soon as he could get his young arse back to Kingston and ask for her hand.

He broke the wax wafer and unfolded the letter. He was instructed to equip himself as a commission officer and report aboard HM *Shrike*, brig o' war, twelve guns, Lieutenant Lilycrop master and commander, with all despatch or risk the senior admiral's displeasure. Failing that, he was to communicate to the flag any inability to comply either in accepting a commission or fulfilling his orders, with the threat of immediate loss of income and dismissal from the Fleet.

"Yes, by God!" he repeated, reading it through once more and savoring the words. "Cony, go below and start packing my sea chest."

"Yer a officer, sir?" Cony goggled.

"Yes, I am," Alan replied in exultation.

"Beggin' yer pardon, sir, but you'll be a'goin' into another ship, then? You'll be a'needin' a servant, sir, an' I'd be that proud ta be yer man, sir," Cony offered.

"Then you shall be. I must see the captain. Off with you."

He went down to the gun deck and aft to the main entrance to the captain's quarters where a fully uniformed Marine sentry stood to serve as guard and tiler.

" 'E's wif t' pusser, Mister Lewrie," the sentry told him.

"Even better." Alan grinned. "Tell him Lieutenant Lewrie is here to see him."

"Oh, Lor', Mister Lewrie, don' you be japin' now," the sentry chided from long familiarity with a young man who was to his lights not much more than a jumped-up younker half his own age.

"No jest," Alan said, waving the parchment as proof.

The sentry shrugged and came to attention, banging his musket butt on the oak decking and shouting at the top of his lungs. "Lef'ten't Lewrie, sah!"

Freeling opened the cabin door immediately and Alan entered the great cabins, where Railsford and Cheatham had been going over the books and having a glass of wine together.

"This is not your idea of humor?" Railsford asked, his face somber but his eyes twinkling.

"No, sir. The flag-captain has promoted me a commission officer into a brig o' war, the *Shrike*," Alan told him proudly.

"My stars above," Cheatham said, rising from his seat to take Lewrie's hand and pump it excitedly. "How *marvelous* for you!"

"Freeling, fetch an extra glass," Railsford instructed. "We'll take a bumper in celebration. Sit you down, Mister Lewrie. Or should I say, Alan. By God, it is marvelous news."

"Thank you, sir."

"Sorry that we have to lose you, though," Cheatham sighed after they had drained their glasses and sent Freeling digging into the wine cabinet for a fresh bottle to toast his good fortune. "But, my word, what fortune you have had in the last year with us."

"Yes, I shall miss you both, sirs," Alan replied. "You've done so much for me, both professionally and personally, I'll feel adrift without you as my mentors."

Damme if I won't miss them, he thought ruefully, realizing at that moment that he would indeed be leaving *Desperate*. Much as he feared remaining near Kenyon and his wrath, he would be departing the first ship he had (mostly) enjoyed service in, where Railsford had always been there, believing in him and turning away Treghues' original ill humor toward him, where Cheatham had done so much to clear up his family problems back in London and get him absolved of the false charges that had led to his arrival in the Navy. They've been good to me, he thought, and what'll a new ship be like without 'em?

"Well, you'll be on your own bottom," Railsford said. "But if you continue as you have lately, I'm sure you shall prosper. It's the Navy's way of snipping the leading strings. Really, there wasn't much more you could learn here, and no way the Navy could promote you an officer in the same ship in which you served as a junior warrant."

"The letter says 'with all despatch,' sir," Alan told them. "Does that mean that I depart instantly? I would appreciate it if you gave me one more fair wind to steer by in this regard."

"Let me see," Railsford said, taking the precious document. "Hmm, you shall have to go aboard the flag to get your certificate of commission, since it is not here. Mister Cheatham shall have to square away your accounts, and I shall instruct my clerk to arrange your pay vouchers and prize-money certificates. Go aboard the flag now and see the pertinent clerk or flag-lieutenant. There's daylight enough for you to take a night's lodging ashore and get to the tailors."

"You might see Woodridge's," Cheatham suggested as Freeling got the fresh bottle circulating. "He has a fine selection of ready coats, and I know you may trade your old midshipman's jackets in partial payment." He concluded with a knowing wink, "Tell him I said to go easy on you and you may get away for less."

"Thank you, Mister Cheatham. I seem to be forever in your debt."

"And you shall square every penny of it before we let you get off this ship, sir," Cheatham japed. "I shall go calculate the reckoning."

Once alone, Railsford leaned back in his chair and flung a leg over the arm and studied Lewrie closely. "You know, this is a fine moment for me. To see you with a commission."

"And for you to be promoted to commander with *Desperate* as yours," Alan countered.

"Ah, 'twon't last." Railsford grimaced. "The war may end soon and I may not be confirmed before it does. *Desperate* shall pay off in another year no matter what happens, and I shall most likely go back to being a half-pay lieutenant, liable for stoppages on commander's pay."

"But there is a power of prize-money to soften the blow, sir." Alan grinned. "And war enough still to get you made post."

"Aye, there's that, God willing, if we pitch into the Frogs and Dagoes sharp enough, and I intend to do just that. Damme, it's fine to think of you with a commission, though. I remember when it happened to me. Up and out of a ship I'd served in for three years, into a new one full of strangers. God, I missed *Hercules* for months! I don't know this . . . Lilycrop, is it? God help the poor man with a name like that. But I tell you truly, Alan, he'll be getting a good officer."

"You do me too much honor, sir," Alan confessed. "I'm proud as hot punch, but scared to death at the moment. And I feel like such a little fraud, and sooner or later someone's going to find me out, sir."

" 'Tis only natural to be nervous about all the added responsibility," Railsford said, comfortingly, leaning forward on his desk. "And you'll no longer have patrons in your new ship to protect you. God knows, you have been more in need of protection than most. But it was worth it, I think. You've turned out main well, with nothing to be ashamed of."

"Thank you, sir, thankee kindly," Alan replied, choking up at the thought of being adrift from the cosseting he had gotten.

"Well, one bad part about this Navy of ours is that when you make great friends they get transferred to the other side of the world and one never sees them again, while the dross keep showing up, one commission after another." Railsford harrumphed, stifling his own emotions. "Another thing is that, as the Bard said, 'parting is such sweet sorrow.' Best do it short and direct, and have done. There's a power of errands you must run before reporting to this . . . *Shrike* . . . so let us say our farewells now, and let you get on about your business. But keep in touch. Drop us a letter now and again. Who knows, at this rate of advancement, I could be coming to you for a favor someday, when I'm still a long-in-tooth lieutenant and you're a high and mighty post-captain."

They stood and shook hands, almost equals now for the first

time, and Railsford did him the grace to walk him to the door.
"By the way, I meant to ask you something. Lieutenant Kenyon
wasn't exactly enthralled with giving you suitable recommendations. Do you know of any reason why he should have been
loath to sponsor you? He said he didn't want to lose you, but he
acted deuced odd about it."

Damme, that's the trouble with such a died-in-the-wool rogue
like me being around decent people like Railsford and
Cheatham, Alan thought. Sooner or later their ways rub off and
keep you from doing the sensible thing.

He could square Kenyon's yards by mentioning his sexual
preferences, what he had seen that night in Kingston, and end up
ruining the man's career, removing him as a threat to him forever. But, he rationalized, he was out and away from him, and
would probably never cross his hawse again in this life. *Shrike*
would be his escape, and if he did good duty in her, no one
could ever threaten his standing in the Navy, not with the record
he had posted so far. So he relented.

"He mentioned that Mister Claghorne had committed suicide
after he gained his commission and command of old *Parrot*, sir.
But other than that, I can think of no animosity," Alan said with
a straight face.

"Oh, poor fellow," Railsford sighed. "Still, some people are
made to handle the solitude of command and some go under.
No, this poor Claghorne was not your problem. And as I remember you saying once, Kenyon was down with Yellow Jack
at the time. He most like blames himself for not being able to
give the benighted soul leadership at such a stressful moment,
which broke his spirit. Well, off with you, you rogue! Make a
name for yourself in this *Shrike*, and we'll see *you* a post-captain
yet."

Chapter 7

Thank God for looking glasses for vain cock-a-hoops like me, Lt. Alan Lewrie, RN, thought to himself with a smugness matched by the smile that greeted him in the hall mirror of the Old Lamb Tavern as he entered.

The cocked hat which had adorned his head nigh on for nearly two and a half years had lost its plainness with the addition of the wide vertical gold strip of lace, held by a gold fouled-anchor button, under which a stiff little bow of black silk riband stuck up above the rim of the brim in a commission officer's "dog's vane."

Black neck cloth over the stock, and the longer tailed naval blue coat with its low stand-collar trimmed at the edge in white. The pristine new broad white turn-back lapels that ran from collarbone to his waist, also adorned with gold buttons bearing the fouled anchor device of his Service. He reached up a hand to remove the cocked hat and could not help but admire his sleeve, dressed with a wide white cuff, a widely spaced row of three large gold cuff buttons.

Damme, but I make a fine-*looking* officer, he preened.

" 'Ere fer the commission party, sir?" one of the tavern's daisy-kickers asked, wipping his ale-stained hands on the universal blue publican's apron. "Take yer 'at, sir?"

"Yes, thankee, yes I am. Guest of honor, actually," Alan said, sneaking one last look in the mirror to see if his light brown hair was in place, the black silk riband tied properly around his now long and seamanly queue of hair at the back of his collar. He could not help winking one blue-grey eye at himself as the servant took his hat away for safekeeping.

"Right 'iss way, sir," the servant beckoned, leading him from the common rooms to an upper private suite overlooking a cool patio.

Alan shot his lace to show the proper amount of ruffles on his wrists, tugged the waist-coat down, and entered.

"Huzzah!" The occupants raised a cheer, some already standing atop the long dining table.

"Marcus Aurelius was right," Lt. Keith Ashburn, now fifth officer of the fifty-gunned 4th Rate squadron flagship *Glatton* japed from his perch atop a chair seat as he waved a bottle of champagne and a glass in the air. " 'How ridiculous and what a stranger he is,' " he quoted, " 'who is surprised at anything which happens in life!' "

"Wet the bugger down, somebody!" Jemmy Shirke, a former shipmate aboard *Ariadne*, Alan's first ship, suggested. Shirke was still a midshipman, now about eighteen or nineteen by Alan's recollections. Only the fact that he was a passed midshipman who had yet to find a suitable opening allowed him to be away from his ship.

Wine was sloshed in his general direction, soaking his shirt and fine new coat—thankfully Alan had had the money from his hidden cache of guineas to purchase four. A glass was shoved into his hand and quickly filled with champagne.

The only other officer present was Lt. William Mayhew who Alan had worked for briefly when that poor young fellow had served Adm. Sir Onsley Matthews as flag-lieutenant. Mayhew had come ashore with Ashburn.

"Get down from that chair, Keith, you're making me dizzy," Alan jested, stepping up to shake hands with him after nearly a year of separation.

"Never did have a head for heights. Same's the day I ran you up the mast for the first time," Keith hooted, jumping down with easy grace. "Goddamn my eyes, you of all people, a commission officer!"

"I thought pretty much the same of you at the time," Alan replied. "Mister Mayhew, is he worth a tinker's damn yet?"

"Oh, for God's sake, call me Billy, will you, Alan?" the ginger-haired, permanently sunburned young man snapped impatiently. "No, he's no more use than the duck-fucker. Never will be. Good to lay eyes on you again, that it is, Alan. And congratulations on passing the board. I'm told not one in five passed, and not one in ten got an immediate commission. Lucky bastard, you are, I'll tell you."

"And we had to be at sea when it happened, more's *my* luck,"

Jemmy Shirke complained. He had passed the previous board, but wasn't in port when the blessings were handed out this time.

"You know all good things come from the flag," Ashburn stated, and that was pretty much true. Promotion came more rapidly for those fortunate officers in a commodore's or an admiral's wardroom than it did for two-a-penny lieutenants in lesser ships, no matter how good their records. And the same could be said for lieutenants' vacancies dropping from heaven to midshipmen who were more favorably placed and endowed with the proper connections; those who had, got.

"Aye, damnit, I do," Jemmy Shirke grumbled, and Alan wondered why Ashburn had suggested inviting him, if he was still the same surly, practical-joking lout he had been in *Ariadne*. They had been mess-mates, but never true friends, not like he and Keith had been. Time had not seemed to have changed him much, either.

"Last I saw of you, dear Jemmy," Alan said, hauling a chair out from the table to take a pew, "you were still lashed up like a fished course yard, pumping away like a stoat on some dark-haired wench. God, must have been July of '81? What did they assign you once you healed, after *Ariadne* was condemned?"

He meant to be pleasant to the fellow—after all, he was paying part of the reckoning for this party.

"And the broken arm didn't slow you down much, as I remember," Keith stuck in.

"Told you to get me a gentle one and I'd take my fences same as anybody," Jemmy mellowed. "No, once my flipper was healed, I went into the *Admiral Rooke*. She's a hired brig o' war, duration only, but she's not bad. They've made me an acting master's mate. No Marines, just the captain, first officer, master and two midshipmen. Only eighty or so in the whole crew."

"That's grand for you, Jemmy," Alan enthused for him. "You're learning scads more than most. Like I did when I went into *Parrot* with Mister Kenyon. And I was an acting master's mate not too long ago, too."

"Promotion may come faster in the bigger ships," Shirke said with returning pride after his brief sulk, "but you can't beat service in a small ship for making a real seaman of you. Only thing is, some of us rise faster than others."

"It'll come," Alan assured him, not sure who Shirke was needling; him, or Ashburn and Mayhew.

"So, what ship are you getting?" Mayhew asked.

"*Shrike*," Alan said grinning. "Twelve-gunned brig o' war."

"My stars, you're to be a first officer right out of the starting gates!" Mayhew goggled.

That was news to Alan. He had believed a brig o' war would be big enough for a first *and* second lieutenant. Jesus, he said to himself, I hadn't thought about that! They're going to find out what a total fraud I really am!

Still, Railsford must have known what it meant, as did the admiral's secretary who made the appointment. Railsford had said that he'd prosper and told him to his face that this new captain would be getting a good officer.

"Not *all* good things come from the flag, I'm thinking," Alan told them with a lazy drawl and a grin that he didn't quite feel. He looked at Shirke, who appeared to have been kicked in the guts by the news, and at Ashburn, who was not exactly overjoyed, either. His appointment had come from *Barfleur*, Admiral Hood's flagship, while Keith Ashburn, for all his connections, his family's money, and "interest"—lifeblood of a successful career—left him a junior officer in a 4th Rate ship, no matter that he had been commissioned a year-and-a-half longer. It hinted at high-flown connections back home with Admiralty, with Hood; else why did not a more senior and deserving man not get the appointment, even if it was in a small brig below the Rate?

"Now, what had we planned for this celebration?" Alan asked in the dumbstruck silence. "I must own I'm famished."

"A page taken from your favorite book, Alan," Keith said, regaining his composure. "That's why we are having it here at the Lamb in Falmouth Harbor, 'stead of over the ridge in English Harbor. Less chance that a naval watch will break things up. And a better run of whore over here."

"God bless you, Keith, you read my mind. I haven't had a good ride since Charleston last August, and damn-all blood and thunder in between. *Rake's Progress* for us, tonight, eh?"

There was a knock at the door. "That must be the mutton," Billy Mayhew hoped aloud as he rose to answer it. Sure enough, the bare-back riders had arrived. More glasses were called for, and more wine, while they were introduced. There was Hespera (most Mother Abbesses ran to the same classical bent as Ashburn when it came to naming their stock-in-trade with Greco-Roman sobriquets), a slim and lanky young blonde of about seventeen, with straight hair. There was an older woman of about thirty, rather hard-faced but blessed with a promising body—she went by Pandora—who appeared to be the bosun's mate in charge of the distaff party. There was a girl with hair so red it had to be hennaed, short and talkative as soon as she got through the door—Electra, she insisted she be called. And there was Dolly.

Alan took a sudden like for Dolly, if only because she probably was using her own name for variety's sake. She appeared to be about twenty-five, just a few years older than Alan. And she was beautiful, rather than merely pretty, and stood out from the rest like a peacock in a barnyard. A high, clear brow, high cheekbones and a slim, almost thin face that tapered to a firm little chin; a slim straight nose cleverly shaped, and a Cupid's Bow of a mouth that showed her upper teeth in repose, and widened in a hesitant smile to show pure, healthy white. And she had the most peculiar dark green eyes and hair the hue of polished mahogany, and just as lustrous and full. She was also much better dressed than the others; not just in splendor—any whore could buy splendor from a rag-picker's barrow or a used dress shop, and these had—she wore a dress less gaudy than the others, almost respectable enough to take out on the town, with fewer flounces and fripperies. One, at first glance, might take her for a proper young woman, or a wife.

"You done us proud tonight, Keith," Mayhew commented.

"Yes, Keith usually has the taste of a Philistine," Alan said.

"Gentlemen, choose your partners," Ashburn ordained loftily. "As our guest of honor, let Alan have first pick."

" 'Oo shall 'ave this 'un, then," Alan chuckled, mimicking the "love call" of the lower deck when they paired off with their temporary "wives" whenever a ship was put out of discipline and the doxies came aboard. The blonde looked promising, but her straight hair reminded him too much of Caroline Chiswick from Wilmington; the others were the usual run-of-the-mill whores one could have any day of the week—he had only one clear choice.

"Mistress Dolly, if you would be so kind as to grace my side during supper?" Alan asked, bowing in congé deep enough for a duchess and taking her hand.

"If you wish, sir," she replied in a voice so soft and meek he almost had to ask her to repeat herself. So she's one of those that'll play the virgin, is she? he thought. This could be interesting.

"Sport?" Shirke suggested after picking Hespera the blonde.

"Oh, let's sup first," Alan said, and Dolly relaxed from a sudden stiffness at his side as he led her to the wine-table. "Take a pew, my dear. God knows what we're eating tonight, but it'll not be short commons. I hope you brought a bounteous appetite."

"I did indeed, sir," she replied, taking a glass of champagne.

"Oh, h'ain't never 'ad bubbly wine afore!" Hespera giggled loud when she took a sip of wine across the table. "H'it tickles me nose!"

"That's not all we'll tickle before the night's through, I'll wager!" Billy Mayhew promised his choice, which made them all roar with laughter.

The supper was more than palatable. There was a poached local fish the servitors called grouper, firm as lobster and just as succulent, served with a melted butter and lime sauce. That had been preceded by a green salad and ox-tail soup. The fish was followed by some small wild fowl, then a domestic goose. Then a smoking joint of beef which was not as stringy and lean as most island cattle. And with it all, there was hot and crusty bread, small potatoes roasted and boiled, native chick peas and broad beans, young carrots in butter and parsley.

Washed down, of course, with several bottles of hock with the fish and fowl, captured or smuggled burgundy with the beef, and more champagne when things got slow between courses.

For those with a sweet tooth, a servant wheeled in a huge raisin and citrus-fruit duff, soaked so long in brandy it was a threat to sobriety of itself, and that was followed, once the cloth was removed, by a fairly fresh cheese, apples, extra-fine sweet biscuit, and port or brandy.

"Drinking games!" Ashburn announced, climbing back onto his chair and striking a pose like a ship's figurehead. "Electra, name me a ship's mast."

"I don't know nothin' 'bout ships," the girl pouted.

"Wrong answer. Drink a full bumper in punishment! Drink, drink, drink!" he shouted, and they took up the chorus while the girl tipped her wine glass back and poured the stuff down like water, and gave her a great cheer when she showed "heel-taps" and nothing left, and they pounded their approval on the table and stamped their feet as loud as a thirty-two-pounder gun being trundled across a wooden deck.

"Alan, sing us a song!" Keith shouted. "A good, dirty one!"

"I couldn't carry a tune in a bucket, Keith," Alan complained. "Look, this is all very well for you, but I have to report to my ship early tomorrow, clear-eyed and somewhat sober, if I know what's good for me."

"Wrong answer! Drink!" Keith ordered, and Alan remembered once again what he had forgotten in long absence; Keith Ashburn was the sort of take-charge bastard who had to have control over everything.

Wine was slopped into his glass from long-range, and some of it got onto Dolly's gown. She half-rose to complain, then took her napkin and tried to sponge it out quickly, while Alan stood and, to the thump of fists and feet, and the encouraging shouted chorus, tipped his wine up and drained it, displaying it was empty by balancing it upside down on his head.

"Song, song!" Mayhew called. "Girls, sing us a song! Serenade us before we strum and serenade you, ha ha!"

During the dinner, Alan had learned that Dolly was, until three months before, the proper, if somewhat youngish wife of an officer of the infantry named Capt. Roger Fenton. He had left her with no debts when he was carried off by a fever soon after their arrival in the islands, but he had left her no money, either, and so far, there had been no word in answer to her tearful letters back to England to his last living relatives. She did not have the money to pay for a passage back home, and was, no matter how she might try to economize, quickly running out of money, and faced penury in the near future.

> *"Heart of oak are our ships*
> *heart of oak are our men,"*

"No, no, that's not the way it starts!" Shirke corrected Hespera after she tried to sing.

"Would there be some of that sparkling wine left, please?" Dolly asked Alan, her voice almost lost in the sudden din.

> *"Come cheer up, my lads, 'tis to glory we steer*
> *to add something more to this wonderful year;*
> *To honor we call you, not press you like slaves,*
> *for who are so free as the sons of the waves?"*

"What?" Alan had to shout back at her.

"I've heard sparkling white wine may remove stains," Dolly said near his ear. "Would there be some left, please?"

"Oh, certainly. Make free," Alan said, snaking a half-used bottle off the sideboard. He handed it to her, and was amazed to see that her eyes were full of tears.

"Heart of oak are our ships,
heart of oak are our men,
we always are ready;
steady, boys, steady;
We'll fight and we'll conquer again and again!"

"What's wrong?" Alan asked, leaning closer.

"Gentlemen, gentlemen!" a servant called from the door. "And yer ladies, if ya *will*! We call this tavern the Old Lamb fer a reason, ya know! Would ya please 'old down the noise, sirs, they's other patrons complainin', an' one of 'em's our magistrate!"

"It is my last good gown, Mister Lewrie," Dolly informed him, "I have had to sell the rest, and now it's spotted, and . . ."

"We'll buy you another," Alan assured her. "Your guinea from this evening could fill a whole wardrobe."

"We ne'er see our foes but we wish 'em to stay,
They never see us but they wish us away;
If they run, why we follow, and run 'em ashore,
For if they won't fight us, we cannot do more.
Heart of oak are our ships,
Heart of oak are our men."

"I mean it, gentlemen! We run a clean, sober, house! Any more noise an' they'll call the watch on you'ns!" the man shouted in parting and slammed the door. Shirke heaved a breadbasket at the door in salute.

"Keith, for God's sake," Alan intervened before they tried to start another verse. "You're going to get us arrested. And I don't think we paid *that* much for the bloody rooms, to let us caterwaul to our hearts' content."

"Yes, Keith, let's have a little dec . . . hic . . . decorum or what the devil you c . . . call it," Mayhew managed to say. "Potty old men with cudgels always put me off my stroke."

"Let's build a galley, then!"

"Oh, who'd sit still for that?" Shirke griped. It was a cully's game for the newlies, to be named figurehead and smeared with shit before the others ran.

"The galley's built," Keith said swaying over the table, thumping it with his heels. "I'm standing on the bloody quarterdeck, but we need a figurehead. A contest to see who's the best!

Pandora, you've a huge set o' cat's-heads. Hop up here and show us your carvings!"

The older Pandora was helped up onto the table, allowed Keith to undo her buttons, and shucked her sack-gown down to her ankles, and bared her breasts to the room, kneeling on one end of the table and bracing herself with the tall back of a chair to lean forward like a ship's figurehead. Candles were fetched to that end of the room so the men could judge better.

"Marvelous!" Keith said. "I'll give her points for size, at any rate. Bit low-slung, though."

"Not a bit of it," Mayhew said, kneeling on the floor and looking straight up at them in awe. "Easier to get to whilst doing the blanket horn-pipe! Like ... hic ... swivel guns!"

"Alan, trot your piece out next, she looks promising!" Shirke crowed. "Nice swellings, there under her bodice."

Alan turned to her, and she shook her head in the negative, rather forcefully; the first sign of any strong reaction she had shown all night. Fresh tears streaked her lovely face.

"If you'd rather not," Alan said, putting an arm around her.

"Thank you." She almost shuddered. "I'd really ... the mistress said it would be a nice supper, and ... I'd really like to go, if I may, please? This is so ..."

"Alan, come on!"

"Try Hespera," he said over his shoulder. "She looks like better pickings." He led her to the dark end of the room and sat her down on a chair. "You've not been long at this trade, have you, Dolly? Tell me true. I've heard enough whore's lies before to know."

She turned away from him and began to sob as quietly as she could, and he knelt down to put an arm around her once more.

"D ... don't call me a whore," she wept.

"Well, what would you call it when you show up at a private party for four men and four women?" Alan asked.

"I don't know," she muttered in a little girl's timbre. "I was happy to ... submit to my husband's desires, as a ... p ... proper ... wife. I thought it would be no m ... more unpleasant than that!"

"But this is low and common." Alan softened, pulling her head over to rest on his shoulder, and she submitted easily, though one of her hands took hold of his coat lapel and wrenched it into a knot from the strength of her humiliation as she trembled and wept on his coat.

"Huzzah for Hespera!" Shirke hooted. "I'll name my next

ship for you, if you'll pose for the wood-carver, m'dear! Marvelous young poonts you have! Alan, you must come and see. They're like two in one. Round little darlin's, with little pink domes atop 'em for dugs. And another little mound of nipple atop that, would you believe? Mm, tasty, too!"

"Areolae, Shirke," Ashburn informed him at the other end of the room. "Mm, you're right, most delectable in form and succulence. From the Latin, you know. Juvenal loved 'em, as do I, better'n oysters!"

" 'Ere, wot 'bout mine, then?" Electra complained, slinging her garments to the four winds. "Thort yew wuz sweet h'on me, me chuck!"

"Hell with it," Mayhew shouted. "All s . . . strip fer a boardin' action!"

"Let's get you out of here," Alan said. Damned if he was going to board any woman in public for someone else's amusement. And damned if he was going to get anything from Dolly under these circumstances.

"Oh, thank you, thank you!" she uttered brokenly as he lifted her to her feet. He led her toward the door, stopping to pick up his hanger and clip it to his belt frog on his left hip.

"Ought to have some music with this," Shirke said. He went to the door clad only in a loose shirt and shouted down the stairs at the top of his voice, a quarterdeck voice that could carry forward in at least half a gale of wind, "Any fiddlers down there? Hoy, we want music up here, can't strum without it! Shake a leg, shake a leg, wakey wakey, lash up and stow! Stir up your dead arses, you farmers!"

The girls were shrieking with laughter as they were pursued in mock chase about the room, all of them now totally nude, and the males shedding what little they had left upon their persons as they ran and made the floor shudder.

Then, there was another wooden sort of thunder; the sound of many heavy feet pounding their way up the stairs.

"Shirke, your musicians are here," Alan said, grabbing Dolly's hand and running for the only other door to the room.

"Bloody good!" Shirke said, breaking off and opening the door to face an obese (and very outraged) magistrate, his bailiff, and a pack of old gammers from the watch. "The Charlies!" Shirke screamed and slammed the door in their faces. "All hands, prepare to repel boarders!"

Alan wasn't prepared to stay and take the consequences. He led Dolly into a small bed-chamber, from which there seemed to be no other mode of escape, unless they wanted to consider shinnying down a drain-pipe from the narrow window to the courtyard below.

"Damn!" he hissed in the darkness. He felt along the wall with his free hand until he came upon a small door set into the wall facing the hallway, about three feet square. It was the closet for the chamber-pots, so that servants could pick them up from the hallway and empty them without disturbing the lodgers. It had not been used, so it was empty. Alan took the two tin pots to the door to the dining room and slung them onto the table.

"You'll need these, I think," he said, slamming the door again. "Through there, quickly, Dolly."

"Oh, God!" she quailed weakly.

"Oh, for God's sake, follow me, then."

He crawled through, saw that the coast was for the moment clear, and stepped out into the hall, almost dragging the young woman in his wake. They straightened their clothing in the small mirror of a hall table at the bend of the corridor, and he then quickly led her away from the noise.

"Damn!" he hissed again. There was no outside entrance from this hallway. They would have to go back the other way, which meant running into the disturbance, which by now was beginning to sound like a full-sized melee. "Look, wipe your tears, Dolly, and look serene, or we're taken for fair."

"I'll try," she promised, taking a deep, steadying breath and groping in her small bag for a handkerchief. "There, do I look calm enough?"

"You look lovely," Alan told her, knowing it would buck up her spirits, and it did. And damme if she don't, he thought.

They advanced on the mob in the hall. Old men with cudgels from the watch, a huge bailiff the size of a plow-horse, the magistrate, several tavern servants, and many patrons, who were yelling for either peace and quiet, or more drinks. Shouts could be heard in favor of lynching the riotous heathens in the dining room, or the magistrate and his churls, or both.

"Excuse us, excuse us, if you please," Alan said with a fixed smile as he led Dolly through the press, leaning back as the door was finally booted open and the party responded with a shower of crockery, glassware, a chamber-pot, and several gobbets of raisin duff. "Will you let a lady pass, please, there's a good fellow."

The Charlies from the watch were not having it all their own way. They could not use their cudgels, and were knotted in the door like a beer bung, even with the bailiff's huge shoulder applied to shove them in by force. Alan put his own shoulder to the back of one old man and pushed, and the Charlies finally gained the bulwarks, but it was a bad mistake, for drunken whores and revelers could fight when cornered, better than the poorly paid dodderers.

Once on the first-floor level, Alan fetched his own hat and led Dolly into the street.

" 'Oy, ain't you one o' them?" a servant cried out as they began to walk away. "Yes, you is! Hoy, the watch! 'Er'es another o' the bastards!"

"My dear fellow, I don't know what you're talking about," Alan countered. "But, here's a guinea on my reckoning, and please inform your cook that it was a *splendid* supper, thankee very much."

The servant bent over to pick up the guinea from the mud, and Alan booted him in the face, which sent him sprawling, out cold.

"Can't be too careful, you know," he said smiling at Dolly. "Now, let's walk in that direction, as quick as damnit."

"But what about your friends back there?" she asked, showing her first signs of amusement all night. "What will happen to them?"

"With friends like that, who needs enemies?" Alan shrugged. "To the devil with 'em. Hurry!"

Her lodgings were in English Harbor, so they took a coach over the ridge, and Alan paid the driver to carry a note to his own inn to his man Cony, telling him not to wait up, but to come fetch him at first light.

Dolly's room was in a ratty, cheap inn halfway up the hill overlooking the harbor. There was one small window, a set of sprung chairs and a small round table under it, a wardrobe which contained only a pair of dresses and a morning bedgown, two large chests, one of which she used for a table for her toilet with a tiny mirror propped up on it, and a high, narrow, curtained bed-stead and nightstand.

"I must apologize for this," she said modestly as she lit the one foul candle on the table below the window. "When Captain Fenton was still alive, we had a set of rooms, in a better lodging house. I tried to keep them for a while, but they were simply too dear. This is all I can afford for now, though Mistress Olivett tells me I may stay in her establishment for very little."

"That's the Mother Abbess you started working for?" Alan asked, removing his coat.

"Yes, she is," Dolly replied, calm enough about it.

"And how long have you been working for her?"

"Only a fortnight," Dolly sighed. "It hasn't been so bad, not until tonight, at least. I go with the others to call upon gentlemen who wish companionship. Oh, God. I suppose I shan't get my money for tonight, after all. A whole crown I've lost, and I've nothing left."

"You're getting only a crown out of the guinea we were charged for your services?" Alan gaped. "What a gyp!"

"A guinea?" she gasped. "And I thought you were japing me when you said that earlier! Oh, how cruel she is, when she knows my need!"

"I'll give you a guinea, and it's all yours, Dolly," Alan promised her. "The night's still young." He pulled out his watch and took a peek at the face—barely gone nine. "Let's get into bed."

An expression of disagreement appeared on her features for a moment, then she sighed and acquiesced, and turned away to undo her gown. Alan shucked his clothing quickly and flung himself onto the lumpy mattress. She came to him after carefully hanging up her gown in the wardrobe. She turned her back and he unlaced her stays for her, then she sat on the edge of the bed and undid the silk ribands that held her knee-length silk stockings up and she folded them as though they were precious gems. He watched her slim back while she worked, and admired the Venus dimples of her lower back. She reached up and took the pins from her hair, letting it fall thick and lustrous down her back almost to her waist.

"Could we lay under the sheet, please, Alan?" she asked in her meek little voice again. "I know it's a rather warm night, but : . ."

"If you wish, dear," he said gently, finding himself in thrall at the sight of a woman undressing for him, and feeling unwilling sympathy for her. She was too ... nice ... a woman to be forced to prostitute herself, far above the regular girls who entered the trade, and he felt for her.

She slid under the sheet with him and lay stiff as a board by his side as he slid over to her. He put an arm behind her head and drew her to him so that they lay facing each other, and he ran his free hand up and down her ribs and her hip. Reluctantly, she put an arm over him as well.

"This is what I liked best with the Captain," she whispered, and the catch in her voice told him she was about to cry again. "The being close in the night, when he had . . . that part was sometimes almost enjoyable, but . . . I'm sorry."

She almost sprang from the bed, but he restrained her and took her in both arms to let her weep on his bare chest, thinking himself such a bloody fool.

"What was he like?" Alan asked minutes later after she had quieted.

"He was much older, in his forties," she sighed. "Such a kind, good man! So patient with my frailties and my ignorance. I'm afraid I wasn't much of a catch for him. No dowry, no lands or rents. His family called him a fool to his face, a foolish colt's-tooth to take a younger wife with no prospects."

"And your own family?"

"They passed over. I was earning my way as a housekeeper in Woolwich when the dear Captain came to visit my people. Not a month later, we were married and at sea on the way here to Antigua. And six months after that, he died of the fever. Ah well, at least we had almost a year of peaceful existence together before . . ."

He kissed her cheek and felt the cool dampness of smudged tears. He kissed her neck, and it was a nice neck, long and graceful with so many interesting hollows to explore, as were her shoulders and collarbones. Firm, yet yielding, apulse with young life.

"Say my name, Alan," she whispered.

"Dolly," he obeyed. "Dearest Dolly. Poor, lovely little Dolly."

Her arms went about him, then, and she allowed herself to be rolled over on her back. Their lips met, and no longer merely acquiescent, she returned his kiss, warming to him and beginning to breathe heavier, to stir her arms, her hands, and her body against his.

He explored her from brow to knees with his fingertips, with his lips and tongue, and she began to writhe and moan, to whimper and chuckle as he tickled or en-fired her by turns. All through it, he praised her, praised her beauty, talked to her gently as one would approach a wary puppy or colt, and she responded with stronger moans and delighted sighs of impending bliss.

He kissed his way from her knees, up both smooth, firm young thighs and over her muff, teasing and nipping until she was panting and grasping for him, and she opened her thighs wider as he slid up to nuzzle her breasts. Such fine young breasts with large, oval aureoles and taut young nipples that cried out for suckling.

A moment's dispassionate reach for the sheepgut condom on the nightstand, and then he was pressing against her netherlips, and she arched her back and lifted her hips to press back, and he was sliding down that endless tunnel that led to the seat of heaven itself, and she cried out like a virgin on her wedding night, though she writhed and clung to him like a limpet, matching his every movement.

"Alan, say my name, please, Alan, say my name!" she panted with her mouth against his neck. "Ah, yes, ah! I never knew . . ."

"Dolly, yes, it's good, so good, you're such a good girl, such a YES!"

He could feel nothing but belly and breasts, perhaps her fingers digging into his shoulders, and their groins; hear nothing but her cries of pleasure and the quick wash-deck pumping noise of lovemaking until she shouted and kept on shouting in an utter transport of joy, not long after his own forge-hot release.

"Dolly, yes, lovely Dolly," he muttered soft against her neck as he lay spent on elbows and weak knees over her.

"Alan, my Alan dearest," she giggled back, trembling still, and showering him with smile-widened kisses.

"If lovemaking could always be this way," she said much later after their third bout, after they had sent down for some wine to cool them.

"My dear girl, it's supposed to be," Alan snickered, pleased as punch with himself. "Leastways, I've always found it so."

"If it could be, I could almost bear the shame of being . . . a whore. Until I hear from Roger's relatives, of course, and get the money to go home." She sighed.

"Think they like you that much?" Alan asked, not meaning to tease her.

"No," she replied, sitting up to hug her knees with the soggy sheet falling to her waist. "Oh, Alan, I've written and written, and there's never a word back from them. Nothing on the packet ships for me. I almost despair sometimes that I'll be bound to this life for all time!" She lay her head on her knees, hiding her face in her hair.

"Wait a minute," Alan said, propping himself up in the bed on a pile of thick pillows. "He only died three months ago, you say? Hell, it's three months by ship back home. Say, here to

Bermuda to pick up a favorable slant from the highs. Then on to New York from there. And for reply, the packet would sail down to Portugal and then run west to Dominica first. They wouldn't even have gotten a word about your poor Roger's demise yet. And it'll most like be another three or four months before you can even expect any kind of answer."

"And I must endure more of this cruelty?" she gasped. "Oh, I cannot bear it! I shall have to enter that woman's dreadful house, after all. It's the only place that will take me."

"There's housekeeping, still," Alan suggested. "Quite a few households here on Antigua would hire a young widow who's experienced at caring for children, or such like. It's not as if you had debts."

She fell back to lay her head on his stomach and hug him.

"Do you think I have not tried, Alan? They have slaves here, not hired servants. And if hired, paid less than a dog's dinner."

Here comes the sly little hand on my purse-strings, Alan said to himself. Yet she stayed silent, hugging him like a child in her parent's lap. Alright, I'll say it for her and get it over with. Damn fool.

"I could loan you a little to tide you over, Dolly."

"I'll not hear of it, Alan Lewrie," she replied, looking up at his face in the gloom. "If I needs must, I can deal with the humiliation of this shameful trade for a short space, and there are still things to sell of my possessions. Thank you, but the answer is no. I must own that I am only a weak, stupid woman, but I can guess what you may think of me if you do loan me money. I'd like you to think better of me than that."

"You're serious!" He gaped in astonishment.

"That I am," she agreed. "After this delightful experience with you, I would not do anything to cheapen our memories of each other. I'd rather starve first. Oh, how masterful you were, and how kind to me, to take me out of that place rather than shame me by making me behave as those others. I've been such a fool to think that taking money for men to pleasure themselves is possible, even for a little time. You have opened my eyes to how low and base I would have become had you not saved me. I shall treasure you forever for that. And for this." She teased with a shy smile, and reached down under the sheet to touch his belly and lion's mane.

"Another man may wish you to be his and his alone. Have you heard of mistresses, Dolly?" Alan asked, sounding her out to see if she still rang true, that it was not a whore's lie yet.

"It would be gentler, and safer, would it not?" she asked. "But, I can think of only one gentleman that I'd care to keep house for."

Another light brush of her fingers over his groin.

"What about your husband's things, then. Have you sold any of that yet?"

"I have his chest here. But Alan, I could not bear to part with all that I have left of that gentle, wonderful man," she objected sadly. "To auction him off to the highest bidder, all that represents what's left of him, it's too horrid to contemplate."

"Let's see what there is," Alan said, sliding out of bed. "Which chest was his?"

"The one with the mirror atop," she told him, and wrapped the top sheet about her as he put on his long-tailed shirt. They knelt and she unlocked his chest with a key, lifted the lid with all the reverence of a parson opening the bread-box of a Sunday, and he helped her pull out the top tray, which was full of papers and correspondence.

There wasn't much, really. Hats and uniforms of the infantry unit he belonged to. Breeches and stockings, a high pair of boots more suited to a dragoon or horse artillery unit. A cheap watch, and the man's sword, one of middling quality.

"Twenty, twenty-five guineas for the sword," Alan said with a heavy sigh. "The boots might go for five, and the watch for ten. The chain and fob are worth more. Maybe one hundred pounds all told."

"But, Alan, that's one hundred pounds more than I have now," she said with a childlike burst of hope. "Though I do hate to part with his sword and watch. I mean, a man's honor, his . . ."

"Twenty pounds at the least is twenty pounds. He won't be needing a sword where he's gone, and there's no son to inherit," Alan said with a harsh rasp. He sorted through the papers in the top tray while Dolly fetched their wine glasses and topped them up, bringing a second candle Alan had ordered to better light his perusings.

"At least he didn't leave you any bills from the mess or from his tailor's," Alan jested. "Did you contact his fellow officers? What did they say they'd do for you?"

"What any man would pay for." Dolly frowned. "They thought him a little silly, I think. And . . . he wasn't exactly that popular with his fellow officers. I don't know why, but I always got that feeling when we were around them. Some jealousy, some argument or something."

"Goddamn!" Alan exclaimed, after he had folded out a large sheet of paper all hung with ribands and wax seals. "You've not talked to them at all?"

"I was afraid they'd sneer at me, Alan," she whispered.

"Not while you hold his commission document, they wouldn't!"

"What is that?" she said, with all innocence.

"My dear Dolly," he began, rocked back on his heels by her naivety. "You know that officers in the British Army *buy* their commissions. Umhumm, and do you know that they pay a lot of money for the privilege of never doing a decent day's labor again? Keep the bloody sword, hang the watch in the window for pigeons to peck on, here's your real money!"

"I meant to have it framed, as a memento, but I couldn't afford to yet," she said, staring at him goggle-eyed with building wonder.

Why, dear Lord, is every woman I meet and hop into bed with as feeble in the brains as cold, boiled mutton? he wondered to himself with a shake of his head and a reflective grin.

"It costs an ensign in a good regiment three hundred pounds to buy a commission. A lieutenancy goes for about five hundred, and I have it on good authority that a captaincy is worth nigh on a thousand pounds, Dolly. As dear Roger's nearest living relative, the one he's most like willed everything to, you now own it, d'you see, girl? It's like a small-holding, it's yours to sell." She stared at him as if he wasn't quite getting through to her. "For *money*."

"Oh, Alan!" she shrieked and flung herself on him, bearing him over on his back on the cold bare boards to straddle him and chortle with glee while she rained kisses and squeezed until he thought he might see stars. "I'm saved! I'm saved! You saved me, you dear man, you wonderful, lovely man! How can I ever repay you, dearest Alan?"

"Well, if you put it that way . . ." He laughed heartily with her.

"I can go home to England! I don't have to be anyone's mistress, or anyone's whore! Oh, out of my darkest night, God has shown me the way to security! How can I ever thank you?"

"I'm just glad I could do something . . ."

"I won't have to drudge as someone's domestic back home. I can live well, if I watch my pennies, and I'm not a spendthrift,

I know how to economize and manage. I did well enough on Roger's pay and the pin-money he allowed me. I made a good home for him, and I can make a good home for myself. Or"—she calmed—"I could make a good home for you. Yes, I could, Alan. I could stay here on Antigua, take a tidy set of rooms, nothing grand, no need for servants . . . well, maybe a maid to help me clean. I'm used to cleaning for myself, Alan. And she would not have to be a live-in, just a day-servant. What's that, six pounds a year, and a dress and shoes? Oh, would it not be grand, Alan? You would come in from your ship, and we could be together again."

Hmm, he considered hard. She's a wonderful gallop, no question about that, and it wouldn't cost me tuppence. How many men can boast of free mistresses. Even if she does stray, or take in someone while I'm at sea, it's nothing more than I'm used to already. Had I bought her, I'd worry about that anyway.

"Dolly, my dearest, loveliest girl, I'll be gone for months on end. I'd love to see you again, but it would be so cruelly lonely for you. Best you go home to England, much as I could wish . . ."

"And if I just happened to be here, Alan dearest? Would we be able to share things? There's no one else in your life?"

"Of course we could, Dolly. And no, there's no one else."

"Oh, you have made me the happiest woman tonight. In all ways, my wonderful Alan. I had not hoped to aspire to so much joy in my life ever again. I shall love and cherish you while I have you, and you shall know how much joy you've given me by how much I give myself to you. Like now. Say you're not so tired, dear Alan. Can we do that again, could we please, my love?"

II

"Thou wilt soon die, and thou art not yet simple, nor free from perturbations, nor without suspicion of being hurt by external things, nor kindly disposed towards all; nor dost thou yet place wisdom only in acting justly."
Meditations IV-37
—Marcus Aurelius

Chapter 1

His vouchers and records were under his arm, and in order in a sailcloth bundle. He had traded off his midshipman's rigs, sold that now decidedly shoddy dirk that had once gleamed with "gold," and had his new uniforms in his sea chest.

There had been a need to dip into his hidden cache of guineas to pay for his new finery, to equip himself with the luxury of a personal telescope, cases of wine, fresh cabin stores such as cheese and jam. And he had spent money on his man Cony's rig as well; new shoes and buckles (pinch-beck but serviceable), a new tarred hat, short blue jacket with brass buttons and slop trousers.

He had not gotten much sleep, in the end. Between the party that had turned into a drunken brawl, his escape, his passionate night with Dolly, which had lasted until dawn, and then a hectic round of chores, he was just about done in. Up and out on a crust of bread and a single cup of tea to move her to his old lodgings, which were a bit more expensive but much nicer and more refined. A quick meeting with his shore agent to deal with her affairs with her husband's regiment, a gift of twenty pounds to get her settled and tide her over until she could sell Roger Fenton's commission. And, lastly, a quiet word with the agent to tell him to advance her no more than absolutely necessary if she could not sell it.

At least, he decided, gaining his first easy breath of the day in the hired boat, he did not have a debilitating hangover. Her send-off, while the coach waited in the street to take him to the docks, had damned near killed him, and had he partaken as heavily as Ashburn and the others the night before, she damned well might have then and there.

"Da's de *Shrike*, sah," the black boatman told him as he

sculled his small bum-boat across the still harbor at first light. Around them the watch-bells chimed from over thirty vessels as the morning watch ended and the forenoon began. Alan consulted his pocket watch and grunted in satisfaction that he would report aboard his new ship just a few minutes after the last stroke of eight in the morning.

Shrike, he could see as they got close, was foreign in origin, probably a prize. She sported two masts crossed with square-sail yards, but on her after main-mast he could espy a brailed-up sail on the lowest yard, the cro'jack, which on the three-masters he had served was usually bare. On a brig, though, they would need that main course for more speed, for there would be only the fore-course forward which might be winded if the ship sailed in a stern or quarter wind. Her spanker boom and gaff were also much larger than anything he had seen before, and were fixed to an upright spar doubled to the main-mast, which officially made her a snow instead of a brig, possibly an alteration any captain could make in the rig of his ship without upsetting higher authorities, as long as it did not cost the local dockyard too much in government funds or supplies.

Shrike's jib-boom and bow-sprit were different also, steeved at a much less acute angle to the deck, which would give her larger heads'ls, and, with the big spanker, more windward ability.

"Damme, but she's a shabby old bitch," he was forced to admit to Cony.

The hull was dark, almost black, but, like an old coat, showing a rusty brown tinge from years of exposure to weather and gallons of paint and linseed oil. The gunwale stripe might at one time have been buff, but had faded to a scabbed and blistered dingy off-white. And where one expected to see gilt paint around the beakhead, entry port and transom carvings, white lead had been applied in lieu of a prosperous captain's gold. Her masts, though, and her running and standing rigging, were in excellent shape, bespeaking a captain poor in pelf, not care.

"*Shrike*, the butcher bird," Alan commented to Cony as he spotted the figurehead and pointed it out. The bird's wings were fanned back as part of the upper beakhead rail supports, clawed feet extended in the moment of seizure of prey, and the hooked bill open to reveal a red tongue. It too needed a paint job to restore the white, grey and brown tones of the real bird.

"Seen 'nough of 'em at 'ome, sir." Cony grinned in remembrance of his forest-running days in Gloucestershire. "Spikes their kills ta thorn bushes. Mayhap we'll be a'spikin' some Frogs an' Dagoes the same, sir."

"We'll see."

"Ahoy the boat!" came a call from *Shrike*'s entry port.

"Aye aye!" Cony bawled back at them, showing the requisite number of fingers to alert their new ship's side-party to the proper show of respect to be presented.

The bum-boat chunked against the ship's side, and the native bargee and Cony held her fast to the chains while Alan squared himself away and took hold of the man-ropes, which were hung old-style from the entry port, without being strung through the boarding ladder battens. It wasn't much of a climb, though, nothing as tall as a frigate's sides, and he made it easily without tangling his hanger between his legs or otherwise embarrassing himself.

The bosun's pipes began to squeal and the Marines slapped their muskets to "present arms" as his head came up over the deck edge, and he was about to congratulate himself on arriving with the proper amount of dignity. It was at that moment that an impressively large ginger ram-cat with pale gold eyes of a most evil cast accosted him at the lip of the entry port. The cat took one look at him, bottled up, arched his back, laid back his ears and uttered a loud trilling growl of challenge.

"Fuck you, too," Alan gasped, almost startled from his grip on the man-ropes. "Shoo. Scat!"

The cat took a swipe at him, then ran off forward with a howl, there to take guard upon the bulwarks and wash himself furiously as he thought up a way to get even.

"Lieutenant Lewrie, come aboard to join," Alan said, once he was safely on his feet on the upper deck. There was very little gangway overlooking the waist, just high enough above the upper deck to clear the guns.

"Ah'm Fukes, the bosun, sir," a male gorilla in King's Coat told him, knuckling his rather prominent brow ridge from which sprouted a solid thicket of white eyebrows over a face only a mother could love. "This'ere's Mister Caldwell, the sailin' master. Lef'ten't Walsham o' the Marines . . . an' you'll be the new first lef'ten't, sir?"

"Yes, I suppose I am. I'd admire if you could lend my man Cony a hand with my dunnage. Is the captain aboard?"

"Aye, sir, 'e's aft in 'is cabins. Ah'll 'ave ya took there directly, sir," Fukes went on, turning to pause and spit a large dollop of tobacco juice into a spit kid. " 'Ere, Mister Rossyngton, show the first officer aft."

"Aye aye, sir," a rather well turned out midshipman answered. "This way, if you will, sir."

Some ship! Alan thought with a sudden qualm of nerves. Fukes and the other senior warrants he had seen on the gangway had been much of a kind; overaged, craggy and white-haired, way senior to him in sea experience. Caldwell, the sailing master, was a gotch-bellied little minnikin in his fifties with square spectacles at the tip of his nose.

Walsham, the Marine officer, was only a second lieutenant, a boy who appeared no older than the run-of-the-mill midshipman, while his sergeant looked old enough to have helped shoot Admiral Byng in the last war. And the doddering old colt's-tooth who sported a carpenter's apron and goggled a drooling smile at him in passing had to be seventy years old if he was a day!

"Mister Pebble, the ship's carpenter, sir. Mister Pebble, the first officer, Lieutenant Lewrie," Rossyngton introduced smoothly.

"Ah de do, sir, ah de do!" the oldster gammered through a nearly toothless mouth, what little hair he had left on his bare head waving like strands of cotton in the slight wind. "A' firs' un died, ye know, o' the quinsy, warn't it, Mister Rossyngton?"

"His heart, Mister Pebble," Rossyngton prompted.

"Ah, 'twuz Curtiss died o' quinsy. Shame, Mister Lewrie, young man like Tuckwell a'dyin', an' 'im not fifty," Pebble maundered wetly.

"Do they do a *lot* of dying aboard *Shrike*?" Alan asked as Rossyngton led him below to the cabins under the quarterdeck.

Rossyngton hid his smirk well, not sure of what sort his new first lieutenant was. "They keep you awake at night, expiring with loud thuds, sir."

"Ah," Alan managed to say, fighting manfully to keep a straight and sober face as was proper to a ship's officer. Rossyngton looked to be the product of a good family, a manly get of about seventeen or so years, and someone with whom Lewrie would have felt at home in shared outlook; and by the devilish glint in Rossyngton's blue eyes, he would have been a mirthful companion, were circumstances different.

The Marine sentry at the cabin doors announced him loudly with a smart crash of his musket butt, and a voice bade Lewrie enter.

Well, he ain't Noah, there's a blessing, Alan thought as he beheld his new master and commander.

Lieutenant Lilycrop had to be the oldest junior officer that Alan had ever laid eyes on, and he had seen some beauties in his time. He was near sixty, with a face as withered as an ill-used work glove, a pug-nosed, apple-cheeked Father Christmas whose chest and belly had merged into a massive appliance round as iron shot. He wore his own hair instead of a wig, and that hair was curly and cotton-white, but clubbed back into a seaman's queue that even plaited reached down to his middle back. Lost in the mass of wrinkles about his eyes, two bright orbs of brown could now and then be glimpsed.

"Lieutenant Lewrie, sir. Come aboard to join, sir," he said, producing his ornate commission document which warned ". . . nor you nor any of you may fail as you will answer the contrary at your peril," his orders from the flag to come aboard, and his pay and certificates.

"Well, sit you down, young sir," Lilycrop growled in a voice gone stentorian and hoarse from a lifetime of barking orders. "Mind the kitty."

Alan halted his descent into the chair and looked down to see a black cat stretched out in the seat, tail lazily curling and uncurling like a short commissioning pendant. Not knowing what to do, and never being terribly fond of cats anyway, he gently shoved it out of the chair so it could hop down on its own with a small meow of disappointment.

"That's Henrietta, oh she's a shy 'un, she is, but she'll take to you soon enough," Lilycrop said, beaming at the black cat, dropping into baby-talk as he addressed her directly. "Henrietta takes time to make up her mind about people, yes she does, don't you, sweetlin'. Now Samson, here"—Lilycrop changed tone to introduce Alan to a black-and-white-and-grey parti-colored ram-cat which had jumped up onto his desk to be stroked and picked up—"Now Samson, he's a standoff-ish young lout, won't have truck with none but me, d'y'see? There's a good boy."

Goddamme, somebody in the flagship must have it in for me in the worst way, Alan sighed to himself. I've seen saner people eat bugs in Bedlam. Was there some back I didn't piss down right? Some grudge getting paid back on me? Did they mix me up with somebody with two heads? God rot 'em, I thought I'd go the least senior officer into a real ship, not this . . . Ark!

"Let's see what he's made of, this young'un of ours, Samson."

While Lilycrop bent over to peruse his records, Alan took the time to look about the cabin, and it was spartan in the extreme. Paint the color of old cheese coated the walls and interior partitions, the result of mixing what was left over from various lots. The deck was covered by sailcloth painted in black-and-white squares, and plain sailcloth made up the curtains over the stern windows. But there was no embroidered coverlet over the hanging bed-box, no padded cushions on the transom settee. The desk, the dining table, the chairs, were all harshly simple and dull, as utilitarian as a wash-hand stand. There was no wine cabinet present, and Alan suffered another qualm as he considered that his new captain was one of those evangelizing tee-totalers.

The sword that hung on the pegs on the wall next to a shabby grogram watch coat was a heavy, older straight sword more suitable for an infantry officer in a Highland regiment. Evidently, Lieutenant Lilycrop did not have two farthings to rub together other than Naval pay, and that none too good for a lieutenant in command of a small ship below the Rate. Come to think on it, mine's low enough at two shillings six pence a day. Alan grimaced. What does he get, four or five at best?

Now that his eyes had adjusted to the gloom of the cabins, he could see that there were more cats present; a lot more. Cats of every color and constitution, some old and grizzled from fights and amours, some spry and young, and at least four kittens being nursed by their mother on the captain's berth. And there was a barely perceptible odor.

"Ah, you've done a lot in a little over two years' service," Lilycrop finally commented, laying down the documents. "But not much more practical experience than a half-cooked midshipman."

"Aye, sir. Sorry if I do not please, but I shall endeavor to do so as we progress together," Alan said, on guard at once but making keen noises.

"A fledglin' just outa the nest. Nay, more a chick fresh from the shell," Lilycrop maundered. "My last first officer . . . oh, now there was a tarry-handed young cock . . . 'twas sorry I was to lose him. But, we do what we can with what we're given, an' if the flag says you're to be first lieutenant into *Shrike*, then growl I may, but agree I must."

Damme, I ain't that bad, Alan thought sourly. And if he don't like the cut of my jib, can't he toss me back for someone else to catch?

"Aye, sir," he replied, noncommittal.

"Well, sir." Lilycrop left his sulks and got suddenly and alarmingly business-like. "*Shrike* is Dutch-built, took by my last ship off St. Eustatius a year ago. She's eighty foot on the range of the deck, ninety-eight foot from taffrail to bow-sprit, an' you'll note she's beamy, like most Dutchies—twenty-seven foot abeam. Barely ten foot deep in the hold, of two hundred and ten tons burthen. She wasn't a fast sailer 'til I had her jib-boom an' sprit steeved lower, an' larger fores'ls cut. We added the horse an' the short trys'l mizzen to the main-mast to make her more weatherly, so she's a snow, now, tho' still rated as a brig-rigged sloop. Started out a tradin' brig, made of good Hamburg oak. She don't work much in heavy seas, don't need much pumpin' out, an' bein' just a quim-hair under ten-foot draught, an' her quick-work flatter'n any English shipwright'd loft her up, she can go places another ship'd dread to go. You'll find her a fiddler's bitch close-hauled, but she'll weather *and* head reach on any fuckin' frigate that ever swum, an' off the wind long's you keep her quartered, an' not 'both sheets aft,' she'll run to loo'rd like a starvin' whore. But I warn ye now, take your eyes off her to play with yourself just a second, an' she'll scare hell out of you if you let her have her head. Flat down wind, we've had her surf up her own bow-wave in a half-gale, an' that with the main course brailed up, and if you let her get away, she'll broach on you faster'n you can say 'damn my eyes, ain't my fault.' "

"I see, sir." Alan marveled at the change that had come over Lieutenant Lilycrop as he got on professional matters.

"We've two little four-pounders on the fo'c'sle, all she'll take for end weight, and only twelve six-pounders for the main battery, and two of those shifted aft into my quarters to get her stern trimmed down so the fuckin' rudder'll bite, so she's not so crank. So she'll tack right smart now. She looks *en flute*, 'cause there were two more guns aft once, but they wuz bronze trash I'd have no truck with, so I had 'em put ashore. Two gunports right forward on the weather deck're empty, too, to lift her bows proper. Damned Yankees, tryin' to make a sixteen-gunned privateer out o' her. Silly fools. Yankee Doodles. Ya know, the Jonathons, the Rebels," Lilycrop explained as he used the nickname with which Alan was not familiar.

"Aha," Alan nodded.

"Pierced for sweeps along the gangways above the gun deck, too. You'll find 'em damned handy for workin' outa harbor, or off a lee, but with so little quick-work you'd best not try 'em when it's too windy or she'll get away from you under bare poles. Ever use sweeps?"

"No, sir," Alan had to admit.

"Well, shit," Lilycrop grumbled.

"Sorry, sir, you were saying?"

"Like most ships commissioned from prizes on foreign stations, *Shrike* has her share of no-hopers." Lilycrop frowned. "Most of her warrants are a bit spavined, but with lots of practical experience. My crew was as scrofulous a lot as I've ever seen, even after my former captain let me have ten prime hands from old *Bonaventure*, the usual surly and slack-jawed louts you'd expect, with more'n average her number of Island Blacks, and half of those probably runaway slaves in the first place. But we've pulled together, and I'll touch 'em up sharp when needed. I'm not a Tartar when it comes to plyin' the cat, but I by God'll flay a man raw when he needs it, not like some of these Goddamn psalm-singin' hedge-priests in disguise you see clutterin' up quarterdecks these days. I don't splice the mainbrace nor cosset the people 'less I see a choir of angels to larboard announcing the Apocalypse. You're not a hedge-priest are you now, Lewrie?"

"Hell no, sir." Alan grinned. "Ow!"

Henrietta had made up her mind that his leg, encased in brand new silk stocking, was a scratching post.

"Ah, she's takin' to you, good girl," Lilycrop said softly, laying his head to one side in admiration of his cat. "Let her have a little lap to make friends with you. Go on, pick her up. She'll purr like a snare drum. Now, you ain't a Tartar, either, are you?"

"No, sir," Alan said, gingerly lifting the cat from his side to sit in his lap, where Henrietta began to lay down her head and rub to mark him, scattering a handful of black fur on his snowy-white breeches. "Firm but fair was the motto I was taught, sir."

"Good for you, then, laddie," Lilycrop nodded agreeably. "Now, as to the people. Caldwell is a sour little shit-sack, but a good master, a bit of a hymn-singer and in another life he'd turn evangel on us, so don't plan on getting much joy out of him in the wardroom. Walsham, well, he's a tailor's dummy, God help him, but what can you expect from Marines. His sergeant is good, though, but deaf as a country magistrate. Master gunner Mister Cox is a sharp'un, and Fukes is a good bosun, but we're thin in mates. Mister Lewyss the surgeon is competent but a horrid drinker, bein' Welsh, and if I hear that damned harp and his quavery fuckin' voice lollopin' out those mournful dirges in the mess past eight bells o' the second dog, I'll kick your young arse so you can kick his. Mister Henry Biggs the purser is the biggest weasel I've ever come across, and that's sayin' somethin' after fifty year at sea, man and boy. You'll watch him like a hawk, and if you discover how he prospers, you'll be the first. Midshipmen're just about what you'd expect, one stupid as cow-pats and t'other too clever for his own good."

"That would be Rossyngton, the clever one, sir?" Alan said as Henrietta draped herself over his chest like a warm blanket and began to vibrate and snore, her paws kneading his shirt front with *sharp* little claws.

"You're smart as paint, Lewrie. T'other, Mister Edgar, is not too long off the dung wagon, and I s'pect if it was rainin' claret he'd have a colander to catch it in, and he'd drop that. Clumsy young bastard. Stepped on Pitt's tail t'other day."

"Who, sir?"

"The ginger tom lives forrard."

"We've met, sir," Alan stated.

"Worst disposition in a cat I've ever seen," Lilycrop confessed. "Know why I named him Pitt, hey?"

"No, sir."

"Because I absolutely despise the bastard!" Lilycrop boomed with a short bark of laughter at his own wit. "Rapacious, sir, most rapacious mouser I've ever seen. Got the soul of a master-at-arms, though. Come to think of it, those are good traits in a Prime Minister, too."

"With so many cats aboard, I should think *Shrike* would not be plagued with rodents like other ships, sir."

"Their tribe stand no chance of prosperin'," Lilycrop boasted.

"Then what do the midshipmen eat, sir?" Alan asked.

"Ha ha, you're a wag, sir!" Lilycrop boomed again. "I can tell we'll get on, if there's a brain hidden behind all that dandy-prattery. Well, I'd expect you'd like to get settled into your cabin and get all squared away. You'll find my Order Book and all that bum fodder to look over, and then I expect you'll go over the ship and make your acquaintances, see what we have to work with, God help us."

"Thank you, sir."

"Got any questions, see me on the sly," Lilycrop commanded. "Can't let the people or the warrants think you're slack-witted or not experienced enough. Would you like a kitten?"

"Um, not right now, sir."

"You're not one of those people who can't abide the little darlin's, are you, Lewrie?" Lilycrop looked at him sternly.

"Oh, no, sir," Alan assured him quickly. "It's just that none of my other ships ran to pets, and I do want to find my feet first."

"Well, keep it in mind, we've four new'uns ready for weanin' in a week or so. That'll be all, Lewrie."

"Aye aye, sir," Alan replied, standing up and trying to disentangle Henrietta from her death-grip on his shirt. She finally scaled his back, scratching him on the nape on her way down to the chair where she re-ensconced herself and began to wash.

Lilycrop turned to stare at a large, shallow wooden box by the quarter-gallery and bawled for his steward. "Gooch!"

"Aye, sir?" a wizened little mouse of a man asked, popping out of the captain's pantry by the chart-room.

"Cat shit, Gooch!"

"Aye aye, sir, right away, sir."

I've always believed it, Alan told himself as he pored over the captain's Order Book of set instructions in his small cabin. Not one captain on the face of this earth is dealing with a healthy mind. They're all daft as bats. This Lilycrop makes Treghues look sane as a banking house. What did I do to deserve this? Who did I fuck, who did I *not* fuck?

The officer's wardroom was not in the extreme stern in *Shrike*, but aft of the main-mast and ahead of stores rooms. As a single-deck ship, she had to cram all her holds and stores onto one deck, along with all her personnel accommodations. There was a solid deck under the fo'c'sle, broken aft of the galley into a capacious hold to allow her to stay at sea for up to three months. Seamen were berthed above the stores kegs and barrels on a temporary mess-deck flooring, swung in hammocks, with the last two rows furthest aft reserved for the Marine complement.

Aft of the Marines, there was room for the officers and senior warrants, with the main after hatch leading down just before the deal partitions that screened it off from the Marines. The captain was kept in his rather spartan splendor in what was called a hanging cabin under the highly steeved quarterdeck, which had a break much like a three-foot-high poop deck near the taffrail to give him standing headroom.

This cut the wardroom off from all sunlight, even though it was above the waterline, but the only openings to the outside were gunports that were kept tightly sealed unless the ship cleared for action.

Alan's cabin was right aft on the larboard side, hard up against the after bread room, spirit store and fish room, which added to the miasma of cat droppings and the usual human odors.

If he thought that promotion to lieutenant would get him any more splendor of his own, he was sadly mistaken. The cabin was six feet wide, which left room for a wash-hand stand and his sea chest, about six feet six inches long to accommodate a fixed berth raised up high enough to give him some storage underneath. Near the door at the foot of the bed there was a tiny portable writing desk, a three-tiered bookshelf already filled with the accumulated reading of an entire commission, and a stool to sit on while he wrote letters or conducted ship's business. Across from his cabin the surgeon, Dr. Lewyss, was housed. The next two cabins were for the sailing master to larboard, and the purser to starboard. Forward of those, the cabins got smaller to make walking space around the fixed dining table and the hatchway to the orlop stores. Walsham the Marine officer, the captain's clerk, Fukes the bosun, Cox the gunner and Mr. Pebble, the enfeebled carpenter, had those cabins. The spare cabin that completed the starboard tier was wardroom stores and the captain's servant and the wardroom servant swung their hammocks in there above the personal food and drink for the officers and warrants.

The many cats may have cut down on the usual rat population, but the ship teemed with cockroaches; small ones, admittedly, since the cats would chase anything large enough to entertain them.

The only blessing for the crew, who normally had only twenty-eight inches in which to sling a fourteen-inch-wide hammock, was that the ship was not at her full-rated complement of one hundred and ten people, but was six hands short in seamen, and four in servants, and that the Marine party, which would not normally be aboard so small a brig, was only sixteen privates, two corporals, a sergeant, and Walsham. Being rated a fourteen-gunned ship in official records could be a blessing.

Alan lay propped up on his bunk, reading. The surgeon was stoking up his harp and singing some Welsh song of unrequited misery, accompanied by someone on a flute who was as mournful a specter as the doctor. Alan didn't think he would enjoy wardroom life, if that was the best entertainment they had to offer. Besides, Lieutenant Railsford had warned him to stay aloof, hard as it would be on his congenial and garrulous nature. Eager as he was for companionship, and no matter how old the others were in the wardroom, he was senior to them, and could only damage his credibility and authority if he was to join in their simple pleasures. He was the captain's voice in all things, the one who would brook no dis-satisfaction with a captain's decisions or allow anyone to carp or cavil.

No wonder old Lieutenant Swift in *Ariadne* was such a dry stick, Alan sighed, wondering if he was up to all the demands that would be made on his abilities, getting lost in the knowledge that he was pretty much in charge of all the various punishments books, logs, charts, pay vouchers, rating certificates, prize certificates (damned few of those, he noted grimly), quarter-bills, watch bills, and professional records of the entire crew.

It really would have been much nicer to have been second officer in a slightly larger frigate than *Desperate*, even the fifth or sixth lieutenant in a ship of the line, where he could hide and enjoy the joyous spirit of a drunken officers' mess without having his young arse on the line at all hours.

The paper work was, as usual, putting his mind into full yawn, and he wasn't through half of it. Once more he felt as if a terrible mistake had been made by a clumsy or inattentive clerk in the flagship, putting such a pompous little fraud as himself into such responsibility. No matter what Railsford had said, he felt like a total sham only waiting for the awful moment of truth when he would be exposed to the world.

"Supper," the servant called from beyond the door.

He tossed the paper work to the foot of his bunk and shrugged into his coat to join the others. Cony was there helping out in serving, and the two midshipmen had come up from their small dungeon in the after orlop where they usually berthed with the surgeon's mate, master's mate and other junior warrants. Rossyngton looked presentable, but Alan had a chance to get a good look at Mr. Edgar, and he was a perfect example of pimply-faced perplexity, all elbows and huge feet, a uniform that appeared to be wearing him instead of the other way around, and that none too clean.

He was introduced to Biggs, the only senior warrant he had not met on his first rounds of the ship, and saw why the captain considered him a weasel. The purser was a slovenly man of middle height who gave an impression of being much shorter and rounder, due to his furtive posture and constantly shifting eyes and hands.

I wouldn't sport a bottle for any one of these bastards if I saw them parching in Hell, he thought glumly.

"As senior in the mess, may I propose a toast to our new arrival," Caldwell the sailing master intoned somberly.

"Senior, my eyes, damn yer blood," Mister Lewyss snapped.

"Don't let your dog-Latin go to your head, Lewyss," Caldwell cautioned. "I'm not much of a drinkin' man, but 'tis the spirit of the occasion."

"Since I am seated at the head of the table, let's have done with talk of who is senior, Mister Caldwell," Alan quipped. "And I thank you for your sentiments, but I would prefer if you give me first opportunity to propose a toast instead . . . to *Shrike*."

"Aye, to *Shrike*," they mumbled, a little abashed that Alan had too pointedly reminded them of just who *was* senior in the mess, young as he was.

Supper wasn't too bad, really. There was an Island pepperpot soup seasoned with every variety of pepper known to man and flavored with shredded bits of fish; roast kid and fresh bread instead of the usual hard biscuit, along with a wine that could only have been fermented from vinegar, cat droppings and bilge scrapings.

"My word, that's terrible," Alan sputtered after his first sip. "Mister Biggs, do you think this wine failed to travel well, or was it dead before boarding?"

"Nothing' wrong with this wine, young sir," Biggs stated as if he was addressing one of the midshipmen. " 'Tis not claret, but suitable for Navy issue from ashore, same's every other ship in harbor."

"The wine stinks, Mister Biggs," Alan said with as much severity as he could summon. "And you shall address me as 'sir,' without the added modifier of 'young.' It tastes to me as if it had been diluted with water, scrubbing vinegar, and a dollop of poor French brandy to give it a disguising character. Do you concur with that, Mister Lewyss? You're a medical man—see what your nose tells you."

"*Ratafia* for sure, sir," Lewyss said after dipping his long nose into his glass, and pointedly making sure that he addressed the first lieutenant correctly. "As to the water, it is not the usual kegged water from the holds, but it is a *thin* wine, that cannot be disputed, sir."

"How many gallons of this do we have aboard, Mister Biggs?"

"Um, of this particular lot, that is . . . ?" Biggs got shifty.

"Yes, of this particular lot," Alan went on.

"Why, I believe there was thirty ten-gallon barricoes or so," Biggs replied in a much more humble tone of voice, almost wringing his hands, with his eyes shifting from one side of his plate to the other, unable to match glances with the others at the table. "Got a good price on the lot, but not so much as to make me suspicious of the seller's goods, sir."

"Tomorrow morning, following breakfast, you, the master's mate and the bosun shall hoist all of those barricoes out and taste them to determine their suitability. Mister Fukes, may I trust your palate in judging good wine or bad?"

"Oh, ah kin tell good wine, sir." The gorilla beamed, spreading his mouth so wide it looked like a hawse hole.

"Perhaps a *medical* opinion as well, sir," Lewyss volunteered.

"Thank you for your generous offer, Mister Lewyss, yes, you may consider yourself one of the judges. Now if it's all bad, mind, I want it condemned and returned to the seller. I shall inform the captain of unsuitable stores . . . I assume the hands are issued this poor excuse for Black Strap as well, Mister Biggs? Well, that'll never do. Turn it in and you'd best let Mister Lewyss and the bosun taste whatever you find in replacement. I trust this shall not upset your books too much."

It would be a bloody disaster! Biggs probably had not paid three shillings a gallon for the stuff, though the ship's books would show a larger sum, of that Alan was sure after being Mister Cheatham's pupil in *Desperate* long enough to learn how many "fiddles" an unscrupulous "pusser" could work. Biggs would make no money on this exchange.

"Cony, would you be so good as to go into my personal stores?" Alan bade his servant. "I took the precaution of providing myself with a small five-gallon keg of captured Bordeaux, and in place of this lot, I would be happy to offer it to assuage our thirsts, this evening at least. It's not a really fine vintage, but more palatable than this."

Biggs was the only one who did not cheer Alan's munificence, but he did put away a fair share of it when it arrived for decanting. Among eleven of them, it went fast, but there was opportunity to send ashore on the morrow for replacement, so Alan didn't think it a bad trade at all. He had stuck a baulk in Biggs's spokes, put him on guard that he would be closely scrutinized from then on, and in so doing to one of their number most despised (as most pursers were), had won a slight bit of grudging respect from the other members of his mess for such sagacity in one so young.

After supper, though, after he had stifled Lewyss and his infernal harp, and Walsham's bloody flute, there were still ship's books to study. He was the only one to keep a lamp burning after the 8 P.M. lights out, listening to the others fart in their sleep, belch, groan and snore prodigiously, listening to the ship as she creaked now and then, and the sound of the harbor watch on the deck over his head, the chime of the bells as time progressed—and several slanging matches between cats who had decided on animosity during their nocturnal turns of the deck.

There wasn't much in the Punishment Book, the log of defaulters and how many strokes they had received for their sins, at least not in the last few months. Ships' crews usually settled down after a while, even the worst collections of cut-throats, cut-purses and foot-pads, once they got used to a master and his ways. There were no entries for less than two dozen lashes, except in the case of boy-servants and the midshipmen, who got caned bent over a gun with a more gentle rope starter. But there were also several entries for three dozen, four dozen, mostly for fighting or drunkenness or sleeping on watch, and some rare insubordination. A captain could not impose more than two dozen lashes with the cat by Admiralty regulations, but Alan had also learned long before that no one at the Admiralty would even open one eye from a long snooze to hear of a captain assigning more; captains were much like God once at sea on their own, and their judgement was mostly trusted unless they were patently proven to be one of God's own lunaticks.

Likewise the log; it was boring in the extreme, capable of being read by flipping through the pages almost without looking, for the ship had seemed to cruise on her own without seeing a damned thing or taking part in any action since her commissioning. There was a convoy or two, some messages run north to the Bahamas or west to Jamaica, and suspicious sail seen but never followed up aggressively, and once they disappeared below the horizon, lost to mind.

Not a penny of prize-money, Alan sighed, thinking of how much he had made (legally and illegally) in *Desperate* and even in *Parrot*. Lilycrop must be the most contented man with Naval pay in the whole world. How long's he been in the Navy, anyway, fifty years did he say, man and boy? Joined at—eight, say, and probably thirty, thirty-five years a lieutenant? With the war almost lost in the Americas, this is the only command he'll ever hope to have, most like. But then, why not be ambitious and make the most of it? If he stayed in the Navy all those years in hopes of advancement, why not parley this little brig into a twenty-gun sloop of war, commander's rank, even a jump to post-rank? All it takes is one bloody, victorious action, God knows. Look at that idiot Treghues! Is he afraid of getting her rigging cut up and untidy? God help us, would it scare his precious cats? More like it, is he afraid of losing her?

That must be it, he decided, congratulating himself on what a sly-boots he was to figure this out so early. At the end of this commission in two years, or the end of the war, which might come at any time, Lilycrop would go onto the beach with a small pension, carried on Admiralty records still as a half-pay lieutenant unless he *did* something to blot his copy book; a commission was for life unless one resigned it or was caught in some terrible error in judgement. A man close to even so little financial security would not err either in commission or omission; he would not jump either way, and end his days snug as houses.

But if the war ends soon, there's only so much time left for me to do something, Alan fretted to himself. Damme, it's happening, I *am* taking me seriously. But I'm first lieutenant of a brig o'war, and if we come across a foe, I could goad him into action. Now that I am commissioned, why not make the most of it while there's still a war on?

Too weary to read any longer, he blew out his lantern, a new pewter one with muscovy glass panels he had purchased the day before, and stretched out to sleep until Cony came to call him at the end of the middle watch at 4 A.M. so he could supervise the morning cleaning.

It took him a while to drop off, though. William Pitt had run across another ram-cat in his night-time perambulations and they had a protracted melee that went from the taffrail to the fo'c'sle and back, and damned if he didn't think the harborwatch wasn't betting on them and egging them on!

"We shall be gettin' underway tomorrow on the ebbin' tide," the captain had told him, and Alan had sweated blood trying to determine if *Shrike* was in all respects ready for sea. The duties of a first officer were galling in the extreme, taking nothing for granted, forcing the warrants to swear to his face that they had all they needed, and if not, then why didn't they say something earlier? Which had prompted another flurry of activity to complete stores until he could go aft and inform Lilycrop (and Samson and Henrietta and Mopsy and Hodge and the so far un-named kittens *et al*) that yes, *Shrike* was indeed ready to go to sea.

Then there had been another utter frenzy for Lieutenant Lewrie to see to everything that could be seen to. Were the braces, lifts, tops'l halyards, tacks, sheets coiled down and ready for running? Were there enough belays? Were the lower booms swung in and crutched? The log-line, hour-glasses and heaving lines had to be brought up. The yards had to be got up for the t'gallants and royals, and the stun'sl's ready for deployment. Chafing gear had to be renewed on yard slings and quarters, on anything that could rub and chafe aloft. Had old Mister Pebble sounded the pump-wells, checked the scupper flaps, hawse bucklers, fitted the gunports with splash-boards, etc.? Were the boats secured and the yards squared, and all the safety equipment laid out for the hands? Were the guns securely bowsed down, with tompions in? Had the quartermaster put the helm hard-over a couple of times to see if the tiller-rope ran freely? Were the catting and fish-tackles rove, and the main capstan and jeer capstan over-hauled? If one little thing went awry, it was the first lieutenant's fault; if everything went well, then it was the captain's credit. Alan was trembling like an aspen in a high wind by the time he had finished his last-minute checks, and his hands were best off in his pockets where they would not betray his nervousness.

"Ready for sea, Mister Lewrie?" Lilycrop asked lazily as he came on the quarterdeck. He had one of the kittens in his hands.

"Aye aye, sir, ready for sea," Alan stammered, already reduced to a shuddering wreck.

"Shouldn't be too bad at slack water, just afore the ebb," Lieutenant Lilycrop surmised, sniffing the slight breeze. "Very well, then, you may proceed, sir."

"Me!?" Alan gaped, staring at him slack-jawed and trying to think of the proper commands.

"Yes, you, sir."

"Bosun, pipe 'all hands,' stations for getting under way."

God, it was a mad-house on that single deck crowded already with guns and their assorted tackle, with all the running rigging in flaked heaps, the tops'l halyard men already snarling at the fo'c'sle captain and his crew for walking space, the hands around the capstans and the nippermen ready with the messenger.

"Capstan's ready!" some kind soul shouted back, or Alan would have never thought of it.

"B . . . bring to, the messenger!" Three and a half turns of the lighter line were wound about the capstan and the nippermen seized the lighter messenger line to the thicker cable.

Thank bloody Christ somebody knows what they're doing, for it sure ain't me! he thought as he saw men manning the bars, dropping them into the pigeon-holes, securing the drop-pins and breasting to the bars.

"Fleet the messenger!" And two men on each capstan plied their middle-mallets to force the turns of the messenger up the drum of the capstan to make room for the turns to come as they heaved in. Bloody hell, makes me wish I'd paid more attention to these things before! thought Alan.

"Heave around!" he shouted, trying to keep his voice from breaking. The pawls clanked slowly as the men walked about the drums of the capstans, chests pressing against the bars with their hands gripping the wood from below, thumbs turned outward to avoid injury.

"At long stays!" came a wail from the fo'c'sle.

"Heave chearly!" Alan encouraged them as the cable came in at a much steeper angle from the bottom.

"Short stays!"

"I'd not forget the dry nippers for the heavy heave," Lilycrop said at his elbow suddenly as he held up the kitten to observe so much activity. "Ain't it a show, littl'un?"

"Do you wish to set sail at short stays, sir?" Alan asked.

"I leave it to you, Mister Lewrie. Proceed."

God rot and damn the man! Alan thought, ready to weep.

"Dry nippers, ready for the heavy heave! Surge ho!"

"Up an' down, sir!"

"Heave and pawl!"

Suddenly, the men at the capstan bars leaned forward and the pawls began to clank faster and faster. The anchor had broken free of the bottom and was on its way up, and the ship was under way under bare poles in the light wind in English Harbor. And just as suddenly, Alan Lewrie realized that it was an incredibly *crowded* English Harbor. There was an armed transport big as a bloody island astern, not one cable off, toward which they were slowly drifting, an anchored line of seventy-fours to starboard, and a line of warping posts to larboard, upon which some newly repaired 3rd Rate line-of-battle ship was making her way toward the outer roads, and *Shrike* was in the way of her towing boats.

"Hee hee!" Lilycrop laughed softly as he read the angry hoist from the post-captain whose way had been interposed. "He's not happy with us, I can tell you, Mister Lewrie!"

"Anchor's awash!"

"Heave and awash, then."

"Cat's two-blocked, well the cat!"

" 'Vast heaving," Alan ordered. "Bosun, make sail, topmen aloft!"

It was really comfortable being a midshipman, even being a master's mate, Alan thought in despair as that armed transport loomed even larger as they made a slow stern-board down onto her.

"You'll not fuck up my transom paint, will you, Mister Lewrie?" Lilycrop asked as if he were out strolling Piccadilly or St. James's Park.

"I'll try not to, by God, sir. Loose foresails! Head sheets to starboard! Lead out tops'l sheets and halyards! Ready aloft? Lay out and loose!" *Shrike* obstinately refused to turn, still making her slow stern-board, and the loosed fore tops'l went flat aback, giving her even more impetus to ram that damned armed transport.

"Spare hands to starboard," Lilycrop whispered sagely. "Run out number-one gun to starboard."

Having no better idea in mind, Alan repeated the command, and he was amazed that the bows slowly inclined right as men and Marines and an artillery piece canted her deck slightly in the same direction.

"Let fall aloft! Hands to the braces!"

"Don't forget the bloody anchor, mind," Lilycrop whispered once more, allowing the kitten to climb on his shoulder and tenuously balance.

"Man the cat and haul taut!"

"They've *done* that," Lilycrop advised.

"Rig the fish! Quartermaster, how's her helm?"

" 'Ard up ta larboard zurr, no bite. Nah, 'ere she coom, zurr."

"Sheet home and hoist away tops'ls, lay aft to the braces, port head, starboard main, port cro'jack!"

"The anchor?" Lilycrop prompted. "And we don't *have* a cro-'jack."

"Man the fish, haul taut!"

Alan had a chance to glance around and his heart leaped into his mouth and he chilled all over. They had succeeded in getting her stern-board stopped, the bows around, but she was close enough to the transport to make out features of the people on her rails as *Shrike* began to go ahead slowly.

"Walk away with the fish! Brace up the head sheets! Ease the helm, quartermaster. Lay us to windward of those anchored seventy-fours."

"Aye, zurr."

"Well the fish, sir!"

"Belay, ring up the anchor, unrig the fish!"

Thank God, Alan could only gasp, and that to himself as he dug out a handkerchief to mop himself down. The ship was now under way, clear of that transport, away from that frustrated post-captain, well up to windward from the anchored ships of the line. The mess on the deck was being flaked down, the yards were braced up, the head sheets and spanker were trimmed up, and the bower was secured forward. But the ordeal was only beginning, for the exit from English Harbor to the outer roads and the open sea was a tortuous dog-legged channel framed by high hills and that meant capricious winds that could veer from one beam to another at a second's notice.

"I'd not like to get a nasty letter from his excellency Admiral Hood 'cause you forgot passin' honors to the flag, Mister Lewrie," the captain said.

"Oh God," was the last thing Alan remembered he said. The gun and flag salutes to Hood, to Comdr. Sir George Sinclair, the forts by the outer roads, the trip down the roads and out to sea, getting the courses on her, selecting a passage northabout to Antigua's lee for the Bahamas; it all passed in an unreal fog that he could never recall, even in later years, and every time he thought of it, his skin crawled.

He turned the watch over to the sailing master Mister Caldwell and went below to sponge himself down with a bucket of seawater and to don dry clothing, his previous garments wringing wet with perspiration.

"Passin' the word fer the first lieutenant!"

Oh God, here comes the axe, Alan thought with a heavy sigh. He went aft to the captain's cabins. Lieutenant Lilycrop was looking comfortable in old and patched slop trousers rolled up to the knees, a loose shirt without stock, and at the moment, no stockings or shoes, either.

"Sit ye down, Mister Lewrie. Sip o' somethin'? Black Strap? Miss Taylor? Got some right nice cider, all fizzy an' tangy."

"Cider, sir," Alan said, grateful for Lilycrop's obvious show of good cheer. Maybe I won't get a cobbing, he thought hopefully.

"Ah, good. Gooch? Cider for Lieutenant Lewrie, and small-beer for me. That'll be all, Gooch," he added as the drinks were put out on the desk. They waited while Gooch finished his puttering and departed the cabins. Lilycrop picked up his mug of beer and took a sip; Alan tasted his cider. They sat and sipped and looked at each other for what felt like about a full watchglass.

Lilycrop belched loudly to break the silence. "Well now, this mornin', gettin' under way," he said softly. "That was—damme—that was *entertainin'*, sir."

"I'm sorry, sir. I know I must have made a total fool of myself," Alan confessed, burning with sudden shame. " 'Twas a shambles."

"I don't think 'shambles' really does it justice, 'pon my soul, I don't," Lilycrop told him sadly, but with a trace of a wry grin as if he truly did find some cruel amusement in Alan's discomfiture.

"I thought I had the ship ready to weigh, sir, but I never had a thought you'd trust me to take her out the first time and I wasn't ready," Alan tried by way of explanation.

"She was ready to weigh, I'll give you that," Lilycrop agreed. "But your choice of timin', and the way you parroted the commands like you'd read 'em out of a book, 'thout understandin' a word you were sayin' . . ."

"It was the first time I was ever allowed to weigh anchor and take a ship out, sir," Alan said, trying to defend himself.

"God help me, then, what's the Navy thinkin' of, to send me a newly so unprepared," Lilycrop spat, that wry grin now gone. "As for givin' you the deck, how am I to find out what sort of sailor you are if I don't test your abilities? Why the hell are you wearin' the coat of a commission officer if you have to be warned to be ready for any eventuality? You should *know* to be prepared."

"I don't know, sir," Alan said in a hoarse whisper.

"You come from money?"

"No, sir, not really."

"Got relatives to give you interest an' place?"

"No, sir."

"But you made master's mate, an' then lieutenant, in a little over two years," Lilycrop carped on petulantly. "Done some brave things, by your record, been in some fights, brought up like a hot-house rose on blood an' thunder and not proper shiphandlin'. I know there's a war on, but even so, I'd not like to think that a panel of hard-nosed post-captains would pass a total fool an' then shove you into such a responsible position 'thout they saw somethin' in you worth promotion."

"One would hope they knew what they were doing, sir," Alan said, hanging onto that scrap of legitimacy.

"You're not somebody's favorite protégé, are you?"

"Um, I exchange letters with Sir Onsley Matthews, sir, and Lord and Lady Cantner, but no one of note locally."

"So if I tossed you back for the fish to play with, nobody'd have my head for it, would they now?" Lilycrop demanded.

"No, sir," Alan had to admit, his eyes stinging at the thought of being turned out of his first posting as a commission officer within a week as an incompetent. Damme, he thought, I don't love the bloody Navy any more today than I did a month ago, but I'll be damned to hell if I'll suffer that humiliation. At least, God, let me leave this shitten mess with my credit intact, with my pride still attached.

"If it is your intention to ask for a replacement, sir, I shall understand, but damme—" Alan could not go on without breaking down as the sick shame of it overwhelmed him and his stomach fermented.

"Well, I have no intention of doin' so at present," Lilycrop told him. He belched once more, drained his beer and padded in his bare feet to the pantry, where he fetched out a squat, leather-covered bottle of brandy. "You've been prize-master in that frigate your captain took, prize-master in another ship last year, and you managed that well enough, as the records say, 'quite resourcefully.' You've stood in charge of a quarterdeck as master's mate."

"There is that, sir."

Lilycrop sipped from the neck of the brandy bottle as he paced about his day cabin, pausing to pet the odd cat. He peered into Alan's mug of cider and topped off what little was left with a liberal potation of brandy, then sat down behind his desk once more, feet up on the top.

"I come up from powder-monkey," Lilycrop informed him. "Then boy servant, midshipman and master's mate. Spent ten years a passed midshipman an' only made lieutenant after

Pondichéry under Pocock in '61, an' that was more due the death rate in India. Beyond Navy pay, I've not got the means to even burn good candles 'stead of rush dips. I should despise your fortunate young arse, sir."

"Aye, sir," Alan nodded, looking down and sniffing the brandy fumes, unable to face the man.

"But fifty years in the Fleet has taught me one thing, boy. The Navy don't let politics interfere when it comes to promotin' fools or gettin' rid of 'em. The rest of our society is trash, spendin' and gettin', schemin' and back-stabbin' but by *God*, sir, the Navy is one of the few institutions the Anglo-Saxon race ever produced that kept its hawse clear of most of that, 'cause if we go under someday an' put the titled gentlemen back in charge with the *real* sailors on the orlop, then England is gonna end up some Frog king's playground."

"Aye, sir."

"So I'll trust the examinin' board for now an' allow as how they know what they saw in you. You'll stay my first officer until you either improve or you prove that you're a fraud and a sham and I'll have you out of my ship before you can say 'Jack-Ketch.'"

"Thank you, sir," Alan almost gushed in sudden relief.

"Now for starters, you'll not dash about gettin' in what little hair the warrants have left tryin' to tell 'em their jobs. They never'd even have their warrants if they hadn't proved themselves already, and I'd have booted 'em back on the beach if they were frauds, too."

"Aye, sir, I'll not. But—"

"Yes?"

"I mean, as first officer, I have to know if they're ready, or how may I present the ship to you as a going concern? I was taught to check up, sir."

"All you have to do is ask, or order, not go below seein' to every little piddlin' detail like you did yesterday. Hell, boy, there're as many ways to run a ship as there are captains, and most of 'em work. We may look pinch-beck, but we're set up Bristol-fashion and nobody can fault our little ship, nor any man in her. So you do like I say from now on, and trust your warrants and mates. You give 'em trust, they learn to trust you. 'Course, it never hurts, once you got your course steady, to find 'em out in some little somethin', to prove you're on the hop. Stir up one division a week at Divisions or an exercise, an' they'll not let you down when it comes to the major stuff."

"I see, sir."

"And, God help me, I'll trust you, long as you don't go off and do somethin' damn-fool lunatick with my ship. As for this mornin', I'll say no more about it. We're at sea now, and you've already proved you can handle that," Lilycrop relented. "My Order Book tells you when I should be called on deck, an' you'll have noted already that I want to be summoned anytime we have to reef, make sail or alter course, so you aren't totally on your own bottom, not yet anyway."

"Aye, sir."

"Good. Now, I'll be wantin' you to shake this crew of buggers up for me, Lewrie. We've spent three weeks in port, an' had four days outa discipline with the doxies aboard, an' that's bad for 'em. They've gone stale on quim an' drink. What's more, the ship's most likely full of shore bugs, an' I can't abide a lousy ship. Just got rid of most of the fleas, an' I don't want the cats to go through another bout of all that scratchin' an' nibblin'."

"Aye, sir," Alan replied, much more forcefully, now that he knew he had been given a second chance. He even ventured to take a sip of his "cider-and" and savor the bite of the brandy. "Smoke and scour in the day watch today, sir?"

"That's my lad," Lilycrop nodded with a bright smile. "An' in the mornin' watch tomorrow, start bringin' 'em to heel an' brightenin' 'em up. Sail drill. We'll need to go close-hauled to make our eastin' for New Providence, so we can practice tackin' 'til 'clear decks 'n' up spirits.' "

"Gun drill in the afternoon, sir," Alan suggested. "So I may discover how good your gunners are."

"Exactly! You'll find Cox is a capable shit-sack, but inclined to be a little lazy. Live firin', if you've a mind. There's a keg or two of powder from the bottom tier that's suspect I wouldn't mind expendin', though we might find some island on passage to serve for a target an' get more practical use from the firin'. I'll leave the rest up to you as to what drill, an' when. Might throw in a night fire drill after 'lights out'; we haven't done that in a month. Take one thing at a time, mind," Lilycrop warned, wagging a finger at him. "Don't over-finesse an' end up confusin' 'em. Nor confusin' yourself."

"I won't, sir," Alan swore. "I suppose I need the practice as much as the crew does."

"Aye, you do, an' I'm hopeful if you may admit it so chearly," Lilycrop rejoined. "What watches you down for?"

"Middle and the forenoon, sir, alternating the dog-watches," Alan told him. It was an easy schedule, except for having to stay up and awake from midnight to 4 A.M. on the middle watch, for he could nap in the first or second dog-watch, perhaps snooze away a little of the afternoon after drills while supposedly overlooking ship's books, and get about five hours sleep in the evening before having to take over the deck at midnight, a watch in which almost nothing ever happened in fair weather.

"No, you're the first lieutenant. Run the drills in the forenoon an' let Caldwell or Webster the master's mate have that watch," Lilycrop ordained easily, his eyes crinkling in seeming amusement once. "Dinner, then drills again in the day watch. You put yourself down for the evenin' watch an' the mornin'. Those were Tuckwell's. You can sleep midnight to 4 A.M., an' caulk a bit during the dogs, everythin' bein' peaceable."

"Aye, sir," Alan nodded, full of outward agreement but fuming at the loss of sleep he would suffer between watch-standing and running exercises.

"That'll be all for now, young sir," Lilycrop told him, picking up Henrietta the black cat as she meowed at his side for attention. "Let us pray you find your feet in the next few weeks. Then we may look back on your performance this mornin' an' laugh about it together. It did have its mirthsome moments, indeed it did, hee hee!"

Once Lewrie had left his cabins, Lieutenant Lilycrop allowed himself a soft chuckle of congratulations, and lifted the cat up to his face to nuzzle whiskers with her.

"Now, did I put the fear of God into that upstart whelp, or did I not, puss? He ain't worth a tinker's damn right now, I'll tell you truly. Maybe he's got the makin's, maybe not. What do you think? Will he do, sweetlin'? I'll promise you this, by the time I get through with him, he'll be a sight better, or you an' the kitties can feed on his tripes, would you like that?"

Henrietta would, and licked her small chops with a pink tongue.

On the quarterdeck, Alan Lewrie felt as if he had *already* been eviscerated for his tripes. He looked at the dour little sailing master and his minions, who sidled down to the leeward side out of his way and whispered among themselves; most likely it was conventional ship's business they were discussing, but at the moment, he was sure they were re-hashing his shambles in secret glee.

God, how much worse a showing could I have made, or is

such a thing possible? he scoured himself. Well, I didn't sink us, there's a hopeful thought. What *were* they thinking of to put me here? Or is *Shrike* such a collection of no-hopers that they thought I'd fit right in?

Much as he disliked the deprivations of Naval life, cared not a whit for most of the drudgery, the lack of sleep and the excruciatingly demanding level of skill necessary to merely survive in the Fleet, there was in his nature a stubborn streak. The more he replayed the cobbing he had received, the angrier he got; with Lilycrop for being so amused, and then with himself for providing the older man with such a pitiful show of seamanly competence. And the worst thing was that he knew he wasn't all *that* bad. The Navy had beaten competence into him, dragged him kicking and screaming and complaining from former disdain into knowledge of his profession; maybe he was in way over his depth at the moment, but at least he had been given a second chance, if only because there could be no ready replacement available until they got to New Providence, or back to Antigua, and God knew when that would be. If there had been a ready escape, he might gladly have chucked the whole thing right then and there, but since there wasn't, he could try to satisfy the eccentric old man back aft. His pride was on the line, along with all the good credit he had made for his name.

How can I go back to London after the war, a failure even at this? he wondered. Railsford's right; it's a gentlemanly calling for such as me. I've no head for Trade, for Law or Parliament, not enough money to live an idle life, no one to sponsor me if I blow the gaff as a Sea Officer. Right, then, I'll take the proverbial round turn an' two half-hitches, and I'll stop that cat-loving sonofabitch from sneering. I'll go back home a half-pay lieutenant, former first officer, and hold my head up against any of those lazy bucks I knew before, damme if I won't. But laugh about this later? I *sincerely* fucking doubt it!

Chapter 2

Shrike saw nothing of interest for the next two months other than islands, and those only in passing. After a trip to New Providence, they patrolled the extreme edge of the hunting grounds split between the Leeward Islands Squadron and the Bahamas Squadron, north of the Mona Passage, beating to windward far out to sea above the Danish Virgins, snooping north of Puerto Rico. Given the reputed volume of smuggling going on, the number of privateers on the prowl, and the threat of Spanish or French warships, they should have seen something, but the sea remained achingly empty from one distant landfall to the next, and they never went close enough inshore to see anything more, using islands only as convenient proofs of the accuracy of their navigation.

During this time, Alan couldn't have cared less if a Spanish treasure galleon had come right aboard and begged to be looted, and that galleon replete with a traveling Viceroy's brothel. The initial shame and humiliation still gnawed at him, try as he did to put it behind him and concentrate on the job at hand, and the job often threatened to swamp him.

After those two months, he was sure that he was the most despised man aboard the brig of war. He had run his drills and gotten his breath back, and riled the gunner and his mates in the process, even if he knew artillery as well as they. Cox and his minions didn't like being drilled so often, with so many live-firings at floating kegs or empty coops. It fouled the guns, it made work to clean, to sew up new cartridge bags, to shift powder kegs out of the hold. He had forced them to sway out the swivels and drill with them, which created more work. *Shrike* had been loafing along for months with no real effort put to her warlike nature, much like Alan's first ship *Ariadne* had been, and the gunnery department resisted his wishes to spruce up.

Fukes the bosun glared daggers at him, worrying if he was going to order stuns'ls rigged out, top-masts struck, or merely work the ship from one point of sail to the other at a moment's notice.

But, he reassured himself, Lilycrop had told him to smarten the people up, and showed no signs that he disagreed with Alan's timing or choice of drills.

During those two months, they went through several half or full gales, nothing like the terror of autumnal hurricanes, but scary enough to pucker Alan's fundaments as he stood on deck watch after watch with no chance to go below, frightened that each helm command or action on his part would put them under in the twinkling of an eye. *Shrike* did not help, for she truly was a bitch, pitching about like a wood-chip in the heavy seas, rolling on her beam ends since she was so light and had so little below the waterline, unlike his previous ships. And Lilycrop had been accurate in his description of how she would almost run away with them in brisk winds unless they watched her helm, or kept too much sail up too long.

God help him, even the weather seemed to conspire against him. Order masts struck too soon, and the threatening squall lines of early afternoon would blow out and the sky would be painted with lovely and pacific sunsets. Trust that it would do so again the next time the horizon gloomed up and they would be ankle deep in rain and foam breaking over her rails as they fought to reef down until it blew over.

And through it all, there was Lilycrop, damn his blood, eyeing Alan's efforts with that maddening little smile, his eyes atwinkle and another kitten being strolled about the decks; sometimes that tiny "hee hee" could be heard from the skylight or the companionway. Lilycrop didn't spend much time talking to him, and when he did, it was the same sort of needling he had gotten after his disaster in leaving English Harbor. Oh, there was some pithy bits slung in now and again as admonitions to not do something like this or that (depending on which exercise or evolution they had been forced into), but nary a word of praise, even the faintest sort, even when Alan had the time to realize that he had done something close to right, and frankly, he was getting damned tired of Lilycrop's attitude. It got to the point that when the captain was on the deck watching Lewrie perform, Alan tensed up so much he could barely keep his victuals down, and his mind would go blank under that amused stare. To utter the right commands was a daily victory over his unsteady nerves.

They were over halfway through their supplies. Another two weeks of patrol and they would have to go back to Antigua to resupply, and Alan had absolutely no idea if he would be retained, or chucked out for incompetence. Alan was sure Lilycrop would wait until the last moment after they dropped anchor to tell him he was out, and the uncertainty was enough to make him want to scream.

Finally, on a fine day while the hands were enjoying their rum ration, he stirred up his courage and accosted Lilycrop on the quarterdeck, perversely wanting to know his fate, though dreading it.

"Dine with me tonight, then," Lilycrop said, ending his stroll about the deck and going below, still wearing that enigmatic twinkle.

"Aye, sir," Alan replied, trying to sound cheerful for the invitation, the first of its kind since he had come aboard. Probably tell me with the port, so I can weep in private, he quailed sadly.

But he showed up halfway through the second dog-watch, turned out in his best kit, and let the Marine sentry announce him and pass him aft into the great cabin to hear his fate.

"Ah, right on time, I see." Lilycrop beamed at him, waving him to a chair. "Gooch, get the first lieutenant a glass of whatever strikes his fancy." Lilycrop had tricked himself out in his best uniform as well, and the white coat lapels, shirt, waist-coat and breeches gleamed in the candle and lantern light.

Dressed for my execution, Alan cringed to himself.

Alan got a glass of poor Black Strap—Lilycrop's purse did not run to claret or Bordeaux—Lilycrop was already slurping away at a mug of brandy, and from the harsh reek of the fumes that Alan could smell all the way across the cabin, it was no better than captured French *ratafia*, the raw stuff they issued their wretched sailors.

"We're havin' a joint of pork tonight, Mister Lewrie," Lilycrop told him genially. "One of the shoats escaped the manger and took his death dive down the forrud hatchway. Thought pigs'd survive a fall such as that. 'Tis kitties that land on their feet, ain't it, Samson? But I don't tell you nothin' you don't already know, do I, Mister Lewrie?"

"No, sir," Alan agreed, having seen the accident, and having heard the uproarious cheer from the hands when it was known that the pig had succumbed and would be fresh supper for all. There was a rumor on the rounds that the pig had been "pushed," and how he had escaped the foredeck manger was still a mystery. "Perhaps it was Pitt killed him, sir," Lewrie japed, hoping he could cajole Lilycrop into leniency.

"Wouldn't put it past the young bugger, indeed I would not." Lilycrop laughed heartily at Alan's small attempt at humor. "A clever little paw on the latch peg, a scratch on the arse, some judicious herdin' ... he'll get his share, same as the others. I do believe that cats are smarter than most people give 'em credit. Gooch, how long now?"

"Not half a glass, sir," Gooch answered from the pantry by the small dining alcove. The table had already been set with a somewhat clean cloth, wide-bottomed bottles to anchor it down after it had been dampened to cling to the wood, and plates and utensils already laid out. *Shrike* was on an easy point under reduced sail, so they would not have to fight the table for each morsel that reached their mouths; she wasn't heeled over ten degrees from upright and her motion was easy tonight. Cooling sunset breezes blew down the open skylight and through the quarter-gallery windows.

They chatted ship's business for a few minutes, interrupted often by the antics of the various cats or kittens that shared the captain's quarters, until Gooch announced that supper was ready.

There was a soup of indeterminate ancestry, most likely "portable soup" reconstituted from its boiled-dry essence. The biscuits were the usual weevily lumber that took much rapping to startle out the occupants and some soaking in the soup so they could be chewed. But the leg of young pork arrived to save the day, crackling with fat and running with juices their bodies craved after weeks of salt-meat boiled to ruin in the steep-tubs. There was pease pudding, too, and a small loaf of fresh bread they sliced thin as toast so it would last, something the cook had whipped up for the captain alone.

"The sweetlin's gettin' theirs, too, Gooch?" Lilycrop demanded.

"Um, aye, sir," Gooch tried to say through a mouthful of pork from the pantry, taking his pleasure with some slices that had been intended for the platoon of felines, who were crowding around his feet and yowling for their tucker.

"Damn yer blood, Gooch, stop stuffin' yer ugly phyz an' feed those cats their rightful share before I come in there an' hurt you," Lilycrop bellowed, turning to wink at Lewrie as though it was a huge joke. "They'll be cracklin's enough for the likes of you later!"

"Aye, sir," Gooch sighed.

There were still cats enough who jumped up on the table to take what they thought was their "rightful share," who refused to stay shooed. And between gentle remonstrances to their gluttony, and his reminiscing about his career, Lilycrop carried the conversation, while Alan guarded his plate with both elbows and nodded or grunted in agrement all during supper.

Then the dishes were removed, the table cloth snatched away and the cheese and port set out. Lilycrop poured himself a liberal measure and passed the decanter down, then patted his thinning hair and looked at Alan carefully, as he poured his own glass.

"Now, young sir," Lilycrop said after they had both lowered the levels in their glasses.

Here it is, Alan sighed, going stone cold inside.

"Tomorrow, we shall alter course. We've been out over two months, an' need to put into port for fresh supplies," Lilycrop said.

"Aye, sir," Alan nodded, nose deep in his glass again.

"Do it at first light, just after standin' down from dawn Quarters—no sense waitin' for sun sights, we know pretty well where we are, an' no hazards this far offshore."

"Aye, sir, I'll see to it," Alan replied, steeling himself for the blow. "Sir, I suppose . . . well, I *have* been doing a lot better in the last few weeks. Whatever you decide, I am grateful I had the chance to be a first officer, if only for a little while."

"What's this, you resignin'?"

"If you think that best, sir," Alan whispered. God, he thought, Lilycrop don't just want to chuck me, he wants me out of the Navy altogether!

"Don't know why you'd want to do a thing like that," Lilycrop told him, cocking his head to one side. "Thought you wanted to get on in the Navy. Can't do it if you cash in your chips on your first commission. Is it you're unhappy in *Shrike*?"

"I thought you wanted me to, sir," Alan stammered.

"Now why would I want a thing like that?"

"Because I'm bloody awful!"

"You are?" Lilycrop gaped. "Couldn't tell it by me."

"But . . . the way you've treated me the past two months, I never knew how I stood with you, sir, and . . ." Alan fumbled, feeling relief flush him like a quick rain-shower, and the beginnings of an anger that Lilycrop would string him along in this manner. "Damme, sir, you've had a good laugh at my every effort, and I've been on tenter-hooks all this time, waiting to let my guard slip and make some mistake, and . . ."

He could not go on, his tongue dangerously close to letting go something that could be construed as insolence or insubordination, as much as he wanted to rant and slap the old bugger silly.

"Want your mammy's teat to cosset you?" Lilycrop scowled as he topped up his glass again. "Want me to pat you on the back an' tell you how marvelous you are? Damme, you're a commission Sea Officer, there's no room for your bloody feelin's. There's the ship, her people, an' the Navy that comes first before makin' you feel good."

"I . . ." Alan started to say before clamping his mutinous trap shut once more.

"You started on the wrong foot, but that didn't last a day," Lilycrop continued. "I told you I'd say no more about it, and I haven't. 'Sides, 'tisn't my nature to go around praisin' somebody to the skies. You do your duty an' that's all I expect of any man. If you do your duty proper, you know it, an' you can pat yourself on the back if you've a mind. 'Sides, you learned, didn't you?"

"I . . . I think so, sir," Alan said realizing it was true.

"Found your feet, got a firm grip on the hands, found out how to run *Shrike* to my satisfaction, what more would you be wantin'?" Lilycrop shrugged. "More port?"

"Aye, sir. But how can you—most people respond to some sign of encouragement, sir. They have to hear that they did something right now and then, just as they need to be told they did something the wrong way if they make a muck of things." Alan floundered.

"Life's an unfair portion, ain't it, Mister Lewrie?" Lilycrop chuckled, slicing himself a morsel of cheese, which he plumped down on a thin slice of the remaining bread in lieu of extra-fine biscuit. "I told you once I don't splice the main-brace without I see the angel Gabriel close abeam. Now what would you a'done if I'd said 'you're doin' splendid, laddie' when you weren't? Gone all smug an' satisfied before you had it down pat. I gave you instruction, let you find your own way, an' you've come around to be a man I'd trust with this ship. Mind you, I had my doubts when you first came aboard. Um, good cheese."

"So you'll not ask for a replacement, sir?"

"Oh, Hell no. You'll do." Lilycrop grinned through a mouthful of cheese and bread.

"Well I'm damned!" Alan exhaled heavily, leaning back in his chair.

"No, you've turned more competent, an' you've gotten the ship smartened up right clever. I'm satisfied," Lilycrop sniffed.

"Even if every hand hates my guts, sir," Alan said, smiling, feeling he was ready to burst into hysterical laughter at his redemption.

"Oh, give 'em no mind, they always hate the first officer, an' don't you go tryin' to be their bosom friend, either," Lilycrop told him, wagging a finger down the length of the table at him. "They despise you, they tolerate me, and beside you an' your fault-findin' an' carpin' I'm a fuckin' saint in comparison. You didn't come aboard to be popular. You came aboard to be efficient in runnin' my ship for me. You're not a heavy flogger, nor are you a hand-wringin' hedge-priest. Firm but fair, you said your motto was, remember, young sir?"

"Aye, sir, I do."

"You're not half-seas-over are you, Mister Lewrie?"

"No, sir," Alan assured him of his relative sobriety.

"Then wipe that lunatick smile off your face and tip up your glass. Gooch, trot out another bottle of this poor excuse for port!"

I'm safe! Alan rejoiced inside as the servant puttered about and drew the cork from a fresh bottle. I'm safe in my place. He'll not chuck me. I'll do, he says! That must mean I'm not at all bad, even if he did half-kill me. Now, can I keep this pace up? Don't I ever get a chance to relax?

Ruefully, he decided that he probably would not. That was Lilycrop's sort of Navy, where one labored long and hard with not one whit of praise or encouragement, ready at all times to care for the ship first, last and always, with little chance for letting one's guard down.

"Now, sir," Lilycrop sighed after he had sampled the new bottle and sent Gooch off for his own supper. "I get the feelin' you may disagree with me 'bout how to train men. Maybe were we talkin' of raw landsmen, I might soften my methods, but 'tis the way I was brought up, you see. When you've a ship of your own to run, you may employ your own methods, and I give you joy of 'em. But I've never seen a sailor yet who was worth a cold-mutton fart for bein' cossetted like he was still in leadin' strings. You just have to make 'em get on with the work, trust your mates and warrants to pound 'em into line, and see they don't get brutalized, nor pushed too fast. Nor do you want 'em dandled on daddy's knee and told what good lads they are when they ain't."

"It varies with the man, some say, sir. What's sauce for the goose isn't sauce for gander all the time, sir," Alan replied, laid back at complete ease for the first time in two months, his breeches tight about his middle after a splendid repast, and his head light with wine fumes.

"But you never have time to train 'em, one man at a time. Some never'll do, no matter what you do with 'em." Lilycrop frowned. Samson leaped up on the table and arched his hind-quarters into the air as Lilycrop stroked his back. "I've seen boys come aboard so starry-eyed for bein' at sea you'd have thought they'd seen Jesus in the riggin'. Some made it, some didn't. Raw landsmen, midshipmen, pressed men, we make sailors of 'em all if we can, or kill some of 'em in the process. When the shot starts to fly, you don't have time to make allowances for a weaklin', you got to have men you can count on. Take yourself."

"Me, sir?" Alan asked, back on his guard again.

"You have *brains*, Mister Lewrie. You can learn, even if you have to get hurt in the process. Now young Mister Edgar, he's been in the Fleet four years, and God help the poor young ass, he'll never make a Sea Officer 'thout somebody on high parts the waters to let him cross over. I had to depend on you right from the start. No way you can have a first officer you have to spoon-feed. So you got your feelin's hurt, an' had yourself a weep now an' again. Well, this is a hard Service, an' I'm damned if I'll go to my grave seein' the ones that come after me have it easy an' soft, a mewlin' pack of children too weak an' whiny to serve our Navy, when it needs tarry-handed *men!*"

"This has been the absolute worst two months I have ever spent in the Navy, sir," Alan confessed as the wine crept up on him.

"And twenty years from now, you'll know you learned somethin'." Lilycrop nodded in agreement, all good humor gone from his face as he spoke with absolute conviction. "By God, sir, you'll be grateful someday you had it this hard, 'cause the worst times later'll feel like a stroll in Vauxhall Gardens. Not that I'm through with you, sir."

"Oh?"

"I said you'll do, but you've still a way to go. Everybody

does. Don't go smug and satisfied on me. Well, you've the evenin' watch?" Lilycrop snorted, busying himself with Samson up on his chest.

"I exchanged with Webster, sir, so I'll have the morning."

"Heel-taps, then, and I'll let you go to your rest," Lilycrop said, lifting his glass and draining it.

"Goodnight, sir. Thank you for supper. And for . . . everything."

"Goodnight to you as well, Mister Lewrie."

Alan left the cabin and went out on the quarterdeck, where the night winds soughed and sang in the rigging, bringing a touch of cool dampness to what had been a warm day. *Shrike* loafed along, speared by the trough of a waxing moon, and the tropic skies were a blue as deep as his officer's coat, littered with stars that burned clear and cold.

He stopped at the wheel long enough to check the binnacle for a peek at the course and the dead reckoning of the day's run on the traverse board, scanned aloft at the set of the sails to see if they needed adjusting, and exchanged a few words with the watch. Then he took himself forward along the larboard gangway, until he was up on the fo'c'sle, where the spray sluiced and showered now and again as the ship's bow rose and fell so gently.

I'll do! he thought, smiling in the darkness. By God, that old bastard! All the worry and fear I've suffered, all the humiliation, and all he says is, you'll do! Well, maybe I shall, at that!

The Leeward Islands Fleet was in when *Shrike* sailed into English Harbor, and so *Shrike* had to take a mooring in the outer roads, for the inner harbor was full, for which Alan sincerely thanked God. He got the ship up into the wind and anchored without having to short-tack up that narrow channel through a city of warships. There were a few ships he had not seen before, including a huge three-decked 1st Rate, and he was so intent on them that he realized he had gotten *Shrike* safely in without his usual qualms. After that supper with Lilycrop, and his grudging acceptance, Lewrie was amazed at how much easier things had gone for him, how much more assured of his abilities he felt.

"A three-decker, sir," Alan said. "Do you think Admiral Rodney has come back? Maybe they're ready to try another pass with this de Grasse."

"Look more closely," Lilycrop suggested, passing him the telescope and uttering one of his semi-stifled titters of amusement.

"My God!" Alan exclaimed as the name on the stern placque leapt into focus. *"Ville de Paris!"*

"Think they have met," Lilycrop barked, rubbing his round nose in delight. "Now, would you be so good as to have my boat brought round to the entry port so I may go aboard the flag and report?"

"Aye, sir, immediately. Fukes?"

They had met indeed, on April 12, and the French fleet had been scattered to the four winds, some running back to Martinique, some for Cape Francois or Havana. Five line-of-battle ships had been taken at the Battle of The Saintes, including *Ville de Paris*, and de Grasse was now a British prisoner. Admiral Rodney had returned shortly after *Shrike* had left on her patrol, had taken Hood and his ships down to St. Lucia, and had dogged the French bases until they sailed. Much like Mr. Clerk's tactics treatise had suggested, Rodney had broken the order of the French line when a God-sent shift of wind had taken the French aback and forced them to luff up helpless while the British squadron still had wind to spare.

From de Grasse and his captured officers, it was learned that the French and Spanish from Havana were to have linked up and invaded the island of Jamaica in a joint expedition. Now that was foiled, for all the siege artillery had been taken at The Saintes in the ships now lying in English Harbor as prizes. Never before had a 1st Rate ship of the line of any nation been taken in battle; never had an admiral other than Rodney taken a French, a Dutch and a Spanish admiral prisoner in his last three actions. There was some carping that breaking the French line was an accident, not planned. There were rumblings that Rodney could have taken a dozen, two dozen prizes if he had released his line in General Chase. Still, it was a magnificent victory, strengthening England's hand after such a long drought.

And for Lewrie, the parties ashore were heaven. Dolly Fenton was still there in his lodgings, having sold her late husband's commission to another officer for twelve hundred pounds, and she had waited for him instead of going home. She did live frugally, as his shore agent could attest, and she was so full of love and passion for him it was all he could do to crawl to the boat landing each morning when Lilycrop allowed him to sleep out of the ship.

And damned if she didn't make a snug and pleasant little home for him, such a nice little abode that he invited Lieutenant Lilycrop to dine with them one night, and Dolly captivated the man from the first sight of her. They dined her aboard *Shrike* in the captain's quarters, asking the senior people from the ward-room in as guests, and she felt so honored she almost wept in the boat back to shore.

The best night was Sir Admiral Hood's levee for Vice Admiral Paul-Joseph, Comte de Grasse, and Alan squired her to that in a new gown and his gift of a gold necklace and earrings he had made her that day. She floated on air, she laughed shyly, and she trembled with joy to be on his arm, and to be ogled by all the other officers and their wives at the levee. She even capti-vated Admiral de Grasse in the receiving line.

It was a fairly quick trot down the receiving line among offi-cers more senior to him, but it was worth it. The Frog was huge, well over six feet tall (it was reputed he had lifted the tall Rebel General Washington off his feet and hugged him, calling him "mon petit general") round as a beef cask, and weighed over twenty stone, with a round chubby face and tiny, pursed, almost porcine lips.

"Lieutenant Alan Lewrie, of the *Shrike* brig. And Miss Dolly Fenton," the officer to his side said as he passed them on. "Lewrie was at Yorktown, and the Battle of The Chesapeake. He escaped after the surrender."

"Milord," Alan said. "Nice to meet you at long last."

"Dolly, vot a pretty name, ma cher!" de Grasse said, kissing Dolly's hand and showing no signs of letting go. "Vee dance later, hein? Vee sing songs of eternal joy! Most beautiful of En-glish beauties!"

"Lewrie, of the . . . oh, the hell with it," Alan sighed.

"Might as well bugger off, Lewrie," the officer who had intro-duced them said. "Be sure to get her hand back when you leave."

And Dolly was so entranced by meeting such a celebrity, by the music and wine and dancing, and the interest shown in her, that by the time they got back to his lodgings, it was all Alan could do to keep a shirt on before they got out of the hired coach.

Damme for a fool, he thought, late that night as she lay by his side, exhausted at last by their frenzied lovemaking, if I ain't coming to enjoy this maybe a bit too much. Damme if I'd ever marry her, not with Lucy Beauman out there, but this could be pleasant enough for the meantime. Only problem is, Dolly needs a man to cling to, and the way she wants to cling is the perma-

nent anchorage. I'm way too young for that. Ain't I? Yes, yes,
I am, I'm sure of it.

And not a week later, they were sent orders to prepare for sea
once more. Lieutenant Lilycrop came back aboard from *Barfleur*
with a thick packet of orders under his arm, canvas-wrapped and
bound up with official ribbons and sealed, and from the way he
carried them, they had been weighted with grape shot to speed
their descent into the nether-depths if *Shrike* were accosted by a
foe.

"Despatches for Kingston," Lilycrop told Lewrie after he had
stowed them away in a locker in his transom settee. "Hood and
Rodney'll be on their way west after us, just in case the Dons
and what Frogs escaped still have plans for Jamaica. We'll crack
on all the sail she can fly, and I'll be wantin' to warn you again
'bout how *Shrike* can get away from you in a stiff blow to
loo'rd."

"Aye, sir," Alan replied. "Sail on the next tide?"

"Yes. Are we ready to put to sea?"

"Aye, sir," Alan said, proud that he had the ship ready in all
respects, in between the riotous celebrations ashore.

"By the way, the flag-captain informs me a terrible mistake
was made two month ago, Mister Lewrie," Lilycrop went on,
tossing off his heavy coat, kicking off his tight shoes, and picking up a cat to stroke. "Seems a midshipman assistin' a flag-
lieutenant—which is like a blind man helpin' a cripple cross a
busy road—sent a Lieutenant Lyles, a man of no little experience, into the *Amphion* frigate, and sent you here as my first.
Upset their little wardroom order with no end of shit."

"I see, sir. So I am to exchange with this Lieutenant Lyles?"

"Not a bit of it. Told 'em I preferred you, now we were used
to each other's ways," Lilycrop growled, busying himself with a
bottle of wine. "If they got their books wrong, it's no fault of
mine, I told 'em. If Lyles got the wet end of the stick, it's their
problem."

"Thank you, sir." Alan beamed, puffing up at the compliment.

"Didn't think an ambitious young fella like yourself would
care to be third officer in a thirty-six, when you could be first,
even in a little brig like *Shrike*."

"I do prefer it, sir," Alan replied, realizing it was true, even
if being third officer in a 5th Rate would be easier on his constitution.

"Thought you'd say that." Lilycrop smiled, his eyes gleaming.

"Gooch, come open this damned bottle! I'm dry as dust! That's why I said you wished to stay in *Shrike*. I don't misrepresent you, do I, sir?"

"No, sir." Alan grinned back.

"Good. Now go stir up the warrants an' tell 'em we're gettin' underway at slack water tonight. And Mister Lewrie, do try an' not be as amusin' when we sail this time, eh?"

"Aye, sir."

"Oh, got the extra barrel o' sand for the kitties?"

"Clean sand from low tide, sir, nothing from further up the beach."

"Good, no reason to bring sand-fleas aboard. That's all, you can go. Think I'll sport a nip for you? Drink your own damned claret."

"Aye, sir," Alan replied, then broke off his exit. "Um, excuse me, sir, but did the flag say how long we would be at Jamaica?"

"Got calls to make there, Mister Lewrie?"

"A few, sir." Alan grinned.

"Well, you keep it to yourself, but we're bein' transferred to the Jamaica Squadron." Lilycrop sighed, as Gooch got the offending bottle open and poured him a liberal measure. "And no tales out of school for you, either, Gooch, damn yer eyes."

"Aye, sir," Gooch replied a bit insulted, as Lilycrop treated the whole affair as a joke. Most cabin servants from the wardroom or captain's quarters could trade information on the sly for favor with their shipmates; no matter how secret a matter was, it was uncanny how quickly everyone on the mess decks could hear all about it within seconds of the officers.

"Pity about Mistress Fenton," Lilycrop said. "Well, off with you, Mister Lewrie. I'm sure you have duties? And go ashore if you think it best."

Alan took himself out on deck, exulting in this stroke of good luck. He would be allowed a shore visit at Kingston, surely, to see Lucy Beauman, the perfectly lovely, and perfectly rich Lucy Beauman. Finally, he could pay court to her whenever the ship put back into Kingston, every eight weeks or so if their last cruise was anything to go by. It was all very well to have made lieutenant, have a decent rate of pay, and the annuity from his grandmother, but Alan knew his tastes and how expensive they could be; a gentleman with any pretensions to the good life back home needed three hundred pounds a year or he couldn't begin to exist. Lucy's parents were rich as Croesus, and were not adverse to a match, now that he'd made something of himself;

they could not deny their beautiful little girl anything she wanted, and from the tone of her last letters, Lucy Beauman most especially desired one Lt. Alan Lewrie. She would bring a settlement, back home in England most likely, of enough land to set themselves up as property owners, ones who rented land to others, instead of the other way around. There would be a house in London, too, fashionably close to St. James's, White-hall or the Strand, and in between smashing bed furniture in ex-uberant lovemaking, they could attend drums, routs, levees, and suppers, go to the theaters and the amusements of the world's greatest city, with the money to live the heady life among the titled and the elite.

"By God, but don't life just surprise the hell out of me some-times," Alan breathed in anticipation. "Four parts of it beshit, and then Fortune drops a whole slew of guineas in your lap! Oh, shit!"

There was Dolly. Trusting, adoring Dolly. God, how could he bear to part from her! Yet it had to be. He wouldn't be coming back to Antigua anytime in the near future, and, wonderful as she was, she was (he had discovered) twenty-seven, older than he was. That was fine for the ego, fine for the libido, but not for a long-term relationship. Lucy was only eighteen. While Lucy would not even hit her full beauty for several years, Dolly could look forward to only a few more years of superb loveliness be-fore she began to fade and lose her freshest bloom. And, unfor-tunately, she wasn't all that wealthy.

"But she's the sort that stays lovely for years and years," he argued. "We could . . . no, best we break it off now, damnit all. Best for her, really. Best she goes back to England and finds a man closer to her own age, someone who'll want to marry and make her happy, a man of substance to add to her husband's commission money."

Shit, he thought. Listen to me worrying about what a woman feels. Who'd o' thought a rogue like me'd ever worry about that? Oh, this is going to be devilish hard. I really am fond of the silly little mort. Yes, I really am. Fuck it, let's get it over with quick.

"Bosun, bring a boat round for me!" he shouted.

Chapter 3

Shrike thumped away bravely as she fired her salute to Adml. Sir Joshua Rowley's flag, ran down her Red Ensign, and trotted out the White, rounded up under tops'ls and spanker, and let the anchor go in as polished a performance as any ship of the line three years in active commission, which brought a grunt of satisfaction from Lieutenant Lilycrop and a large whoosh of relief from Lt. Alan Lewrie. Almost before the hook was on the bottom inside the Palisades of Kingston Harbor, the gig was alongside the entry port, the coxswain and his oarsmen turned out in the best uniforms they possessed (or could borrow from the purser's stores), and Lilycrop was safely into his boat and on his way to the flagship.

"Harbor gaskets on the yards, Mister Fukes," Alan ordered.

"Aye, sir," Fukes rumbled. " 'N, could I be a' borryin' a boat ta row about n'see to squarin' away the yards, sir, while we set kedges?"

"My pleasure, Mister Fukes."

It would be a long row to get ashore, Alan noted, but Lilycrop had insisted that they anchor far out from the main anchorage, far off shore so the night miasmas that brought fever could not reach them, so they could still have a sea-breeze at night to keep the number of insects down. It would also reduce the thoughts of desertion among the hands, none of whom were strong enough swimmers to reach that tantalizing shore.

"Rig the awnings now," Alan said. "It'll get a lot hotter this afternoon."

There was still work to do, rowing out kedge anchors to hold the ship without swinging all about the compass on her bower rode and fouling another ship, tidying up aloft, coiling the miles of sheets and halyards, clews and buntlines down into

141

neatly flaked piles or hung on the bitts and pin-rails. Then boats would have to go ashore for fresh water and firewood, and every department had needs which the purser would have to refer to the captain, hoping to keep the expense down in some cases, and seeking a way to make extra money in others. Biggs was already rubbing his dry hands together, expense ledgers under his arms, and eyeing the shore with an expression that could only be described as avidly expectant.

But for now, Alan could relax. The ship was at anchor, and nothing short of fire or hurricane could disturb her, which meant he could lower his guard from active trepidation to wary ease. The life of a first officer was onerous when one considered all the things that could go wrong, but, tentatively, he was beginning to admit to himself that he could cope, most of the time, at least. Tedious, some matters were, but no longer a reason for a dry mouth. Exacting, some chores might be, but no longer a cause for shaky limbs. When Alan had time to think of this change (and those times were damned rare) he supposed it had come about after the supper with Lieutenant Lilycrop. Being told that he was passably acceptable had removed the greatest part of the fears he had suffered, allowing him enough personal breathing room to grow into the job instead of staggering from one possible disaster to the next with the feeling that he was about five steps behind the acceptable pace. Witness their last passage from Antigua to Kingston, which had gone past in six days of (mostly) tranquility, giving Alan time to savor sunrises and sunsets, the joy of sailing over an inspiritingly benign ocean with winds enough for a glutton under a sky of Wedgewood blue. He had even begun to enjoy the banter in the wardroom, though he could not join in as joyously as was his usual wont when japes, liquor and high spirits were aflying.

Lilycrop was not fussy about uniform dress when *Shrike* was out of sight of the fleet, so Alan had served his watches and supervised the unending drills in old breeches and a shirt loose to the waist, minus stock, coat or stockings, and a woven sennet hat to ward off the sun. Lilycrop believed a large towel was clothing enough on some days for his own august personage, wrapped about his rotund body like some Roman senator's toga, and a pair of native sandals. The crew had gone about in rolled up slop trousers, belt and head-scarves like so many bloody buccaneers, except for Divisions and the rare turn-to to witness punishment in the forenoons. Now they were all chafing in full clothing, and the flesh that had been exposed to the sun was itching under the requisite layers of uniform, no matter how Red Indian–copper they had become with long service in tropic waters.

"Bum-boats comin' alongside, sir."

"Tell 'em to sheer off until the captain returns," Alan snarled. "And tell . . . no, the master-at-arms knows to keep drink from being passed inboard," Alan said, grinning at himself, "At least he'd better."

William Pitt came sauntering aft along the larboard bulwarks to take a perch by the main chains and sharpen his claws on a shroud dead-eye. The cat ignored Alan until he strolled to the railing to peer down into the bum-boats which were offering their usual gew-gaws; small bottles of rum, flowers, cheap shirts, parrots and caged birds, pocket watches and shoe buckles (most likely stolen) and the women who helped scull the boats. When Alan got close enough, William Pitt had no more patience. He bottled up once more, spat and hissed, then took off forward in a ginger streak, uttering a low trilling growl.

"I hate that damned cat," Alan growled.

"Ah, he hates you, too, sir," Caldwell, the sailing master, told him with a wry grin, polishing his square little spectacles. "But then, there's not a soul aboard I've ever seen him warm up to, not even the captain. If he weren't such a deuced clever mouser, he'd have been over the side a year ago, and good riddance to bad rubbish."

"Not a half-bad idea, to trade the little bastard for a bird or something." Alan laughed.

Their captain returned about an hour later, and by the expression on Lilycrop's face as he heaved his bulk through the entry port, and the way he took his salute so testily, he obviously had not had a good time aboard the flagship.

"Mister Lewrie, attend me, sir!" Lilycrop snarled.

"Aye aye, sir," Alan replied, wondering what he had done to earn this new enmity. Had the more dubious parts of his repute made their way as far west as Jamaica? Once aft, though, he was pleased to discover he was not the reason (this time, at least) for Lilycrop's ill humor.

"Poxy, woman-handed little bastard!" Lilycrop barked, slinging his hat toward the hanging bed-box. Cats scattered to the four winds. "Insufferable arse-licker!" The shoes followed, caroming off bulkheads and decorating the sickly paint with streaks of blacking. The shirt stock nearly made it out the transom sash-windows. "Gooch!"

"Sir?" Alan asked, standing well back from this barrage of attire.

"Not a morsel of welcome, sir, not a morsel," Lilycrop gloomed. "Oh, aye, I've grown accustomed to small portions of hospitality in my years, but . . . Gooch, come open this damned bottle before I crack it over your empty head!"

"Aye, sir!" the servant bobbled.

"I'd not expect to be dined in, sir," Lilycrop went on, almost tearing the buttons from his waist-coat as he removed it and slung it in the general direction of the pegs. "That's for post-captains an' the titled fools, but nary a drop of comfort was I offered, sir, not one drop for a newly arrived master an' commander."

"Most inhospitable, sir," Alan commented as Gooch got the hock open and deftly stripped Lilycrop of his heavy old sword as he raved about the cabins, drinking from the neck.

"D'ye know, Mister Lewrie, we're the first vessel in with word of The Saintes, and their salvation from the Frogs and the Dons," Lilycrop raved on. "While they couldn't stir their arses up an' put half a dozen sail o' the line to sea to save their souls. A battle ye say? Truly, sir? Defeated de Grasse, did they? Capital doin's, but more important, who d'ye like in the Governor's Cup Races? Pahh!"

"Perhaps the flag-captain was drunk, sir."

"An' maybe he's an addle-pated, light-footed, silk-kerchiefed sodomite fool!" Lilycrop roared. He flung himself down on the transom settee, but calmed enough to accept a mug from Gooch, who had been weaving a circumspect course to avoid his captain's wrath. "Then this dandy-prat had the gall to look down his nose an' wonder what Rodney was thinkin' of to transfer little *Shrike* to Sir Joshua Bloody Rowley an' Billy Graves' fuckin' damn flag! 'My dear sir,' he says to me, 'I know not to what avail a brig o' so little worth shall answer, but given enough time, we shall discover her uses, perhaps in the guarding of the harbor entrance, or the coast an' revenues'! Goddamn them!"

"Graves, sir?" Alan started. "From The Chesapeake?"

"The same. A vice-admiral servin' under Rowley, if you can imagine what a come-down that is for him." Lilycrop wheezed humor.

Alan shrugged philosophically, approaching to within throwing distance as Lilycrop poured half the bottle of hock into his mug and began to sip. "Perhaps they still perceive a danger, and thought themselves more in need of ships of the line, or a brace of larger frigates to add to their strength."

"What bloody danger? Rodney'n Hood put paid to those Frogs off The Saintes. Scattered their fleet Hell to Huttersfield, took the ships loaded with the siege artillery. Jamaica's safe as houses now."

"Yes, sir, but where did those other ships escape to, the ones we didn't take?" Alan pondered. "Up to Cape Francois, or Havana? There are still ten Spanish sail of the line in the Indies. And the Dagoes were to provide troops for the expedition. Who's to say they might try yet, sir, strictly a Spanish adventure, with help from one of de Grasse's junior admirals and what ships he's collected after The Saintes? When you consider that, they might look upon Rodney offering them one small brig of war as an affront. Perhaps there's bad blood between Sir Joshua and Sir George, and you the intermediary between their animosity."

"Goddamme, but you're a *political* animal, Lewrie," Lilycrop spat.

"Aye, sir, but it's a learned habit. Society runs on rumors and grudges." Alan grinned, now on solid ground. For all his seafaring skill and his tarry-handed knowledge, Lilycrop was a child when it came to the ways of English "Society"; childishly proud of his lack of familiarity with the back-alley routes to success, money and "place." In contrast, Alan had cut his milk-teeth on the practice, raised as he was in the shadow of the mighty, the titled and the wealthy. Lilycrop wanted his Navy to be immune to what he thought was unfair and scheming, but the Navy was a microcosm of the society which it protected, and its officers came from families who had to play "The Game" to get ahead. Until the society changed, the Navy would reward those who knew how to grease the wheels with unctuous words. In a sudden flash of insight, Alan saw the reason why Lilycrop had named the ginger cat William Pitt. He had been a champion from the commoners, but on retirement he had accepted the King's gift of title as Lord Chatham, and all the perquisites of the wealthy Tories against whom Pitt had dueled, betraying Lilycrop's simple faith in ordinary men rising by their own abilities. No bloody wonder he was a lieutenant all this time, Alan thought a bit sadly. The wheel that squeals the loudest never gets the grease. He rubs everyone the wrong way—God help him, he's even proud of it.

"Damn Society," Lilycrop groaned, lifting his beak from the

mug, but he had calmed himself. "Think you, though ... we were too small an offerin'?"

"I'm sure of it, sir. Perhaps Admiral Rodney offered larger ships, or Drake's small division of line-of-battle ships for later in the despatches we carried, but we don't know that."

"Nor should we have," Lilycrop nodded firmly. "So I was the bearer of bad tidin's, the one the Roman emperors used to kill. Uriah smugly bearin' his death warrant from David to place him in the thickest fightin' so Uriah's wife would be a widow for David's pleasure."

"Um ... something like that, sir," he shrugged, at a loss.

"Nothin' more'n I'd expect after fifty years in the Navy, man and boy, watchin' ..." Lilycrop squirmed as he realized he could not expose himself or his life-long grudges to anyone, much less to an officer from that very background that seemed to spawn the successful, while he soldiered on without seeming rewards. "Stores complete, sir?"

"Ah, aye, sir," Alan replied, caught off guard by the sudden shift of topic. "Or, that is, they soon shall be, sir. The purser is ashore, and should be returning soon."

"Once we're replenished, be so good as to hoist 'Easy Discipline' so the doxies can come aboard, then," Lilycrop directed wearily. "The hands've shaped up main-well, the last two months. They've earned a few rewards. Mister Lewyss to check for pox'n fleas, mind."

"Aye, sir."

"Far's I know, we could tup'n sup out here 'til we sink at our moorin's, for all this admiral cares. Shore leave tickets for the senior warrants first, junior warrants second. Leave tickets for those hands deservin' afterward."

"Aye, sir. Um ..."

"Aye, I mind you've calls to make," Lilycrop said, frowning. "I'll take a turn ashore myself, but my needs're simple. You've earned your chance for a wench and a bottle as well, young sir."

"Thank you, sir, but ..."

"Then you don't wish shore leave?" Lilycrop teased.

"Not at all, sir! Of course, I want shore leave! It's another matter, sir. About *Shrike*. About the admiral, sir."

"Spout away. Sit you down an' have some hock, then."

The cabin cats had sensed that the rant was over, and emerged from their hiding places, tails flicking for attention. Samson and Henrietta and Mopsy and Hodge and the kittens made for

Lilycrop, and this show of affection mollified him most wondrously.

"Who says we're useless, sir?" Alan began.

"Every poxed mother-son of a gun in the flag, damn their eyes."

"You once said *Shrike* could go inshore, where a frigate or sloop of war would fear to go, sir," Alan schemed on. "Now, I see no ships in harbor capable of that."

"Small ships . . . ketches'n cutters'n such . . . they're possibly out on patrol," Lilycrop waved off as Gooch brought another mug to the desk and poured Lewrie some of the wine.

"Could the Spanish have some siege artillery of their own, sir?"

"Oh, aye," Lilycrop agreed. "Every fuckin' fort on Cuba'r Hispaniola's full of heavy guns. Poor local-milled powder, maybe old stone shot, though. Be a bitch to dismount and build field carriages."

"But they could improvise a siege-train from them, if they were of a mind, sir. And the easiest way to transport them would be by sea, along the coasts, would it not?"

"Aye, they'd kill a thousand bullocks haulin' 'em on what pass for roads in the islands." Lilycrop perked up.

"Exactly, sir," Alan pressed. "But what sort of ships would be available to carry siege guns to Cape Francois or Havana? How many ships of worth do they have in the Indies they'd risk in coastal waters?"

"Not that many, I grant."

"Too strong to be taken by a small ketch or cutter, sir, but just the presence of a well set up brig of war could run them back into harbor. They'd think themselves safe from a frigate close inshore, but we are pretty fast, sir, and we can go into less than three fathoms to chase them down."

"Damme, but you're a nacky little'n, Mister Lewrie," Lilycrop marveled. "I misjudged your wit, an' for that I apologize. Aye, *Shrike* could stir 'em up like the Wrath of God. If," he cautioned, "if we were allowed. I'm sure this Admiral Rowley has his own favorite corsairs; bought in some shallow-draught vessels as tenders to the flagship to line his pockets with prize-money already. We'll swing at our anchors 'til next Epiphany waitin' for the call to glory."

"A respectful letter to the flag, suggesting suitable employment for us could take the trick, sir." Alan smiled. "Prize-money for us and the admiral, a reduction in the bottoms available to the Dagoes, some repute for us, and . . . if there is some grudge between Parker and Rodney, we could mollify it. Rowley needs to be seen doing something to save Jamaica, doesn't he? Rodney'll have all the glory at the victory celebrations, and . . ."

"Now you're off in fictional speculatin'," Lilycrop scoffed. "We know no such thing. Still . . ."

"Beats waiting for employment at the admiral's pleasure, sir."

"Hmm." Lilycrop stroked his chin, now shaved of the usual crop of bristly white for his appearance aboard the flagship—usually he only laid steel to whiskers once a week for Sunday Divisions.

Alan took a sip of wine while Lilycrop pondered the matter. He could see the battle going on between the need for recognition and some small bit of fame before the war ended (and his hopes of future service in the Navy with it) and the desire to safeguard what little he had. The want of prize-money for retirement, and the risk to his ship and the loss of what grudging respect he had won if he failed.

"Too deep for me, Lewrie," Lilycrop scowled finally. "It smacks too much o' schemin' for 'place,' to suit me. An' what sort of fool may I look to go clamorin' for action when there's others more senior or deservin'? In the Navy, you'll learn to take what comes as your portion an' not go wheedlin' for a chance to shine, sir."

"They do wish us to be ambitious, sir," Alan allowed with a shrug, thinking he had disappointed his captain by being too forward.

"In our actions, yes, once given a charge," Lilycrop cautioned. "But not in advancin' our careers 'thout earnin' the right to do so."

"Well, it was just a thought, sir," Alan sighed. "But it would gall me terribly to think we had to sit out the rest of the war with no opportunity to do something useful."

Did I mean that? Alan wondered even as he uttered it. It was the proper sentiment a fire-eating young officer was expected to display, and he thought he had said it rather well, so well, in fact, that Alan felt a hard kernel of truth in it. He sometimes thought it was his curse that he could sit outside himself and judge his performance on the stage of Life like a disgruntled theater-goer waiting for a chance to get rid of the rotten fruit carried in with him, ready to jeer and heckle a poor reading, or cheer when a scene was carried off well.

It would make little difference if *Shrike* did spend the rest of the war at her moorings, or off on boresomely empty patrols. He had fulfilled his present ambitions; a small measure of fame for cool bravery, a commission, some prize-money, and now his post as a first officer, even in a small ship. He had seen the razor-edge of terror often enough to know how mortal he was, and like any sensible person could give war a great big miss the next time, to save his own skin.

If *Shrike* did stay in Kingston Harbor for some time, he could get ashore to court Lucy Beauman and make a firm pact with her about their future together. And from the tone of her latest letters, that would be best, before her circle of swains and admirers monopolized her to his detriment.

So why am I urging the captain to get us active employment? he asked himself, when anyone with any sense would want to stay out of danger and go courting one of the most beautiful young women of the age. It's daft, but this Navy stuff must be getting to me.

It made him squirm to face it, but he was indeed, through no fault or wish of his own, a Sea Officer of the King. He was getting rather good at it. And it was an honorable profession, not just the Guinea Stamp admitting him to the society of other gentlemen, but now a small yet burgeoning source of pride in his abilities. God knew he had had few reasons for pride before. It was demanding, dangerous, but it was his. There was no reward on earth for meekness, so why should he be content to stand on the sidelines crying "well played, sir" to some other ambitious young bugger with better connections, when there was a chance for advancement? There were prizes to take, money to be made, further fame to be won which would ease his passage to—to what?

Post-captain? He scoffed at his speculations. Admiral's rank? A bloody knight-hood? The peerage? Why not make the most of it while I may. Lewrie, what a *hopeful* little fool you are! But then again, why the hell not? We could sweep the seas so clean we could come back like that Dutchman Tromp with a broom at his mast truck. Just goes to show why one shouldn't encourage people like me. Once they got a taste of something, damme if they don't aspire to the whole thing.

"Lieutenant Alan Lewrie, of the *Shrike* brig!" the major-domo announced over the sound of the lawn party, to which announcement very few people took notice, being too intent on their pleasures. The sun was low in the sky and the tropical day had lost most of its heat to a sea breeze that swayed the paper lanterns in the trees, toyed with the wigs of the revelers and ruffled the intricate flounces of the women's gowns. String music (something by Purcell, Alan decided after cocking an educated ear) waxed and ebbed, depending on the wind or the thickness of the throng in front of the musicians in the gazebo to his right.

He stood at the base of the brick steps that led down from the tiled and sheltered back terrace of the house, surveying the crowd and searching for Lucy Beauman. Her parents' town house, which was no town house at all but a second mansion large enough for a titled lord, was aflutter with bunting and Naval ensigns in celebration for Admiral Rodney's victory at the Battle of The Saintes. There was enough red, white and blue material to make commissioning pendants and ensigns for every ship in the active inventory of the Fleet. As he had come through the central hall, Alan had seen a dining table decorated with a line of pastry and confection 3rd Rates, candied sails abillow and marzipan guns belching angel-hair powder smoke, a card table as a center-piece amid the buffet items with Winged Victory bearing a trident and flag, roaring lions at her feet, with a gilt helmet overlaid with the laurel wreath corona of triumph.

"Damme, but the Beaumans know how to spend their money, don't they?" he muttered, happy they had the pelf with which to entertain their burst of patriotic emotions. "Wonder they didn't just gild the whole damned house?"

There must have been over two hundred guests, the luminaries of Jamaica: prominent officials or high-ranking Navy and Army officers, and leading citizens with the government, title, place or sufficient money and lands to be included. Men strolled languidly in silk and satin suitings, women glided and tittered and fanned themselves, showing off their most stunning gowns and jewels.

Somewhere in that mob, Lucy could be found, and Alan felt his pulse quicken at the thought of seeing her again. He looked for the densest clutch of young men; Lucy would be sure to be in the center of them, flirting madly, if Alan knew his average young tit.

The wind picked up briefly, and a gust played with the tail of his long uniform coat. A black servant in cloth-of-silver and silk livery offered him a tray that bore delicate flutes of champagne, trying to balance the tray and keep his fresh-powdered white tie-wig from scudding somewhere off to leeward at the same time.

It would rain soon, Alan knew, a heavy tropical downpour fit to run all these revelers indoors, but not a threatening storm. If there had been any ominous signs to the weather, Lilycrop would have pulled his pug-nose and not allowed him ashore, invitation or not. But Lilycrop had had his own run ashore, and had come back aboard in the "early-earlies," breeches half buttoned, with what appeared to be rouge or paste on the fly, and most cordially "in the barrel," so he could not deny his first lieutenant his chance.

Alan took a sip of champagne—it was a suspiciously good vintage from France, a nation with which they were at war, and he smiled wryly as he imagined what under-handed practice had brought the wine to this occasion. He stepped out into the crowd, bowing slightly to people now and again if he caught their eyes, or they took notice of him, a cordial smile plastered on his phyz.

Aha, he thought, hearing a small shriek of laughter from the left, near a span of side-tables loaded down with delicacies and drink.

"Young Lewrie!" a voice boomed, interrupting his progress in that direction. Alan turned to see Mister Beauman. If anything, his host (and hopefully, prospective father-in-law) had gotten even stouter, and his taste in clothing had not improved much. It had been a sweltering spring day, and still felt clammy despite the cooling breeze from so much rain due soon, but he was tricked out in a massive older wig awash in side-curls down past his ears, which gave off puffs of flour every time the wind came up. His coat and breeches were white satin, and he wore a *sleeved*, older style waist-coat of pale yellow silk heavily embroidered with vines and flowers. How he kept from melting away, Alan could not ascertain.

"Mister Beauman, sir," Alan replied, as though he was the very person for whom he had been searching. "How grand to see you once more. May I express my heartfelt thanks for your kind invitation!"

"Don't ye look a sight, sir!" Beauman whooped. "Bless my eyes, a commission officer! Give ye joy, me lad."

"And to you, sir."

"Heard ye'd made lieutenant. Hard service in Virginia? Damn all Frogs." Beauman rumbled on, snatching another glass of claret from a passing tray. "Still, skinned the bastards, hey?"

"Indeed we did, sir," Alan agreed.

"Saved Jamaica," Beauman pronounced between slurps. "Took part in it, did ye? Grand sight, and all that?"

"No, sir. *Shrike* was up north patrolling between the Bahamas and the Virgins when . . ."

"Oh, too bad," Beauman interrupted. "Not your fault, I expect."

Alan wondered once more if the man had ever completed a full sentence instead of lopping them down to the pith. The Beaumans, except for their dear Lucy, were "country" types, shootin', huntin', dog-lovin', tenant tramplin', slave-bashin' Squires with more money than *ton*, and Alan felt a twinge at the thought of having to spend more than a day in their presence if he were fortunate enough to wed their daughter. He vowed he'd live in London and let them pursue their own amusements, preferably as far away as possible, as long as possible. Had it not been for their money, he'd have sneered at them for being such a pack of "Country-Harrys" and "Chaw-Bacons."

"Come meet the missus, Lewrie," Beauman ordered, turning his back and leading off through his guests, and Alan had no choice but to take station on Beauman's ample stern-quarters and follow.

"So this is young Mister Lewrie of which we've heard so much," Mrs. Beauman exclaimed after they had exchanged greetings.

Mrs. Beauman was the source of Lucy's beauty, Alan saw, fair and petite, a bit gone to plumpness, but still a fine figure of a woman in spite of her age. Her choice of attire was much better than her husband's, as well, though a bit old-fashioned. Hugh, the eldest son, was a younger replica of the father, hard-handed and hard-eyed as he finally met the upstart suitor for his sister's hand; the welcome from him was a chary one. The younger son resembled Lucy in his short stature and fair complexion, a bit of a dandy-prat in grey and maroon shot-silk coat and breeches, exaggerated sleeve cuffs and coat tails, and blue leather shoes with red heels trimmed in gold.

"Alan Lewrie, haw haw," he offered. "Ain't you the fortunate buck! Escapin' Yorktown and all, what?"

"Cut his way out!" Beauman, Sr., boasted. "Through fire and steel! My youngest boy, Ledyard, Lewrie."

"Delighted," Alan replied, offering his hand.

"Y're servant, sir, haw haw!" Ledyard rejoined inanely.

There was a middle daughter named Floss, bearer of the worst traits from the father's side of the union, ill-favored and swarthy; but her husband seemed happy enough, perhaps mollified by her father's gold. Master Hugh Beauman was married as well, to a rather good-looking young piece who evidently had realized it was impossible to get a word in edgewise in such a family, and had stopped trying. Anne gave him a sympathetic shrug, and a bit of a wink that in other circumstances would have had Alan scheming for a space of time alone with her.

There followed some rather uncomfortable minutes of chit-chat, with Alan the unwitting victim for not knowing any of the people or events they referred to, a common fault in people full of themselves. And Alan should have known about that, from monopolizing past conversations, but it was a wrench to be on the receiving end. There was no chance to break away and go searching for Lucy, the prime object of his trip ashore.

"Think it'll rain?" Mistress Anne asked him as the tops of the trees began to sway, and the sky turned gloomier.

"I would not doubt it at all, ma'am," Alan replied.

"Then we must see to getting the side-boards indoors before it begins. And I see you are out of wine, sir," she offered.

"Ah, yes I am," Alan noted. "May I escort you, ma'am?"

"I would be deeply obliged, sir."

Alan bowed his way out of the family circle and offered his arm to walk the fetching Anne Beauman towards the buffets.

"Daunting, ain't they?" she smirked once they were out of earshot.

"Daunting is a good description, ma'am," Alan smiled back.

"And I doubt you'd care to spend the rest of the evening with them, when Mistress Lucy is the reason for your visit?" Anne rejoined.

"I had hoped," Alan agreed, waving the servant with the askew wig over to service them with a tray of wine. He traded their glasses in for two fresh flutes of champagne and offered her one.

"We have heard much of you, Mister Lewrie," Anne continued. "From Lucy's description, and from your letters—those portions which Lucy thought relevant to relate to us—I would have expected someone much older. More . . . weathered."

"As my captain says, ma'am, I've only been in the Navy little more than a dog-watch."

"Dueling for Lucy's honor, saving a ship and her distinguished passengers, escaping Yorktown . . ." Anne raised an eyebrow in appreciation. "You have led an active life. And now you wish to enamor yourself to the Beaumans?"

Damn the bitch, Alan thought. I didn't come here to be mocked by some *parvenu*.

"Lucy and I developed a great fondness for each other last year on Antigua, ma'am. Her father allows me to call, but as for . . ."

"Don't call me ma'am, Mister Lewrie," Anne assured him with a touch of her hand on his sleeve. "I am Anne, and you are Alan. With luck, we shall be related, so why not start out on your best foot? A bit of advice?"

"Thank you."

"Don't take them seriously. If you do they will infuriate you beyond all reason." Anne frowned. "Hugh is a good enough man, the best of the lot in many ways, but in better circles they can appear a bit crude. A little too rustic and earthy."

"It is hardly my place to judge yet, Anne. I'm sure Lucy has many admirers, and as for my hopes—well, we shall see."

"How romantic!" Anne gushed, with just a tinge of sarcasm. "To hang the larger issues and let love dictate your desires. You are a paragon, Alan. *Always* pay attention to the family. Daughters turn out remarkably like their mothers, and sons become their fathers, in most instances."

"You sound disappointed," Alan said, cocking his head to one side to study her more closely. Yes, there was definitely a come-hither glint to her beauty; long dark hair and dark eyes, skin more olive or tinted by the sun than was fashionable. A wide mouth, high cheeks and a face that tapered to perfection, spoiled only by a few small-pox scars, but altogether a damned handsome woman near his age.

"Walk with me," she insisted. "I shall lead you to your Lucy."

"My pleasure."

"Island society, as you may know, is not what one would choose if given the choice of a Paris salon or a London drum," Anne told him, her hand resting maddeningly on his left sleeve, her fingers prying at the broadcloth gently. "There is a difference between hiring servants, and owning them outright. It makes for a callousness. Wield the whip often enough and flayed flesh becomes commonplace. The same goes for emotions, for souls. And the civilizing influence of literature, of music and manners is only a thin veneer. Thinner here in the islands than at home."

"I stand warned that they are all brutes and ogres," Alan quipped.

"They have their charms, even so," Anne replied with a small shrug. "And they are hardly that bad. I apologize for being gloomy."

"And you are not from the islands originally, I take it?"

"No. My father was secretary to the Governor-General, and we came out here in '72, before the war," she told him. "The lure of sugar planting got him, and we stayed. Hugh and I have been married for four years now. We have two fine children. I am quite content."

The hell you are! Alan thought. That's about as broad a hint as I've heard in six months. She's bored beyond tears.

"As I hope to be, Anne," Alan told her.

"Ah, here's your Lucy," Anne said, pointing out a group of young men in high finery almost eclipsing the figure of a young girl with blonde hair. "Such a darling girl."

"Amen to that," Alan agreed heartily.

"Lucy?" Anne called. "Look who's here."

Lucy peeked from the crowd, gave a small gasp, fanned herself, and stepped through to rush to his side.

God Almighty! he thought as he took her in. How could she have gotten *prettier*?

Lucy Beauman's bright aquamarine eyes lit up, her lips parted in a fond smile, showing her perfect little white teeth. Gloved hands touched his arms, there was a whiff of some maddening scent as they stood gazing at each other. He noted her high-piled hair, so delectably honey-blonde, the perfection of her neck, her shoulders, the white and pink and maroon gown she wore daringly off the shoulders (the proud swell of her breasts against the gown even more bountiful than formerly); he took in how petite and lovely her figure was, how round and inviting her arms were.

"Lucy," he breathed, all other sights gone from his ken.

"Oh, you are here!" she sighed, like to faint, her lips trembling. "I shall die of happiness, surely."

Much as he wanted to crush her to him, he had to stand back and hold hands with her, his own hands trembling with emotion. Money be damned, she was so beautiful, so much more beautiful than he even remembered, that he would have carried her off that moment if she didn't have two ha'pennies to rub together.

"You look so grand as a lieutenant," she admired. "The uniform suits you so *well*!"

"And your gown is delightful," Alan complimented in return. "But no gown could hold a candle to your beauty, Lucy."

"You are *such* a rogue, Alan," she gushed, blushing prettily but mightily pleased that he took the time to notice. "Oh, I have missed you so much!"

"And I you."

"You must come and meet father," she told him.

"I already have. I would have been at your side long before, but I was intercepted. Father, mother, Hugh, Ledyard, Floss . . ."

"Oh, good then. And you have met Anne as well?"

"Yes."

"She is such a dear. Oh, I fear I am neglecting the other guests, the gentlemen who . . ."

"Damn their blood, I say," Alan growled.

"Alan!" she whispered, pretending to be shocked, with a glance over her shoulder in the general direction of her miffed admirers.

"I haven't seen you in almost a year," Alan insisted, leading her further away from the disgruntled pack of suitors towards the back of the garden, where there looked to be a bit more privacy. "Why would I wish to make acquaintance of your other worshipers?"

"You are *so* forward!" she protested, but not very much.

"Forgive my eagerness, but it has been a long time."

"Of course, I forgive you, Alan. And you would never do anything to cause undue comment." She acquiesced, matching him stride for stride. "Oh, do tell me everything. Your last letter said you had left that ship *Desperate*, and had made lieutenant. And you were in a new vessel, the name escapes me?"

"*Shrike*, a brig o'war. I am first officer."

"You captain your own ship?" she gaped. "Already?"

"Uh, no" he had to admit. "The captain is a Lieutenant Lilycrop, but I am next in command, *his* first officer, you see."

"Oh, but that is marvelous for you." She beamed. "Now you are no longer a midshipman. And you have an annuity. And your grandmother's inheritance. Oh, Alan, I could never have dreamed things would turn out this way. Dad can have no objections now. And do they pay you?"

"I'd hardly do it for fun, now, would I?" Alan teased. They reached a wall of lush tropical plantings, heavy with flowers and thick with bouquet. There was a narrow path that led under and through the thicket, and Alan grinned at her as he cocked his head in that direction. Lucy met his eyes and grinned mischievously in reply. They were just about to step through for some real seclusion, when the rain that had been threatening began to spatter on the lawn and the leaves.

"Oh, my gown!" Lucy wailed. She stood up on tiptoe to kiss him briefly on the lips, then tugged him into a dash for the house as the rest of the guests ran for cover as well, and the servants gathered up what they could before the storm ruined furniture and tablecloths.

They made it to the porch, where Lucy bewailed the state of her dress and her hair, sure she had been disfigured by the raindrops; and from the sound of it, was sure the condition was permanent.

"I must go change," she told him as he mopped his hair and face with a pocket kerchief. "I hope my maid may be able to salvage it."

"Hardly spotted," Alan pointed out as the rain gusted and blew in on the porch, swirling in the late afternoon light on the yard and the steps and railings. "It'll be fine."

"Just like a man to think so!" she snorted back, tossing her head as though her hair was still down in a more casual style. "Now you entertain yourself for a few minutes while I go change into something dry. But do not be *too* entertained. There are quite a few other young women here, and I should not like to see you being too charming."

"You have nothing to fear, Lucy, I swear." He told her with all innocence. She smiled once more, looked about to see if anyone was watching, and pecked him on the cheek. He kissed her hand, and she blushed again, before darting off, calling for her maid-servant.

Damme, what a lovely little minx! he crowed in silent congratulation at his good fortune just to know her, and to know that she was so fond of him. Ain't she fine, just! Lord, she's so perfect, so beddable, and admirers be damned, she's as good as mine. This time there'll be nothing to tear us apart. And if she don't fetch five thousand pounds for her portion, I'm a Turk in a turban!

There was a lot of fetching of towels, a lot of shaking of powdered wigs that left a slurry of wet flour on the terrace tiles as the other guests tended to their ruined finery, though no one looked particularly wet to Alan's viewpoint. Let 'em stand on a quarterdeck with me in a gale of wind, and I'll give 'em "wet"! he thought with a touch of contempt for lubberly civilians.

Lucy Beauman's conception of "a few minutes" was obviously not everyone's; the time passed slowly, forcing him to check his pocket watch to see how long she was taking to change. Alan occupied himself with a couple more glasses of champagne.

"Mister Lewrie?" A familiar, throaty voice spun him about.

"Ah," Alan managed to say, "Mrs. Hillwood?"

"I am so gratified you recall me," the older woman said. She was still lovely, in her lanky fashion, a bit less smooth-complexioned than he remembered from nearly two years before, when they had met at a supper-dance at Sir Richard Slade's. He had gone to her house the next day, after debauching himself to the wee hours with . . . whatever the little chick-a-biddy's name had been (it had been that sort of a party) . . . and Mrs. Hillwood had damned near killed him with kindness. If it hadn't been for her penchant for neat gin, which had put out her lights and let him dress and escape, she might have put him under for good.

"How delighted to see you once more, Mrs. Hillwood," he told her. "You are looking marvelous, as always."

"You are too kind, young sir. But what is this? You have made lieutenant. Still in that despatch boat?"

"No, ma'am. I left *Parrot* soon after docking at Antigua."

"And how is that young scamp we knew," she simpered, laying heavy stress on "knew," since she had "known" both Thad Purnell and Alan Lewrie, in successive evenings. "Thomas? No, Thaddeus."

"I regret that I must inform you that Thad Purnell passed over to the Yellow Jack on that same voyage, ma'am."

"Oh, how terrible." She frowned, dropping her teasing air. "He was a dear friend of yours. So young, too."

"That seems to be the way of the world, ma'am," Alan agreed somberly.

"Once you sailed, I never heard from you again," Mrs. Hillwood went on. "I am sure so much of note has happened to you. You must let me entertain you, perhaps come for tea, and tell me all about what you have been doing since last we had the pleasure of each other's company."

Damned if she hadn't been one hell of a bare-back rider, bony about the hips or not, chicken-chested or not, Alan remembered. It had been two months since he had even gotten a whiff of womankind, and he would not be doing much more with Lucy than holding hands and sighing a lot, he realized. Memories sprang up, like how predatory she looked with her face beaming a wicked smile up from his groin as they lay in bed and she coaxed him into just one more bout; the noises she made as she rode St. George on his member and stirred her hips and belly like an island woman grinding corn.

"Nothing would give me greater pleasure," he told her, and

she grinned in delight, curving up those talented lips. In repose, her face, with an unfortunately hawkish nose her only mar, could appear fierce, but a smile restored the great beauty she had once possessed.

"I am certain it would, Mister Lewrie," she cooed softly, as she toyed with her fan, using it to touch him on the cheek by his faint scar. "And you must tell me all about that. Your address?"

"The *Shrike* brig."

"You mind where I live?" she asked. "Not quite? How forgetful of you. I trust I shall not have to write it down more than this once."

"I am certain you shan't." Alan grinned at the meaning of that threat, and his groin got tight just thinking about it. "And Mister Hillwood is still inland, I trust, being—agricultural?"

"As far as I know," she sighed. "His particular passions require greater secrecy than mine."

"Ah, Alan," Lucy said as she re-emerged from the house in a new gown of creamy pale yellow satin with gold bows and trim. Her hair had been let down and brushed dry as well.

"A few minutes, hey?" Alan teased. "Half a dog-watch, more like. Lucy Beauman, I believe you know Mrs. Hillwood?"

"We have not had the pleasure, though the name is familiar to me," Lucy replied, looking somewhat vexed. "How delighted to make your acquaintance, Mrs. Hillwood."

"And I yours, dear. My, what a lovely gown. You are fortunate not to have gotten it wet in the rain showers," Mrs. Hillwood cooed.

"I had to change." Lucy frowned.

"Would that I could, my dear. Or at least sponge this down."

"I would be happy to offer you the use of my chambers. Did you bring your maid with you?" Lucy suggested.

"You are too kind!"

"Think nothing of it, ma'am. I would be only too happy to give you my every assistance," Lucy purred. She clapped her hands quite briskly. "Tyche?" she called without looking, and her black maid-servant came on the run to attend her. Lucy gave her instructions to allow Mrs. Hillwood the use of her toilet, and for Tyche to help her rearrange her habiliment. Mrs. Hillwood headed off for the stairs, and Lucy glared at him as he said his goodbyes.

"Alan, how could you?" she demanded in a soft voice, but one tinged with a certain menace.

"How could I what, Lucy?" Alan asked, wondering if he looked half as innocent as he was trying to look.

"Mrs. Hillwood is really the *most* despicable woman," Lucy told him with some heat. "I say woman rather than lady, despite her airs and her pretensions."

"Well, how was I to know that, Lucy?" Alan shot back. "I met her once before, near on two years ago at one of Sir Richard Slade's suppers."

"My God, it gets worse and worse!" Lucy spat. "The most infamous . . . I cannot find the strength to name the man's sinful predilictions . . . no proper lady could. And what were you *doing* in such a place?"

And just where did this termagant mort come from? Alan wondered, amazed at the change from the sweet and gentle and cooing lovely girl he thought he had known and desired.

"My captain in *Parrot* knew him from school, and I and another midshipman were invited to join him for supper." Alan shrugged it off.

"And were you not scandalized by all the goings-on?"

"I saw none." Alan tried to scoff. "We had a feed the like of which I had not seen since London, and the victuals held more interest. After a year of Navy issue, I'd have dined with the Devil himself if he set a good table." He chuckled.

"If you sup with the Devil, as you say, I trust you used a long spoon." Lucy fumed.

"Now look here, Lucy." Alan attempted to bluff it out when he saw that dumb innocence would not suit. "She came up to me and introduced herself. All I know of her was she was several chairs down from me at table nearly two years ago. I've probably gone into the same chop-house as notorious murderers back in London, but that don't make me guilty of murder. How could you think such a thing? As for this un-named prediliction of Sir Richard's, well, I know nothing of that, either. You use me rather ill, I think."

"Oh, Alan, I'm sorry." She mellowed suddenly, allowing him to offer an arm to lead her toward the buffet tables. "What must you think of me, to accuse you of encouraging such a woman. It is only that I have missed you so much. And I come back down to find you in the clutches of a trull whose reputation is no better than it should be. What a welcome I've given you. Please forgive me, but I was suddenly so jealous I could hardly utter a civil word, to her, or to you."

"Jealous, is it?" he coaxed gently.

"I shall own to it," she whispered, leaning close as they went to a side-board and began to pick at the delicacies to load on their plates. "After months of only letters from you, I could not let anyone steal one precious minute of our time. Perhaps the tales about Mrs. Hillwood aren't whole cloth, but you can understand why I was so uncharitable about her. Come to think of it," she smiled, poking him in the ribs with her fork, "you were not so charitable to those other young fellows I was with. Damn their blood, did you say?"

"And their eyes and kidneys, and anything else they have they can spare," Alan assured her.

"So you were jealous, too. Admit it," she prodded.

"I own to it, too," he muttered so others could not hear. "You don't know half of what I've been through since Antigua, with only your letters for comfort, and those months apart."

As soon as I decyphered 'em, he qualified to himself, for Lucy was what one could charitably describe as an *inventive* speller, with a quick, darting penmanship that started out in neat round (horribly misspelled) words, and when she got to the exciting bits, went mystifying as the scratches on Stonehenge.

"And you must tell me everything, darling Alan," she begged. "Was it really so terrible?"

"It was pretty rough," he allowed modestly. "There are some things you'd best never know, some of the things that happened during the siege, and during our escape are unsuitable for a lady to hear."

"And I wrote of silly social things while you were being racked by shot and shell." She sighed. "How could I have been so cruel or thoughtless? Yet I wrote you often. You did not get them?"

"Well, the mails never caught up with the fleet before we left New York, and then we were stuck in the Chesapeake," Alan told her. "The Frogs and the Rebels weren't about to trot out the penny post for us. There were dozens of letters to you I never could post myself, some the Rebels captured I suppose."

"You mean those uncouth, quarrelsome people have read my letters?"

Conversations with her take the *strangest* bloody twists and turns, he sighed to himself, and had to cosset her out of her pet. But for the rest of the evening, during the strolling about in the suffocatingly hot rooms, the dancing and the card games and a brief tour of the side-terrace for some air, where they could indulge their need to hold each other and kiss passionately, he managed to keep her happy and positively glowing. As he paid his respects to the family, they treated him as almost one of the family, though nothing concrete had been settled, but that was sure to come, in time.

All in all, except for walking back to the docks with an erection he could have doubled for a belaying pin, it was a good run ashore. And there was always Betty Hillwood and her invitation to "tea."

Chapter 4

There were a lot of "teas" in the next week or so. Once more Alan was thankful that in harbor officers stood no fixed watches, and once what few duties were done for the day, could absent themselves to their own amusements.

If I spend the rest of my career doing this, I shan't cry, Alan thought smugly as he lay back on the soft mattress, panting for air in the close tropical heat. The linens clung to them, crinkled with perspiration, and he fanned them with a corner of the sheet.

"You insatiable beast!" Betty Hillwood uttered with a gasp for air herself. "Pour us something cool, Alan dear, whilst I try to recover my senses."

He hopped off the bed and filled their wine glasses with lemonade—she was a lot more fun if he kept her out of reach of the gin, or at least cut down on her consumption during the early hours of their trysts. He stood over her and offered her a glass, enjoying the slim form, still beaded with mutual perspiration, and her incredibly soft skin reddened in all the most interesting places by having his body pressed so close to hers. Over forty or not, she was more woman than most men could stand and live to talk about.

"The pot calls the kettle black, love?" he told her as she took a sip. "Now who's insatiable, damn my eyes."

"You're even more impressive than I first remembered," she said, shifting to sit up on one elbow and pile pillows behind her head. She gave a delightful groan when she said it. "Before, you were a randy boy, for all your eagerness."

"Clumsy, was I?" he chuckled, climbing back into bed and laying against the footboard pillar so their legs entwined.

"No, my chuck, just . . . exuberant," she crooned, plying her toes around his groin playfully. "A year's hard service has made you even more a man to suit my taste. Harder . . . leaner . . . the most impressive and satisfying fuck I've known."

Once out of polite society, and her clothing, Betty Hillwood had always had the mouth of a farrier-sergeant. Perhaps it was the gin that loosened her tongue and her inhibitions, if she truly had any.

She demanded pleasure as her due, since she would not get it from her husband, who preferred to live inland on one of his plantations and bugger the field hands and the house-boys. There was no longer any coy pretense of seduction between them, no more teasing conversation or tea to be poured, no guests to shoo off so he could return after he had made a proper goodbye, so they could play innocent for Society. He came to her after a morning or afternoon with Lucy and her parents, sometimes came to her direct from the ship, and the black servant let him in and then took her leave. Betty Hillwood met him in morning gown or her bed-clothing, under which she tantalizingly wore nothing. They would have a drink, no more than one, while she let her clothing fall open, and they would be grappling with each other within a quarter-hour, making it to the bedroom at the back of her cool apartments most of the time but not always—there was a good assortment of settees and chairs to roger on, an escritoire of just the right height to support her small buttocks, and a marble-topped breakfast table by a shuttered window that made a cool change if the day was too hot.

Every visit was a revelation, a learning experience in just how many ways two people could give each other pleasure, and Alan Lewrie was all for education—look how much the Navy had taught him already. It beat whores all hollow, in his estimation, didn't cost him more than "fiddler's pay"—compliments and wine—and took the rapacious edge off his manners with Lucy Beauman, whom he would have ravished by this time if he had not had another outlet for his frustrations. Being around, and tantalisingly near, such a delectable young girl with no chance to grapple would have killed lesser men by this time. One could hardly be considered a respectable suitor to conjoin with such a fine (and wealthy) family if he spent all his time goggling at Lucy's breasts, or fondling her on the sly. Not that they hadn't played lovers in daring, and heart-breakingly brief, moments of privacy. The common wisdom said that too much spending of one's vital fluids in fornication made a young man spineless and weak—his breath shallow, his eyes watery, and his general condition little better than a victim of consumption—but Alan was of the opinion that too *little* spending made one so full of humors that one would explode if restrained from the sport too long. Either that or begin to squirt semen from one's ears. If too much spending led to pathetic lunacy, then so be it; he could drool and cackle with the best of them, sooner or later.

"I have something for you, my chuck," Betty whispered, once she had gotten her wind back. She slunk out of bed, brushing her body the length of his, kissing him open-mouthed, then skipped coquettishly out of reach and down the narrow hall to the parlor as he grabbed at her. She returned with a small package and held it out to him, then busied herself at the bedroom wine-table to pour herself a drink while he undid the ribbon and opened it.

It was a watch-chain, a particularly fine one, with rectangular links of small and cunning workmanship. Depended from it was a braided band on which rested a small fob of silver and gold damascene worked in a fouled anchor over crossed cannon. It was beautiful. More to the fact, a well-made chain from an expert craftsman could cost more than a watch did.

"God's teeth!" he exclaimed in delight. The silver and gold chain, the dark blue ribbon, and the silver and gold fob were magnificent, and he told her so. "Whatever possessed you to do me so much honor?"

"You're truly pleased?" she asked, flinging her arms around him and drawing her delightful body the full length of his.

"And flabbergasted," he admitted. "It's so damned grand! How may I ever thank you for it?"

"By doing what earned it in the first place, my chuck." She nibbled on his ear, reaching down with one hand to dandle his member against her belly. "You have given me so much pleasure, and so much delight, I had to reward my darling lad. Ah, there's a stirring of gratitude, methinks? Shall I be rudely speared for my pains to please?"

"Methinks milady is right," Alan growled, seizing her buttocks and hauling her in closer.

"Pitiful, tearful beseechings have no avail," she whispered as she steered them backward toward the bed once more. "Even offers of gold cannot soften the heart of a barbarian bent on rapine."

Damme, here she goes with another of her bloody fantasies, he thought, more than willing to oblige, but tiring of her ripe imaginings in which he had to play so many parts.

"A tender senator's wife, with Hunnish blades at her children's throats. Tender white skin assaulted so wickedly by callused hands and brutal urges ... ah!" she urged, playing at fending him off. "No, please ... Rome lies open at your feet. Spare me this, I beg you!"

"You lay open to me!" Alan grunted, trying to be rudely Germanic.

"No, please!" she cried, but not too loudly. They mock-fought, and she fell face down across the mattress, and Alan knew his duty. He flung himself down on her, forced her legs apart, and entered her dog-fashion, gripping her hips and lifting them up off the sheets, and she panted and pretended to weep until the "virtuous Roman senator's wife" was overcome with pleasures she had never experienced on the bridal couch, and the game had its usual ending. Betty groaned and sobbed, rolled her hips and thrust to meet him as he knelt between her thighs, tore at the bed-linens with her nails until she shivered and cried out in ecstasy, gasping for air once more, and dropped away limp.

"Oh God, but you're a bloody stallion, dear Alan!" she sighed in a swoon. "So long and thick and hard, and ..."

He rolled her over, and she chuckled as he lay down between her legs, which flopped aside in exhaustion.

"Alan!" she protested as he raised her knees and slid back into her hot wetness. "I am spent, truly."

"Hermann ist gut, ja? Hermann not through." He grunted as he began to plunge at her again for his own satisfaction, which she finally shared, all protests aside, and she clawed at his back and shoulders and uttered a thin keening cry until they lay still once more.

They finally rose and sponged down with a bucket of cool water left standing by the shuttered bedroom windows, snacked on some cold tongue and chilled hock for him, some "Blue Ruin" for her in a large glass. They lay down together to nuzzle and purr until the urge came on them again.

"Would we could do this always," she said softly.

"I have to sail eventually," Alan whispered back. "Or at least I hope we do. This idleness isn't doing the crew much good."

"To where?"

"Oh, up around Cuba or the Florida Straits, maybe over to the Windward Passage."

"And how long would you be gone, dear?"

"Near on three months if we don't take prizes to sustain us," he reckoned, half asleep. "Back in two weeks if we take enough ships to deplete the hands for prize-crews. Wish we could—I could use the money."

"You are short of cash?"

"Well, not short, really. I was thinking of after the war when I'll go back to England. London wouldn't have gotten any cheaper. I've enough now for my needs, what with naval pay and my remittance." He shrugged and snuggled closer. "Enough as long as I stay at sea three months out of four, that is."

"Perhaps I can help," she told him, rolling over to look down on him. "I have money of my own, and as long as my dear husband may indulge his pleasures in discretion, and I play the proper wife, he allows me to spend as I will. He has bags of money. Perhaps the only endearing side to him," she concluded sourly.

"Here, now," Alan replied, warning her off as he got an inkling of a change in their relationship beyond the physical.

"As long as you pleasure me to utter ruin, I could support any desire you have," she promised. "You would be at sea part of the time, but once back in port, you could lodge ashore with me. No more visiting and having to skulk away."

"But what would that do to your good name in Society?" he protested, sitting up and fluffing up the many pillows to sit upright.

"This is not my only residence, dearest Alan." She chuckled, rising to get herself some more gin. By this time, she was a trifle unsteady on her feet, and he was sure it was the drink that had given her courage enough to make her proposition. "I have property of my own, mostly rentals. I cannot count on my husband to play me fair should he have the good grace to die. There are children to consider. But over the years, I have provided for my own security. Now I could lease you a lovely flat . . . I own this building entire. Would you prefer a suite here? Or would you like a set of rooms with a harbor view, closer to the piers. You tell me, and I shall move my things next door to you. We shall be no more than friendly neighbors, should anyone remark on our companionship. Of course, the rooms would cost you nothing. And I could furnish them to your taste, and put it down to my fondness for you. And the way you bull me all over the lot. The fob and chain are only a token of what I could offer the young man who so eagerly tops me so well . . . and often."

Her smile was positively vulpine, though she meant it to be seductive; the hawkish nose had a lot to do with it.

"Whew," Alan wheezed. "That's a damned handsome offer, from a handsome piece of woman, I might add."

"Then you will?"

"Seems a waste, when I'd get ashore so seldom." He stalled, gaining time to think this over. "And people would talk anyway."

"Aye, people would," she allowed breezily. "People already do, no matter what one does in Society. Rumors are more interesting than truth, don't ye know, and the naughtier the better. There's not one woman on this accursed island who hasn't been whispered about, only half of them with good cause. Only fools marry for love, unless they both have wealth and security of their own, or know how to pile it up, as I have. That victory celebration at the Beaumans' . . . I know more than two dozen women there who already have their own pleasurable arrangements with other men, and their husbands have theirs as well. God, don't admit you're truly an innocent!"

"No one in their right minds has ever called me innocent." Alan laughed.

"The only important thing about our wretched English society is to be discreet, and one may do anything one wants," Betty Hillwood said with a sneer. "And if one has money, then no one will even utter one peep of remonstrance. You won't hear sermons preached against anyone like me, as long as I give to the alms box and pay the Poor's Rate on time. One only gets exposed when one goes broke."

"Or gets too careless?" Alan finished for her, taking a sip of wine from an offered glass.

"Exactly, though I hardly have to tell you that, Alan dearest. You're discreet in your visits to me, I trust."

"Completely," he assured her. The last thing he needed was for anyone to know that he was courting Lucy Beauman and rogering Betty Hillwood at the same time.

"Who knows, you may even wish to return to England with me."

"Eh?"

"After the war, when the seas are safe, I'll go back to London where I may live in a proper style," Betty prophesied, downing her gin and pouring another. "You shall be on half-pay by then, and as you say, London will not have gotten any cheaper. My husband can stay here and rot for all I care ... he's probably peppered to his eyebrows with the pox by now, anyway. You would have servants, fine clothes, anything your heart could ask. And you would have me. And I could have you, every night and day. We could live together, or apart, but only a bit apart. I would want you to spear me and split me until I scream for sheer joy."

Now what do you say, fool? Alan thought, trying to plaster his most disarming smile on his face as he pondered this new development. She may be a good ride, but I'm damned if I want a steady diet of Hillwood mutton. And I'm not so poverty-stricken I need to be supported. 'Tis flatterin', I'll grant, but she's a little long in the tooth for more than a few hours.

"You must know, Betty, that I've been up to the Beauman place quite often." He temporized, trying to be honest without hurting her feelings. "Their daughter Lucy and I ... well, nothing's been said one way or the other, but eventually, I would wish to settle down and wed ... somebody, wouldn't I? And where would that leave you? I mean," he added with a sudden burst of inspiration, "it takes an Act of Parliament to get a divorce, and your husband could maybe stand going his own way, but no man wants to be known as an outright cuckold. Why risk his anger and your reputation going for more than we have now?"

"He's been cuckold since '72!" Betty declared, exasperated with his sudden cold feet. "Not, I'll grant, by anyone that could even approach your talent at it, dearest. And as for the Beaumans ... that pack of 'Chaw-Bacons'! For all their airs, they've not been long off the hay-wagon, with the manners of stable-hands. Oh, they're rich, I'll allow, and you see security with that little chit, do you? Well, let me tell you, she's not been pining away for you to sail back into her life. No party is complete without her, and her pack of admirers just slavering for a grope at her, and she's not exactly been shy at being groped at, I'll wager."

"Now hold on!" Alan grunted, not wanting to hear anything bad about Lucy. He was indeed fond of her, money aside, and the last time Mrs. Hillwood had given him the dirt on someone, Lieutenant Kenyon for instance, one of his grandest illusions had been shattered. He would hear no smear on Lucy's character. "You may dislike the whole family. And frankly, they are a bit rough around the edges, I'll admit, but that's no reason to slander her."

"Oh, poor dear Alan," Betty muttered cynically. "Do you think you're the only buck pawing the ground she's walked on? She's young, beautiful and ungodly rich into the bargain. But could she ever give you half the pleasure I've given you just this day? Or would she most likely be so shy and inexperienced a jaded rogue like you would scare the breath out of her? Though where she gets her purity is beyond me."

"What do you mean, damnit?"

"Peace, my love. I speak of the Beaumans, of course. Father off with a girl he keeps . . . in one of my apartments, I might add."

"Really?" Alan blurted, sitting back on his heels at some really lively gossip.

"Hugh, the eldest son," Betty smirked, swaying her hips seductively as she came back to the bed and stretched out near him, "he's right fond of 'fancies,' he is."

"Fancies," Alan stated; he'd heard the term before back in the Carolinas with the Chiswick family, but hadn't known what it meant.

"Very pale, very elegant-looking Samboes. House-servant quality, half white or almost white. You've seen them around town." She chuckled, swinging her glass back and forth, without spilling a drop. "Hugh can't get enough of them. Over on Portland Bight, where they have one of their sugar plantations, Hugh keeps a stable of them; not in the house except when Anne and the children are in town, though. I believe Mrs. Beauman is the only one that doesn't know about her own men-folk, but I could be wrong. But then, many women suffer in silence for the sake of the children, or their security. Unlike me."

"Well, stap me," Alan said, amazed at the ways of the world, though he should have known better by then. "The whole damned family?"

"Mrs. Beauman, no," Betty sighed. "She really is a sweet thing, but not too observant of most goings-on. Anne, Hugh's wife . . . well, I think she's aware of it, but as long as she doesn't have to be *enceinte* over and over, I doubt she minds that much. No woman wishes to have a child a year and never have another hope of anything else until her womb shrivels. There was the most delicious doings two years ago, my dear!"

Betty snuggled closer to impart her intimate information.

"Do tell," Alan replied, leaning closer.

"During the slave revolt, all the women-folk came into Kingston for safety, while the men were off with the militia and the troops." Betty snickered in glee. "And there was this one *glorious* young officer from the garrison, a captain, who took a particular fancy for the handsome Anne Beauman. As far as decorum allowed, they were inseparable."

"And did you rent him rooms, too?" Alan mocked.

"No, but it was powerful wondrous how often Anne had to go out to shop, and never found anything worth buying, and how often young Captain McIntyre was away from his quarters. A friend of mine, Mrs. Howard, the frumpy one you met? Well, servants may come and go with no notice, and she set her maid to watch, and it appears that Captain McIntyre would enter certain lodgings every day, and soon after, the lovely Anne Beauman would enter those same lodgings and stay for three or four hours at a stretch. Then they would leave separately, she first, and him about a quarter-hour later."

"So what happened?"

"Ah, the estimable young captain was carried off by the Yellow Fever after he went back into the field, and Mistress Anne was seen no more about Kingston for about a year, off to Portland Bight, no matter that the slaves were still in revolt. 'Twas said Hugh came back in a furious choler and dragged her off."

"Damme, that's amazing. I'd have never thought her capable."

"When disappointed or crossed, anyone is capable, Alan dear," she told him condescendingly. "Not only capable, but eager and willing to do almost anything to get their own back."

He succeeded in getting the subject changed to one she liked a whole lot better, which did not require words, avoiding any more speculation on her offer as well. And once she took on a larger cargo of Holland gin than was good for her trim, he could leave her snoring it off. He sponged down once more, dressed and headed out, and the servant girl slipped back in the door as he slipped out, still as silent as the Sphinx. Down the steps to the courtyard with its fountain, fish pond and flower beds off which all the lodgings opened, then out the double iron gate to the bright street, which shimmered in heat.

He stood there a moment, almost sneezing at the change from a fairly cool, thick-walled building, to the sharp warmth of late afternoon.

I'm going to break this off, he decided. Good as Betty Hillwood wanted to be to him, and as wanton a ride as she was, her proposition was nothing he wanted to be part of. While he did not consider himself one of God's innocents, Betty Hillwood could make him feel like a gawking choir-boy with her sour, jaded outlook on the world, and he wasn't sure he was ready to share her state of mind.

"I mean, damme, pleasure's fine, but my God!" he groused as he began to stroll off, trying to stick to the shadows where the sun did not strike with such ferocity. I've never heard a good word pass her lips 'bout anyone or anything, have I?

He had just finished four straight hours with a woman who would fulfill his every desire, and he should have been skipping and laughing with delight at his good fortune. She had given him a chain and fob worth an easy fifty or sixty guineas, but he had little joy from it.

"I'm not one for the Blue-Devils," he muttered, pondering his moodiness. "Must be her, the sour bitch. No wonder her husband took off for the back-country, if that's the sort of thing he had to hear all the time. Well, thankee for the gift, and thankee for all the quim, Betty dear, but that's the last time I sport with you, or give ear to your poison."

Besides, he assured himself, looking for a cause for joy, wasn't he handsome and pleasing enough to have a younger and prettier wench if the humors took him again? Didn't Lucy Beauman go faint at the sight of him? He had bigger fish to fry, and Betty Hillwood was a possible embarrassment if word got out about their affair. She would be nice to look back on, but that was all.

He headed for "The Grapes," the cheery red brick inn and public house at the foot of the docks and the landing stage, for a last cool mug of ale or beer before taking a bum-boat out to *Shrike*.

The heat was killing, and all his pleasurable exertions had left him loose-hipped and a trifle weak in the knees, so when hearing the clatter of a coach coming down the road from behind him, he gladly shifted over towards the nearest wall, into a patch of shade, and leaned on the wall to take a breather. He turned to see if the coach would miss him in the narrow lane, and was amazed to see that the light open two-horse carriage bore Mrs. Anne Beauman and her maid. He lifted his hat and gave a bow as they neared, and the carriage squeaked to a stop, rocking on its leather suspension straps.

"Mistress Beauman, a good day to you, ma'am."

"Mister Lewrie." She beamed back at him, looking fetching in a white and pale-blue gown, and a wide straw hat that echoed her colors. "Are you forced to walk in this oppressive heat, sir?"

"Shank's ponies, ma'am, for journeys too short for a coach," Alan laughed lightly in reply.

"So formal, Alan," she admonished. "And just two days ago it was Anne. Get you in and we shall deliver you to your destination."

"My undying thanks, Anne," Alan said, as the footman got down from the rear postillion, folded down the iron step and opened the low door for him. Alan settled into the rear-facing forward seat next to a large, wrapped bundle. "I am only going to the docks, Anne, if that is not too large an imposition on your time."

"None at all," she replied, reaching over to touch his knee with her large laced fan as the coachee whipped up. "You come ashore, though, without paying court to our dear Lucy? How remiss of you," she teased.

"I only had the few hours today," Alan replied, reddening slightly.

"Then I shall not tell her I saw you, or she would feel slighted, no matter the reason." Anne chuckled, going back to fanning herself. With one backward glance, she got her black maid to adjust the large parasol over her head so the sun would not strike her and ruin her complexion.

Now why, Alan speculated in appraisal, would Hugh Beauman want to dally with one of his fancies, when he could sport with this one any night?

In bright sunlight, Anne Beauman appeared even more exotic than before, her hair and complexion dark, making Alan wonder if she were the off-spring of some island racial mix herself. Possibly some Spanish blood, or sprung from those "Black Irish" sired by the survivors of the Armada? There had been damned few Black island women that had tempted him, and he could not think why anyone would spurn the charms of such a handsome woman for those of some slave in the back-country, even if the slave was close to European. But then, why was he fond of chamber-maids and willing widows? he asked himself. Perhaps it was an acquired taste.

"Not much wind today," Alan observed as the coach clattered on its way towards the center of town. "I wonder you're out yourself."

"House-keeping errands, I'm afraid," she replied with a brief frown. "My newest gown in that bundle next to you was spotted with soup, and no one seems to be able to get it out. I was hoping my dress-maker could run up a new panel so I could wear it Sunday. And what brings you ashore?"

"Oh, just some shopping."

"Only poor shops up the way you came," Anne pointed out. "You must have been in search of a bargain."

"And a little sight-seeing. Just to get off the ship for a few hours, see some new faces."

"And did you see anyone interesting? Any new sights?" Anne rejoined, mildly amused, as though she knew what he had been doing, and with whom.

"Not much up that way, you are right," Alan replied, flushing with heat under his clothes at her probing. "Might I offer you some reward for saving me from a long, hot walk? A cool drink, perhaps?"

"There is no need to reward me, Alan, though I must admit something cool would feel welcome. I had no idea it was this hot!" Anne said, plying the fan more energetically. "Where would you have in mind?"

"Well, there's 'The Grapes,' " he suggested, unable to think up anyplace else on short notice—he had not been ashore in Kingston often enough to know all its establishments.

"Hmm," she frowned, "a sailor's haunt, I fear. Not quite genteel, is it."

"I thought it was rather nice." Alan shrugged.

"A bit too many Navy officers and merchant captains, trading factors and such. There are few places a lady may go away from home. Ah!" She brightened. "There is, however, a small public house near my dress-maker's. Baltasar's. The emigré Frenchman who is the proprietor styles it as a *restaurant*, quite the latest thing in Paris, he says. No lodgings, just food and drink. Can you imagine?"

"The hard part is imagining how the man turns a profit," Alan said, grinning. Chop-houses and public-houses were usually close by *bagnios*, had rooms to let for private dining and discreet sport with dinner companions, or could trot out a chambermaid or a prostitute for their patrons. Without that sideline, he could not see how money could be made, not in a harbor town, at any rate.

"If you do not mind me seeing to my errand first?" Anne

asked, as though eager to try the place. "If I do not delay you from returning to your ship at the proper time?"

He was forced to walk her into the dress-maker's shop, where several island ladies of social note were taking rest from the day's warmth, gossiping and killing time, while fabrics and laces were considered, the latest points of style were admired or denigrated, and the small staff bustled about to fetch out requests. Alan felt like a total fool standing by the door with his hat under his arm, feeling the cool gaze of the women. They glanced at him, scowling a bit at the effrontery of a man to invade their sanctuary from husbands, shot glances at Anne, and then shifted to gaze most significantly at each other.

Damn all this feminine truck! Alan fumed, trying to look patient, calm, and innocent, though he felt as examined as if he had gone in naked as the day he was born.

The *restaurant* a few doors down was almost empty, thank God, but not a bad sort of place, screened from the street by a high brick wall and an iron gate, with a second false wall behind the gate for discretion. The small front garden was sheltered from the sun by thin slats of wood in an overhead screen supported by trellises, all adrip with vines or hung with flowers in hanging baskets. There was another fountain to cool the air. A series of French doors at the back of the garden terrace led into the main dining room and kitchens, and more doors and windows overlooked the harbor from a back terrace with the same sort of screen overhead. Except for a small brass plaque on the iron gate, Alan would have never known it was there; he had walked by it before and thought it a residence.

They were seated at a small table near the back terrace where the shadows were deepest, and the thick walls of the building, the stone floor and the light harbor wind gave the impression of coolness.

The proprietor, a Frog dandy-prat who appeared lighter in his pumps than most, tripped over and bowed deeply and elegantly, making the usual gilt and be-shit flowery words of salutation to what were probably the only new customers he had seen in a long afternoon. And he was disappointed that they did not wish to sample his solid fare, but only wanted drinks. He did, however, serve them a treat he told them was known in the Spanish Indies as *sangria*, a fruit juice and hock concoction, made to a recipe he had received in Havana during his service to the court of the Captain-General himself.

"It's quite delicious," Anne said after taking a sip. "And most refreshing. I have been told that too much acid fruit is bad in a hot climate, but I never saw the sense of it."

"Hmm, not bad," Alan had to agree. "Must keep it on ice. It's almost cold."

"Or in a hanging ceramic jar," Anne told him. "Everyone in the islands learns that if what the Spanish call an *olla* is hung in shade where there is a chance of wind, water or whatever it seems to cool on its own. One may see beads of water on the outside, and it feels cold to the touch. Quite remarkable, really."

"Hmm, one could do that aboard ship, below decks, and God knows out at sea, we'd have bags of wind."

"Your shipmates would think you quite ingenious, Alan," Anne promised. "Well, I hope you were not bored by the sights of our poor city today, or by having to escort me to the dress-maker's."

"Oh, not at all," he assured her.

"You looked as if you would strangle back there," she teased.

"Well, they did make me feel dawkish," Alan had to admit, easing back in his chair. "All those ladies eyeing me like I had the King's Evil. And at you. I hope my presence gave them nothing to talk about."

He almost bit his cheek in alarm when he realized he wasn't to know about her alleged past dalliance, and his comment made it sound as if he did. "I mean," he qualified, "they looked like an idle lot. People like that usually misconstrue the most inno-cent event and turn it into a subject for gossip. Bored to tears with their own miserable lives, I expect."

"Yes, I suppose they could." Anne looked at him directly over the rim of her glass. "But since there is nothing between us but the hope of you becoming a member of our family, what harm?"

"Well, none, I suppose." He shrugged and hunched back for-ward over the rim of the table, trying to look innocent once more.

"Are you as worldly as you sound, then? Does our Lucy have cause to worry?" she asked softly, with a grin at his discomfort.

"Now you are teasing me," he said. "I've seen gossip-mongers in action before, though. And I would hate to do any-thing that would jeopardize the Beauman family name. Or do anything to hurt my chances, either."

"Then you shall be making a formal proposal for Lucy's hand? Perhaps I should tell her I saw you after all. And how you poured out your heart to me about your fondest desires." Anne smiled.

"Now you really are teasing me," he protested.

"I'll own to that." She laughed. "Are you that eager for her?"

"I'd not come traipsing by two or three times a week if I was merely entertaining myself, Anne. Let me try to explain." He began, trying to form the words carefully so he would not be misunderstood. "At first, on Antigua, I thought Lucy was the most beautiful girl I had ever seen, and the sweetest. But at the time, she was only a girl, my admiral's niece. I had no idea if I had a future in the Navy, much less what would happen to me when the war ended. I had a small annuity from my father, but no hopes for anything else. Lately though, there is a larger annuity from my grandmother, and an inheritance. Mostly her personal goods and paraphernalia. And I've prize-money coming due when I go on half-pay, so I can now offer something other than 'cream-pot love.' Never even thought I could really court Lucy and be taken seriously before, though we were allowed to correspond. I don't know what will satisfy the Beaumans, but I am willing to try my hand, even if the war isn't over yet. Maybe my timing is bad, but we may sail soon, and God knows when *Shrike* puts back into Kingston."

"Allow me to play the Devil's Advocate for you," Anne offered. "If you do not mind me prying, what is your estate?"

"Near on twenty-five hundred pounds in prize-money," he said, adding in his hoard of stolen guineas. "Twice that in inheritance, and two hundred pounds a year. Not a stick of land or rents, though, but . . ."

"Godamercy!" Anne laughed, throwing back her head. "Even if a girl brought nothing but her linens, you're a prime catch, Alan. For half a tick, I'd be interested myself, were I not already settled."

Don't say tempting things like that, he thought quickly.

"So I do stand a chance?" Alan asked. "I've not been too abrupt so far, have I? Do they doubt my feelings for her, or think me too poor to pay serious court to her?"

"Well, I would say you stand as good a chance as any, more so than most of the local lads," Anne told him. "I know they were concerned when they brought Lucy back from Antigua that you had no lands or inheritance. Yet you had fought a duel for her honor, and Uncle Onsley and Auntie Maude spoke well of you, both professionally and for your personal qualities."

"Thank God for that."

"Compared to some of the island boys of good family, though, her prospects would be better with one of them," Anne cautioned. "You must know there are many who've squired her. You compare more polished, more refined a gentleman to them. Educations and manners in the Indies can't match a Home-raised young man. But."

"Yes?" Alan almost groaned at that qualifying "but."

In sympathy for his cause, perhaps, or to calm his fears, she laid a cool hand on his wrist and let it linger. "You must know that her parents are just as interested in a suitor who brings profitable connections. Plantations, new opportunities for trade. Money to put into ships and cargoes, or places to raise new capital. 'Tis a curse of our Society that even now, after years of seeing the wretched results of marriage formed on pecuniary interests instead of worry about a young woman's eventual happiness, parents still follow their own desires. They may say they are looking out for Lucy's happiness and security, and certainly I am sure they shall, when the time comes, but you must know the Beaumans," she pressed, a slight sadness coming to her voice and her huge dark eyes. "It is just as easy to find contentment and a good life with a man more endowed with the means to security. To them, that may mean someone of their own station, even someone older and more settled in his affairs, as you should well know."

"I see." Alan nodded. Betty Hillwood had not put him in the most jovial mood he had ever experienced, and he wasn't exactly cherry-merry at this new information, either. "It's changing back in England, you know. As long as the suitor has stability, they seem to let the daughters have more free will."

"Would that was always so!" Anne exclaimed, sharp enough to make the nodding Frog proprietor glance up briefly, and she took hold of his wrist instead of merely resting her hand on it. "Wedding for love, all other things being equal, surely causes no more distress than marriages without it, and gives more reasons for sweet contentment later."

She seemed to speak from painful personal experience, but Alan was cautious enough to keep his rebellious trap shut.

"And finally," she said, seeming to wilt back into her chair and removing her hand to toy with the stem of her wine-glass, "there is your age, and Lucy's. They believe neither of you is old enough to know your own minds yet."

"Bloody hell!" Alan spat softly, too crestfallen to guard his choice of words. Was he truly wasting his time courting Lucy, and would be denied the joy of her company forever? Potential wealth be damned, he suddenly felt the need of someone sweet and young and unspoiled, someone even naive and in love with the world, instead of trulls like Betty Hillwood and their weary cynicism.

"And when, pray, do they think we should be old enough to know our own minds?" Alan asked sourly. "And please them into the bargain?"

"It's a rare girl who weds before her mid-twenties, even here," Anne told him gently. "With enough wealth, that may not answer, but I'd think even the most ardent swain from the best family'd have to content himself with a wait of at least three more years, till Lucy's twenty-one."

"Whew."

"And father Beauman has been talking of retirement lately," Anne went on. "Of going back to England and leaving the family business to Hugh, with Floss' husband to help him. They're thinking that Lucy and Ledyard would benefit from a couple of years in London society to put some *ton* on their manners, and give them a better future."

"Oh bloody—" Alan sighed.

"Could you wait that long, Alan?"

"I'd hoped not to," he growled. "I mean, God knows what could happen in the meantime, half a world away, even if the war ends and I pay off at home."

"You might meet someone more pleasing to your nature in that time, Alan," Anne said. "Lucy could meet someone else, and I know how much the thought of that causes you pain. But, perhaps it is not meant to be. No matter how fond we desire something or someone, there is always a just reason that we do not attain our wishes. We must trust that things may turn out for the best, though the pangs of our heart blind us to admitting the truth of it."

"You know, Anne," Alan scoffed, "every time I've ever heard that line of reasoning, it's been from someone who *already* had what they wanted. Like telling the poor that eating regular's a bother, when you get right down to it."

He was surprised that Anne chuckled with amusement at his statement, and after a moment, he had to smile in spite of his feelings of doom and gloom.

"It was presumptuous of me to preach at you, I'll own," Anne said with a smile. "It was the way you said it that tickled me. You must know I meant no cruelty at your disappointment."

"Oh, I know," he said, patting the back of her hand without thinking, and was surprised for a second time when she did not draw back from his touch. "At least I can still laugh. I think. I'm sure we've both heard what other people think's best for us. Off in some future we'll find something or someone better than what we wish now. But Lord, it's a wrench! T'will make a better man of ya, me lad!"

She laughed once more at the pompous tone, which he had meant to mock his father's pronouncements.

"You sound like my own father," Anne confessed, still not trying to disengage his touch. "You not so much younger than I, and I can assure you it wasn't so long ago I suffered these self-same pangs, in the name of love, and heard the same platitudes."

"That is comfort, coming from you, anyway, Anne."

"Though I must admit that what I yearned for, and what I have now, are close to the same sort of pleasurable contentment," she finally said, and slowly drew her hand back to her lap.

"It's just that I don't believe I've ever been in love like this before, Anne," Alan went on, fiddling with his own glass and topping up their drinks from the sweaty pitcher of wine. "Come to think on it, I'm not sure I've ever been in love at all."

"So jaded, so young." She shook her head in mock sadness.

"I ran with a rather woolly crowd back in London. Love was just a game one played to learn how to do it at parties. We were more interested in the baser aspects, and if we fell in love, then it happened two or three times a week. And then, the Navy's terribly down on it."

"Dear me, perhaps I should warn the family after all. I wish it was women who could treat love so casually and prosper."

"I've become a *much* more responsible person since joining the Navy, mind," Alan pointed out, with a grin.

"Oh, sailors always do turn saintly, do they not. Then tell me, pray, if you are so reformed, why would you associate with Betty Hillwood?"

"Ah. Eh?"

"Those were her lodgings I saw you leaving. Or do you know another party in that building?" Anne asked, not quite sternly, but not exactly amused, either. "That would not endear you to the Beaumans, should they learn of it. Not from me, Alan, surely. But perhaps you should consider reform, if you wish Lucy's hand."

Good Christ, she's got me by the short and curlies! he thought wildly. Had she led him on with all the hand-holding, to see if he was going to rise to her bait? Had the Beaumans put her on him to smoke him out, and had he blown the gaff to the bloody horizon?

When in doubt, lie like blazes, he decided.

"I made her acquaintance a year ago," Alan replied, trying to toss it off lightly. "And she was at your father-in-law's party. She invited me to tea, with the hint that some shore lodgings could be obtained cheaply between voyages. But she really is the most vindictive person I ever did see. And damme, but I was the only guest at what I thought was to be a tea. Frankly, she more than hinted at some fondness she said she'd developed for me. Not my sort, really. I heard more scandal in half an hour than I'd heard in London in a month."

"It sounds innocent enough," Anne commented with a skeptical cast to her features.

"I have already admitted to you that I'm no calf's-head in relations with the ladies, but I doubt a bosun's mate'd be that desperate," he told her with what he hoped was a disarming grin of rough honesty. "If I would have consort to answer brute nature, I'd do better than Mrs. Hillwood, surely. Excuse me if I distress you with my choice of words, Anne, but I'd like you to understand me plain."

"I am not shocked, Alan," she said finally, shaking her head. "You would have to speak much plainer to rival anything I've heard in what passes for genteel conversation in the Indies. I must tell you, I was pained to recognize you leaving her gate. I would not like to think that your talk of true love and your eagerness to pay court to Lucy was a fraud, based on mercenary designs on the Beauman guineas."

This mort reads me like an open book! he thought.

"As you said yourself, one must always consider the family as well as the young lady," Alan said, scooting his chair up closer to the table for more intimacy for his confession. "I have no lands, no rents, and I'd be a fool to think Lucy and I could live on moonbeams. But with Lucy's portion, and my inheritance, the land could come, and I can't deny that the thought of what is necessary to keep her in her proper station hasn't crossed my mind. I don't want to sound harsh, but reality has a way of being harsh. I'd not even persist if I had no hopes of providing for her. And you mustn't doubt the depth of feeling I hold for Lucy!"

"I love her dearly as well," Anne relented. "So you must see my concern that she isn't fooled and her heart broken by someone who cares more for her dowry than her feelings. No, I don't doubt your affection for her, and I'm sure she has high regard for you as well, though it will be years before she may realize ... I just don't want to see her hurt, that's all, Alan. Nor would I wish to see you hurt."

"So you are saying I should not aspire to too much too soon?" Alan asked, frankly puzzled by her statement, and her sad look. "Or is there something else I should know? A serious rival?"

"Just that you should learn to be patient," Anne said with an expression that was close to misery, and their hands found each other again in unspoken sympathy, and this time her fingers wrapped around his firmly. "And don't close yourself off from all the other young ladies you may encounter in the time you have to wait. I don't say you should behave without license, but you have time to be sure of your feelings and your desires before committing yourself. Once wed, it's not a thing one may change. If one makes a mistake, one has to make the best of it, even if it's sometimes unpleasant."

He gave her fingers a squeeze in commiseration, and she responded with a firm grip on his. "I'm sorry you didn't get what you wanted, or what you thought you'd have, Anne."

"What?" she snapped, almost jerking free of him. "Certainly not!"

"You sounded so bitter before. I thought you spoke from experience," he told her softly. She was trying to tell him something, and he didn't know quite what she meant; a warning that he was wasting his time with Lucy for some unknown reason, and telling him to spare himself some future pain? That he would never be truly considered for Lucy's hand? Whatever it was, he was grateful to her for trying to express herself. And he felt a flash of sympathy for her, married to Hugh Beauman, who had not been her true choice, it seemed, if he read her hints correctly. And then she had found comfort with that Captain McIntyre, or so Mrs. Hillwood said. Had she been ready to run off and leave Hugh Beauman for him before he died? She was a proper lady, not given to aimless amours for the sake of amusement or quick gratification, a woman with two children to think about, and a place in society she would lose. She must have been deeply in love, he decided.

"Not bitter, Alan," she finally said after a long silence. "I am content. I'm sorry if I gave you a wrong impression. I thank you for your kind intentions, but they aren't necessary, though I think more of you now for saying what you did. There's more to you than I first thought. The girl who gets you shall be lucky, if she knows how to keep you interested."

"The right girl wouldn't have much trouble, if I let my heart rule, instead of my brain. Too much pondering is bad for you."

"And too little, dear sir, is just as bad." She grinned quickly. "Now, I'm sure your captain has need of your talents, and I must be on my way home. And when next I see Lucy, I shall praise you to the skies, if you are certain in your affections."

"Praise away!" Alan laughed and rose to dig into his coin purse for the reckoning. "With such an ally, how could I worry? If you will keep me current with what the Beaumans think of me."

"I shall," she promised. "And should you wish to discuss the progress of your suit with someone who truly likes you, you have but to drop me a note, and I shall make time for you. Feel free to call on me at any time should you have need."

He walked her out to her carriage and handed her in.

It was only after he was ensconced in "The Grapes" near the cold fireplace with a pint mug of beer at his lips that he thought again about what implications Anne Beauman had left unsaid. Surely, Lucy was daft about him. But what had she meant by describing Lucy's feelings as only "high regard"? Anne had warned him off Betty Hillwood, but had left the barn door wide open should he find someone else to dally with, as long as his intentions were sure, had practically shoved him into sampling what the wide world had to offer before he made his final choice and gave up his freedom.

Oh, surely not, Alan thought. She couldn't be suggesting that she and I . . . Lewrie, you're cunt-struck! If they smile at you, you want to put the leg over right then—it don't signify they want you. Best put that thought out of your lust-maddened little mind. Let's not try to bull every bit of mutton in the entire Christian world! Besides being related to Lucy, Anne's a real lady, no matter how unhappy her marriage is.

If ladies were willing, Alan Lewrie would be the first in line to alleviate their unhappiness. He had almost cut his milk-teeth on the ones who cast about for comfort and pleasure, but to work at seducing a properly respectable woman who had no mutual wish to initiate an affair had always struck him as a caddish deceit. Damnit all, he thought, I've *some* scruples, don't I? (Hell, maybe I really do, after all.) Why ruin a lady's reputation, and get an angry husband chasing me with pistol or sword, when there's battalions of 'em trailing their colors, just waiting for a rake like me to give 'em the eye? Not Anne—she's not one to give anyone a tumble or two and then walk away. Nor is Lucy, bless her. Right, I've had my fun for now. Let's do up our breeches and keep 'em done up, Lewrie lad. No more Betty Hillwood, no thoughts of Anne. Concentrate on Lucy.

The decision made him feel more grown up, more in control of his urges and his choices in life, though he doubted he would remain a celibate, but that was a different matter. And as he finished his beer, he could congratulate himself that he was finally becoming an adult with a clearer idea of what he wanted in life.

Chapter 5

"Jesus Christ!" he breathed, as he read the note again. More to the point: notes. One from Lucy:

> *I noe nott wat Cusstoms are in yur circels back home in London, but imagin howe distressed I was to lern from a Sorse who shal remane name-less that a yung man I thaught werthy of my Love coud make sutch shameless and lood Advanses to my own ~~estima~~ vertuus Sister-in-law Anne!! I never herd the like of howe yu Carreed On with her in Publick to yur everlasting Shame and the Ruenashun of her Good Name!*
>
> *Mine eys are nowe opend to wat sort of Corinthian yu reely are, and I must say, it braks my Hart to think I wuns ~~consi~~ thaught we wood one day be ~~congoy~~ Mareed!*

There was much more in the same vein (some of it indecipherable, of course), suitably tear-stained, but the meat of the missive was that she never wanted to see or hear from him again, and would be sorry when brother Hugh put him in the cold ground for dallying with his wife.

"But I didn't *do* anything!" Alan ranted in the semi-privacy of his cabin. "God Almighty, for the first time in my life, I'm *almost* innocent!"

To make matters worse, there was also a note from Hugh Beauman, advising Alan that if he did not relish dying on the point of his sword, he should make himself available as soon as possible to explain himself and the report of his conduct towards a happily married woman of distinction. Mr. Beauman, Sr., had put in his own post-script denying him any more welcome at his home, or any further contact with any member of his family, until the matter had been cleared up one way or another.

And I've been so bloody . . . good lately! he thought sadly as he let that collection of epistolary misery fall to the bunk from almost nerveless fingers. He had stayed aboard ship for the last week, with no more trips to Betty Hillwood's, and had answered her written invitations with pleas of duty. He had gone up to Lucy's and played the virtuous young swain, listening to Lucy and Floss butcher music on last year's harpsichord, which the tropic damp and the termites had soured even before their untalented fingers got hold of it. He had drunk innumerable gallons of tea and simpered politely at the social chin-wagging. He had acted properly respectful to everyone that called, especially Anne Beauman when she and her husband had been there, too.

"Damn, damn, damn!" he moaned. "Now, what do I do?"

He needed to think hard, and the stuffy cabin below decks was not conducive to logic. He threw on his coat and hat and stepped out into the wardroom, where several of the others were lazing about.

"Summat troublin' ye, Mister Lewrie, sir?" Caldwell asked him with a sly smile as he looked up from one of his charts he was updating, and Walsham the Marine lieutenant gave him a half-hidden smirk.

"Nothing particularly, Mister Caldwell."

"Nothing a fellow of so much dash may not solve," Walsham said with a titter.

"Damn your eyes, sir!" Alan spat. "How come you by that?"

"Nothing, sir." Walsham sobered, or tried to. "Only that I hear you've cut a dashing figure ashore lately. Some poor girl with a 'Jack-in-the-box'? Well, twenty guineas'll take care of it."

"I'd tread wary, Walsham," Alan snarled, leaning over the table to face him. "You might be slandering someone dear to me with your feeble japes, and I'll not stand for it."

Before Walsham could re-raise his fallen jaw, Alan spun

about and trotted up the accommodation ladder to the gun deck, then up to the gangways where he could pace furiously. William Pitt hissed at him as he stamped around the fo'c'sle belfry.

"Get out of my sight, you worthless little hair-ball!" Alan roared, and Pitt laid back his ears, shrank away and ran forward, while the crew on watch sprang to whatever duties they were performing lazily a moment before.

"Mister Lewrie, sir?" the quartermaster's mate asked, keeping back just in case the first lieutenant exploded at him for interrupting.

"What?" he barked, stomping to a stop.

" 'Is note come h'aboard fer ya, sir," the man whispered in terror of his possible wrath, offering another one of those damned letters.

"Bloody hell, another one?" Alan growled, snatching it from him and raising a finger to the brim of his cocked hat in rough salute so the man could shrink away.

This one was from Betty Hillwood.

That's right, pile it on, why don't you? Alan thought, casting his eyes towards heaven. My God, things could not possibly get much worse, could they. Wonder what the old mort wants?

After opening it, Alan discovered that yes, indeed, things could get worse. A small whimper of pain escaped him as he read it.

You must come ashore and meet me or suffer such dire consequences as you may not imagine to your reputation and your hopes for surviving the troubles you are in. If you do not confront me by sundown today, I shall be forced to tell all.

"Sufferin' shit!" he hissed. "Now what?"

"What's all this about?" Alan demanded after he had gotten his captain's leave to absent himself and had gone to Betty's lodgings.

"You've been a fool, Alan dear," Betty Hillwood told him with a cool air. For once, she was properly dressed, fit for genteel company, and had the tea service on the breakfast table for them.

"Oh, I'll grant you that," he fumed, declining her offer of tea and heading for the sideboard for a glass of wine. "But I did nothing with Anne Beauman. It was totally innocent!"

"I was not speaking of any troubles you are in with the

Beauman family." Betty frowned. "I am talking of the trouble you are in with me!"

"Look Betty . . . Mrs. Hillwood." He fumbled. "We had a lot of pleasure, but . . ."

"You beg off seeing me, yet you continue to court that simpering fool, that mere chit of a girl Lucy Beauman," she intoned icily.

"Anne Beauman saw me leaving your apartments, that's why I didn't come back," Alan exclaimed. "She threatened to tell the Beaumans, out of concern for her younger sister-in-law."

"You refused my offer of companionship and support, Alan, no matter the circumstances," she drilled home archly. "No one spurns me. Alan. No one."

"Surely, you see that it's impossible," Alan stated, aghast at her attitude. "And I was kept aboard by duties. The Navy don't let me come and go as I please!"

"Ah, but the Navy allows you time enough ashore to woo your little Lucy, does it not? So don't lie about having no time for me. It won't answer."

"But Anne will tell the Beaumans. About us."

"Yes, she will, if she has any sense." Betty chuckled. "What better way to dispel the gossip that you squired her about town and practically pawed her at the Frenchman's."

"But I didn't, damn you!" he snapped.

"Oh, I am sure you did nothing so crude." Betty laughed. "That's not your style, dear boy. But what people bruit about as truth and what is real are totally foreign to each other. Our boresome little circle has a juicy new scandal to twitter about, and I'm sure they'll work it to death before they're through."

"I can explain everything," he insisted, feeling cornered but game. "And I can't believe Anne would throw me to the wolves. It isn't her style, either."

"In some ways, you are so innocent," she cooed. "But either way, you are finished with the Beaumans. No more hopes of a profitable match with that simple young tit, even if you could explain everything."

"My God, you're jealous!" he burst out in sudden understanding. "Did you have anything to do with this rumor getting started?"

"Not I, Alan. You did that yourself, you and Anne. With more common sense and discretion, you would not have gone into the shop with her," Mrs. Hillwood explained. "One does not appear so publicly with a married woman. You should have gone on to the *restaurant* and waited for her, or found a more private place to do your talking. Perhaps gone for a carriage ride, which would have appeared unremarkable."

"You're jealous of Lucy, aren't you!" he reiterated.

"Not at all," she replied lazily. "I would never have denied you such a hopeless pursuit, as long as we could continue our pleasurable couplings. With proper discretion, of course. You must have known it was hopeless from the start. Impressive you may be, but your purse isn't deep enough to suit the Beaumans' idea of a suitable mate for their daughter. I'd suspect *them* of starting the rumor."

"The hell they would!" Alan ranted. "It hurts them just as much as it does me. Far easier on everybody to make you and me public."

"For all I know, we probably already are," Betty informed him breezily. "Now do sit down and have some tea with me. And then we shall go to my chamber for something more fun."

"Good God, I've got a daddy and a husband sharpening their swords for a crack at me, and you want to get diddled?" he complained.

"It will come out alright, Alan, sit down. Just as easily as one rumor can get started, I and my friends can start another that you did nothing. While I cannot get you back into the good graces of the Beauman family, I can save you from further harm." She patted the settee beside her. "You would not have Anne Beauman suffer because you did not take my advice, would you? And how may I whisper what you need to do if you do not sit down here and let me get on with it?"

"Sorry, but I intend to go see Hugh Beauman and Mister Beauman and get this straightened out right now, while I have shore leave," he replied heatedly, setting down his glass and tugging his waist-coat straight.

"And do you also intend to continue refusing me?" she asked.

"I don't see how it would be possible," he told her. "And yes, I did consider your kind offer. I'm really flattered and grateful you find me that attractive, Mrs. Hillwood, but I must decline. I must be my own man, d'ye see."

"I am sorry you feel that way, Alan, and so shall you be. Very sorry, indeed." She frowned, setting down her cup. "I shall give you one chance to reconsider, after I have told you something else to help you make up your mind."

"And what, pray, could that be?" he snapped, eager to be

away, and a trifle afraid of what she might come up with. "You cannot force people to shower their affections."

"As you said, we are probably an item of gossip, Alan, but as long as we maintain a certain decorum, there's no problem. Everyone knows about my marriage, and what two estranged people do, two people with money and high position, is their own business."

"So?" he sneered, getting impatient to leave.

"But, if a certain upstart young naval officer, who has already caused a storm of comment by his brash lust," she narrated with relish, "was to write a note to a lady of breeding and position, another lady at the same time, expressing how much he would like to couple with that lady, in graphic detail and language even uncultured men would flinch from, then how much more trouble do you think he could get into?"

"What the hell are you talking about?"

"Last year, before you sailed away to glory, you left me a note, Alan. Do you remember it?" She smiled in victory.

"Oh, Christ." Yes, he did remember it. She had finally gone off into gin-induced slumber, and he had left her a letter on her pillow, thanking her for bedding him, and hoping to repeat the experience the next time he was in port. And, to match her own lusty vocabulary, he had phrased the contents in pure bosun's mate Billingsgate, of good, well-known English words of mostly four letters in reference to her body, his body, what was done with them, and certain favorite variations in technique or novelty he would like to perform again.

"Let me get this straight. If I walk out of here without giving you what amounts to permanent possession of my prick, you'll hold that note over my head?"

"Exactly."

"You silly bitch, what would people say about you if it got to be common knowledge? You'd be cutting your own throat! Go ahead!"

"I might remind you it's undated, Alan. If I say I received it just yesterday, then it has nothing to say about my reputation, but everything to say about *yours*."

"You wouldn't!"

"And while my poor husband couldn't care less if I open myself to every man and boy in Kingston, he could not ignore such an insult to the *honor* of his wife," she went on remorselessly with a pleased smile at her cleverness. "Discreet fucking is no fucking at all, but importunate addresses from a scandal-ridden

Corinthian such as you would be more than he could stand. It would be a killing offense. While I may play the shocked matron. It may even appear that I spurned *you*, and you wrote that note in desperate want of me, to convince me to bed you. In that instance, my repute could work for me. While I have been known to succumb to charming gentlemen, I most certainly do not have to entertain foul-mouthed gutter-snipes."

"You really don't care what I say, do you?" Alan muttered, in shaky awe of just how low she could go. "If I give in, you force me to stay with you, and destroy my chances with Lucy Beauman. If I refuse, I still am denied Lucy, and you get your revenge. Either way, it's not that you want me so much, as you don't want me to dismiss you before you're ready. I see your game. You don't want to be jilted for somebody younger and prettier. My God, do you really think you'd make me perform like a trained terrier? Roll over, boy. Good boy, here's a treat. Cock-stand, boy, big 'un!"

"So what is your answer, sir? Stay and survive this *contretemps*?" she demanded evenly. "Or go and be destroyed utterly. Either way, you may forget any arrangement with Lucy Beauman. I do not mean to ruin you. And as you may remember, I can be forgiving and sweet to you. Face facts and stay, Alan dear. And I shall treat this as just a little domestic argument that occurs between lovers."

"Either way, as you put it, I'm looking at a duel. Hugh Beauman or your sodomite of a husband." Alan sighed. "All to assure yourself of some energetic sex? To salve your pride?"

"Would you deny me my pride?" She laughed, thinking her victory complete as she watched him vacillate, almost deflate with resignation. "Stay with me and answer my desires, and you'll be safe from further scandal. And I shall reward you with all the fondness of a satisfied lover. I shall dote on your every whim. And spare you the necessity of a duel, if you fear such."

He was indeed halfway to giving in to her will, of taking the most logical and safest course, reminding himself that she *was* an impressive and pleasurable ride; it wasn't as if he would have to get re-enthused about mounting her, even with a gun to his head. He had blown away any hopes of marrying Lucy Beauman now or in the future, so what was the difference. Yet in his weakest moment, she struck sparks on the flinty core of his stubbornness with her comment that questioned his courage. By God, no one did that and lived to tell of it!

"Damn you to Hell for that!" he spat. "You can't buy me like a joint of beef, and you can't threaten me. Bring your husband on and I'll chop him to flinders! If he wants to blaze, I'll put a pistol ball right through him! If that makes you a deliriously happy widow into the bargain, then be damned to you!"

"You shall regret this," she rasped, her face paling. "I thought you were a young man of my own tastes, grown beyond the petty strictures of our hypocritical society. But I now see you're just another *common* sort. A secret hymn-singer with no courage to live his own life."

"Better that than a draggled whore who has to hire men to top her." He grinned, finished his wine and flung the glass across the room to shatter on the stuccoed wall. "Damme, have I ruined the set? A pity, ain't it. Bye, love."

On his way to Hugh Beauman's town house, he bought a light gutta-percha cane, little thicker than his index finger. When the servant announced him, Anne came running out into the front hall.

"Hugh is not here, Alan. And you should not be," she warned.

"Where is he, then?" Alan asked. "I have things to discuss with him."

"He went to father Beauman's. Oh, surely, you won't fight him! He's ready to kill you! Do anything but fight him."

"When he asks, tell him this. You took the risk to your repute to warn me off Betty Hillwood, do you understand?" Alan told her. "You knew, you would have sent me a letter, but you saw me in town and took the risk. There is nothing between us and you touched my hand once."

"He would not believe me," she almost wailed, sure that blood would be spilled before the day was out.

"Blame it all on Betty Hillwood, remember that. She started the rumor, her or her friends, to get even with me."

"He will not speak to me, so how may I tell him anything?"

"Because of Captain McIntyre?" Alan asked.

"How . . . Oh God."

"I'll not see you hurt any more, Anne," he promised. "I've most like lost any chance with Lucy, but I'll get you out of this. Remember what I said."

"Lieutenant Alan Lewrie, sirs," the butler announced, and Alan stalked past him to confront Hugh Beauman and his father, both of whom looked shocked that he would even dare show his face to them. But after they got over their shock, their angry expressions prophecied a hanging.

"There, sir," Alan said, flinging the gutta-percha walking stick to the parqueted floor at Hugh Beauman's feet. "If you feel the need to use that on me, feel free. Should you wish it occur in the main plaza, we may go there, and I shall be completely at your disposal. I shall not defend myself."

His boldness disarmed them, as he thought it might, allowing him to present his case before they dredged their thoughts back into order.

"Mister Beauman, Master Hugh, I have been a complete, callow fool, and I humbly beg your forgiveness for any taint of scandal that might have touched your family. But I assure you as God's my witness Mistress Anne Beauman is completely blameless. If you will indulge me?"

"Um, yes, little privacy, what?" Beauman, Sr., stammered, waving his hand towards a small parlor or study off the main hall. Once the doors were shut, Alan took the offensive once more.

"I would take a public whipping to settle this if that is what it takes," he repeated.

"You squired my wife about the town, sir," Hugh began, working up his anger once more, now that they were in private. "You were seen fondling her, sir. What manner of man would expose a proper lady to that, dragging her into a public-house, sir?"

"Because I needed warning, sir, and she took the risk to her reputation to repair a greater risk to the Beauman family reputation. You should be thanking her, as I do."

"Warnin'?" the older man scoffed. "About what?"

"About Betty Hillwood, sir," Alan replied. "That's what I was a fool about. I was visiting her, to work off the humors of the blood."

"Ah," Mr. Beauman coughed. "I see. You an' . . . at clicket, eh?"

"Like foxes, sir," Alan admitted with a worldly smile. "Better her than a public-house whore—less chance of the pox."

There was a chance they would understand; the Beaumans were an earthy lot. From what he had heard of them, they could empathize.

"Being in the company of such a beautiful young lady as your Lucy raised my humors to the boiling point, and I thought it best to release that tension, sirs. And if my suit was to be a long one—and you note I use the past tense, sirs, since my foolish behavior has raised such a tempest I doubt you could entertain my hopes further—I feared the frustration would cause me to do something untoward."

"Damme, you're a bold 'un!" Mr. Beauman gaped. "You sport with another woman to avoid rapin' my daughter if your ... bloody humors ... get outa hand, and I suppose you think we should be thankin' ya?"

It was the longest and most complete sentence Mr. Beauman had ever uttered, and it stopped Alan cold in his tracks for a moment.

"What man, faced with a long courtship of a sweet and proper young lady, could do otherwise, sir, and retain his sanity?" Alan asked them. "In your own courting days, Mister Beauman, was there no release for you? Did not the long delay of hoped for satisfaction drive you to distraction?"

"Well, there was a tavern wench'r two . . ." the older man began to maunder.

"Father, that's not the bloody point! He's ruined Anne's good name, and I want satisfaction," Hugh barked, bringing them back to the meat of the matter.

"But Mrs. Hillwood *is* the point, sir," Alan doggedly went on. "Who do you think started the rumor in the first place? Her and her friend Mrs. Howard, sending their servants to peep and pry and report back with gossip to liven their lives, or give them an advantage. I met Anne as I was leaving Mrs. Hillwood's. She would have warned me off with a letter, but she took the risk to accost me, then and there. I rode in her carriage down to the dress-maker's and went inside with her. I stood by the door, feeling like a damned fool to even be in the place. Not a word, not a gesture of anything improper occurred, sir. We then went for something cool to drink to revive her as she was wilting in the heat, and to find a place where she could impart her timely warning that I should best stop visiting the woman, not only for the good of the Beauman family name, but for mine own. To stress how important it was, as she spoke of her fondness for Lucy and the Beauman family, she touched my wrist once. And as I poured out my own problem with Mrs. Hillwood, I admit to taking her hand and beseeching her what to do about the mess I had made. That is all that passed between us, Master Hugh. I did not think that an establishment so seemingly refined as the Frenchman's ... what you may call it ... a *restaurant* ... would be looked upon as a public place. Back in London, it has become the custom that ladies may frequent eating establishments, as long as they do not contain rooms to let. All the quality do so, and I didn't know it was any different here on Jamaica."

When in doubt, trot out the aristocracy as an example, he told himself. No one wants to appear out of the latest fashion.

"You swear on your honor?" Hugh Beauman demanded, unready to relent.

"For a gentleman to *say* it is to swear to its truth, sir," Alan shot back, a little high-handed at the slight of his honor, though he sometimes doubted if he truly had any to slight or get huffy about. "If you demand more, then I swear on my honor as an English gentleman and as a commission Sea Officer that events happened as I said."

"What problem with Betty . . . Mrs. Hillwood, sir?" the older man asked.

Thank bloody Christ for you, Alan though gratefully. "The lady became a bother, Mister Beauman. She took a greater fancy to me than I thought was good. She gave me this chain and fob, and promised more of the same, if I became her kept man and topped her regular. When I told her no, she vowed to get even, no matter who got hurt. If not by this rumor she spread about me and Anne, then by another means, a letter I was foolish enough to write her."

"What sort o' letter?" Mr. Beauman asked, fetching out a squat brandy decanter and beginning to pour himself a drink.

"A rather risqué . . . no, I don't think risqué does it justice. Pornographic, would be more like, sir," Alan confessed, putting on his best shame-face and hoping they would eat this up like plum duff. "She dictated it, I wrote it. As a game, you see. Between bouts."

"Ah?"

"In her bed, sir."

"Aha!"

"With her belly for a writing desk, sir," Alan finished with a shrug of the truly sheepishly guilty, a gesture he had practically taken patent on in his school days.

"God's teeth!" Mr. Beauman, Sr., exclaimed, settling down into a chair with a look of perplexity creasing his heavy features. "With her belly . . . *on* her belly, sir? Well, stap me! Don't see how it can be done, damme if I can. 'Course, I never tried *writin'* down there."

"It's a rather firm belly, sir," Alan commented.

"Aye, that'd help, I suppose," the man nodded, beginning to grin slightly at the mental picture.

"Father, for God's sake!" Hugh exploded. "Whatever the reasons, no matter how innocent they were, people have taken a tar-brush to our family's good name and reputation, our social standing!"

"Start some gossip of your own, sir," Alan suggested.

"Damn you, sir!" Hugh Beauman snarled. "We'll decide what's best for this family, not you. You've done enough."

"And I would be willing to do anything to assist you, sir."

"What sort o' rumor?" the father asked, slopping back a large swig of brandy and waving the bottle at them in invitation, which Alan agreed to readily; he was dry as dust from nerves, and three men drinking together and consorting on how to solve something were not three men who would be trying to stick sharp objects into each other.

"It was Mrs. Hillwood's pride and vanity that brought this about when I rejected her offer," Alan said, taking a pew on the corner of a desk with glass in hand, though Hugh Beauman was still averse to showing him any leniency. "She didn't want me paying any attention to Lucy. I think the woman was jealous of anyone younger or prettier. Not so much that she was truly in love with me, but she disliked *losing*, d'ye see. And I don't think she cares much for the Beauman family in general, if you can believe the things she told me, trying to destroy my respect for the lot of you. Terrible things best left unsaid."

"Like what, sir?" Hugh required. "Speak out."

"She called you ignorant 'Chaw-Bacons' and 'Country-Harrys.' People with more money than style. She'd have me believe there's not a Christian among you, a one to be trusted. She blackened every name in the family with some back-stairs scandal. You, Hugh, Anne, Floss' husband . . . even Lucy. She intimated all your morals were nonexistent."

"Goddamn the bitch!" the father roared. "She said all that?"

"Not in one session, sir, but over the course of time."

The Beauman men looked righteously outraged, but a little queasy as well; they knew their own sins well enough, and knew that Betty Hillwood was probably privy to most of them.

"Show me claws, would ya, hedge-whore?" Mr. Beauman ranted. "I'll give ya claws right back. Blacken me children, will ya? I'll hurt ya where it hurts the most, by damn if I don't!"

"In her pride, sir," Alan prompted, feeling safe now from physical harm. "She wouldn't like people in her circle to know that she had a lover spurn her, or that she had to buy his affections and then threaten so much to get him back, no matter who got hurt. It may not matter to anyone about Mistress Anne—anyone would have done for her purpose to try and ruin me, d'ye see. Clearing Anne's good name is only incidental, too."

"It's not to me, damn your blood!" Hugh barked.

"If the gossip sounds like an attempt to clear Mistress Anne, it will fail, sir," Alan told him, familiar enough with what stuck in the mind in all the scandals he had chuckled over back in London. "It will ring false. But, if enough shit flies and sticks to Betty Hillwood, Anne becomes an innocent victim in contrast. A month from now, they'll still be chewing on *la* Hillwood's bones, and if they ever think of my part in the affair, or Mistress Anne's, it will be favorable. If the affair is handled properly, of course."

"Aye, t'would kill her soul, the crafty old witch!" Beauman, Sr., chortled with a cruel grin of anticipated pleasure at Betty's demise in Society. "Why, we'd skin her alive!"

"My God, you're too clever by half!" Hugh marveled, disgusted.

Alan didn't know quite how to answer that, so he kept silent for once. People with brains were usually mistrusted when they showed off.

"Perhaps it's best this happened after all, if only to spare us a son-in-law so scheming, father," Hugh added, smiling slightly in some form of satisfaction that he wasn't going to be related to anyone as "smarmy" as Alan Lewrie. "You must know that you have totally ruined your hopes of eventual marriage with Lucy, no matter how this comes out."

"I do realize that, sir," Alan nodded, suddenly sobered. "And I must say it is the greatest regret of my life, and hopefully shall be from this moment on. I truly love her, you see."

The frank admission shut them all up for a long moment, broken only by the sounds of brandy being slurped, as they all looked away and communed with their own thoughts, abashed by such a personal revelation usually left unspoken by English gentlemen, who would be the last men on the face of the earth to confess their love for anything other than horses, dogs or some institution larger than themselves.

"If there is some way you could convey to Lucy my regrets as to how this came about, and how I feel about her . . ." Alan whispered, going for the brandy decanter unbidden. "And to

Mistress Anne my regrets as well that she had to involve herself at such a risk. And my undying thanks, tell her."

Would they relent, he wondered with a final tug of hope? Was there some way he could still see Lucy in future, once this was all blown over? He had spoken the truth (mostly), and he had couched events in such a way that he did not appear a *total* rake-hell; a young and foolish buck, but not a complete wastrel.

"Aye, I'll tell her," Mr. Beauman intoned sadly. "'Twasn't all your fault, though ya did show bad judgement. Like Hugh says, fer the best, mayhap. Few years from now, who knows? Good lesson fer ya, what?"

"Aye, sir," Alan replied with a sad shudder of his own. "Well, I'd best be going then."

"Father," Hugh said as Alan finished his drink and picked up his hat from a side table, "if we mean to save our good name, we cannot send Mr. Lewrie away in shame."

"Hey?"

"At least escort him to the docks. Make a show of being fond of him, a public show. Otherwise it still looks like we have a reason to duel him, or whip him," Hugh went on, distaste curling his mouth at his own words. "Not that he's welcome here in future, but . . ."

"Best for Anne, aye. Best for us," Mr. Beauman concurred.

They rode in an open carriage, to outward appearances a dumb show of three gentlemen of like minds, cracking japes and laughing together in public before the startled eyes of the quality who had business about the town. They dined at the Frenchman's, shared some wine, and saw Alan into a boat out to his ship, waving goodbye chearly with bonhomie plastered on their phyzes like a painted chorus seeing off a hero in some drama. But it was very final sort of good-bye.

Alan gained the deck, took his salute, and went aft where the captain was lazing about under the quarterdeck awnings, slung in a net hammock of island manufacture, with one of the half-grown kittens in his lap.

"Come aboard to join, have you, Mister Lewrie?" Lilycrop asked with a droll expression as he walked up and saluted him.

"Sir?"

"We've seen so little of you," Lilycrop teased as he dandled a black-and-white tom-kitten. "Wasn't sure if you'd jumped ship or been transferred."

"Sorry, sir, but there were some . . . personal problems ashore."

"Woman trouble, I heard. Finished, is it?"

"Finished, sir. Yes, woman trouble. A devilish power of 'em."

"A day'r two of pushin' does for most of us, you know." Lilycrop smirked. "No need to make a meal of the doxies. Saves you from angry daddies an' husbands, too."

"Aye, sir, I shall remember that from now on."

"God knows, they're mostly only good for one thing, an' you may rent that," Lilycrop went on. "Give 'em guineas enough an' they'll be fond of you for as long as you want, then take your leave before they turn boresome. They've no conversation worth mentionin', so why go all cunt-struck by some mort who'll most like put horns on you the minute you're out of sight?"

"Surely not all women, sir," Alan sighed, about as deep into the Blue Devils as a young man could be over a girl.

"Aye, there may be a gem somewhere, but the likes of me never could afford 'em or run in the right circles to find 'em. No loss at this stage of the game. So you're back with us for a while? The delights of Kingston have lost their luster, I take it?"

"Aye, sir. I could use a few months at sea. God help me, I never thought I'd say this, but is there any way we could sail, sir? I stay out of trouble at sea, mostly." Alan groaned with a heartfelt ache of desire to escape into Duty, to lose his crushed hopes in a long spell of seamanship and possible action.

"Well, top up your wine cellars, Mister Lewrie!" Lilycrop said with a bright smile, rolling out of his hammock and handing Lewrie the kitten as he adjusted his uniform. "Admiral Sir Bloody Joshua Rowley remembered we're in his bloody squadron after all. Had you been around, and had an ear cocked like a real first officer, you'd've heard of it before. We have orders to head for Cuba, to harry coastal shippin'. Let us go aft and I'll show you the orders. Then you can indulge another form of lust, on our good King's enemies."

"Thank bloody Christ, sir."

"Don't forget to have the purser obtain a barrel of dried meat for the kitties, and you'll not forget the beach sand, hey?"

"Aye aye, sir."

III

"Dicantur mea rura ferum mare; nauta, caveto!
Rura, quibus diras indiximus, impia vota."

"Let my lands be called the Savage Sea;
beware, O Sailor!
Of lands, whereon we have pronounced
our curses, unholy prayers."

"Dirae"
—Virgil

Chapter 1

They spotted her at first light rounding Cabo Cruz, a fine ketch of what looked to be about eighty tons burthen. Lilycrop thought she was on passage from Santiago de Cuba to Cienfuegos, and had taken the pass outside the chain of islets and reefs of the Gulf of Guacanayabo, a safer voyage most of the time, but for this instance.

She was a little ahead of them, too far out to sea to scurry in-shore for safety, a little too far west to turn back for Santiago de Cuba. And with *Shrike*'s shallow draft, even shoal water would offer no safety from them.

"Hands to the braces, Mister Lewrie!" Lilycrop snapped. "Give us a point closer to the wind and we'll head-reach the bitch!"

"Aye aye, sir! Hands to the braces, ready to haul taut!"

Grunting and straining near to rupturing themselves, the hands flung themselves on the braces to angle the yards of the square-sails, the set of the fore-and-aft stays'ls, jibs and spanker to work the ship as close to the wind as she would bear, to race as close inshore of the enemy vessel as they could, denying her the chance to round up or tack once north of Cabo Cruz to shelter.

"Helm down a point, quartermaster," Lilycrop demanded. "Mister Caldwell, what say your charts?"

"Deep water all the way, sir," Caldwell finally announced, just before Lilycrop turned on him. "With this wind outa the east'nor'east, neither us or her'll make it into shoal water."

"Unless she tacks, sir," Alan cautioned.

"And if the bitch tacks, we'll be gunnel to gunnel with her before she can say 'Madre de Dios'!" the captain laughed.

Shrike was indeed the butcher bird, rapaciously hungry, and her prey displayed on thorns was Spanish coastal shipping.

201

There were so many ships, so little time, and Lilycrop seemed determined to make the most of any opportunity, very unlike the first image Alan had formed of him and his ambitions. Now the ship's log read like an adventure novel of ships pursued, ships taken as prize, or ships burned to the waterline to deny the enemy their use. Admittedly, the number burned greatly exceeded the number sent off in the general direction of Jamaica, but that was not their fault. The roads inland on Cuba, on the west coast of Spanish Florida, were abysmal, and everything went by sea, mostly in small locally built luggers, cutters, ketches and schooners, with only a rare brig, snow or hermaphrodite brig making an appearance.

Alan had expected a cruise with little excitement. But one lovely sunset evening, they had come across a merchant schooner off Cayo Blancos on the north coast, a small ship headed for Havana, and Lilycrop had run her down before full dark. She hadn't been much, but the captain had acted as if she were an annual treasure galleon, and the ease of the capture had fired his thirst for more. If his orders were to harry coastal shipping, then harry them Lilycrop would, but suddenly following orders could be profitable.

There were no despatches to run, no schedule to keep, and Lilycrop slowly had discovered the joys of an independent, roving commission for the first time in his long career of being held in check as a junior officer. In their first cruise of four months, extending their time at sea by living off their prizes' supplies, they had taken four decent ships, and burned nearly a score more. Small traders, fishing boats, anything afloat no matter how lowly had fallen victim to their guns, and the crews allowed to row ashore as their livelihoods burned like signal fusees.

Like Alan's first piratical cruise aboard *Desperate*, the only limiting factor was warm bodies to work the ship. Once enough men were told off as prize crews and sent away, *Shrike* had to return to port. It had happened once before, and now, only two months into their second cruise, it was about to happen again, if the ketch proved worthwhile.

Alan already had a revised watch and quarter bill in his coat pocket for just this eventuality, and his only concern at the moment was just how many extra hands the ketch would take from him.

"He's crackin' on more sail, damn his blood," Lilycrop noted.

"Don't think it'll do him much good, sir," Alan commented,

eyeing the enemy through his new telescope. "He's hoisting his stays'ls. That'll push him down off the wind more than if he'd stayed with the fore'n'aft sails. And push his bows down maybe a foot. That'll slow him down."

Minutes passed as the Spanish ketch, now trying to emulate some sort of square-rigger, held her slight advantage, though *Shrike* was making better way to windward.

"We're makin' too much heel, sir," Lilycrop spat, impatient to be upon their prize. "Not good with a flat run keel."

"Run out the starboard battery, sir," Alan suggested immediately, "and I'd take a reef in our main tops'l. We're canceling out the lift on the bows from the fore course and tops'l."

"Make it so, Mister Lewrie." Lilycrop nodded in agreement.

"Bosun, and mast captain! Lay up and trice out! First reef in the main tops'l! Mister Cox, run out the starboard battery!" Alan roared through his brass speaking trumpet, and he could not help feeling pleased with himself. When they anchored at Kingston the first time in early May, he was still uncomfortable and daunted by his lack of experience, but now by mid-December 1782, such decisions had begun to come naturally to him, based on a growing wealth of knowledge about seamanship, and how *Shrike* reacted in particular. Lilycrop occasionally pinned his ears back for over-reaching to keep him humble, to remind him he did not yet know it all, but those admonitions were rarer.

Once adjusted properly, *Shrike* settled down on her keel a few more degrees and made the most of her longer hull form. The Spanish ketch grew in size, bringing all her hull up over the horizon as the Gulf of Guacanayabo opened out before them. Try as she might, she did not have the sail power or the length of hull to make enough speed to escape.

"Ahoy the deck, thar!" came a call from the lookout aloft. "Sail, three points off the starboard bow!"

"Rossyngton, get aloft and spy him out," Alan barked, and the well turned out midshipman paused for a moment as he considered how dirty his white waist-coat, slop trousers and shirt were going to get from the tar and slush of the standing rigging.

"Today, Goddamn you!" Lilycrop howled.

Rossyngton was off like a shot, pausing only long enough to take a telescope with him as he scampered up the shrouds to the top and almost shinnied up to the cross-trees.

"Guarda Costa sloop, sir!" Rossyngton finally shouted down. "One-master!"

"Must have been on patrol out of Manzanillo, sir," Alan said, hanging from the shrouds himself for a better view. With his heavy glass, he could see a small ship, as Rossyngton described a single-masted sloop or cutter, with a large fore-and-aft gaff-rigged sail and one square-rigged tops'l above that, and a long jib-boom and bow-sprit that anchored three huge jibs. Even in the protected bay, she was hard at work off the wind, pitching noticeably.

"Fifty, sixty foot or so," Lilycrop speculated, leaning on the starboard quarterdeck bulwarks by Lewrie's feet with his own telescope. "Maybe two heavy guns forrud, nine or twelve-pounders, and little four-pounder trash abeam. That's why she's pitchin' like that."

"She'll interpose our course, sir, to save that ketch."

"Damned if she will!" Lilycrop chuckled. "Mister Lewrie, beat to Quarters. We'll take her on first, then have our prize."

Shrike did not run to a richer captain's private band replete with fifes and drums. Her single young black drummer rattled his sticks, first in a long roll, then broke into a jerky, cadenced beating of his own invention that sounded like a West Indies religious rite or revel.

"She'll try to fight us like a galley, Mister Lewrie," Lilycrop informed him once the ship was rigged for battle with all unnecessary items stowed below (and his precious cats ensconced with Gooch in the bread rooms). "Keep her bows aimed at us to let her heavier bow guns bear."

"We could fall off the wind, sir," Alan suggested, scanning the tactical set-up and trying to solve the puzzle of three ships, each on its own separate course and proceeding at different speeds. "We've room enough to windward of the chase now."

"No, she'd still get within range, or chase after us, and damme if I want my stern shot out," Lilycrop replied. "Stand on as we are, and give her broadsides close aboard. Mister Cox, I'll want three shots every two minutes at your hottest practice, double-shotted, mind!"

"Aye aye, sir!"

"On this course, the chase'll get inshore near Santa Cruz del Sur, Captain," Caldwell told them, waving a folded up chart at them. "There's a battery there, I'm told. About forty miles before we'd be in their range, though, sir."

"The bitch'll never make it," Lilycrop said confidently. And before a half-hour glass could be turned, the Spanish Guarda Costa sloop was within range of random shot, and her heavy bow chasers barked together. One shot moaned overhead and forward of the bows to raise a large feather of spray to leeward. The other ball smacked into the sea abeam of *Shrike*, but about a quarter-cable short, and skipped once but did not reach her.

"He'll go about now, or we'll leave him behind," Lilycrop said.

Shrike was racing nor'nor'west, with the sloop to her right side, about a mile east of her, and about half a mile ahead, bound on a course roughly west'sou'west. She did not have the speed to pass in front to rake *Shrike*, so she would have to turn soon on a parallel course and bring her guns to action down her larboard side.

"She's leaving it a bit late if she is," Alan observed as more minutes passed. The sloop's heavy fo'c'sle guns spoke again, this time raising splashes much closer, though once more without harm. Her bows were pitching too much for proper aim even as the range shortened.

It was a beautiful day for it, Alan noted with pleasure, unable to believe that the small sloop could be much of a menace. The sea was sparkling blue and green, azure near the eastern shore, and the hills around the small port of Niquero, and the mountains of the Sierra Maestras were a vivid, luscious green after the last heavy rains of the hurricane season, sweeping fluffy trails of cloud above them in a perfect blue sky.

"There!" Lilycrop pointed as the sloop finally foreshortened in a turn as she came almost abeam of *Shrike*'s jib boom, not half a mile away now. "Mister Cox, skin the bitch!"

"Aye, aye, sir!" Cox agreed joyfully. "As you bear ... fire!"

The small four-pounder chase gun yapped like a terrier, then the more substantial explosions of the six-pounders of the starboard battery pounded out. Caught in the act of wearing ship, controlling that huge fore-and-aft mains'l and those over-sized jibs, the broadside shook her like a shark's first bite as ball after ball hammered into her. The sloop seemed to tremble, then swung about quickly, almost pivoting on her bows as her mast, the tops'l yard, and the mains'l gaff came down in a cloud of wreckage, and the uncontrolled jibs billowed out to drag her bows back down-wind. For a second, she had heeled like a capsize.

"That's one way to gybe a ship!" Caldwell exulted.

"Bit rough on the inventory, though," Lilycrop chuckled in appreciation. "Well done, Mister Cox! Hit her again!"

They passed her at long musket-shot, about one hundred yards, as the sloop was tugged down to them bows on, and iron round-shot tore her to lace, flinging light scantlings into the air in a cloud, ripping her bow and fo'c'sle open.

"Luff up and hit her one last time, sir?" Alan asked, excited at how much damage they were doing.

"She's a dead 'un," Lilycrop scowled. "Let's get on to our prize. If we've a mind, we might come back for her later. She's not goin' anywhere but down-wind and out to sea, away from rescue."

"Mister Cox, stand easy!"

"'Bout another hour to catch yon ketch, Mister Caldwell?" Lilycrop surmised with a practiced eye.

"Hour and a bit, sir," Caldwell agreed.

"Secure from Quarters. Issue the rum and a cold dinner."

They did catch the ketch, nearly one hour later, prowling up to her starboard side with the advantage of the wind-gauge. One ball from the larboard battery settled the matter, splashing close abeam to ricochet into her upper-works and shatter a bulwark, raising a concerted howl of terror. The ketch lowered her colors and rounded up into the wind quickly, while the howling continued.

"Jesus, what's all that noise?" Alan wondered aloud as one of the boats was led around from being towed astern to the entry port.

"I suspect yon Dago is a slaver, Mister Lewrie," Lilycrop said sadly. "We're upwind where we can't smell her, but keep a tight hold on your dinner once you get inboard. Now, away the boardin' party before they change their feeble minds."

The winds were freshening, and the sea heaved a little more briskly as Alan sat down on a thwart in the cutter. The captain's cox'n got the boat's crew working at the oars, and within moments they were butting against the side of the ketch, and Alan was scrambling up the mizzen chains to swing over the low rail, glad to have pulled it off without getting soaked or drowned.

"Jesus!" He gagged once he was firmly on his feet, and the men from the boarding party were following him up onto the ketch's decks.

It stank like an abattoir, brassy with corruption, almost sweet like decomposing man-flesh, mingled with the odor of excrement and stale sweat, of foul bilges and rot. Most ships smelled to a certain extent, but he had never, aboard a prize or a well-found Royal Navy ship even after a desperate battle, smelled the like, and his stomach roiled in protest.

An officer walked up to him, a sullen brute in rumpled and

soiled breeches and shirt, legs exposed by lack of shoes or stockings. He began to rattle off a rapid burst of Spanish, which was definitely one of the world's languages that Alan lacked, and Alan waved him off, trying to shut him up.

"You the captain?" he asked when the man took a breath.

"Capitano, si." The man swept off a battered cocked hat small enough to fit a child, dripping though it was with gold lace and feathers, and introduced himself with a deep congé. "Capitano Manuel Antonio Lopez, Capitano de *Las Nuestra Señora de Compostela*."

"Lewrie," Alan said bluffly as an Englishman should. *"Shrike,"* he added, pointing back toward his ship. "Royal Navy. Your sword, sir."

All the man had to offer was a cutlass stuck into a sash, which Alan passed on to his man Cony. There was one passenger, a man of much more worth, by his clothing. He was tall and slim, partly Indian in his features, but adorned with a stiff waxed mustache. He, too, offered his sword, this one a slim smallsword awash in pearls and silver wire, damascened with gold around the hilt and guard. He was elegant, a dandy-prat in the height of Spanish fashion.

"Señor, I must talk to your captain," he began in passable English. "It shall be of great value to him."

"And what brings you aboard this voyage, sir?" Alan asked, fanning his face to push away the stinks.

"She carries my cargo, señor."

"Slaves?"

"Si, señor. Fifty prime blacks bought in Santo Domingo."

Alan took a look about the deck. The ketch (and he could not even begin to remember her name, much less pronounce it) would have been a well-found vessel, if she received a thorough cleaning. The rigging was thin as a purser's charity, but that could be set right. There were only four carriage guns, bronze or brass three-pounders—no value there. Most of her armament, he noted with surprise, consisted of swivels and bell-mouthed fowling pieces aimed down at her hatches and waist, evidently to control the slaves should they get loose.

"I must speak to your captain, sir. You are?"

"Lewrie, Lieutenant."

"Allow me to introduce myself, señor. I am Don Alonzo Victorio Garcia de Zaza y Turbide." The man rushed through a formal introduction. "I assure you, Teniente, it shall be most pleasing to your captain if I am allowed to speak to him."

"Pleasing how?" Alan asked, getting rapidly fed up with the over-elegant posturing of this stiff-necked *hidalgo*.

"To his profit, señor," the man beamed back with a sly smile.

"I think a well-found ketch and fifty prime blacks for resale in Kingston is profit enough, don't you?" Alan smirked.

"I do not care about the blacks, señor. The world is full of slaves," Don Miguel sneered. "Nor do I much care about this little ship. But if I go to Kingston, then I am prisoner, sí? And there is no profit for me in that. I ask, as a gentleman, as a knight of Spain, to be set ashore. I can pay well, señor. In gold," he added.

"By all means, Don Thingummy, talk to my captain. I'm sure he'll simply *adore* talking to you!" Alan laughed. "Cony!"

Alan sent the aristocrat, the ship's captain, and her small crew over to *Shrike* for safe-keeping, while he and the rest of the boarding party sorted the freed lines out and got a way on the ketch, headed out to sea, with *Shrike* following in her wake. He had half a dozen hands, half a dozen Marines, and a bosun's mate, plus his man Cony to keep order aboard. Once he got his people apportioned at duty stations, he led the rest to search the ship.

"Godamercy, sir," Cony gasped as they opened the hatch gratings.

Crammed in between bales and crates of cargo were fifty slaves, naked as the day they were born, chained together with ankle shackles into two rows on either side of the hold, their wrists also bound by cuffs and lighter chain. They were squatting or lying in their own filth that did not drain off into the bilges. They glared up at him angrily, some begging for water with cupping motions by their mouths, some rubbing their bellies for food and miming the motions of eating.

"Godamercy, sir!" Cony said again. "Hit's devilish the way them Dagoes treat people. We oughter feed 'em, sir. Give 'em water an' some air. 'Tain't Christian ta do otherwise, sir."

"Well, they don't look exactly glad to see us, Cony."

" 'Course they ain't sir!" Cony burst out. "I 'spect they thinks we're Dagoes, too, Mister Lewrie."

"Corporal?"

"Sir!"

"Fetch 'em up, one coffle at a time. Use those swivels and such if they get out of hand. Cony, break out a butt of water and see if there's some food about," Alan relented.

The slaves were fresh from Dahomey or some other port on

the Ivory Coast, for they cringed away from their liberators just as they had from their captors. They drank the water, ate the cold mush and stale bread as if it was manna from heaven, but stayed in a tight clutch of flesh away from the muskets of the Marines and sailors who kept an eye on them. Easy bantering from sympathetic English humors did nothing to reassure them, even if they could have understood the words.

"Murray, take charge of the deck," Alan told the bosun's mate, and went below to search the captain's quarters and those of the distinguished passenger, who was by now getting his ears roasted by Lieutenant Lilycrop for trying to bribe a Royal Navy officer.

He gathered up all the papers he could find, not able to read a word of them, hoping Lilycrop or one of the warrants had some Spanish for later scanning. The captain's quarters were spartan in the extreme, not from the usual sailor's suspicion of anyone given to too many airs and comforts as was rife in the Royal Navy, but from poverty, he assumed. Even the captain's wine cabinet could offer nothing better than a locally grown wine of dubious palate, and some fearsome rum. After one sip, he spat the mouthful on the canvas covered deck and put the bottle back in the rack.

Don Thingummy's cabins, though, were a different matter. Some attempt had been made to pack away valuables, for all the chests and trunks had been locked, and Alan was just about to search for a lever with which to pry the first of the locks and hasps off when the sound of gunfire erupted from the deck, forcing him to sprint back topsides.

"What the hell happened?" he demanded, sword in hand.

"This'un went for t' corpr'l's musket, sir." Murray panted from excitement or sudden exertion. "They wuz beginnin' t' smile'n all, sir, an' then, when we wuz gonna put 'em below once agin, this'n jumped us!"

One of the slaves lay stretched out and dead on the planks, bleeding like a spilled wine keg, another keened and rocked with agony after being shot in the shoulder; the others tried to draw back from the casualties to the full extent of their leg chains.

"Christ, what a muck-up!" Alan sighed, sheathing his sword. "Pop him over the side, then. Corporal, can you get the shackles undone? And see if anything can be done for the one wounded."

"Aye aye, sir."

"I saw some keys in the captain's quarters. Try there. And I also saw some rum. He might feel like a drop. Fetch that, too."

Cony knelt down next to the wounded slave and tried to staunch the flow of blood from the purple-plum entry wound, which was not bleeding all that badly. He gently pushed him down and rolled him a little so he could see the back, where the ball had exited high up.

"Shot clean through, sir," Cony said with a grin. "No ball in 'im ta fester, there's a blessin'. Easy now, bucko, lay easy. Rum's a'comin', cure for damn near ever'thin'. You'll be alright."

The corporal came back with a huge ring of keys and fiddled at the shackles until he found one that unlocked the dead man from the coffle. He then knelt at the feet of the wounded slave and undid his ankle shackles.

"Stap me, sir!" Cony wailed in disappointment. " 'E's dead!"

"Dead? Of that?" Alan asked, bewildered as the next man.

"Guns is magic, sir," Murray the bosun's mate said softly. "If'n 'e wuz island born an' used ta us'n, 'e'd a lived, but direck from 'is tribe not three month, if'n yer shot, yer killed, so 'e believed 'e wuz dead an' that's that."

"Jesus, they believe that?"

"Aye, sir. Ask Andrews, sir, 'e were a slavey," Murray insisted.

Andrews was one of their West Indian hands, signed aboard as a volunteer, an almost white-skinned Negro, like one of Hugh Beauman's favored bed-partners.

Alan turned to look at him, and Andrews shrank away, after glaring at Murray with alarm. Alan thought there was more to his sudden fear, so he crossed the deck to stand beside him and speak softly.

"Is it true they die so easily, Andrews?"

"Aye, sah. Dey b'lieve a witch can put a curse on 'em an' dey lays down an' dies of it. First dey see o' white men, dey learn about guns. Sometimes dey die o' just bein' shot *at*, sah. Just feel da bullet go pas' an' lay down an' die," Andrews informed him.

"Poor bastard."

"Aye, sah, poor bastard. All of 'em."

"You were a slave?"

"No *sah*, Mista Murray got it wrong, sah. Ah weren't no slave!"

"You're a freeborn volunteer. But you must have talked with slaves to know what you know," Alan pointed out.

"Freeborn volunteer, sah," Andrews insisted.

"But not a sailor, eh? Before?"

"I worked wit' my father, sah, fishin' sometimes."

Were you, indeed, Alan thought, skeptical of Andrews' claims. The man had written his name instead of making his mark when he signed aboard; Alan had offered the book to him himself. If he was not a runaway servant, then Alan was a Turk in a turban.

He was a well set-up young fellow, near an inch taller than Alan's five feet nine, his skin the color of creamed coffee, and his eyes clear instead of clouded. A former house-servant run off for his own reasons? Alan wondered. Whatever his background was, he wanted to keep it quiet.

"Well, you're the Navy's now, Andrews, whether you were a prince of Dahomey . . . or a runaway slave," Alan said softly, so the others would not hear, and Andrews' eyes pinched a bit at the last. "Don't worry over it. Prime hands are hard enough to find—we'll not be letting you go so easily."

"Aye, sir," Andrews replied, letting out a pent-up breath and relaxing a little.

"Mister Murray?"

"Aye, sir?"

"Andrews tells me he may be able to calm the slaves down a bit. Place him and Cony in charge of tending to them, if you please."

"Aye, sir."

Andrews gave him a short grin as he went below to talk some gibberish language to the slaves to calm their fears. Between him and Cony, whose simple farm-raised gentleness and caring were already evident, Alan was sure that he had made the right decision.

"Mister Murray?"

"Sir?" the bosun's mate said, coming to his side near the tiller.

"How did you know about what black slaves believe?" Alan began. "It's so incredible to me that people should die simply because they were shot at. He was barely hurt. That ball went in clean, maybe broke a bone, and exited high at the top of the shoulder."

"Served in the Indies a lot, sir," Murray told him. "Seen lots o' slaves turn up their toes fer a lot less, sir."

"I am grateful for your knowledge, Mister Murray. Never hurts to pick up a little lore from here and there, does it?" Alan cajoled.

"Nossir, hit sure don't, an' thankee fer sayin' so, sir." Murray almost preened at having gained favorable comment from his first officer.

"Well, with Cony and Andrews tending to them, they'll go quiet from now on. Oh, about Andrews. Do you *know* if he was a former slave?"

"Well, nossir, but hit's been my experience 'at mosta the West Indian 'ands is, sir," Murray said with a wink at the age-old practice.

"Good sailor, is he?"

"Nary a topman, sir, but 'e'll do fer most duties, an' good in a fight wif a cutlass, sir."

"Then we wouldn't want to get him into trouble by announcing he's a former slave. People might think he's a runaway, whether he is or not, and he might be tempted to run. And with nigh on a third of the hands West Indians, it might stir up resentments," Alan suggested.

"Aye, sir, least said, soonest mended."

"Thank you, Mister Murray, that'll do, I think."

Shrike put back in to Kingston a few days later, preceded by her prizes, the trading ketch *Nuestra Señora de Compostela*, and the Guarda Costa sloop *San Ildefonso*, which they had run across on their way seaward from the coast of Cuba. She had barely been repaired enough to hoist a jury-mast with her main boom serving as a vertical spar, and a tattered tops'l employed as a lugsail. She had fallen without a shot being fired, all resistance blown out of her earlier in the day.

It made a proud sight, the small convoy of three ships rounding Morant Point, threading the Port Royal passage past the forts on the Palisades and into the harbor with the Ensign flying over the white and gold flags of Spain. As soon as all three ships had dropped anchor and begun to brail up their sails, Lieutenant Lilycrop took a boat over to the flagship, strutting like a peacock at his success.

Alan was left to deal with the officials from the Prize Court, and the Dockyard Superintendent about repairs. The slaves from the trading ketch were removed, to be auctioned off at some time in the future, and they would fetch a good price, since the island of Jamaica was badly in need of prime slaves to support a wartime economy, and the supply from Africa had been cut to a trickle by Spanish and French privateers. After the recent slave revolt, unaffected slaves were doubly welcome.

Admittedly, Alan suffered some qualms at seeing them led off, still in their original chains. He had not known any slaves in his former life in London—there they were more of a novelty or an affectation of the very rich, employed as house-servants and body-servants, with the mannerisms and voices of failed Etonians who had to work to keep body and soul together. There were a few slaves in the Carolinas he had met, the Hayley sisters' maid Sookie, who had nearly been the death of him after he and the Chiswick brothers had escaped Yorktown, Caroline Chiswick's "Mammy," who was cook, nurse, housekeeper and more a family friend than a slave. And the West Indian hands and ship's boys, who were mostly good-natured cheeky runts or diligent workers as good as any volunteer signed aboard back in England.

" 'Tain't right, sir," Cony commented once more, coming to the rail by his side as the huge harbor barge bearing the slaves got underway from *Shrike*'s gunwales, ironically being rowed by hired freeborn blacks.

"No, it's not right, poor bastards," Alan agreed in a mutter.

"They get took from their 'omes back in Africa, clapped inta irons an' shipped 'cross the seas, an' them that live gets sold like dray 'orses," Cony lamented. "Worked ta death, sir, whipped ta death, and not a Christian 'and raised for 'em."

"And we capture them from the Dagoes so we can sell them for a good knock-down price," Alan went on. "By damn, I love prize-money good as the next man, but I don't know as how I'll feel right taking money for them. The ketch, yes, and all her fittings and cargo, but not them."

"That's the truth, it is, sir, an' you're a fine Christian for a'sayin' it, sir," Cony spat. "I been talkin' ta Andrews, sir, an' 'e says nigh on two hundred men and women're crammed in front ta back an' kept below for months on the Middle Passage. 'Tis a good voyage iffen only a quarter of 'em die, an' contrary winds'll end up a'killin' 'alf."

"You'd think, with all the talents mankind has at his disposal, there'd be someone working on a machine to harvest sugar cane instead of causing so much misery. As if life isn't misery enough already."

"God, wouldn't that be grand, sir!" Cony beamed. "An' I'll lay ya odds, it'll be an Englishman what does invent it, sir. Britons'll never be no man's slave, so why 'elp make other people our'n?"

In the months during the siege of Yorktown, in their escape, and ever since Cony had become first his hammockman in the midshipmen's mess and later his personal servant, it was only natural that Alan would become familiar with the young man. It was no longer an officer/common seaman relationship, nor was it strictly an employer/servant relationship, either. Cony had little education, no philosophical practice, but a strong sense of justice and decency, and had learned that in most instances, Lewrie was willing to give his opinions a fair hearing, which had encouraged the lad to speak out when he felt something strongly enough.

Perhaps it was because they had shared misery together, or the familiarity had come from Alan having so few people he could relate to on a professional basis; his circle was limited to the captain and the other officers in the wardroom, and he had to be standoff-ish with those or suffer a loss of respect. Decorum demanded he stay aloof, and it was only with Lilycrop that he could let down his hair, him and Cony, though he had yet to ask Cony for an opinion or advice—that would be going too far, he thought. One could be seen, warts and all, by a servant of long standing (which was probably why people changed them so often, he thought) but an English gentleman was drilled from the cradle to not get too close to the help, and never allow his dignity to slip before the servants.

A few warts were allowed, then, but if Cony really knew him for the rake-hell he was, he was sure Cony would lose his awe of him in short order.

"What else did Andrews say?" Alan asked, still intrigued by the man.

"Well, sir, 'e said back on the plantations, they beat 'em for almost anythin'," Cony went on, now that he was bid to speak further. "Rice an' beans, some truck they grow in their own time maybe, an' now an' agin some salt-meat . . ."

"Most likely condemned naval stores, that," Alan stuck in.

"Aye, sir. An' new clothes but once a year, after ever'thin' else's rotted off 'em." Cony sighed. "Treat 'em like beasts, sir, an' th' way they abuse the women, sir, is somethin' shameful. Ya know, sir, I can expect the practice o' the Frogs an' Dagoes. They's just cruel ta the bone with 'orses an' dogs an' people, but sometime 'tis 'ard ta see Britons a'doin' it here in the islands, or in the Colonies. Remember them escaped slaves what 'elped us build an' man the battery at Yorktown? Like whipped puppies they were, sir, grateful for what little we could share with 'em. Come away ta us ta escape their masters, poor old things. Wonder what the Rebels did with 'em after Cornwallis surrendered?"

"Same as today, most like," Alan scowled. "Them they didn't flog or hang for an example. Same they do with a runaway apprentice, hey?"

"That's differ'nt, sir," Cony insisted. "A 'prentice made 'is own choice o' master, made 'is contrack an' give 'is bond-word. Nobody asked those poor buggers. An' a 'arsh master deserves his 'prentices runnin', long's they don't steal nothin' when they go."

"Damme, Cony, you sound like one of those Leveling Rebels!"

"Nossir!" Cony defended himself. "They wanta give ever'body, the unlettered an' the poor the franchise, don't they? An' fer all their 'igh-tone' talk o' freedom, they still keep slaves ta toil for 'em sir. Seems ta me, iffen they mean all that guff, an' don't do away with slavery, they won't 'ave much of a country. They may o' been English once, sir, but livin' so wild an' rough musta addled 'em, an' I couldn't 'old with 'em now."

"Well, it didn't affect the Chiswicks," Alan said. "They're still our sort."

"Oh, aye, them Chiswick lads 'ad their 'earts in the right place fer King George an' all, sir, even if they were so fearsome. And you'll pardon me fer sayin' so, sir, but young Mistress Chiswick was fair took with you, sir. She was a *real* lady." Cony blushed at his own daring.

"And certain people of my acquaintance aren't?" Alan frowned.

"Not my place ta say, sir. Beg pardon, meant no disrespeck."

"The hell you didn't, you sly-boots." Alan laughed, even if his servant had come too close for comfort. "Off with you now, and keep an eye on Andrews for me, will you?"

"Aye, sir, that I will. 'E's a pretty good feller. An' 'e was grateful ya didn't pay 'eed ta what Mister Murray said about 'im, sir."

"So you think he ran from some slaver, too, Cony?"

"Aye, sir, I thinks 'e did," Cony almost whispered. "Not from the fields ... mebbe a 'ouse servant'r such ... ya know, sir, 'e can read and write? Now ain't that a wonder! 'E never goes ashore 'cept h'it's a workin' party. Maybe 'e's afeard o' bein' took back."

"Well, he'll not be, you can tell him that for me," Alan vowed.

"Aye, sir," Cony replied, looking mightily pleased.

Once the main bustle was over, and the shore authorities took charge of their prizes, *Shrike* stayed at her anchor stowing fresh provisions, with Lewrie keeping a wary weather eye cocked on Henry Biggs the purser for any peculiarities in goods or book-keeping.

Lilycrop strutted about, pleased as punch with himself for taking so many prizes and burning so many more. Their captured Don Thingummy had related that *Shrike* was becoming feared from one end of the coast of Cuba to the other. And Adml. Sir Joshua Rowley, who took an eighth share of any prize his squadron captured, had made a pretty penny from Lilycrop's new-found zeal, so he was most pleased with his junior officer. Which meant that Lilycrop was pleased with the world, and with his first lieutenant. Alan, however, did not know just how far that pleasure extended until one afternoon after *Shrike* had completed provisioning and placed the ship out of discipline so the whores and "wives" could come aboard. Alan had been primping for a run ashore. Even if he was *persona non grata* with the Beaumans and Mrs. Hillwood (who was reported to have gone inland to her husband's plantations to ride out the scandal that had redounded to her total discredit in Society) there had to be a company of willing mutton ashore to choose from.

"Passin' the word fer the first l'ten't!" came a call from the upper deck, and Alan uttered a soft curse at the interruption of his planned pleasures. He tossed his fresh-washed sheepgut condom back into his sea chest and slammed the lid in frustration. Damme, it's been two months! he sulked on his way topside.

"Cap'n warnts ya aft, sir," the messenger told him.

"Thank you." Alan shrugged. He was turned out in his best uniform, and was grateful for the awnings rigged over the quarterdeck so he would not sweat his best clothes clammy, but it would be hot and close in Lilycrop's great cabin.

"You wished to see me, sir?" Alan asked once he had been admitted.

"Yes, Mister Lewrie. Sit ye down. You know where the wine is, by now. Fetch yourself a glass."

Alan poured himself some hock which Gooch had been cooling in the bilges, shoved a cat out of his usual chair, and glared at the rest, as if daring them to climb up on him and leave a quarter-pound of hair on his fresh breeches.

"You had plans to go ashore this evenin', I see," Lilycrop said, noting how well he was turned out.

"Aye, I did, sir. But if there's any service I may do you . . .?"

"Oh God, but you look such a choir-boy when you do that," Lilycrop chuckled. "You'd rather be stuffed into some willin' wench than do me a service, an' well you know it. More to the point, so do I, by now."

"Aye, sir," Alan admitted, allowing himself a small smile.

"Can't say as you didn't earn your fun, Mister Lewrie," the captain went on, leaning back in his chair with both feet on his desk and a cat crouching on either leg. "Fact is, though, you may have to delay any hopes of fuckin' yourself half-blind, at least for this night. I've been bade dine aboard the flag, along with my first officer."

"With Admiral Rowley, sir?" Alan asked, perking up at the news.

"One may assume so. Seems we've been active little bodies, all but winnin' the war single-handed or such," Lilycrop hooted in glee. "And it don't hurt our cause we've lined the admiral's purse with prize-money, neither. Six month ago, he didn't know who the bloody hell we were, and I expect he'd like to show a little appreciation to us. Now, you can pass up a crack at the whores for a night for that, can't you, Lewrie."

"Oh, aye, sir!" Alan preened, excited at being known personally to the flag. "Lead me to it. And I'm told he sets a good table, too."

"You have my word on that," Lilycrop replied, for he had dined aboard the flag once before. "Fine things can happen yet, even if this war of ours seems to be peterin' out."

"Time enough for a lieutenant master and commander to be made post, perhaps, sir?" Alan hinted.

"I'll not hold my breath on that, mind." Lilycrop shrugged, but Alan knew the hope was there nevertheless. "Just wanted to catch you before you went ashore. Have my gig ready at seven bells of the first-dog. And since you're dressed to kill already, I'll not have to tell you to do so. That'll be all, Mister Lewrie."

"Aye, sir."

Chapter 2

Amazing how quiet we are, Alan thought to himself as he sipped his soup in the admiral's cabins aboard the flagship. It was a small supper party, and not one prone to much conversation. Lieutenant Lilycrop was head down and almost grim with determination not to make an ass of himself, and as long as he was silent, his first lieutenant should keep his own mouth shut, if he knew what was good for him.

Adml. Sir Joshua Rowley presided at the head of the table, a man of some girth and seniority. Next to him on his right was a Lieutenant Colonel Peacock, commanding one of the regiments that garrisoned the island of Jamaica, resplendent in polished metal gorget, scarlet waist sash and red regimentals. To the admiral's left sat a civilian in a bottle-green silk suiting, a Mr. Cowell.

The next pair of diners were, on the right, a Captain Eccles of Lieutenant Colonel Peacock's regiment; at least, to Lewrie's eyes, their regimental button-hole trim matched. Across the table from Eccles was another civilian named to them as a Mr. McGilliveray, a young man in his mid-twenties or so. From the poor quality of his snuff-colored suiting of "ditto"—matching coat, waist-coat and breeches—Alan assumed that he was Cowell's secretary, or something menial.

Then came Lewrie on the admiral's left, and Lieutenant Lilycrop across from him on the right. There had been a place laid for the admiral's flag-captain at the foot of the table, but he had not been able to attend at the last moment.

There had been some conversation, of the dullest and blandest sort, when they arrived, and the admiral traded gossip at the head of the table with his more distinguished guests, which did not extend to the people below the salt. From Cowell's com-

218

ments, Alan gathered that he was not long from London. Turning to McGilliveray, his dining companion on his right, Alan said, "I take it you're out from Home recently?"

"Not in about a year, sorry," the man replied with almost a guttural slurring of his words, which led Alan to wonder if he was drunk as a lord already.

"Ah. I'm from London, you see," Alan went on. "Thought you might know something entertaining about things there."

"Oh, London," McGilliveray brightened slightly (but only slightly). "Yes, six months ago. About the same sort of thing as usual. Crowded, prices too high, much too noisy."

"My dear fellow, that's exactly what I like about London!" Alan said with a small laugh. "No, I meant some new scandal or something."

"I don't follow Society," McGilliveray sniffed, prim as any Scottish deacon, which put paid to any more hopes of conversation from that source.

Damned odd sort, Alan thought, trying to find a niche for the man in his mind. He was dressed almost poor (and had an excruciatingly bad tailor) but carried himself without deference to Cowell. With a name like McGilliveray, Alan expected him to be a Scot, but if he was, he was a Scot/Dago, for the man was almost coppery red in complexion, with the blackest hair Alan ever did see, parted in the center and drawn back into a long, almost seamanly queue that reached down to the middle of his back. His face was broad, and his nose was hooked as a hawk, broad as it was to match those high cheekbones.

Alan turned away as the soup was removed and a smoking joint of mutton made its appearance on the table. Liveried servants passed behind the diners with small boiled potatoes and peas.

Lilycrop rose and hacked at the joint to carve the diners their choice. As a meal, Alan could not fault it; the mutton was followed by boiled lobsters and fresh-dredged crabs, with the Bordeaux replaced with bottles of cooled hock. Before the hock was removed, it went well with the small game birds, and claret replaced the hock to be served with the roast beef without which an English meal would not be complete. To sweeten the palate, slices of tropical fruit were served, then the cheese and biscuit.

The water glasses were removed, and servants topped up their glasses with claret. Admiral Rowley cocked a weather eye at Lewrie.

As the most junior officer at table, Alan knew his duty. He rose to his feet and raised his glass.

"My lord, gentlemen, the King," he said as they rose.

"The King," they chorused, Lieutenant Colonel Peacock almost smashing his skull open on an overhead deck beam, and whispering "God Bless Him." Obviously Peacock was from one of those regiments that were allowed that nicety by their sovereign in times past.

They sat back down and the tablecloth was whisked away and the last of the claret drunk while the port was set out for them, along with a large silver bowl of nuts to join the cheese and biscuit.

"Should nature have her way with your digestion, I urge you to attend to your needs now, gentlemen, so we shall have no interruptions," Admiral Rowley said, more in the way of an order. It took about ten minutes before everyone had voided whatever irked them and were back at table. Rowley sent the servants away rather pointedly.

"Gentlemen, I trust you have enjoyed what bounty I was able to offer?" Rowley began once their odd assemblage were the only people in the huge dining alcove of the great cabins. "Now, let us turn our heads to business. Lieutenant Lilycrop, Lewrie; Mister Cowell is a representative of His Majesty's government. Sorry you were kept in the dark, and the dinner conversation did not sparkle, but certain precautions had to be taken so that word of our meeting did not get round to the wrong people. Mister Cowell, sir. If you would be so kind as to explain your purpose."

Cowell was one of those people who thought better on his feet, or felt he had to pace when he orated, like a Member of Parliament.

"Gentlemen, I am sure you are aware as I this war is lost," he began rather dramatically. "Not the one against our classic enemies, the French, Spanish or Dutch, but the war in the Colonies. Our last armies gone except for the New York and Charleston garrisons, Lord Shelburne in charge now that Lord Rockingham has died, and our ambassadors treating at Versailles. The official end could come soon, perhaps on the next packet from England."

Just what I needed, Alan thought glumly, wondering if he could crack a nut to snack on during Cowell's harangue. A bloody sermon. He settled for a sip of port.

"This is not to say that England shall curl up like a worm in hot ashes and shrivel away, sirs," Cowell said, giving them a slight grin of encouragement, to which everyone grunted their "here, here's," much like a back-bencher Vicar of Bray in the Commons.

"Reports from India suggest we hold the upper hand against the French fleet at long last, have subdued the rebellious sultans, and look to evict the French from Pondichery once and for all," Cowell went on.

"Should never have given it back after the last war," Lilycrop growled, slicing himself a morsel of a rather fresh Stilton.

"I quite agree, Lieutenant," Cowell said, looking anything but pleased to be interrupted. "And here in the West Indies, the Sugar Islands are safe since de Grasse's fleet has been scattered. We hold the old French Canadian colonies and the maritime approaches to the Americas. St. Kitts shall come back at the treaty table, I assure you. No, the government's biggest worry right now is what the Rebels mean to do with their new lands, and how France or Spain may profit thereby."

"The Frogs might try buying territory, you mean," Alan said, almost without thinking, or more like thinking aloud. Cowell swiveled a glance in his direction, obviously unused to being interrupted so often by people below his station in life, and Alan was glad he had spoken. "We took a French ship last year loaded with artillery and draft horses and what-not. She also carried more than seventy thousand pounds, to be used for bribes or gifts to influential members of the Rebels' Congress or whatever they call it," Alan went on.

"I refer more to awards of territory to recompense the French and Spanish for their assistance and material support, sir," Cowell huffed, and the others looked at Alan as though he had broken wind at table—such was simply not done! Lieutenant Colonel Peacock glared as though Alan were one of his junior officers, he'd be in irons that instant.

"We shall not give them one acre, sir, but what the Rebels may do is open to question, and a formal military expedition to express our displeasure at any reward of territory is simply not in the cards. What we may do informally, though, is another matter entirely," Cowell said with a sly grin. "And there are methods by which the French and Spanish, who are already out untold riches, and in financial difficulty by their support of this unlawful Rebellion, may be discomfited and confounded in those territories they already possess, souring their appetites for more."

Cowell turned to stare at Alan, expecting him to open his

mug and make some comment, but Alan had learned his lesson and gave him a beatific smile of encouragement, one of his best eager-but-innocent expressions, which made Lilycrop cough into his fist to hide a smile.

"Pipes, gentlemen?" Admiral Rowley offered, obviously fidgeting for the soothing fumes of tobacco. He rose and fetched out his own tub of tobacco, a large-mouthed stone crock aromatic with Virginia leaf, and then chose a clay church-warden pipe from the ample selection contained in a plush-lined box large enough for a brace of dueling pistols.

"Not for me, thankee, milord," Alan said to his offer.

"Best to learn how," McGilliveray told him. "It shall come in handy soon."

"Well, if you insist." Alan shrugged and took one of the pipes. As the crock made its way down the table, along with the port, he stuffed crumbled leaf into the bowl, got a light with a paper spill from an overhead silver lantern, and fired the pipe up.

Damned silly practice, he thought, after almost coughing his lungs up. From then on, he merely rolled the smoke around in his mouth, not trying to inhale as the others did, slightly sickened by the taste and the sharpness of the hot smoke on his palate, which until then had been doing just fine with supper and wine to savor.

"A blend, Sir Joshua?" Cowell smirked, pacing about the cabins and puffing away like a house fire. "Quite pleasant. Quite."

"Just a touch of Turkey, sir, to give the Virginia some character," Admiral Rowley nodded, pleased at Cowell's opinion of his blend. "From Latakia, I believe. Taken from a prize last month. Usually it's more suited to snuff material, but it does give the blend some fire."

"Yes, it does have bite under the mellow," Cowell agreed. "Now, as to how we may foment confusion to our foes, gentlemen, let us take a look at the Spanish situation in the Americas. If you may allow me to refer to this map." He produced a large map, big as an ocean chart and spread it out on the polished mahogany dining table, anchoring the corners with glasses and bowls.

"We shall most likely lose East, or British, Florida at the Peace Conference," Cowell pointed out. "Spanish forces have evicted us from our last bastion at St. Augustine, and from the mouth of the St. John's River."

"God give them joy of it." Sir Joshua shivered. "A pestilential place, from my experience."

"As you see, just before the war, the southernmost colonies of Florida and Georgia were just beginning to draw colonists," Cowell lectured, using the long stem of his church-warden pipe as a pointer. "Note the topography of the Virginias and the Carolinas, separated from the interior by the Appalachians, all the way down to here, where they end in Georgia, from whence a great coastal plain stretches all the way to the great river of the Mississippi, and probably beyond. The new Rebel nation has not crossed over these mountains yet, though they probably shall in future. To the north, the Iroquois nations, still favorable to British interests and dependent on us for trade goods. They shall give our Rebels pause, should they attempt colonizing westward."

"Bankrupt the devils to maintain a standin' army against the northern Indians," Lieutenant Colonel Peacock barked with amusement. "Let 'em see what the cost of their folly is!"

"With the French evicted from Canada, we can maintain good relations with, and ministries to, the northern Indians, as a check to any Rebel plans for expansion to the north and west," Cowell said with a firm nod or two.

"And we propose to do the same with the southern Indians," the admiral added, puffing away contentedly.

"That is exactly our plan, sirs," Cowell went on quickly. "Now, there will be Rebel influence in the South, unfortunately. Charleston was the center for trade inland for many years. That city's merchant adventurers extended far to the west and south, and we may expect no less in future, a trade, I wish to point out, that shall no longer be British. Where the border shall be drawn, we have no idea, but Spain rules the rest of the coast, West Florida and all. Fortunately for us, they rule pretty much in name only. Their normal methods of conquest, such as they employed in New Granada and New Spain were not followed on the mainland. Small church settlements, a few troops to keep order, but few European settlers, and no *encomienda* system to exploit the downtrodden Indians in slavery on large estates and fiefs. The land does not support the Colonies for that reason, and the Spanish are losing money on the bargain, though the soil inland past the coastal marshes is quite fertile. One of the reasons they have not moved inland is the southern Indians. The entire region swarms with various tribes, some of them powerful enough to give anyone pause, and none of them willing to have anyone settle among them—British, Spanish, *or* Rebel. They are, or could be, a potent counterpoise to any further settlement west of Georgia. Properly armed and trained with European arms, these Indians could provide us with a drain on the new Rebel economy, a force that could limit any westward expansion, and a means to bankrupt the Spanish treasury, making the Spanish think twice about keeping the region; in short, a southern Iroquois League."

"We want to establish good relations with the southern Indians," the admiral summed up, shifting in his chair with impatience at Cowell's plodding oratory. "We wish to give the Spanish fits over their possessions in the South, making them more amenable to our re-taking the region at the peace negotiations. And we want to nail down the western border of the Colonies in the meanwhile so *we* may exploit this great and fertile coastal plain, instead of the Jonathons, the Frogs or the Dons. Look at the possibilities. Great rivers pouring down from the interior. Here at the mouth of the Mississippi, of the Mobile, this bay at Pensacola, even here at Tampa Bay. They could be important naval bases in time of war. Why should the Dons have 'em—or the Jonathons?"

"And, for the nonce, with strength enough, we could bleed both the Rebel and the Spanish treasuries trying to keep large forces on the frontier," Cowell finished with a dramatic sigh, and sank down into his chair as though exhausted by the effort of being so clever and erudite.

"Catch 'em in a nutcracker," Lieutenant Colonel Peacock said chearly, waving a real nutcracker at them. "Canada and a new British Florida, with the Rebels squeezed to death between, ha ha!" To prove his point, he crunched a walnut to nibble on.

"The only problem being," Sir Joshua frowned, "that at present we have no *entrée*, with the Dons in possession of the coast."

"Ah, but a most weak and porous possession, Sir Joshua!" Cowell chuckled. "A few Guarda Costa luggers, little better than fishing smacks. Perhaps one full regiment, supported by native levies of doubtful worth. Had we the troops, and the inclination, we would have swept the area clean years ago, but for Washington and our priorities further north. That is where you two gentlemen come in."

"Us, I see." Lilycrop pondered, slurping some port.

"Can't get there without the Navy, ey?" Cowell laughed.

"So what is it exactly you want us to do, milord?" Lilycrop asked of his admiral.

"Your brig o' war, *Shrike*, is shallow-drafted. You can get close inshore in what . . . two fathom of water?"

"She'll draw about ten foot proper laden, milord."

"Even better. The bays are shallow along this coast, even at high tide, and the passes into the sound through the barrier islands are of a piece with the Bahamas, or the coast of Cuba, which you gentlemen have done such a thorough job of ravaging lately," Sir Joshua Rowley told them. "In addition, you took a Spanish Guarda Costa sloop on your last cruise, of a type not very much unlike anything the Spanish would expect to see along the coast. False flag, false uniforms for your officers. *Shrike* was originally a trading brig, so her presence under Spanish colors would be unremarkable. We propose that you, disguising yourselves as a Don packet-brig and escort, go inshore, drop off a party who shall make their way inland to treat with the Indians. And if the negotiations go well, deliver to the Indians a quantity of arms suitable to their needs, along with such gifts as may tempt them to side with our interests."

"How far inland, milord?" Lilycrop asked, looking a trifle dubious. "And how long are we to linger off this coast?"

"Mister McGilliveray?" Cowell asked.

"The tribe we wish to talk with are the Lower Creeks, sirs," McGilliveray said, swiveling about to look at Lewrie and Lilycrop.

He stood and swung the large map about so the military representatives could see it better. "In the peninsula of Florida, the people are pretty much shattered. Timucua, Ocale, several other tribes mostly reduced by Spanish or British weapons or disease, or rum. West of the peninsula, pretty much the same for the Apalachee. But to the north, there are Muskogean peoples, whom the colonists call Upper Creeks and Lower Creeks. There are also Seminolee, Creek relatives who speak Muskogean. They're fairly powerful on their own. Their influence shall be most helpful to me inland."

"You, sir?" Lilycrop asked.

"Mister Cowell and I are your passengers, sir," McGilliveray said with a small grin. "Do you land us here, sir, at Apalachee Bay east of the Ochlockonee River. There are marshes and mangrove swamps for cover, so we may take the Guarda Costa sloop up-river to where it joins the larger Apalachicola, behind any coastal patrols. Two days on the water, perhaps forty miles? Then we pick up horses from the Seminolee and march two days overland to the large lake formed by the Chatahoochee

River. Or if the sloop will not serve, perhaps a pair of ship's boats with sails."

"And how long to negotiate, sir?" Lieutenant Colonel Peacock asked.

"Two more days, if all the important *mikkos* are available," McGilliveray speculated. "It might be a week if they had to be summoned. They will be cautious, so it might take a total of two weeks altogether before they make up their minds, including the trek inland. Then say a third week to get representatives from the Creeks at the mouth of the river here to pick up the arms. Or pick up our shore party should we fail to convince them."

"Damme, hide a ship in the marshes for three weeks?" Lilycrop almost exploded, turning a cherry hue. "More like hide two ships, *Shrike* at the mouth of the river, and the sloop way up here, assumin' the damned thing may get that far, which is a rather large assumption, ain't it? And just what forces do the Dons have around this Apalachee Bay, I ask you? What about these coastal Indians? They goin' to sit on their duffs and just let us set up housekeepin', or are they goin' to run off and sell us up to the bloody Dons?"

"One would think you had no bottom for the adventure, sir," Lieutenant Colonel Peacock countered grumpily. "Perhaps another officer . . ."

"I think what my captain means, sirs, is that no one could sail in and play 'Merry Andrew' with no knowledge," Alan stuck in as Lilycrop turned scarlet at the slur to his courage. "And what is *Shrike* to do in the time the Guarda Costa sloop is up-river? Lay at anchor and trust a local patrol doesn't happen along? Pray some local informer doesn't tell the Spanish we're there? It sounds as if *Shrike* should lurk offshore, say ten or fifteen leagues out in the Gulf, and never close the coast at all. Let the sloop go inshore alone. Then, if all goes well, *Shrike* could meet her at some prearranged *rendezvous*. I assume, however, that *Shrike* would carry the main cargo of arms and trade goods, and must at some time come inshore to deliver. Or do you plan to take everything along in *San Ildefonso*, Mister Cowell?"

"It would cut down our time in danger on the coast if the sloop bore the complete cargo, sir," Cowell said.

"And how much is to be transported, sir?" Alan pressed.

"There are eight hundred refurbished muskets with all equipage, eight hundred infantry hangers and bayonets, plus forty thousand cartouches," Cowell stated as though reading a manifest. "And powder and ball equivalent to another forty thousand rounds. And we have trade goods. Tomahawks, knives, bolts of cloth, cooking pots, shirts and cast-off tunics, the usual merchant truck the tribes desire the most."

"About four tons altogether," McGilliveray said. "A very light load. The sloop could handle it easily, could it not?"

"Aye, a thirty-six-foot barge could do it easy," Lilycrop agreed.

"Then another two weeks to get the stuff inland and get our party back?" Alan wondered aloud, glancing at Lilycrop.

"No, the Creeks have horses and mules," McGilliverary told him. "And they have their own canoes, you know. They could take it all on their own once we get them to agree to the bargain. Once they show up and we unload for them, the sloop could be gone."

"What about these Apal . . . what-you-call-'ems, then?" Alan asked. "Do we have to hide from them as well? Would they be hostile?"

"I know for a fact that we have no worries about the Apalachee." McGilliveray smiled. "They are too weak on their own. They're allies of the Seminolee and the Creeks. Mostly out of fear of what will happen if they cross them. I shall explain the situation, and I doubt if anyone remaining with the boats at the mouth of the river will have any worries. They have no reason to love the Spanish, either. With some trade goods presented to their chiefs, they'll probably fall all over themselves to help us, as long as the crew that stays behind does not offend them."

"That's a rather big *if*, is it not?" Alan laughed. "I mean, I never heard of anyone who could trust an Indian. They follow their own lights, and be damned to everyone else, don't they?"

"*We* trust the Indians, Mister Lewrie," Cowell sniffed. "We trust Mister McGilliveray. This is his plan."

"Know a lot about them, do you?" Alan cocked an eyebrow at the young man to his right.

"Dear me, I should have told you, Mister Lewrie. I am one." McGilliveray smirked.

"Ah," Alan managed to say, mostly because it could be done with his mouth hanging open.

"My mother is Muskogee, my father Scot, one of those merchants out of Charleston," McGilliveray explained. "With my mother's people I am called White Turtle, of the Wind Clan, the most powerful clan in any tribe or settlement. My grandfather on mother's side is *mikko* where we are going, and my cousins are influential. The Apalachee and Seminolee know me, so we shall be safe from harm from them. I shall try to explain all the particulars you should know on the voyage."

"And how many crew may you need, Captain?" Admiral Rowley inquired to smooth over Alan's gaffe.

"Nine men, plus cook and officer, milord."

"Along with Captain Eccles here, and a dozen men from my regiment as guards with the sloop, and with the party up-river," Peacock added.

"Pardon me, Colonel, but would those be troops of the line, or light infantry?" Alan asked, once he had regathered his abashed wits.

"Why do you ask, sir? What do you know of soldiers?"

"I was at Yorktown, sir, and this affair strikes me as calling for Rifles or skirmishers, not line troops. I dealt with a Loyalist Volunteer Regiment and their light company, armed with Fergusons, sir."

"Rifles, bah!" Peacock spat with some heat. "Bunch of damned irregulars, no discipline. Dependable as chimney smoke. If you run into trouble up there, you'll thank your lucky stars for some steady men of the line who can overawe these savages, men who can fire two shots a minute in volley, such as Captain Eccles may select!"

"Pardon me, sir, but in my limited experience with land fighting, I'd rather fire four shots a minute with a Ferguson breechloader from ambush than stand and deliver by volley," Alan retorted with a smile.

"One of the reasons we chose *Shrike*, you'll remember, is that her first officer does have land-fighting experience, Colonel," Admiral Rowley interjected before Peacock could explode like a howitzer shell with a very short fuse. "Plus her shallow draft, and the record she had made for herself as a fighting ship under her gallant captain, Lieutenant Lilycrop. And since *Shrike*'s officers shall be responsible for getting our expedition ashore and up-river safely, it does seem reasonable to allow them to make suggestions now from their experience."

Damme, that sounds devilish promising! Alan thought with delight at the admiral's praise. Singled out for hazardous duty 'cause I made a name for myself? Won't *that* look good in the London papers.

He shared a quick glance with Lilycrop, who was beaming and nodding his head as he digested the fine assessment the admiral had made of his recent record, looking pleased as a pig in shit.

"No red coats," McGilliveray said in caution. "Your men should wear buff or green anyway. Have some linen hunting shirts run up. And I quite agree with Lieutenant Lewrie about the type of men to go ashore. It would be best if we could procure irregulars, people with some woods-craft. More than *one* British general has come to grief, tramping about the back-country with line troops, Colonel."

"Well, that lets out Walsham and his Marines," Lilycrop said. "And if this mission is to be secret—I do take it to be secret, hey—then why advertise our presence by wearin' uniform at all?"

"A good point, sir," Cowell spoke up, feeling left out on all the martial planning. "Mister McGilliveray, I doubt they could pass at close muster as natives, but clothes do make the man, do they not, ha ha?"

"A most sensible suggestion, honored sir," said McGilliveray, bowing to his mentor. "Perhaps pack uniforms for the negotiations, to appear more impressive to my people, who are delighted by a fine show. But on the march hunting shirts, leggings and moccasins might escape notice by any Spanish patrol we happen onto. Better to be ignored than have to fight, unless it's absolutely necessary."

"You could supply troops, Colonel?" Cowell almost demanded from his enthusiasm and excitement at getting to dress up like a Red Indian.

"I still hope to honor your requests, sir." He frowned, not liking his unit to be slighted so easily from a grand adventure. "There are no riflemen on Jamaica. No Fergusons, either. Well, I *could* assign men from my regiment, even so. From the light company, practiced as skirmishers. Remnants of a fusilier battalion. I assure you they know their way around in the mountains and forests hereabouts, milord. They're acclimated to Yellow Jack and the other fevers by now as well, after chasing after rebellious slaves during the last revolt."

"God. Cashman," Captain Eccles whispered bitterly, aghast at being left out.

"Cashman, did you say?" Admiral Rowley prompted, cocking an ear in Eccles' direction. "And who is that, sir?"

"The captain of our light company, milord," Peacock replied, trying to keep a sober face. "A bit . . . eccentric, but a good man in a fight, I assure you, milord."

If this ass Peacock doesn't like him, then he'll probably be just our sort, Alan thought. Doubt if I could have stood this catch-fart Eccles for more'n a week without callin' him out. And damned if I'd trust one of those battalion-company stallions to guard me out in those swamps.

Alan took it for a given that, as first officer, he would be called upon to guide the little sloop inshore; that's what first officers were for, to risk their arses while their captains stood off and chewed their furniture with worry. It was a rare captain who would give his first lieutenant command of his precious ship and go off on some deed of derring-do just to satisfy his blood-lust. By the time a man had made post-captain, he mostly had blood-lust out of his system, anyway, and was glad to make way for a younger, and more expendable, man.

The conference lasted several more hours, determining that the Spanish sloop would be the only vessel to go inshore, towing a single ship's boat. She could make her way at high tide as far as two miles up the Ochlockonee River with her topmast struck. The two twelve-pounder guns on her fo'c'sle would be dismounted for a brace of four-pounders to ease her sailing qualities. The ship's boat, a standard twenty-five-foot launch, would step a single mast, and would need only six oarsmen due to her shallow two-foot draft. She would also get a couple of swivels should they run into trouble.

This meant that another half a dozen hands had to come along, leaving half a dozen soldiers free for lookouts and protection. Once they left the sloop, six men would stay behind under a quartermaster's mate, with another half a dozen soldiers.

Shrike would never close the coast, but would stand off out of sight of land, and would wait two full weeks from the night the *San Ildefonso* left her and went inshore. If she did not show up within three weeks, they would come into the bay and search for them.

Shrike would not go ashore for good reason; she would be carrying the bulk of the arms. Cowell didn't want to risk everything in one small ship. The sloop would carry fifty muskets, one thousand rounds of pre-made cartouches and musketeers' equipment such as cartridge boxes, fine priming powder bottles, bayonets, swords and baldrics enough to make a fine show, along with knives, pots, blankets, etc., as samples of England's largesse. There would be bolts of cloth and blankets for presents, and all the usual trade goods, but only enough to whet their appetites for more. McGilliveray argued against this, assuring Cowell that he knew best when dealing with his own people in good faith, but finally relented.

"Well, I think that about covers it, gentlemen," Admiral Rowley said with a yawn. "*Shrike* is provisioned for a cruise already. All that remains is loading the cargo, bringing the troops aboard the sloop, and readying her for sailing. Her repairs are complete, and she has been provisioned as well. Lieutenant Lewrie, you had best go aboard her at first light with your selected crew. Mister McGilliveray is going to take care of the disguises for the shore party. Have we forgotten anything? Mister Cowell? Mister McGilliveray? Captain? If anything springs to mind between now and sailing date . . . say two days from now . . . send me a sealed note, or better, bring it yourself to my flag-captain. And I must warn you, not a word of this among your men until you are at sea. You know how fast rumors fly on the lower deck, hey?"

"If they wonder, we'll let out we're goin' to raid the Cuban coast, milord." Lilycrop chuckled, almost leaning on his hand, propped up from the table and looking far past his bed-time. The continual supply of drink hadn't helped. "They'll believe that, and be glad it's the Army goin' ashore 'stead o' them. That'll explain the sloop, too."

"Excellent subterfuge, Captain. Excellent. Well, I'm for bed."

When they emerged on the quarterdeck of the 2nd Rate flagship, it was blessedly cool, and a refreshing little breeze was blowing to remove the funk of the closed cabins. Their boat was brought round, after the crew was awakened, and they rowed back to *Shrike*, keeping an enigmatic silence. It was only after they had gone to Lilycrop's cabin that they could talk freely. Lilycrop stripped out of his uniform and knelt to pay attention to his many cats, who blinked and stretched and made much ado over him after such an uncharacteristically long absence.

"Cats et, Gooch?"

"Aye, sir." Gooch yawned. "Will there be anythin', sir?"

"No, go back to sleep. Bide a moment, Mister Lewrie."

"Aye, sir."

"Wine?"

"Thankee, sir."

"Pour me one, too, whatever you're havin'."

They sat down together at his desk, leaning forward into the pool of light from a single overhead lantern that swayed softly as the hull rode the slight harbor ruffles stirred up by the gentle breeze.

"You feel comfortable with this idea, Mister Lewrie?" Lilycrop asked, his features heavily shadowed by the light.

"Comfortable enough, sir, I suppose." Alan shrugged. "It's a devilish grand opportunity for us, stap me if it ain't. If McGilliveray knows half of what he says, we should be alright once we're ashore. But I worry about the sloop and the men we leave behind. Not just about the Spanish running across 'em, but discipline while we're gone."

"Take Svensen, the quartermaster, as your senior hand," Lilycrop suggested. "That square-headed Swede'd put the fear o' God into artillery. There'll be no nonsense with him in charge. And he's a right clever'un, too."

"Thank you for the suggestion, sir."

"I don't like it, myself." Lilycrop frowned, looking old as Methuselah. "This McGilliveray, or Turtle or whatever he prefers to call himself, come up with this too-clever idea, an' he's got that Cowell excited as a sailor on his first whore to go off'n do somethin' grand an' mysterious. They sailed direct from Portsmouth in the mail packet with all their trade goods, and loped up to Rowley and Peacock with this plan. Now if the government at home is so miss-ish about endin' the war, why did they agree to such a far-fetched scheme, I wonder?"

"You don't think they're legitimate, sir?" Alan perked up.

"Oh, don't be *that* large an ass," Lilycrop grumbled. "Think just any fool can go aboard a flagship and dream somethin' like this up on the spur of the moment? No, this'n has so many official wax seals on it it'd float."

The ship's bell chimed three bells; half past one o'clock of the middle watch, and Lilycrop looked weary to the bone, which explained his testiness.

"Only thing that surprises me is, if Florida's so bloody important to us, why didn't we raise the tribes long ago, when we still had the east coast forts? Why leave it this late?"

"There is that, sir," Alan agreed, too sleepy to worry much.

"I've seen things like this before," Lilycrop went on. "War on the cheap, dreamed up by map-gazers'n quill-pushers safe back in London. I don't know whether our Mister Cowell come up with this himself, or if he's just a nobody wantin' to make his name out of it. He might be some lord's errand boy. And that McGilliveray. A right 'Captain Sharp,' too clever by half for the likes of me. Mayhap he knows what he's talkin' about, an' his tame Apalachee'll treat us like vistin' royalty, and he'll sit at the right hand of God once he's up-river with his people the Creeks. I don't like leavin' the sloop up-river. And we'll have to split our parties again when you transfer to horses."

"You should have said something then, sir."

"Oh, I did enough carpin' for their likes. All that praise we got, like we're Drake'r Anson come back with flamin' swords . . . well, talk's cheap, and so are we. I'm the oldest lieutenant in the Navy, you're nobody, and *Shrike* and the sloop are expendable. Damned expendable."

"You give me chills, sir," Alan said, taking a deep sip of his own mug to fortify himself. "But surely, the admiral has already placed his favorites into larger ships than ours. Everything makes sense to choose *Shrike*. It's a chance to do something really grand."

"And get your name in the *Marine Chronicle*?" Lilycrop sneered. "Hell, nary a word o' this'll ever get out. We're goin' to be as anonymous as spies, no matter how it comes out. Oh, maybe our Lords Commissioners of the Admiralty will make a note of it in our records, but I'll not be made post-captain over it, and you'll not go higher than you are now. There's no way to refuse this duty, but if there was a way, I'd consider it. All that talk of how the Spanish don't patrol. Well, remember, there's troops and a ship'r two at Pensacola, and sure to be a ship o' war workin' outa Tampa Bay. Spies along the coast, some Indian that'll run to the Dagoes to raise the hue an' cry. Sell us out for a fuckin' *mirror*! Jesus weep! Nobody I knew ever prospered who got tied up with damn foolishness such as this. You be sure to watch your back once you're ashore. If you learned anythin' up in the Chesapeake, use it. Take whoever you know is a woodsman an' a scrapper, 'cause you'll have need of 'em. And I'll pray every day for your safety, Mister Lewrie."

"Thank you, sir, that was well said, and welcome," Alan replied with a warm feeling inside for Lilycrop's regard for him.

"Hard enough to break in a first officer. No call to do it more'n once a year, 'pon my soul." Lilycrop scowled, looking away at the antics of his cats on the floor. "I've grown used to ya, d'ya see? Show us heel-taps on your glass, and let us get some rest. We'll need it."

Chapter 3

" 'They are ingenious, witty, cunning, and deceitful; very faithful indeed to their own tribes, but privately dishonest, and mischievous to the Europeans and Christians. Their being honest and harmless to each other may be through fear of resentment and reprisal—which is unavoidable in case of any injury.' " Alan read half aloud from a volume that McGilliveray had recommended to him, James Adair's *History of the American Indians*, published in London in 1776. " 'They are very close and retentive of their secrets; never forget injuries; revengeful of blood, to a degree of distraction. They are timorous, and consequently, cautious; very jealous of encroachments from their Christian neighbors; and likewise, content with freedom, in every turn of fortune. They are possessed of a strong comprehensive judgement, can form surprisingly crafty schemes, and conduct them with equal caution, silence and address; they admit none but distinguished warriors and beloved men into their councils.' "

"Well, that let's me out," Captain Cashman of the light company of the 104th Regiment of Foot laughed easily as they sat at table their second day out from Kingston.

"I quite look forward to our meeting them," Cowell said. Without his wig, and with his shirt collar open, he looked like a balding club waiter out on holiday. "They are an admirable people, much abused by contact with the white man. As the French philosopher Rousseau said, they have a natural nobility. Read on, Mister Lewrie, do."

" 'They are slow but persevering in their undertakings'— Sorry, Mister Cowell, but negotiations may take longer than you think if that's true—'commonly temperate in eating, but excessively immoderate in drinking.' Hmm, sounds like half my relatives. 'They often transform themselves by liquor into the likeness of mad foaming bears.' "

"Can't take someone like that to Covent Garden," Cashman observed.

"Ah, here's the best part. 'The women in general are of a mild, amiable, soft disposition; exceedingly modest in their behavior, and very seldom noisy either in the single or married state.' Hmm, well, maybe it's not the best part at that."

"Adair is amusing," McGilliveray said, looking up from carving his salt beef. "He got that part wrong, at least among the Muskogee."

"Oh, are the women better than he said?" Alan asked.

"Once married, they are subservient to their husbands. That doesn't mean they cannot nag, or raise their voices. Frankly, the older they get, the more they resemble Billingsgate fishmonger women. Very earthy." McGilliveray gave them a tight smile.

"What we're interested in, my dear sir, is what sort of rattle they are," Cashman drawled.

"Lay hands on a married Muskogee, any married Indian woman, and her male relatives will hang you up on the pole and butcher you for three days. One does not even cast a covetous eye on them, for fear of retribution. It's a blasphemy."

"You mean we can't even bloody look at 'em? Here, Lewrie, this is a rum duty," said Cashman, frowning.

"You may notice them, but you can't ogle them, or follow after them, or try to talk to them. If they're in their monthly courses, you won't see them at all." McGilliveray went on sternly lecturing, as he had since he had come aboard. "They hide themselves away from their families and their village, and anything they touch is polluted. A man who looks on a woman in her courses, gets downstream of one, has to go through severe purification rituals to restore his spirits."

"Don't sound like they run to whores, neither." Cashman winked at Lewrie, who was as tired of McGilliveray's pontifications as anyone else aboard.

"No, we don't, and you're becoming tiresome, Captain Cashman," McGilliveray said, controlling his temper, which Alan had just read was supposed to be "immoderate."

"Seriously, Mister McGilliveray, we're going to have seamen and soldiers running about who haven't had anything better than a harbor drab or a toothless camp follower since their last payday. There must be some release, surely. The whole tribe can't live in chastity belts."

"Indian men do, you know," McGilliveray said smugly. "For the good of the harvest, the planting of the crops, good fortune in hunting, success in battle, when someone dies. That's why sexual relations are so strictured. Also, how do you control the urge to adultery among so many people in such a small village unless the whole thing becomes some form of magic ritual?"

He gave them a deprecating smile to show that he was human, which did nothing to convince either Lewrie or Cashman that he hadn't been got at by Baptists.

"At least, once they become warriors, they do, and once they wed. Before, there is allowed a certain license. Among the younger women as well. They can be rather . . . enthusiastic about men before they wed."

"Well, how do you tell the difference, then?" Cashman demanded. "And what do you do, bring her a plucked chicken? Flip tuppence across the fire? Tell 'em to wash the *mehtar*'s daughter?"

"The what?" Lewrie goggled.

"Sorry, I was in the East Indies once. It was a lot easier there, let me tell you. Cheaper too, if you like *nautch* girls with bums and legs like farrier sergeants," Cashman said irrepressibly.

"There's a lot of ceremony in village life," McGilliveray told them, sipping at small-beer, which was all he would allow himself. "At each ceremony, there's dancing in circles around a central fire, and all the unmarried women sort of cluster together and show off their finery. I shall point them out to you. If they fancy you, you'll know it right off. They run things, long as they're single."

"And if Indian men restrict themselves as you say, they must have to make up for lost time after they're married," Cashman said, grinning. "So if she's there, she isn't polluted, and if she fancies a tumble, she'll come over and flash her poonts?"

"It's a bit more subtle than that, Captain," McGilliveray said with a sigh of the truly long-suffering. "Believe me, you'll know."

"I should think it best if we forswore conjugal relations with the natives," Cowell said, a bit prim. "It would be easiest."

"Hardly possible, I'm afraid, sir," Alan stated. "You haven't seen my sailors a'rut." Or me, Alan qualified to himself. "And if the young unmarried females are so eager for it, I doubt a troop of saints could hold out for long."

"You'll have your rut, sir," McGilliveray snapped. "Speaking further of pollution, I adjure you and your men from making water into any body of water. Running water is sacred, you see, where some of our gods dwell. You don't piss in it, or spit into it, or pass excreta into it. No dumping of kitchen scraps, anything like that. You do that on dry land where it won't drain into running waters. Bury it."

"Well, we can go have a wash, can't we?" Cashman asked.

"Oh yes. In fact, if you don't wash daily, first thing in the morning, they'll look on you strangely. It's our way. But, never get downstream of a woman. It's best to conform to our customs for as long as you are with my people, to ease the negotiations, you see. With so many distinguished chiefs gathered together, the slightest upset can make them leery of the whole thing and then they'll not side with us."

"When in Rome, do as the Romans," Cowell suggested. "Now Mister McGilliveray, tell them about the missionary work among the Muskogean. I mind you said once back in London, with the bishop of Chicester as I remember, that only a few of your people have accepted the faith."

"I should be delighted to hear of it, sir, but I believe that Captain Cashman and I are already due on deck," Alan said, referring to his pocket watch. "Musket drill, you know. If you gentlemen shall excuse us? Please stay and indulge yourselves. You have but to ask of my man Cony."

"Jesus bloody Christ!" Cashman sighed after they had got on deck. "I've about had it with that blackamoor. Like being lectured to by a mastiff. A very unfunny mastiff, at that. Sarn't! Trot the buggers out for musketry! And if Navy rum is too tasty for proper aimin', then maybe a Navy cat'll suit 'em better!"

"Sir!"

Cashman was indeed, as Lieutenant Colonel Peacock had said, eccentric. His speech was littered with Army slang, East Indian Hindi expressions, and a pungent sprinkling of profanity that would make a bosun's mate green with envy. He had come aboard armed to the teeth, wearing an infantry-man's short, brass-hilted hanger instead of a small-sword, four pistols stuck into his sash and a pair of converted saddle holsters, a short fusil slung over one shoulder and a French musketoon over the other.

In a world where officers were to be fashion-plates, and the rankers usually clad in rags, Cashman looked as if he had darned his uniform together since he had bought his first set of colors, and once aboard ship, had doffed half of that.

"Quartermaster, the keg paid out astern?" Alan asked.

"Aye aye, zir. Hoff a cable," the blonde hulk named Svensen told him. "Full hundret faddom line, zir."

"Let's get to it, Sarn't."

The men of the light company split off into skirmishing pairs at the stern rail. They pulled their weapons back to half-cock, bit off the twist end of their first cartouches, and primed pans. Poured powder down the barrels, wadded the waxed paper cartridges around the lead balls, and rammed them home, keeping the rammer free in their off hands instead of returning them to their proper place under the barrels.

The first rank fired, raising froth around the towed keg at one hundred yards range, and stepped back to start reloading while their rear-rank partners stepped up to deliver their shots, not in volley, but within a few seconds of each other.

"I like the fusil, if I can't have a jager rifle," Cashman said, tap-loading his charge and snapping the weapon up to his shoulder. "No one knows exactly why, but a short barrel is just as accurate as a long one."

Bam! And down came the piece, drawn back to half-cock on the way to loading position. Alan nodded as he saw that Cashman had chipped the keg, which, half-submerged, would be about the size of a reclining man at one hundred yards.

"With a smooth-bore"—Cashman continued to talk as he bit at his cartridge, blackening his lips—"it's more a problem of obturation, you see, how snug the ball fits in the barrel."

Tap went the fusil on the deck to settle the powder. The right hand had rolled the ball and paper wad together and stuck it in the muzzle as it came up from being rapped. The rammer came up like a fugleman's cane on parade, and everything was shoved home snug with one firm push. The rammer came out of the muzzle and spun in Cashman's left-hand fingers as he brought the weapon up, pulling it back to full-cock. A quick breath, and a second shot rang out, the second in half a minute.

"No parade ground bumf for us, see," Cashman said, even as he was making a fresh cartouche appear as if by magic. "Just get it done. Three, maybe four rounds a minute, fast as your Ferguson breech-loader. Here."

Alan took the fusil. It was a lighter, shorter musket, just a little longer than a cavalryman's musketoon, with a barrel of about twenty-five inches. As Alan loaded for himself, Cashman went on about it.

"Smooth-bore, takes a bayonet, heavy enough stock to knock some poor bastard into next week, but only .54 caliber. Lighter ball carriers farther with a standard Brown Bess powder measure. And if you use the waxed cartridge as a greased patch, like you would in a rifled piece, the bugger carries farther and straighter. Battalion companies with the Brown Bess average eighty or ninety yards for a killing shot, but the fusil will go a bit farther. One hundred twenty, perhaps one hundred fifty yards. Nothing like a rifle. But it only drops about ten inches in two hundred yards. Frankly, I couldn't hit a bull in the ass with a carronade at two hundred yards."

Alan brought up the weapon, pulled it back to full-cock, took aim and squeezed the trigger, and was pleased to see his ball raise a splash just short of the keg.

"Load, quick now! The Indians are breathin' on you!"

"Respectable kick," Alan said, fumbling through the loading procedure and taking a lot longer than Cashman or his men did.

"Lighter piece, same powder charge as a regular's musket. Masters, you poxy spastic, pick up your bloody rammer, man! Don't drop it!"

"Take 'is name, sir?" the sergeant offered.

"No, take his pulse. See if he's dead," Cashman quipped, and his men laughed easily.

After half an hour, with their mouths and faces blackened by the powder they had eaten and the flash from the pans, they took a short rest while the keg was paid out to one hundred fifty yards.

Alan had finally managed to get off three shots a minute, and had hit the keg twice in that period, though the fusil had pummeled his shoulder almost numb. He walked over to the water butt and dipped the long, narrow sipper down through the small scuttle to draw out a measure.

"Your men seem to know what they're about, I must say," Alan commented.

"They're damned good, aye. Best thing about the bloody 104th Regiment," Cashman spat, wiping his mouth and face clean and making a face at the taste of nitre on his lips. "A war-raised single-battalion unit. No home depot, you see. Peacock raised it himself. Tory patriot, don't ya know. Cheap at the price, too, them that survived the fevers and the slave revolt campaignin'. They'll deactivate us, if they even remember we're bloody here, soon's the bloody treaty's signed."

"You were part of it, originally?"

"Hell, no. My light company's all that's left of a fusilier battalion. Got tagged onto them after most of us went under to Yellow Jack. Came off the ship four hundred seventy-seven men and officers strong, and two weeks later, we made roughly two companies. Now I've barely forty left. These are the best of 'em, though it was hard to choose."

"Lieutenant Colonel Peacock and Captain Eccles seemed a little put off that I suggested light infantry, or that you would be the one to go on this adventure of ours," Alan said smiling.

"This was your doing?" Cashman brightened. "Blessings upon ye, then. Anything to get away from those buggers. What did they say?"

"That you were eccentric, but a hard fighter."

"I'm not their sort," Cashman admitted chearly. "Thank God. I'm amazed they reckoned me a good soldier. I didn't know they'd recognize one if he crawled up and bit 'em on the arse. Beggars can't be choosers, though, and they needed a light company to flesh 'em out. If they had a choice, I'd not have been able to purchase a commission with 'em. I was only a lieutenant with my old battalion. A captaincy was a brevet promotion, but if the loot's good, or the cards run right, I might be able to purchase a real captaincy one of these days."

"Back Home?"

"Hell, no. A captaincy costs near twenty-five hundred pounds for a good regiment," Cashman chuckled. "No, unless God passes a miracle, I'll be soldiering in cheaper places. Here in the Fever Islands, back in the East Indies, where nobody in his right mind would want to go. A regiment like that's a buyer's market. Cost me only three hundred pounds to become an ensign when word got out we were going to Madras. People were 'changing or selling out like the hounds of hell were at their heels. But, if it weren't for the loot, I'd have never had enough for a lieutenancy in the Fusiliers. One way or another, the old Regiment'll have to take me back soon as I get home, and when the Army's reduced, there'll be a chance to buy up."

"Thank God the Navy doesn't go for purchased commissions or commands." Alan shivered, thinking how menial he would be that instant if he had had to depend on his father spending money to get rid of him. "Why didn't you give the Fleet a try?"

"Fourth son." Cashman shrugged. "And damn-all inheritance for any of the others. Already had the future farmer, a sailor, and a churchman, and I had a choice of clerking in Ipswich or going for a soldier. Ever been in Ipswich? Last time I was home, I thought I'd freeze my prick off, and that was in summer, mind. And Suffolk's pretty damned dull any time of the year. I love

England well as any man, but there's something about the tropics, if you can survive in 'em. At least it's warm, and not too many churchmen breathing down your neck with their 'shalt-nots.' "

"What do you think of this mission of ours?" Alan asked him.

"Frankly? I think it's a rum'un," Cashman whispered, though the sound of his fusiliers banging away at the keg would have covered his doubts from the men. "If we want Florida back so bloody bad, why not put a couple of good regiments together from the Jamaica garrison and make it a proper landing? Oh, aye, take along some pretties to buy off the locals, maybe form some temporary levies like East Indian *sepoys*. From what I hear, these Creeks'd make good soldiers if somebody took the effort to train 'em. Good skirmishers and woodland fighters, proper armed. Hell and damnation, I'd like to have all my company with me, if that won't serve. We're too thin on the ground to suit me."

"Bring the rest of your present regiment?"

"Peacock and them?" Cashman laughed sourly. "They'd get themselves butchered. Less'n two hundred of 'em, anyway, and not worth a tinker's damn when it comes to skirmishing. Turn that lot loose in the woods and they'd make so much noise, and get so lost, any Indian in the world'd have 'em for his breakfast."

"My sailors won't be much better, I'm afraid. Cony and some of the party coming with us are country lads, one jump ahead of the magistrate for poaching, but nothing like what one needs against Indians and Dago troops who know the country," Alan confessed.

"Here, you sound like you've been around before. Served ashore, have you?" Cashman asked.

"At Yorktown. We escaped," Alan told him with a touch of pride. "With a light company of Loyalists from the Carolinas."

"Whew," Cashman whistled. "So, how do you feel about this trip of ours?"

"I'm a touch leery, too. Oh, it sounded grand when they offered it to us, and we couldn't say 'no,' anyway," Alan told him with a shrug. "Supper with our admiral, being admitted to high plans, you know. But my captain over there is worried, and now he's got me doing it."

"You should."

"I don't like leaving this sloop in the swamps, at the mercy of those Indians," Alan went on. "What happens if McGilliveray, or White Turtle or whatever, can't convince them to keep their hands off while we're gone? From what I've read, an Indian thinks it's his duty in life to lift from strangers whatever's not nailed down."

"Who says we have to leave things laying about to tempt them?" Cashman replied with a twinkle in his eyes. "You know that once we separate from your ship yonder, you and I are equally in command of this mess. You of the sloop and the long-boat, I of the land party. Cowell is no soldier, he's a London paper-pusher with dreams of adventure. And this McGilliveray is only an advisor. They can't order us to do a bloody thing. What do you *want* to do?"

"I'd like to send *San Ildefonso* off to sea under my quarter-master," Alan said after a long moment of thinking. "There's no reason to leave a large, easily discoverable ship in the swamps. The crew could sicken on the miasmas, get over-run by the Apalachees, or the Spanish could find her and bring force enough to take her."

"Best we go quietly on our way up-river," Cashman agreed. "We're going to be dressed pretty much like Indians in these hunting shirts and whatever, so the Dons don't know we're here. So what's stopping you sending this ship back to sea once we're landed, if secrecy is so important?"

"Not a bloody thing," Alan realized.

"And if I wanted to bring another squad with me, so we'd have a round dozen skirmishers, there's no one to gainsay me, either. Out at sea, your ship wouldn't need a party of soldiers left behind."

"What about the samples, then?"

"Oh, we can take 'em up-river, can't we?" Cashman asked.

"Well, this sloop does have a boat of its own, a little eighteen-foot gig. Take five more men to run her under oars, though. Say three minimum, with two of your men aboard as guards."

"I can find enough lads to row her, you just give me one sailor to show 'em what to do. That way, I can take six more men, two as guards as you said, spelling each other, and part of the cargo with me."

"Cowell and McGilliveray might not like it, mind," Alan cautioned.

"The devil with what they like or don't like," Cashman said, sure of himself. "They're only civilians."

"They could ruin your career. And mine."

"There's not much more they could do to ruin mine, the way

things are going," Cashman laughed. "How enamored are you of yours?"

"I don't want to get cashiered," Alan said. "I'm getting just good enough at the Navy to want to keep it."

"You'll end up on the beach on half-pay soon enough anyway. And this whole expedition is a pretty neck-or-nothing thing. It's not like it has much hope of turning things around quickly."

"So why are you here, if you don't like it?" Alan demanded.

"Because I might become a substantive captain out of it," Cashman told him. "And the way things are going, it's the only little piece of the war I've left. Desperate or not, it beats garrison duty back on Jamaica, you see."

"Jesus."

"So don't tell me you weren't thinking about getting a little fame yourself out of it?" Cashman teased him. "Of course, long as we're changing things, who says you have to go?"

"Come, now."

"Seriously. If anybody'd asked me as to how we'd pull this off, I'd have stayed off the river entirely. Rivers are like highways in this country. Might as well hire a band. I'd trade for horses with the coastal Indians, and go overland. Lay up by the day, travel by night, disguises or no. If I'd helped plan this, I'd have asked for the Navy to merely get us here and come back to pick us up later. Just like Peacock not to confer with the ones who have to do it. Sail off."

"Damned if I will!" Alan spat. "Cowell would really have my hide for funking on him. And my admiral would have my hide a week later for cowardice. No sir!"

"Alright, then. We go inshore after it's dark, and we head up-river in the dark, to get as far as we can before it's light," Cashman schemed. "Then McGilliveray can turn into any old sort of Indian he likes and lead us the rest of the way, but without having to depend on this coastal tribe, who're like as not hand-in-glove with the Dons already. We'll have enough on our plate with the other tribes as it is."

"Damn your blood, sir!" Cowell fumed after he had been told of the new arrangements. "This is not what we agreed to at all, damme if it's not! I am charged by His Majesty's government directly to . . ."

"Mister Cowell, Lieutenant Lewrie and I are the senior military representatives," Cashman argued, as the unloading went on. "Now keep your voice down. Or do you wish to draw every bloody Don within fifty miles to this damned inlet? This way, we are much more secure. The sample goods still get up-river, you get up-river, White Turtle gets up-river, and we run the same bloody risks, but we do it on the sly. More than we would leaving the sloop behind to advert our presence."

"I'll have your hide for this, see if I do not, sir!" Cowell raged, but in a sibilant whisper into the tropical stillness. "Once we are back at Jamaica, Sir Joshua shall hear of this. Your captain shall know of your insubordinate attitude as soon as we *rendezvous* with his ship! And your colonel, too, Captain Cashman."

"The exigencies of the situation, sir," Alan said, almost quoting Cashman verbatim from one of their later planning sessions once the sloop had left *Shrike*'s company and made her final run of fifteen miles for the coast that afternoon. "Based on sound military reasoning, and on Captain Cashman's long experience, with which I concur totally."

"I'll send a letter to your captain before the night's out, I will!" Cowell went on. "And a despatch to Sir Joshua. If the sloop is no longer germane to our enterprise, she may serve to inform your superiors of my extreme displeasure with your conduct, sir!"

"Do what you like, sir," Alan replied with a genial tone.

"Mister Cowell, I must warn you to keep your voice down, sir," McGilliveray hissed, coming to their side. "Sound carries a long way at night, and you may be sure someone is watching and listening to every word you say, every action we do, this very minute."

It was hard to think of him any longer as young Mister Desmond McGilliveray, since he had shed his poor suitings for a snuff-brown linen shirt with the sleeves cropped off, a breech-clout tied about his waist with a hank of leather thong, a yellow waist sash, and deerskin leggings and moccasins. The bare coppery flesh of his legs, arms and chest revealed intricate tattoos that had been concealed by a European's togs.

"Do you know what this impudent . . . *puppy* . . . has done, sir?" Cowell raged. "Him and that jack-a-napes, jumped-up gutter-snipe Cashman?"

"Please discuss this below decks, and quietly," Alan cautioned. "And let me get on with the loading, if you please, gentlemen."

McGilliveray almost dragged Cowell to the hatch-way and led

him below, where they stumbled down the darkened ladder to the lower deck.

"Gig iss in der vater, zir," Svensen told him. "Vater butt, biscuit box, zalt meat barricoe, der mast, zails und oars, zir."

"Good, Svensen. Andrews shall take her as cox'n, and the soldiers shall do the rowing. Get the hands started on loading her with the smaller pile of goods yonder. As much as you think best. If we can't get it all aboard, sort out as many different kinds of things."

"Zir?" Svensen begged, unwilling to take responsibility with items unfamiliar to him.

"Then we'll let Mister Cowell or Mister McGilliveray see to that. You'll not keep this ship hidden here, as I first told you. Take her out to sea as soon as we're on our way. Meet up with *Shrike* and tell the captain we didn't think it was safe to leave her here."

"Aye, zir, t'ank Gott, me neider!"

"Give him this letter telling him the reasons for my decision. And I expect Mister Cowell shall have one for you, too," Alan said, smiling. "I shall go below and change."

Alan stumbled down to the hold accommodation deck of the small sloop, and stripped out of his uniform as men bustled about past curtains that served as light traps from the hold where they could at least see what they were doing in carrying goods and weapons to the spar deck.

"This is so damned daft!" he grumbled as he exchanged white slop trousers for an old pair of buff breeches reinforced with leather on the seat and inner thighs, some cavalryman's castoffs. They were much too big for him, but they would serve. A forest-green linen shirt went on over those, a faded blue sash about his waist outside the shirt, in which he stuck a boarding axe, much the size of an Indian's tomahawk, a pair of dragoon pistols he had kept as mementos from Yorktown, and a short dagger. Then came cartouche pouch and musket implements slung over his shoulders, and a baldric for a sword.

He eyed his hanger, the lovely Gill's in its dark blue leather sheath with the sterling silver fittings, the sea-shell design on the hilt and guard, and the gilt pommel of a lion's head. It was too precious to him to traipse about before sticky-fingered Indians, or lose, along with his life, if this expedition went sour. With a sigh, he put it down and exchanged it for one of the cheap Spanish cutlasses from the ship's weapons tub. He went aft to his quarters in the stern and wrote a short note which he wrapped about the scabbard, instructing that if he did not return, it should be sent to his grandmother in Devon whom he had never laid eyes on.

That act convinced him, if nothing else did, that there was more than usual danger in what they were about to do, and he regretted that he had not taken the time to write a few letters. There was Lucy, whom he had been forbidden from seeing since his disastrous actions of the months before. There was his maternal grandmother, who had rescued him from ignominy and poverty. There was Caroline Chiswick, now safely in the arms of her family in Charleston, if they had not already sailed for England by now. Poverty-stricken she might be, but she had been such a sweet and lovely girl, a little too tall and gawky for fashionable beauty, but damned handsome nonetheless, and devilish smart and delightful to converse with. God help him, he felt a pang for Dolly Fenton, and wished that he were back in her bed that instant. She at least had for a time loved him as well as she was able, and that was damned fine. He still regretted that last hour or so with her, when he had to tell her he was sailing away for good, and that her dreams of a little love-nest for just the two of them could not be. She had wept as quietly as she could, clung to him, given him passionate love once more, saving her real tears and squawls for total privacy. She had been so sweet, too, so dependent, yet good of heart, and, thank God, nowhere near as dumb as Lucy.

"Might as well write my fucking will while I'm at it!" he muttered, suffering a premonitory chill even as he said it. His insides cooled noticeably, and his stomach got a touch queasy as he finished gathering up a change of clothes and a few personal items in a sea-bag.

Damnit, this was a bloody undertaking, not like a sea-battle at all, which was gory enough for anyone's tastes. With McGilliveray to lead them and negotiate, they might be safe as houses, or they could end up tortured to death, *screaming* for death, and painted savages dancing about waving their *own* hair and their privates at them in glee!

"Jesus, I'm scared witless!" he whispered soft as he could in the privacy of his quarters, the temporary luxury of untold space in the former master's cabin. He had been frightened before. Any time he had to scale the masts. Before battle was joined, when he had time to think about how he could be mangled. The two duels he had fought in his short life. The shelling at Yorktown, or the horrible battle they had fought with Lauzun's

Legion and the Virginia Militia on Guinea Neck before they could escape. Even the first few weeks under Lieutenant Lilycrop's pitiless eyes as he fumbled his way to competence had tied his plumbing into hot knots, but nothing like this icy dread.

"Damn the Navy, damn King George, damn everybody!" he spat, within a touch of begging off at the last minute. It was all he could do to walk to the cabin door and think about joining his party.

There was a knock on the door, which almost loosed his bowels.

"Enter," he bade from a dreadfully dry mouth.

Cashman stepped inside, clad in pretty much the same rig as Alan, but with the addition of a scarlet officer's sash.

"You look like death's head on a mop-stick," Cashman said with a quirky little cock of his brows.

"How I look is nothing on how I feel," Alan grumbled.

"Then let's liquor our boots," Cashman suggested, crossing to the former captain's wine-cabinet. He drew out a wine bottle and took a swig from the neck, then handed the bottle to Lewrie.

"Ah, that's the ticket," Alan sighed. "Incredibly foul *vin rouge*, my last taste of civilization."

"I hope you've remembered rum for my troops?" Cashman asked. "God knows how anyone could do what we're about to do sober."

"Aye, rum enough for everyone for three weeks, though not the usual sailor's measure. A sip, no more."

"It's beginning to feel a touch insane about now, ain't it?"

"Insane ain't the word for it, sir." Alan shuddered.

"Call me Christopher," Cashman told him. "Growl we may, but go we must, you know. Give me that bottle, if you've had enough. I feel the need for a generous libation to put me numb enough to get on with the business."

"Feeling daunted yourself, hey?"

"Bloody terrified," Cashman admitted easily. "You?"

"I was wondering if I could break a leg or something at the last minute." Alan grinned back at him. Cashman tipped him a wink.

"Either way, it's bloody daft, the way we leap at chances for honor and glory," Cashman said with a belch, and handed the bottle back, which bottle had diminished in contents remarkably in a very short span of time. "Personally, I think it's a lot of balls, but that's what they pay us for. This is the worst time, when one steps out into the unknown. Once we've been shoved into motion, it usually goes much better."

"That's been my experience." Alan nodded. "What about Cowell and McGilliveray?"

"Cowell *sahib* is still scribbling away at his objections, but the Turtle-*rajah* came round at the last, long as the goods get up-river. He suggested the sloop would do better to handle the transfer of goods from *Shrike*, instead of having your ship come inshore with her. Wants you to pass the word to your captain to load her up and stand ready to meet us once we get the *gora logs* convinced to set out the red war pole."

"Could you possibly speak the King's English, Kit?"

"Ah, sorry, not possible, you see. Been too long away from it. I can *pidgin* with any Samboe you want from the Hooghly Bar to the Coromandel coast. I can even get along in Creole with the slaveys up in the Blue Mountains. Who knows, by the time we're done, I'll master Creek, too?"

"Well, we can open another bottle," Alan sighed, tossing the empty onto the coverlet of the hanging cot. "Or we could get started while it's still dark and quiet."

"Best go, then. Or we'll never." Cashman tried to smile.

"Aye. Goddamnit."

"Amen, parson Lewrie."

Chapter 4

Florida pretty much ain't worth a tuppeny shit, Alan thought moodily as they lay up ashore just a few miles short of the head-waters of the Ochlockonee. The past night and day had been miserable. The air was still, and foetid with the smells of marsh and mud, the swamps aswarm with mosquitoes and biting flies, biting gnats. Alligators and poisonous snakes were two-a-penny on the banks, in the water, laying out for a bask on the tree limbs that overhung the banks when they were forced close ashore by a bend in the channel, or snuffling about under the banks in their nests and roaring at them when disturbed.

They had made very good time, though, catching a favorable slant of wind on the first night when the river was wide enough for short-tacking inland. So far they were a day ahead of schedule.

It was only after the sun had come up that they had been forced to row as the banks closed in and rose higher in thickly treed hammocks that blocked the breeze from the sea, and the familiar tang of salt air was left behind like a lover's perfume. The heat wasn't bad, though the air was stiflingly wet enough and humid enough to wring perspiration from them by the bucket, and it was a blessing that the leafy green waters could be drunk safely, or dipped up and sluiced over tired bodies.

Bald cypress, scrub pine, and yellow-green stagnant ponds spread out on either hand under the canopy of the marshes, punctuated by water reeds, sharp-edged grasses, or jagged stumps of prodigious size. Bright birds the like of which the hands had never seen cried and stalked or fluttered below the canopy. Frogs the size of rabbits croaked at them from their resting places. Water bugs skittered on the deceptively calm water as it slid like treacle through the marshes. Now and then a hammock of higher sandy ground loomed up around a bend in the channel, covered with pines thick as the hair on a cat's back, open to the bright sky as the result of a lightning fire, or burn.

Otter, deer, a host of wildlife, lurked along the banks. Alan saw raccoons for the first time, and opposums hanging by their naked tails like obscene caricatures of rats. He had been almost nauseated by McGilliveray's grunted comment that opposums were very good to eat, though he was never one to refuse a bread-room fed "miller" in his midshipman days—at least the ship's rats were decent-sized!

McGilliveray had gone totally native by then, stripping off his shirt to bare more pagan tattooing, wrapping a length of cloth about his head like a Hindi's *turban* as Cashman styled it, naked under breech-clout, and the leggings only covering his thighs, held up by thongs from the single strap that held the breech-clout in place. Most of the sailors had tied their kerchiefs about their heads like small four-cornered mob-caps. The soldiers sported rough imitations of *turbans*, and had taken off their shirts as well, though their skins gleamed almost frog-belly pale in the fierce light, and several were already regretting the expo-

sure, and patting their burns with water. At least in that regard
Alan's sailors were more fortunate, since they had had months
and years of continual tanning by the sun, so they appeared at
first glance as ruddy as any savage.

"Apalachee scout over there," McGilliveray whispered, coming to Lewrie's side. "I shall go speak to him."

"Is that wise?" Cowell asked, almost prostrate with exhaustion, though he had not done a lick of work since plunking his
posterior on a thwart the night before. Alan thought it comical
to see how McGilliveray had tricked Cowell out in breech-clout,
leggings, moccasins and calico checkered shirt, with a *turban* of
his own, like a maggot done up as a man. He could not have
fooled a European at a hundred yards, and any Indian running
across him would have asked him how fast the pitch was at the
new Lord's cricket grounds.

"We have to let them know who we are eventually, sir,"
McGilliveray said. "They saw us land, tracked us up-river. I had
hoped we would make contact with them last night. It's only polite, seeing as how we've crossed most of their territory already."

"If this is the best real-estate they have, they're welcome to
every bloody stick of it," Alan griped.

McGilliveray stood up and waved an arm, calling out in his
odd language, and from where Alan thought only a mosquito
could live, up popped a full half-dozen savages, dressed in
breech-clouts and tattoos only, bearing long cane bows and arrows. McGilliveray took off his moccasins and waded across a
shallow slough of weeds and reeds to converse with them.

"They don't look like Rousseau's noble savages, do they,
Mister Cowell?" Cashman asked, coming to join them as they
stood idly by watching the parley.

"Look how lithe and tall they are, how nobly they bear themselves, sir," Cowell disagreed softly. "One does not need much
clothing in such climes. Mankind, reduced to Eden, without a
houseful of possessions and gew-gaws, with no prating philoso-
phies to occasion rancor, shorn of metaphysics, of confusing science. They are a handsome folk, you'll not be able to deny. All
pretensions of society cast aside, and relying on Nature and our
Creator and their native wit for sustenance. You may speak of
barbarity, of quick anger and bloody-handed murther, but has
Mankind, in all our wisdom, gone far beyond those passions for
all our supposed improvements, Captain Cashman?"

"We don't kill quite so openly and easily, sir," Cashman replied.

"Life, in all its facets, is closer and more personal with them, sir. They are not like us, but we were once much like them, and still are, in many ways yet. The brave man slays with a sword, the coward with an invitation to tea, if I may paraphrase the quotation, ha ha."

"I've never been *scalped* at a cat-lapping," Alan quipped. "Fucked with, God yes, and damned proud of it, mind."

"We are in luck, Mister Cowell," McGilliveray told them when he returned. "There are Seminolee a few miles ahead of us, in a spring camp to fish. Lots of horses."

"Any Spanish?" Cashman pressed.

"None seen this far inland in weeks. Some parties passed north of the swamps and crossed the rivers heading west a few days ago," McGilliveray/White Turtle grunted, having seemingly given up the act of smiling for the duration. "A company of horse, and one of foot, with baggage train. But they were busy driving stolen cattle they took from British colonists far off to the east."

"According to this map, there is a small stream that leads to the Apalachicola River," Alan pointed out, folding out their large chart. "How deep is it? This one that leads west and nor'west."

"Very shallow. Dugout canoes have trouble there," their guide said, after peering at the map, and at Lewrie. "Another change, Mister Lewrie?"

"We've made good time by water so far, why change bets now?" Alan replied, mopping his face with a kerchief. "If it goes our way."

"Best we continue on north." White Turtle scowled, pointing in that direction with a chin jutted over his shoulder. "This river bends easterly to the lake. Where the lake begins we find horses. Leave the boats, and a guard over them."

"Damn, splitting our party again," Cashman spat. "What's odds these Apalachee, or your relatives the Seminolee, would keep them safe for us. For a share of the profits, of course."

"If the Seminolee want something, they take it." He shrugged.

"Well, they can't make off with anything big as a launch and a gig, can they?" Alan japed. "I saw something up at Yorktown, a set of poles lashed together from a horse so it could drag, instead of carry a load. We could take the rations, masts, oars, everything on the drag behind one horse. I assume we'll march?

Right, then. We haul the boats ashore and hide them from the Spanish at least. Then if they rip out the thwarts, we may still make new ones later. Wrap everything else up in the sails and shroud lines, which we can't easily replace."

"You are a paragon, Alan," Cashman beamed. "I'd never have ever thought of anything like that. See how fortunate we are, Mister Cowell, how well the Admiralty has provided for you?"

"Let's simply be on our way. It's stifling in these swamps," Cowell fluttered petulantly.

"Right you are, then. Off we go. Andrews? Back into the boats."

They began to get back aboard, but several of the men from the launch shrank back in fear and scrambled back ashore quick as they could.

"They's a bloody *snake*, Mister Lewrie, sir!" one of the hands yelped.

"Well, kill it and let's go."

"No!" McGilliveray shouted. "Never kill a snake! Bad luck with my people!"

"Wot're we s'posed ter do wif'em,'en, kiss 'em an' tuck 'em inna bed'r somefin'?" one of the older men muttered loud enough to hear.

"I do it. They're poisonous," McGilliveray offered, and climbed into the boat, using a long club to lift the snake out and toss it over the side, after greeting it in Muskogean.

"Notice how his speech is getting more pidgin as we go?" Cashman noted before they shoved off.

"Yes, I had. Must be getting back into the mood of his people," Alan replied.

"Perhaps," Cashman whispered, rubbing his nose. "Perhaps."

After camping at the lake shore with the party of Seminolee men, they started out at first light after a dip in the water and a quick breakfast. The Seminolee had provided some rather good horses, and had known what Alan was driving at when he described a drag. With some of the trade goods left behind, and at least the promise that the boats would be left undisturbed, there was nothing for it but to proceed.

Once out of the swamps, the land opened out into grassy meadows almost like park land, where the heat was not so oppressive and the gentle winds could cool them on their march. It was early January, and the skies were cloudier than before, promising rain.

With a pair of cotton stockings on, rolled down to the ankle, Alan found moccasins rather comfortable to march in. They went in a single file, with soldiers and sailors gathered round the pack-horses, and Seminolee out on the flanks and rear, with a scout out ahead.

"Great warrior, the Raven," White Turtle said, pointing with his chin to the head of the column. "The bravest man. He gives call of a raven if he sees trouble. To the left, the Wolf."

"Who howls, I presume?" Alan replied, meaning to be civil.

"To the right, the Owl, who will hoot. Behind us, the Fox who will yelp." McGilliveray nodded in agreement. "The others should go all in each others' moccasin prints, so it only looks like one man. Might be a big party, might be one man alone. Makes for safety."

"Seems safe enough now."

"Nothing is safe here, you will learn."

"But it's so open!" Alan protested, shifting the sling of his fusil on his shoulder. "Two hundred yards to the trees, and the scouts."

"Hide behind tree, hide in those groves. Lay in the grass. Ten warriors, twenty? They could be on you before you get that gun to your shoulder."

"Delightful." Alan shuddered. "Look, about that snake yesterday. Never kill a snake."

"No."

"Never wash meat in a stream, never piss in one, never put out a fire with water. Never get downstream of a widow, or upstream from a wife. Avoid women in their monthlies like the plague. What else?"

"A great deal more, Lewrie," McGilliveray said. "But it makes sense to us. Women are a separate animal from man. Not like us at all, so we have to be careful we are not defiled. We know the Thunder Boys are the ones who create mischief in this world, and people bring it on because they mixed elements that should not have been mixed. In the world above, everything is perfect, each animal, each plant, and man and woman, larger than us, and perfect. Down below in the underworld, monsters and witches and Water-Cougar, one of everything, but evil. In the right here world, sometimes the perfect comes down, sometimes bad comes up from below, like Spear-Finger, the old woman who kills and steals men's souls to feed on so she can live forever. Even when she was finally killed, she did not really die. The good and the bad always come back, so people must always be on their guard not to defile their spirit, or offend the Great Spirit by defilement. For their own good, their family and clan, and their nation."

"Is that what you believe personally?" Alan asked. "Are you a Christian, or do you believe the native religion?"

"When my father took me to Charleston, and then to England, he taught me about God and Jesus, but I always found it a little confusing," McGilliveray admitted. "Even after a year at Cambridge, I find the old ways more comforting. Mister Cowell and his friends tried to explain the unexplainable as he puts it, but the various points of doctrine are troubling to me."

"Ah well, most people have that problem. Most call themselves Deists and let it go at that." Alan grinned.

"Then you do not honor your God who made you, as we do. To say that God exists, and then continue your life your own way, is to negate your belief," McGilliveray expounded. "Others leap about and speak no known tongue, shake and dance in glory. They raise the Bible on high and declare everyone sinners but themselves. But then they go out and kill eagles for sport, kill snakes, sleep with their women in their courses. All Christians treat the earth as a dead thing to walk upon, and all animals as dumb food. When we kill an eagle to get its feathers for our great men, it takes much prayer, and we ask the eagle, and the Great Spirit, who is most in the birds, and in the eagles of any race of animals on earth, to forgive us for we have to do this. Christians would strip this land bare, chop all the trees, slaughter all the game far beyond what they could eat, because God gave man *dominion* back in the cloud-time before the clans saw their signs. Look here," he said, pointing to a circle tattoo on his chest, which enclosed a four-legged equilateral cross.

"This is the circle of the world between the sky and the underworld. The four principal directions, and where they meet, right here now. Everyone of Indian blood knows here is where he must live if he wants to be good, following the laws laid down by the Great Perfect Spirits."

He reached out and put a hand inside Alan's shirt.

"Hold on, my good fellow!" Alan snapped, unused like any Englishman at being pawed at. But McGilliveray took hold of his small *juju* bag strung about his neck and weighed it thoughtfully.

"How odd. I had expected to find a cross," McGilliveray said with a wary expression. He let go of the bag so that Alan could tuck it back into his shirt. "The white man's cross is off-center. There is no sense of being centered, and the directions lead off to nothing, which is why all white men, all Christians are so unhappy, and want to have dominion. I saw the old roods, the Celtic crosses of your people in the long ago, which had circles around the center, but the directions go beyond the circle. They must have been close to the truth in those days, but even so, they never really knew peace."

"We could have had a fish, you know. What would you make of that, I wonder?" Alan groused, still resenting the manhandling.

"Then it would be a great fish that swims the world's oceans and never knows rest," McGilliveray intoned. "If one cannot find peace, then one will try to run everything to one's own satisfaction in the search for peace. How much better are my people, who live so close and snug to each other, in a great family. We know want, but we share equally, not like you who store up food and wealth from each other and let other men of your kind starve or beg. If our clan or town is rich in food, we all eat well. If there is little, we all starve together, and pray that we have lived well, so that the Great Spirits and the perfect spirits of the deer people, bear people and fish people may come to our hunters and help us by giving us their lives. If a man was starving back in your London, and he came to your door, would you send out a slice of your roast beef to him? I do not think you would, sir. To you, all is property and goods. You are a Christian yourself?"

"Church of England, and damned proud of it, sir."

"So many of your people say that, but they do not really believe in their crucified son of God, not in their hearts. And which God do you serve with your little bag?" McGilliveray asked with the smugly superior tone of anyone who thinks he is more righteous than the next.

"It's a good luck charm, from a young lady of my acquaintance," Alan had to admit sheepishly. "One of her servants made it . . . to keep me safe from drowning, and such."

"Not even representative of any god, then. How sad. What is in it, do you know?"

"No, I don't. And what's in yours?" Alan asked.

"My personal medicine."

"Then please be so good as to leave mine alone in future," Alan spat.

McGilliveray glared and trotted toward the head of the column.

"Bet the Wesley brothers would *love* you," Alan muttered to himself once McGilliveray had gotten far enough off, thinking how absurd it was to be discussing theology with a Cambridge man in breech-clout and scarifications with his bare arse waving about in the breeze.

At the evening stop, not half a day's march from the second lake where they would find McGilliveray's tribal towns, Alan took a tour of his men, seeing to it that they were bedded down comfortably and had a hot meal. Some of the Seminolee had put up some birds and nailed them with their insubstantial cane arrows tipped with fish bones or tiny flints. There was *sofkee*, a hominy meal mush, a soup or stew of the birds, *succotash* of sweet corn kernels and beans, and cool clear water to wash it down.

The men had been issued a small measure of rum, liberally mixed with water to have with their meal, and the Seminolee had crowded round to take a taste, though McGilliveray was leery of the practice, and warned all not to share more with them.

" 'Ere ya go, Mister Lewrie, sir," Cony said, dishing up a bowl of *sofkee* with some of the game-bird stew ladled over it. "H'it ain't bad, really. Better eatin'n we got in the Chesapeake, sir. An' I got yer rum ration laid by, so's the Seminolee won't notice."

"You're a wonder, Cony," Alan said, sitting down crosslegged on a piece of sailcloth by a crackling small fire with the other officers. McGilliveray was at another fire with the Seminolee, stuffing food into his mouth with one hand and talking with the other. Pipes were going on all sides, though it was a rough blend, Cowell stated.

"Well, no one's turned into mad foaming bears yet from rum," Cashman said. "Though I wouldn't mind much."

"One is struck by how much progress we have made," Cowell said, smiling while perched on a fallen log for a seat. "It has all fallen out pretty much as young Desmond said it would. The Apalachee were friendly, and now so too are the Seminolee, giving us an escort and all."

"There is that," Cashman replied, laughing softly. "And the fact that we still have our hair and our livers."

"If one approaches people in a friendly, open manner, Captain, with something of value that they desire, as a prize for good behavior, what else could one expect?" Cowell sniffed. In the firelight he looked, in his Indian garb, much like some haggard bridge troll from a nursery story. "We have not given offense, have we?"

"No, but other white men before us have, and they're not the sort to forget easily, or forgive," Cashman commented between spoonfuls of victuals. "There's still the possibility that someone might be tempted to knock us off for our arms and the goods we carry, and the devil with the rest of the shipment. They have no concept of time, of waiting for things promised when they can get half a loaf now."

"For your information, these Seminolee are going with us to the Creek town," Cowell told them. "To get a share of the spoils, yes, and to visit. Indians either fight or feed you if you show up on their door step. Some of them have second wives among the Muskogee. They've sent for their *mikkos* to come parley. And they let Desmond know that his own *mikkos* are pretty much together at the main town ahead of us. It's some game they play, an annual contest of some importance to them."

"So Parliament's been called to session, and it's Cambridge Fair," Alan offered for a jest.

"It would appear so, Lieutenant Lewrie," Cowell replied stiffly, still on the outs with his naval commander. "I shall be glad to get there, put on a decent suit, and get out of these rags And spend a night under a roof. No matter how exotic and exciting this journey of ours is, I must own to being unused to such discomfort."

"We did have a roof over our heads last night," Cashman pointed out. "That was about all, though, I'll grant you."

The Seminolee had erected a temporary fishing camp, replete with structures they called *chickees*, open platforms raised several feet off the ground and open to the night winds and any flying insects, with a thatched roof to keep off the rain. McGilliveray told them sleeping so high off the ground discouraged snakes that would otherwise crawl into their bedding for warmth, and made the leap too far for fleas. Either way, either the mosquitos or the tiny biting gnats had gotten to them, for they all itched and had broken out in rashes.

"Desmond tells me that as honored guests and ambassadors, we shall probably be quartered in the town house," Cowell went on. "If the visiting *mikkos* have not already taken it. Their winter meeting hall, I'm told, very solid and snug. Much like an Irish sod house, I think."

"God pity us," Cashman said grinning. "All fleas and no whiskey."

McGilliveray came back from the Seminolee fire circle to join them, and sat down gracefully in a cross-legged position. "If you have finished supper, you might wish to try a short parley with the Seminolee with me, sir. Their Raven is not very influential, but you will do great honor to sit with him and smoke a pipe or two. He's gaining note as a warrior, and as a great man, sure to lead a chiefdom in future."

"That sounds eminently sensible, thank you, Desmond, I shall."

Cony and Andrews came in from the dark, carrying large bundles of Spanish moss, which they had harvested from the nearest trees to make a soft mat for bedding, and McGilliveray smiled for the first time that day.

"I wouldn't if I were you, gentlemen. Don't sleep on moss."

"Why?" Alan asked, having used some the night before to make a pallet.

"There are tiny red bugs that thrive in the moss, like very small lice," McGilliveray told them. "They can hardly be seen, but they drive people mad from the itching."

"I was wondering what 'gentlemen's companions' had gotten to us," Cashman said, and Cony and Andrews dumped the stuff immediately and began to wipe their arms and chests down.

"Once we get to the town, I can give you some grease to make them leave you, but for tonight, I am afraid you shall have to scratch." He frowned. "Did you use some last night? I'm sorry, I should have told you. There is so much to know, and so much of it comes naturally to me, that it slipped my mind entirely."

"We could take a dip and scrub them off. I have some soap," Alan offered.

"Not at night!" McGilliveray gasped. "The Water-Cougar . . . !" He paused and pouted at his own reaction. "It's safer to avoid the water after dark. You can't see the snakes until you stumble upon them."

"What a country," Alan snapped, exasperated and now itching fit to feel the need to scream. Damme, I started out being terrified of being gutted and scalped, and now I'm more scared of dropping my breeches after dark than I am of these mangy pagans, he thought.

"It is good country, even so," Cowell said. "Look at these fine meadows, just waiting for herds to graze them. Think of the crops that could be raised in this rich soil. Forests enough to build fine home-steads."

"It is a fine country, sir," McGilliveray echoed. "But, who is to do this farming and cattle-raising? Our people like having wild land around them, land no one uses, except for hunting and fishing. Do not forget that one of our aims is to reach some sort of accommodation with our respective peoples. The lands are just as rich to the east, on the other side of Apalachee Bay."

"You mean this would revert to Indian land?" Cashman asked.

"There are swamps and rivers running north and south to the east. The new American colony of Georgia to the north," McGilliveray pointed out. "If my people, and the Seminolee, are to be your barrier to future expansion here in the south by the Rebels, we must determine where the Creek, Seminolee and others can live in peace, with secure borders."

"Why can't we live together?" Alan asked, trying his hand at politics. "It would be good for your people, would it not?"

"When has it ever been good for Indians to live cheek-to-jowl with Europeans, Lieutenant Lewrie?" McGilliveray asked sadly. "Do you but think back on the history of relations between us since the first colonists. Slaughter, misunderstandings, Indians displaced from their ancestral lands by usurpers. We shall never understand each other. You think in terms of property to buy and sell; my people own everything, and nothing. Our ways are so different. Your people slave to make a living, put up houses to last hundreds of years, while my people do with so little, and all we have is impermanent, taking only what we need. We are clean in our personal habits of bathing each morning, but wear the same single trade-good clothing until they wear out, and have no need for more, just to have something to prove we are wealthy, as you do. I saw your sea chest aboard ship, sir. You carry a lifetime's worth of goods for your comfort. I and any of my people could gather his life's possessions in a single sack, and feel rich."

"Well . . ." Alan began but Cashman shushed him with a nudge.

"Perhaps sometime in the distant future, there will be good relations between us, but until then, it would be best if someone could say, here is Indian land this side of this river. No whites but traders and missionaries go there. Here is where Indians do not go. We Creeks and the Seminolee know our borders, to the north where Upper Creek territory starts, and the Upper Creek know where Cherokee land begins. To the west of here are Chickasaw, Choctaw, Natchez. If white men come among us here, there is nowhere for us to go. If rum comes among us as trade goods, we lose respect for our *mikkos* and mischief comes down with the Thunder Boys. We cannot be with you and stay a people. If you need us, and truly want to live in peace with us, you must realize this. If you want us to take the arms and fight your enemies for you, then you must let us live our own ways on our own lands. To keep our lands and our ways, we need your support and your arms, your soldiers close by."

"But what about the smaller tribes already here?" Cashman asked.

"The Spanish and the French have already destroyed them," McGilliveray said. "They could move to the Indian territories, if they do not like living among the Rebels or the British. People in small groups can always find a home in another tribe easily. And if there is land that you want, then the Upper Creeks, the Lower Creeks, and the Seminolee, tied by trade treaties, supported by British arms, can make war on the smaller tribes with you. The Alabama, Biloxi, Kosati, and some of the tribes along the coast. West of here, toward Pensacola, and the mouth of the Mobile, there are fewer swamps along the coast. If we march together, you take certain lands, and we take certain lands, making sure we have good borders, you get what you want, and we get what we want. When the Rebels come across the mountains, as they will, they will put pressure on the Cherokee, and the small tribes in Georgia, who will be forced to move onto our lands. But if my people have strong allies who will march to our aid and give us weapons, we can say 'no' to them."

"An Indian kingdom," Cowell said, having heard the argument before. "We join hands with *sultans* and *rajahs* in the East Indies so."

"This would give heart to the Cherokee to hold onto their land, to come parley with England for the same sort of help. And you already help the Iroquois League north of them. A solid barrier, all along the great river Mississippi, west of the mountains where the Rebels live."

"Been my experience with *sultans* that they'd rather fight among themselves than eat," Cashman stated, a trifle dubious.

"Then bring officers among us, white officers and sergeants to lead us, to teach us, like the East India Company raises native units," McGilliveray urged, getting excited. "Bring teachers to help us develop our own books, printed in Muskogean. Do you know just how big this continent really is, Captain? How far it stretches to the other ocean? It would take a thousand years to fill it up with people. Think of Indian regiments who could help you take it and hold it. Think of future wars with the Rebels, and how the people east of the mountains could be defeated with our help, not just as irregular scouts and raiders, but as a field army, like Germanic and Gallic auxiliaries who supplied the cavalry to Imperial Rome! And how barbaric were the Germans to the Romans at the time. As barbaric as we appear to your burgeoning Empire now?"

"Gad!" Alan exclaimed, getting dizzy at the thought of it. "Is that what we could start? We'd go down in history, famous as anybody!"

"It is, indeed, Lieutenant Lewrie," Cowell said so soberly that even in his ludicrous togs, he looked as impressive as any togaed Senator of old Rome himself. "So you see why Desmond and I were so worried that neither of you seemed very involved in it, and have altered our carefully laid arrangements."

"Had we been *told*, sir, it would have made a difference," Cashman replied. "Did you discuss this hope with Lieutenant Colonel Peacock? With Alan's admiral?"

"We were not able to make either of them privy to all our goals."

"Damme, Mister Cowell, we should've landed a regiment and come ashore with a band, 'stead o' this rag-tag-and-bobtail. I didn't even bring my regimentals with me. Alan left his uniform behind. From now on, would you *please* consider us in your plans, 'stead o' keepin' it to y'rself?"

"I give you my solemn vow that from this instant, you shall be thoroughly informed, and involved, in our deliberations, Captain," Cowell said, giving them a satisfied smile. "But do you see the implications of our embassy to the most powerful southern tribes? Not simply correcting a fiscal mistake which reduced subsidies when the war began. If we had continued financial aid, the Creeks and Seminolee would have stayed on with us instead of staying neutral, and we would have had the force to retain Florida and Georgia, come the Devil himself against us. God willing, it is still not too late to recover this region. And in the process, establish a fairer, more productive and peaceful relationship between all Indians and all Europeans throughout the Americas, one that shall put to shame near on two hundred and fifty years of the way we have dealt together. The Rebels are married to the old ways, while our new colonists to a renascent

British Florida, untainted by misconceptions of the past, can adjust to the new order of things."

"And I would not worry much about making a grand show," McGilliveray chuckled. "Along the Great Lakes, the 8th Regiment wears Iroquois garb as part of its full-dress regimentals, Captain. My people have seen grand embassies before, and they all led to nothing. What we bring is more important than how well you dress for them. As I remember, I saw a painting in London just before we left. A very famous soldier portrayed in part Hindu garb, part rag-tag-and-bobtail, as you put it. He was Clive of India. Would you gentlemen like to be known to history as famous as Clive? He won England a doorway to India. You could win England the rest of North America."

Chapter 5

Alan had not known what to expect when they got to the Indian town. At best a cluster of *chickees* straggling along the lake shore. But what greeted him was a frontier fortress. Across nearly a mile of bottom land thickly sprigged with new corn stalks twined with vines laden with quickening bean pods, row upon raised row of plantings mixed with gourds and squash, plots of other vegetables and fiber plants he had never seen cultivated before, there was a huge town surrounded by a tall log palisade, with watch-towers every fifty yards or so, and gates cut into the walls with guard-towers alongside them.

McGilliveray informed them that this chiefdom, the White Town, held land about a mile and a half in depth into the forests from the shore of the lake, and ran for over six miles east and west.

In pride of place, McGilliveray mounted a magnificent Seminolee horse and rode at the forefront of their column, with Cowell at his side, now turned out in a bright blue silk suit as neatly as if he were taking a stroll along The Strand. Alan, Cashman, and their troops followed in two columns, somewhat uniform in their forest green shirts and breeches or slop trousers. Seminolee brought up the rear, leading the pack animals, yipping and curvetting their mounts to show off.

"Just like the Romans," Cashman said as they passed through the gate into the town proper. "A fightin' mound just behind the gate with another palisade, you see. Bends us to the left, you'll note, between another long mound. Opens up our weapons side to arrows, and puts our shield side on the left where it wouldn't do any good. It'd take a light artillery piece to force an entry here, if you could get close enough to un-limber under the fire o' those towers. Nacky bastards."

"Just as long as we get safely out," Alan replied, looking at all the Indians who had congregated to watch their arrival. "Goddamn, Kit, do you see 'em? Look at all those bouncers, will you! Not one stitch on above the waist! Oh, Jesus, I'm in love with that'n there!"

"Never let it be said you let a solemn moment cramp your style," Cashman drawled.

"You conquer what you want, and I'll conquer what I want."

"I doubt the Royal Academy would hang that sort of heroic portrait of you in Ranelagh Gardens. Besides, if you keep ogling all the girls, your men will get out of hand. Set an example," Cashman ordered. "For now, at least."

"Eyes to your front!" Alan barked over his shoulder.

The street they paraded was wide as any in London, wider than some in Paris, lined with what seemed to be a definite pattern of buildings. There was a fence of sorts surrounding each plot, an insubstantial thing of dried vines and cane. Behind each fence was a two-story wood house much like a *chickee*, with plaited mats hung from under the eaves, some open and some closed. A more substantial house of thickly woven cane walls daubed with mud sat in each plot, along with one, two or three smaller out-buildings, and each plot featured a home garden of some kind.

But, grand as it looked, the place was rough on the nose. They might bathe every morning, Alan thought, but something stinks to high heaven. It smells worse than London, that's for sure.

The plots were laid out in a rectangular pattern, so many of the plots to each . . . he was forced to call them town blocks, with narrower lanes leading off at right angles from the main thoroughfare. Up ahead was an open area, and what looked like a gigantic plaza raised several feet above the town's mean elevation, upon which sat a large wattle and daub structure, and beyond it a collection of open-sided sheds. Beyond that, there seemed to be a war going on.

Several hundred Creek warriors were whooping and storming from one end of the plaza to the other, all waving some kind of war club, and flowing like waves on a beach, swirling left and right in pursuit of something. It had to be some ritual war, Alan decided, by the way the clubs were raised on high and brought down on the odd head. Now and then, the shrieks and cries surged to a positive tumult as the mob congregated around a tall central pole. The mayhem was so fierce he expected to see bodies flying in the air.

One thing that amazed their party were the many people who looked almost white compared to the run-of-the-mill savage. Not just white men and women who might have gone native while on a trading venture, but a great many scarified tribespeople who sported blue or green eyes, blonde hair, or other signs of European origin. There were also lots of people much darker than average who appeared to have been sired by Blacks, or a few men and women who could be nothing but Black.

Once they stacked their goods by the winter town house and had a chance to look around, Cowell asked McGilliveray about this phenomenon.

"Runaway slaves, sir," McGilliveray said with a smile. "And men from the Colonies who found our way of life more agreeable than slaving for a harsh master. Or the Army."

"Or deserters run from a King's ship?" Alan asked.

"Possibly, Mr. Lewrie." McGilliveray laughed, at ease among his favorite kind. "Captives taken by war parties, too. Our life is hard, make no mistake of that, but it is much less hard than white man's ways. There are many captives who eventually prefer to stay when given the chance to escape. Talk to them, find out for yourself. Every child wants to play Indian, but no Indian child wants to play white man, or go willingly to live among your people. The ball game will go on for hours yet. I shall go find my mother's people, and tell her we are here. You rest here in the shade. Do not raise your hand to any man, or give any offense, I warn you now. Keep your goods safe in the center of your group, and don't wander too far. You are safe, so there is no call to brandish weapons, I swear it. One thing, though," he warned as he left, "don't show any liquor until you are safely housed."

There was nothing for it but to gather their boxes and chests together and use them for furniture. They sat in the welcome shade and fanned flies. Some of the men might have been tired enough from their marches to sleep, but the swarming activity of a whole town full of savages kept them awake and near their weapons.

The Creeks walked by without a care in the world, laughing and pointing to the white party now and then, calling out what seemed to be friendly greetings. Some scowled at them and made threatening gestures from a distance, but the White Town was supposedly, according to McGilliveray, a place of sanctuary and peace, where grudges could not be acted out.

"We should have waited outside the town walls until tomorrow," Cashman finally mumbled, almost asleep.

"Why is that, sir?" Cowell asked.

"We're bein' *made* to wait, sir," Cashman said. "Coolin' our heels in the ante-room. Best they got their damned game over and been ready to receive us at once, with no excuses. We lose authority by being kept waitin' like this. Devilish shabby way to treat an embassy."

"Desmond knows best, surely," Cowell complained.

"Oh, perhaps he does, sir," Cashman grunted, too sleepy to argue about it. He pulled a pipe out of his pack and started cramming tobacco into it.

"Hullo," an Indian boy said, coming up close to them while Cashman got out his flint, steel and tinder for a light. The child was only about five or so, as English in appearance as any urchin on a London street.

"Hello, yourself." Cashman grinned. "And where'd you spring from?"

"Here."

"Before," Alan prompted, not too terribly fond of children, but willing to be friendly, as long as he had to be.

"Before when?"

"Before you came here?"

"Tallipoosa town," the boy said, pointing north.

"Before you were a Creek," Alan asked.

"In belly." The child grinned widely. "What is Creek?"

"Muskogee," Cashman said.

"Me Muskogee!" the boy crowed proudly.

A youngish white man in breech-clout and head band came

over to them, and spoke to the boy in Muskogean. "He botherin' you, sirs?"

"Not at all, sir." Cashman smiled, now puffing on his pipe. "I was askin' him what he was before he was Muskogee."

"He's always been," the man replied, squatting down in their circle cross-legged, fetching out a pipe of his own, this one part of a tomahawk he had in his waist thong. Cashman shared his pouch of tobacco with him. "Ah, 'tis grand, this is, sir, the genuine Virginia article. Beats *kinnick-kinnick*, it does, thankee kindly. Now what would be bringin' a English officer into these parts?"

"An embassy to your *mikkos*," Cashman allowed grudgingly, and Cowell woke up enough to huff a warning to keep their business close to their chests.

"Not seen English about since Fort St. George went under down to Pensacola in '81," the man said, having trouble with his English from long dis-use.

"And how did you know he's an officer, fellow?" Alan asked.

"Same way I knows you are, sir." The man beamed with good humor. "I was a soldier meself, back five-six year ago, at Mobile. I run off. Not much you gonna do about that, is there, sir?"

"Enjoy your honorable retirement, sir," Cashman said laughing lazily. "Good life among the Muskogee, is it?"

"Better'n fair, sir. I was once called Tom. Now I'm part of the Muskrat Clan, me name's Red Coat. Got me a Muskogee wife, and the boy, o'course."

"So what's the life like, Red Coat?" Cashman drawled.

"Oh, Injun men work, sir, don't let nobody tell ya differn't," Tom/Red Coat allowed with a shrug. "Got to hunt, fish, build things now an' agin. Keep a roof over yer heads, food in yer belly. Help with the harvests, though the wimmen tends the fields. Fight when t'other tribes stirs up a fuss. Say, you wouldn't be havin' no rum ner whiskey, would ya, sir?"

"Clean out of it, I'm afraid, Tom." Cashman frowned.

"You bringin' guns an' powder, looks like," Tom observed keenly. "Want the Muskogee to do some fightin' fer ya's? With Galvez over to New Orleans with nigh on four thousand men? Garrisons at Mobile and Pensacola, and patrols all over these parts? 'Tis a wonder ya got this far, and that's a fack. They brung five thousand outa Havana when they took Pensacola, and that's not two days' march from here."

"We're devilish fellows, Tom," Cashman grunted. "What's odds we get put up in this long house here?"

"Wouldn't hold me breath on that. Too many *mikkos* in from the tall timber, Seminolee, too. Who brung ya this far? Had to be a Injun guided ya?"

"White Turtle," Cashman said finally, after playing with his pipe to exchange glances with Cowell.

"White Turtle, hey? He's pretty well connected. Must be somethin' powerful important, then," Tom speculated. "Might get put up with the Wind Clan, and Green-Eyed Cat. Hey, sure ya don't have no whiskey? I could come 'round later on the sly, like, so's the bucks don't get a nose of it. I palaver Muskogean powerful good, sir. Ya might find me a useful man, so's ya don't make anybody mad if yer gonna stay a spell. Be yer interpreter an' such."

"That might be worth talking about." Cashman nodded slowly. "I can't promise anything, mind."

"Wink's as good as the nod, sir, I get yer meanin'. I go." He knocked the dottle out of his pipe, crushed it between his fingers hot, and stuffed it into a small beaded pouch, and stood up. "Oh, by the way, sir. Tell yer friend in the pretty suit not ta sit on his knees like a woman. They been laughin' at him, they has. Sit cross-legged like a man'r he'll not be welcome at the council."

"Thank you, Tom. G'day to you, then."

"Insufferable person," Cowell sniffed, shifting his seating position with a groan. "An admitted deserter, you heard him say it, with a smile on his face."

"Still, he might be useful, Mister Cowell." Cashman shrugged.

"We have Desmond, what need do we have for him?"

"Desmond can't be with us all the time, sir," Cashman said. "And we'll not always be together as a party, not if we're to bathe and do all the things he suggested to ingratiate ourselves. From what I've seen so far, there may be more of his type about this town, willing to give us a bit of advice or translation, for a sip of rum or two. Remember what Lewrie said, about our men and the native women. It's bound to happen, and Desmond doesn't seem willin' to help in that regard."

"Neither do I, sir," Cowell sniffed. "It is not our place to be topping their women. You and Lewrie should issue strict orders that we are to concentrate on the task at hand and eschew their favors."

"One thing I've learned in the Army, Mister Cowell, is never be stupid enough to issue an order I've no hope of enforcin'. What should we do, raise the cross-bars and have one of Lewrie's men fashion a cat o' nine tails? That'll make the Indians eager to join hands in our endeavor, won't it, if we have to flog our men to keep 'em chaste?"

"When in Rome, do as the Romans do, I believe you said not too long ago, sir," Alan stuck in. "And who better to steer us in the proper course than a Roman? Sure, there are a dozen former Europeans from where I sit right now, you can spot 'em for yourself if you've a mind. I wouldn't mind knowing as much as we can learn from them. Our men will want to leave the group now and then. Or we piss in squads by the numbers out in the weeds. Best we had some willing guides, I say."

"Hmm, you may have a point at that," Cowell finally agreed.

They were finally ensconced late that afternoon in one of the enclosed lots not too far from the central plaza, given what McGilliveray told them was an unused winter house belonging to his mother's family. The house was snug, a rectangular building of wattle and daub, with a roof that stuck out over the walls quite far. The door was low, about four feet high, and the way in wound in an L to keep out cold winds. It was dark and gloomy inside, but for a small smoke-hole in the center of the roof, and had it been cold enough to have need of a fire, Alan was sure that it would have been a reeking, smoky hell. There were beds around the margin of the floor space, raised up off the ground about three feet to discourage insects and snakes.

"Snug enough," Cashman said after looking the place over. "We may keep our goods safe in here, with just the one entrance I can see."

"And we're trapped in here if they turn ugly," Alan commented.

"There is that, but we could dig loop-holes through the walls if we had need, and the walls are thick enough to give some protection. I'll post a guard outside, and one just inside the doorway, just in case. No fire in here, not with all this powder. Would you be good enough to hang some of that sailcloth to separate our quarters from the rest, Alan? And before it's dark, we might as well see to settin' out a place to eat outside. Some firewood, too."

That need was being taken care of, though, for several Indian women were bustling about in the yard, laying out woven cane or willowbark mats to sit upon, laying a circular fire, and fetching iron pots to do the cooking in. Some of them were rather attractive, and it was all their party could do to keep their hands to themselves.

The whole clan seemed intent on an outdoor meal, for several fires were already burning in the family compound, and the village was full of drifting wood smoke as it got darker, and other *hutis*, as Desmond termed them, prepared their evening meal. The streets beyond the insubstantial vine and cane fence palings were almost empty, with only a few tribesmen wandering about, on their way to supper with another group for the most part. Dogs and cats lay with their eyes aglow, sniffing and licking their chops as meat sizzled over open coals, and soups and stews bubbled and simmered.

It was a novelty for the troops and sailors to sit cross-legged on their mats before the fire while women did the cooking and fetching for them, instead of the men doing their own kitchenwork.

"Ah, McGilliveray," Alan asked, as he spotted a girl of more than usual comeliness who was smiling at him from across the cheery flames. "You were going to explain to us the difference between an unmarried Muskogee woman, and a married one. And what the customs were."

"These are safe enough, Lewrie," their host announced. "They are my daughters."

"Oh, damn."

"Any younger girl on my mother's side is my daughter to me, no matter the relation, and I address them that way. There are no married women here, except for the older ones directing things. I adjure you, make sure there is no question of force. Let things take their natural way, or the offender shall regret it for what little life he has left. If a man is favored, there is usually no problem among the Muskogee. In other tribes, they take a stricter view towards chastity."

They headed across the town for the edge of the lake before it got too dark to see, and Alan stripped out of his clothing to wade in chest-deep and wash the grit and sweat of the day from his body. There was no soap to be had, but it felt good.

"I say, McGilliveray, what are those things out there with the red eyes?" Alan asked, pointing east down the lake opposite the sunset.

"Alligators," McGilliveray replied, damnably calm about it all, still dunking and wringing out his long hair. "Now you see what I mean about not going into the water at night."

"Damned if I'm staying out here, then," Alan replied, shivering despite the warmth of the water and the soft, humid tropic eve. He thrashed to the shore and swiped himself free of water with his hands. "You staying out there, are you? Well, you're daft if you are."

He turned around to reach down for his buff breeches, and came face to face with an Indian girl, who had come down to the lake to fetch water for cooking in a ceramic pot. She smiled at him. He smiled at her. With his breeches clutched over his groin, it was a tough call as to which of the two wore less clothing. She was clad in a woolly looking short skirt from waist to just above knees, and her smile, of course. Her breasts were high and firm, her hair glossy raven-black and tumbled about her face in two loose braids wrapped in deer fur.

Exotic, he thought inanely, definitely exotic, taking in the coltish slimness of her limbs, the delicate taper of her torso to a narrow waist, and the heartbreakingly lovely swell of her hips and buttocks. Her eyes almost swam open wider and wider as they stared at each other, and her teeth gleamed pearl-white in the gloom.

"By God, I hope you're not his bloody sister!" Alan breathed. She was as lovely a girl as he had ever seen, her russet complexion so fine that even Anne Beauman was put to shame. "Hey, White Turtle, what do you say to a girl when you want to say hello?"

McGilliveray came out of the water and spoke to the girl, who turned her head to look at him. She muttered something back, dropping her eyes and looking at the ground.

"I can barely understand her. Cherokee. A slave," McGilliveray said with a deprecatory sneer. "She's nothing."

"She's damned handsome for nothing. A slave?"

"War captive, maybe, or we traded for her from the Upper Muskogee or Alabamas. I saw her around the houses. You can do better, Lewrie."

"Mustn't let the old school down all of a sudden, McGilliveray?" Alan scoffed. "Hello, my dear, and what's your name? Do you speak English? What a daft question, of course you don't. Alan," he said, thumping his bare chest. "Alan. You? Help me out, will you, McGilliveray?"

He rattled off something guttural and the girl looked down at her bare toes again, and barely whispered a longer reply.

"Rabbit, she is called," McGilliveray said, turning to dress, such as it was. "Among her own people, she was named Bright

Mirror, if I can understand her words. Cherokee cannot speak properly, not a real language like Muskogean. If you want her, there should be no problem. She is a slave, after all, only loosely of the Wind Clan."

"Tell her I think she's lovely."

"I think she knows that already. She has to get back to help with the cooking or she'll make the other women angry."

"Me Alan," he said, stepping closer to her and thumping his chest again. Then he reached out and pointed at her. "You Rabbit?"

She said her name in Muskogean, gave him another bewitching smile, and fetched a heavy sigh, then spun around and trotted back to the town with her pot of water.

"How old do you think she is, McGilliveray?" Alan wondered as he began dressing at last. "Eighteen or so?"

"More like fifteen or sixteen, I should think. Might be careful with her. Cherokee women, even married ones, can bed with anyone they please, and their husbands have to stand it. Such a thing is not done among Muskogee, any more than it is done among your people."

"Why is it that you sound remarkably like a vicar railing against Puck's Fair?" Alan complained as he re-tied his waist sash over his shirt.

"Morals are important among my people. Unlike yours."

They made their way back to the fire circle and took their seats on the mats laid out for them, Alan remembering to sit properly cross-legged, though it was uncomfortable to him. Within moments, food was delivered to them. There was venison enough to stuff an army, hot from the spits, *sofkee* and *succotash*, flat rounds of corn-bread piping hot from the stone baking ovens.

"Nice change from salt meats," he noted, wishing he had a bottle of burgundy to wash things down with.

"Cattle and pigs have no souls," McGilliveray said. "They were not made by the Great Spirits, but brought from over the ocean, and are not good to eat."

"Will you cease your infernal carping?" Alan griped, fed up.

"I am only trying to point out those things that you should know to better deal with my people during our negotiations, sir," McGilliveray sniffed primly. "Most whites have an abysmal ignorance of Indian society, which creates exactly the sort of misunderstandings we are attempting to correct. If I seem to be partial to my mother's people over what you think is your so-called superior white civilization, then I own to that partiality gladly. I think Indian life is more caring of the individual, of the earth and the gifts we may take from it. We live in harmony with Nature; you plow it flat, create your parks and gardens and *call* it Nature."

"A little less of it, please, sir," Cashman sighed. "Our minds are quite overwhelmed already, don't ye know. Give us a rest, eh?"

McGilliveray got the hint and directed his conversation solely to Mr. Cowell after that, or to the various Indians who had condescended to eat at their fire for Cowell's edification.

Alan tucked into his supper with a strong appetite, not without casting his gaze about to see if he could spot the Cherokee girl named Rabbit, and he finally saw her off in the dark tending a cooking pot at another fire where the women had done their work and were now taking their own victuals. She sat a little apart from the accepted Creek maidens, and was not included in their conversations except to be directed to fetch something now and again. But when left to her own amusements, he was gratified and thrilled to see how she looked up and met his gaze with a fawn-like, trusting smile of welcome. And when his plate looked to be empty, she rose quickly and brought a platter of smoking venison to refill it, kneeling down before him gracefully and playing flirtatious looks at him from beneath her down-turned face. By firelight, she gleamed copper, and when she leaned close, she smelled fresh and clean and . . . foresty was the only term he could think of.

"Looks like you've made a conquest, Alan," Cashman said, giving him a nudge.

"I certainly bloody hope so," Alan agreed, not taking his eyes off her. "Rabbit," he whispered, and gave her his best smile.

"Ah . . . Arhlan," she attempted in a voice so soft he was not sure his ears weren't playing tricks on him. Then she was gone back to her fire, stifling a girlish giggle and looking over her shoulder at him.

After supper, there were pipes to be smoked while the women gathered up the cookware. Alan noted that they had been served off tin or pewter, with only rarely a well-crafted native pot or dish being seen. Although some Indians ate with their hands, there were a lot of spoons and knives in evidence to dip into pots or spear a slice of meat with. More wood was laid on the fire in a circular pattern, spiralling outward from the center, and some powdered tobacco was cast into the flames, which were already redolent with cedar and pine resins. The night was now fully dark, and the sky was ablaze with stars above the swirling motes of sparks from the fires. The air was still humid, but cool and pleasant on the skin.

"Best we turn in early," Cowell finally said, his eyelids heavy after such a repast. "We shall have to bathe in the morning, and then attend the square-ground council while all the *mikkos* are still here. 'Twill be a busy day for us, gentlemen."

"Andrews," Alan called to his senior hand. "Bed your people down."

"Aye, sah. Come on, lads."

"You be needin' anythin', sir?" Cony asked.

"No, you turn in, Cony."

"Aye aye, sir."

Alan sat by the fire a while longer, puffing slowly on a pipe to develop the knack of doing so, killing time as the others drifted away. He looked over to the other fire, and saw that the Cherokee girl was the last one left, given the task of tidying up for her betters.

"Where's the necessary closet in these climes, McGilliveray?"

"Back in the woods, if you must. Be sure to dig a small hole and bury it when you're done. And don't use just any leaves. Some of the plants cause painful rashes. Ask the girl for some dry corn husks."

He rose to his feet and wandered over to the other fire, bent down and picked up some husks while she sat on her knees and looked up at him. He walked away into the darkness at the back of the compound where it butted up against some trees and bushes.

A few minutes later, he stumbled his way back towards the fire, and she was there, stepping out from between some corn-cribs and small storage huts in the darkness. He stopped and stood very near to her, and she turned sideways to the fitful light from the fire. The light accentuated her wide and high cheek-bones, the sparkle in her brown eyes, and the way her skin shone. He put out a hand gently, not knowing what the custom was, and stroked her arm with unaccustomed shyness. She stepped up to him and pressed her slim body to his, looking up into his eyes from her short stature, about five feet and no more. Those magnificent young breasts brushed his shirt, driving him mad.

He slipped an arm about her waist and she leaned into him, rubbing her loins against his with a lazy, circular motion. Her face was close to his chest and her breath raised goose-flesh as she inhaled him and gently blew air on his skin.

He bent to kiss her, and she leaned back, unused to the custom, but gave him another smile to let him know that all was still well. He took her hands and she dragged him back between the corn-cribs out of the light, where they could embrace fully, and he could stroke that incredibly firm but downy body. He placed his lips on her shoulder, and she writhed in delight. His searching hands found her breasts and lifted them, rubbing his work-hardened palms across her large dark nipples, and they sprang erect and shivery to his touch. He bent down to kiss and tongue them, and she shuddered and gave a small yip of glee.

He showered kisses along her upper body, across her nose and cheeks, and brushed his lips against hers fleetingly, working slowly at finally bringing their mouths together, and this time she was not startled, but brought her face up to his, her mouth slightly open as she discovered a new thing. Her breath went musky, and her scent of arousal wafted over his senses as he groped a hand under her loose skirt to stroke her firm young buttocks. She reached away from him and fumbled with the latch-peg to one of the corn-cribs and drew him into the dry, moldy-smelling structure, where they sank to the mats on the earth in between large cane baskets of kernels. He kicked the door shut and undid the buttons of his breeches. They rolled back and forth, first one atop then the other as he fought his way out of his clothing, and his hands found the way up between her slim thighs to press against her belly. There was very little hair at all when his fingers found an entry to her body, and it drove him even more insane with wanting her. She rolled onto her back and raised her legs about his waist, reaching down to touch his member, and gave a gasp as her fingers wrapped around it, drawing it to her belly and stroking the tip against her swollen clitoris. She bit her lower lip and cried out softly as her namesake before he lost all control and forced himself against her. She was incredibly moist, yet almost too snug to take his first thrust, and for a moment, he thought it would end right there as he struggled to enter her fully. He tried thinking of the exact wording of the Articles of War.

" 'An Act for Amending, explaining and reducing into one Act of Parliament, the laws relating to the Government of His Majesty's ships, vessels and forces by sea!' " he gasped as she writhed up at him, lifting her legs around his chest and spreading them wider to allow him easier entry. Her fingers were digging into his shoulders and she was moaning with total abandon by then. " 'Whereas the several laws relating to the Sea Service, made at different times, and on different occasions, have been found by experience not to be so full, so clear, so expedient or consistent . . .' Ah, Jesus God Almighty, what a snug'un you are!"

But finally, he was completely within her and forced her to lie still for a moment by putting all his weight on her to hold her down before she bucked him off. After a half-minute's pause in the proceedings he began to thrust gently into her, and lifted himself up to allow her to move. She clung to him like a limpet, grunted and puffed and met his every thrust, squeezing his member like a firm handshake until finally she cried out and mewed in pleasure, and he followed her into bliss.

Except for a few times during the night when she had to run her errand to check the cooking fire and keep it smoldering, they were in each other's arms, napping lightly now and again, but mostly going at it like a pair of stoats in heat. For one so young, she was expert as all hell, and eager to meet his every desire, as he was hers. They did not share a single word in common, but they giggled and teased and tried to talk between their waves of passion. Alan finally dropped off for what seemed an hour or so, and then she was nudging him, rolling over on top of him and molding her maddeningly lovely body to his for warmth in the grey pre-dawn light of a foggy morning.

"Arhlan," she whispered, kissing him. "Go." She exhausted her tiny vocabulary of English words and lapsed back into Creek or Cherokee, he had no idea which.

"Rabbit," he sighed, wrapping his arms around her with his eyes still shut. "Soft rabbit. Bunny."

"Boony," she mocked.

"Soft. You say soft?"

"Soff?"

"Like these," he said, brushing her deer fur braids. "Soft."

"Soff," she repeated, nodding to show she understood at least the sense of what he was saying.

"Soft Rabbit, you. Soft Rabbit."

"Soff rabt," she parroted. "Arhlan. Go." She made a gesture and touched her chest.

"See you tonight, yes?"

She gave him a smoldering kiss and knelt to wrap on her skirt.

He got into his clothes and staggered outside into the thick mist of a river-bottom dawn, almost unable to find the winter house for a moment. People were already stirring, at least from the Indian side of the compound, while a soldier nodded on guard before the low fire of the night before.

"Morning, sentry," he said to alert the man before he jumped up from his nap and shot him.

"Mornin', sir!" The man leaped to his feet like a signal rocket.

"Anyone else up?"

"Nossir, not yit, sir!"

A minute later, while Alan stood there yawning and stretching the kinks of too-little sleep on too-hard a ground, McGilliveray came out of the winter house. "Good, you are up. We go to the lake and take bath. Wake your people, if you please."

"They're not going to be awfully keen on it, mind," Alan told him. "It's barely past first sparrow-fart, and the water'll be cold as charity."

"We agreed, Mister Lewrie," McGilliveray carped like a tutor who had caught him scribbling in the margins of his books again.

"Alright, alright," he said, leaning into the house and duck-walking through the low entrance. "Wakey, wakey, lash up and stow! Show a leg, show a leg, all hands on deck!" After being pestered to death by heartlessly cheerful bosun's mates chanting that dreadful tune aboard ship for years, it did his spirits good to finally get a chance to use it himself. Hmm, just as good I said show a leg, he thought. That part was to determine, when the ship was out of discipline, which occupant of a hammock or pallet on the deck was a hairy male liable for duty, and who was a hairless (mostly) female doxy or "wife" who could sleep in and not be tipped out or roused roughly. The hands had found their own arrangements with the Creek girls during the night, it seemed, privacy be damned; it had been dark enough inside the fireless winter house to allow everyone willing to enjoy a grope on the raised cots the chance to do so, and several cackling young women made their way outside, leaving their men to grumble their way awake.

"Outside and down to the lake, lads," Alan called with false cheer. "Into the water for a dip before breakfast. I know, I know, but the Indians do it, so we have to as well, long as we're here. Nobody ever died of a little less dirt. Let's go!"

"Ah, fook t'Indians," someone groused in a whisper.

"You already have. So let's get down there and see how pretty the rest of 'em are with their clothes off."

It amazed him that sailors could get soaking wet during a turn on deck, could kneel and scrub with "holystones" and "bibles" every morning and revel in the sluicing of a washdeck pump, but would turn their noses up to anything that smacked of getting wet on purpose. They stripped reluctantly, covered their privates with a sudden surge of heavy modesty, and waded into the water an inch at a time, yipping and shying as the coolness crept up their bodies.

Alan walked out, wincing with chill but determined not to make a sound, feeling the soft lake bottom ooze between his toes, stumbling now and then on a twig or reed on his unprepared soles.

Damn fine show, though, he thought, taking in the view.

Indians of every stripe and condition were splashing into the water, the children yelping and making great water-spouts as they dove in. Men congregated to one end of the bank, women much further down, and the negotiating party about midway between, far enough away from the females so they would not enrage a wet husband.

"Please, sir, kin we get out now, sir?" one of the men said shivering with cold, his arms wrapped around his chest.

"Scrub, dunk and get the worst smuts off," Alan said, staring at the dirt that was floating off the man. "*Scare* the lice and fleas if nothing else. Get your hair wet, it won't kill you."

"Aye, sir," the man sighed, looking down at his own scum as if he expected to be drowned in three feet of water. He held his nose and dropped out of sight, to come up puffing and blowing a second later as if shot out of the water. "Oh, Gawd!" he cried miserably.

"Hot breakfast waiting for us, lads. Get dry and we'll eat."

Alan came out of the water, shivering like a dog. He saw his girl trotting off towards the town to be the first to help with the cooking, and he waved at her. She stopped and waved, and he blew her a kiss, and she parroted his motion, laughed, then ran on to her never-ending labors, which raised a laugh out of his miserable crew, at any rate.

"Gawd, sir, yer a ram-cat, sir!"

"And it didn't even cost tuppence," Alan boasted. "When in Rome, do as the Romans do, I've heard. Especially if they enjoy it."

Chapter 6

The square-ground, where they assembled for their negotiations, was a series of open-sided sheds that faced inward towards each other, like huge three-walled *chickees* elevated the usual three feet off the ground, but with tiers of seats added which made them appear like the seats of a European theater. The inevitable fire was burning in the center of the square-ground's sandy expanse which had been trodden bare of weeds or growth; a fire laid out in a circle that would burn from the outer spiral into the center. Alan could only assume that once the fire in the center burned out, the talks were over for the day.

McGilliveray turned up in a pale, almost-white deerskin shirt trimmed in beading and embroidery. He led them to the eastern end of the council ground and sat them down on the front row of the tiered seats.

"On the north side there," he lectured, "that's where the warriors sit. It is called the Red Shed. The *mikko* and some of his Second Men sit on the west facing us, with the principal chiefs in the center shed."

"I thought the *mikko* were the chiefs," Alan commented.

"No, they are the chiefs' principal ministers, usually from one of the White Clans, dedicated to peace. They are to run things evenly, and keep order. If things go badly, they can be replaced without the hereditary chief being blamed."

"Politicians, leaders of the Commons," Alan speculated.

"If you like, it is an apt simile. Now to the south, that's the sheds for the Second Men, who brew the white drink, and that is the white shed side. And scattered on every side are the Beloved Men. The Beloved Men are very old, very wise."

"What's the difference, then, Desmond?" Cowell asked.

"Second Men are officers responsible to the *mikko* who see to

278

the well-being of the tribe, and of the settlement. Beloved Men perhaps once were Second Men, but they could have been Great Warriors or retired *mikkos*. Maybe members of the chief's clan. There are only a few of them held in such regard for their wisdom and good works at peace or war at any one time. You see," McGilliveray said with that smug snoot-lifted expression of superiority that they had all come to know and love, "Indian society is much more organized and thought out than is commonly known, much like your own political systems."

It took a boresomely long time for things to get organized, though, with leaders and warriors and old codgers milling about and saying their hellos right and left. Delegations from other Lower Creek towns had to be seated, and the touchy Seminolee had to be given good seats. Finally a servant came from the south, or white, shed with a conch shell dripping with some hot liquid and presented it to the chiefs and *mikkos* on the west side, crying out "Yahola!"

"The White Drink," McGilliveray told them. "You must drink it so the council can be properly purified in spirit."

When the conch shell was refilled and brought round to them, Alan was repulsed by the smell of it, and said so. "White drink, mine arse, it's black as midnight! What the hell is it, liquid dung?"

"White men call it Black Drink. It is a tea, or a coffee, if you will. It is bitter, but it must be drunk, I told you. Now, Lieutenant, will you please shut up and don't cause a reason to break off the talks?" McGilliveray snapped.

"Lewrie, you and Cashman may run things military, but this is my responsibility, and if you cannot go along with us peaceably, then you had best go back to the house now," Cowell uttered in a low growl.

McGilliveray drank of it, then Cowell, then Cashman, each keeping a grim, set expression on their face at the taste. The conch shell was presented to Lewrie, and he tipped it up cautiously. Damned if it didn't smell a little like coffee, he allowed grudgingly. It was hot, and it was indeed bitter, and it was all Alan could do to screw up his mouth as though he had just bitten into a lime.

"Manfully done, sir," McGilliveray whispered.

"I still say it tastes like boiled turds," Alan whispered back. "I just hope I don't give way."

"It is better if you do," McGilliveray instructed. "And when

you vomit, try to do it in a great arc, far away from you. You
will impress them no end."

"Mine arse on a band-box!"

"The White Drink is very strong," McGilliveray whispered
with evident signs of glee at Alan's discomfiture. "A physician
would say that it is an excellent emetic and diuretic. You will
begin to sweat, and you may feel the need to vomit, since you
are not used to it. It clears the thoughts and stimulates the brain,
you see, so that decisions are better thought out. They will pass
the shell all during the council."

"Oh, good Christ!" Alan said as his stomach rolled over.

A pipe had to make the rounds after being presented to the
east first, then the other cardinal directions, and more White
Drink was handed around, at which point the actual negotiations
began. The *mikko* of the White Town did not speak directly, but
passed everything through his *yatika*, or interpreter. Cowell
spoke for England, and McGilliveray acted as his interpreter as
well, voicing aloud what Cowell said in a softer voice.

The council could have lasted hours; Alan didn't much care
what they talked about or how long it took. His guts were
roiling and the vile taste of the White Drink hovered just below
his throat like some not so veiled threat. Just opening his mouth
to take a puff on the pipe as it circulated was dangerous enough,
and the rough tobacco set his bile flowing with each puff. He finally could hold it no longer. Sweat had been pouring off him
in buckets and his clothing was soaked with it. His heart thudded and his pulse raced worse than the most horrible hangover
he had ever experienced.

"Gangway," he finally said, leaning forward in hopes the contents of his stomach didn't land in his lap, and heaved. There
was a smatter of applause, and some cheerful comments made at
his production.

"Damme!" he gasped.

"Oh, well shot, sir." McGilliveray smirked. "I'd give you
points for distance."

"Wish ya hadn't done that," Cashman grumbled through
pursed lips, and then it was his turn to "cat" like a drunken
trooper. They were rewarded with another of those infernal
conch shells topped off with the latest batch of White Drink.
Cowell turned a delicate pale green color, and sweated like a
field hand, soaking his elegant suit, manfully trying to express
his government's arguments between spasms.

This can't go on forever, Alan thought miserably, eyeing the circular fire and willing it to burn faster so his agony would end. Oh, burn, damn you, burn. Bet we'd get what we wanted double quick, if we could pass the port, 'stead of this muck!

Mercifully, about three hours later, the fire did burn down to the last stick of cane, and the meeting broke up, with the Indians whooping in glee and heading for the gaming ground for another match of their favorite pastime.

"Went well," Cowell stated once they were back in front of their lodge, sponged off and dressed in clean clothing.

"Did it, by God?" Alan sighed.

"Did you pay any attention at all, sir?" Cowell asked.

"Nothin' after my first broadside, I'm afraid," he admitted.

"Well, the gifts went over extremely well," Cowell said, rubbing his hands with a satisfied grunt of pleasure at his dealings. "And their Great Warrior and his war chiefs, the *tustunuigi*, and the big warriors and all liked the idea of having lots of muskets and shot."

"So we could get out of this dreadful place soon?"

"It's not that simple, I fear," Cowell went on. "Desmond was correct in telling us that none of them have any love for European settlers living cheek-to-jowl with them, Spanish or English. The way we've treated them in the past, you see. If pressed, they'd prefer the Dons, who leave them pretty much alone. Horrid thought, isn't it? If one wishes to make something of these climes with proper settlements and industry, even peaceable, that threatens them, while those horrible Spaniards, who so slothfully *siesta* and stick to their few towns are preferable to us, cruel as they have been in the past in New Granada and New Spain. No, what we offered this morning is so novel to their experience that it shall take days, perhaps weeks of conferring."

"God help us, then," Alan sighed.

"There is also the problem of all that we offer being anathema to some of them," Cowell went on relentlessly. "If they take arms with us, let our missionaries and teachers come among them, and agree to new treaty borders and all, they fear they stop being Creeks and become pale imitations of white men."

"Well, what's wrong with that?" Alan griped, fanning himself with a broad split-cane fan. The day was not that hot, but the diuretic effect of the White Drink still made his perspiration flow. "I mean, given a choice of running naked through the woods like an ignorant savage, or settling down and making something of myself, I know which one I'd choose."

"They see nothing good in our system, you see," Cowell said

with a sad shake of his head. "Oh, they're more amenable than most Indians, who don't farm. Left to their own devices, with trade goods in constant supply, they'll have to become more like us eventually. But remember those corn fields we saw. Hill-rows of corn, with squash and gourds and beans vining around them. Plows would do them no good, and our way of growing corn would only exhaust the soil, even of rich bottomland. They have few needs for fancy clothing, solid houses and such. They've taken to the mule and the musket, the iron cooking pot and the pewter plate, but they don't need us or our goods all that badly. Perhaps they may even go for wagons one day, but I doubt it. Poor, sad people," Cowell intoned mournfully. "Doomed, I think. Rum and whiskey'll be their downfall, that and disease, and they know it."

"This town might as well be European, the way it's laid out," Alan countered. "So they don't have private property, but instead hold the land in common. That doesn't mean they can't do some minor adjusting to our ways."

"To adjust is to die, Mister Lewrie. Their only hope is to be so strong, so unified against all comers, that they can preserve their way of life, taking only what is useful from our society, and that'll never do. They're not unified, yet. Nor are they strong enough militarily, even with muskets and shot in plenty."

"Seems to me, then, that this mission of ours is a wasted effort," Alan said, after a long silence following Cowell's remarks. "If you think they're going to go under sooner or later."

"They shall, if they deal with the Rebels solely," Cowell said. "With us as a counter-poise, they have a chance to develop as a society. That's what we're offering, beyond the immediate military alliance to retain British Florida."

"Where would you draw the borders, then?"

"Truthfully, I don't know," Cowell admitted. "That could be settled later, once we get the region back, and fill it with new settlers more amenable to their way of thinking and dealing."

"But Mister Cowell, if they don't like settlers close by them, why should new colonists fare any better than the last batch?" Alan pointed out. "And why should the new settlers be any fairer with them than before? They'll need land, and all the land's Indian. Either that or turn Indian like that fellow Tom, and give up on civilized ways."

"Men of good will and reason may find ways to accommodate with each other," Cowell concluded stubbornly, his face aglow with conviction of the rightness of his purpose. "Ah, dinner! I must own to having developed a devilish appetite."

"One usually does, when one's stomach's been emptied so thoroughly," Alan drawled sourly.

"This is all moonshine," Alan told Cashman later that day down by the shore of the lake.

"It probably all is," Cashman agreed easily. "But it's none of our worry. We do our job of getting Cowell and McGilliveray here in one piece, get the trade goods exchanged safely, and that's that."

"But what do you think of all that talk about a whole new policy of dealing with the Creeks, all this . . ."

"It'll come to nothin'." Cashman shrugged. "Indians'll get the smelly end of the stick, same as usual. I even doubt we'll get the territory back, but then, nobody asks a soldier about diplomacy."

"Not even get it back?"

"Best thing for all concerned is both us and the Dons get kicked out." Cashman laughed at Alan's shocked expression. "Who in his right mind'd want the silly place? Give Florida and the whole damned coast region from here to the Mississippi to the Indians. It's all bugs and flies and alligators, not white man's country, anyway. If they want to live in it, they're more'n welcome, I say. Spain can't do anything with it, least they haven't shown signs of it yet. We can't do anything with it, either, 'less we want to shove an army in here to hold it."

"So much for becoming the new Clive of India," Alan spat.

"They had me goin' there for a minute, same as you, I expect. But once I had a chance to ponder it, I realized it's a forlorn hope at best," Cashman admitted, stripping off his shirt to splash water on his face and neck to cool off. "No, there's more profitable places just as miserable in the world we could do more with. The Far East, India, China. Could we get Capetown away from the Dutch, we'd be better off. Though, I could get to like it around here if it weren't for the Rebels up north. Or so many bloody Injuns down here. If they were a little more civilized, just a touch, it'd do fine for me."

"Go native?" Alan mocked.

"Not a bit of it," Cashman chuckled. "Look around here. See how rich this soil is. Ever see cotton grown?"

"No."

"The East Indies and Egypt's full of it, and it's the coming thing, now we've the water-power looms and such back in England," Cashman enthused, kneeling to scoop up a handful of dirt. "River-bottom land is the best place to grow it, with long hot summers, just like here. I'd stake me out about a shire's worth of land, plant cotton, and cut the distance from India to the mills in half. Bring some Samboes from the East Indies over to tend to it. Corn, horses, pigs, cattle, fruit, sugar cane, you name it and I'd farm it. And while I'm about it, I'd get me a regiment of *sepoys* from the Far East to guard it. No more English troops who die so fast in such a climate. Sikhs or Mahrattas, Bengalis or lads from the Coromandel coast. They're used to hot, wet weather and sweat. And one thing in their favor, they're civilized, in their own fashion, not like these swamp-runners. Then you'd see this land take off and flourish! That's the way to become the new Robert Clive!"

"What about the Indians, then?" Alan smiled.

"That's their own lookout, isn't it?" Cashman replied.

"There's plenty of streams and rivers," Alan said. "Why not put your looms here, then, if you're going to bring over East Indians? Do the whole manufacturing process in one place?"

"By God, that's not such a bad idea, Alan!" Cashman agreed. "Look here, even if the Dons keep the place, a man could do a lot worse than settin' up in these parts. Cotton and flax together, looms and mills, dye-works, ready-made beddings, shirts, everything right here, even our own ships to transport the goods. We'd make thousands, millions of pounds. How'd you like to be a landed gentleman, with a fleet of merchantmen? A big house grand as the bloody Walpoles, bigger'n St. James's if you've a mind? Sure, it's trade, but given a choice of bein' a poor gentleman'r a rich lower-class tradesman, I'd take rich any day. B'sides, once you're *nabob* rich, the gentlemen'll catch your farts for you like you was royalty."

"With a harem in the west wing?" Alan laughed.

"We'd be so wealthy we could rotate 'em in platoons every month," Cashman hooted. "Wouldn't take much to set up, should it. Cotton and flax seed, seed-corn from the Creeks, and we're in business. Maybe only a few Hindus at first, just to get things started. *Sepoys'*d work cheap as a private troop to guard the place. God knows 'John Company' pays 'em little enough as it is. What do ya say, Alan? Want in on it?"

"It's tempting." Alan grinned at Cashman's daydreams. "But we're both impoverished. No way we could settle here, not the way things are."

"It's just as big a dream as Cowell's, and more profitable in the long run. I'll do it somewhere in this world, you see if I don't. And when I'm ready, I'll get in touch with you and we'll do it, damme if we shan't! Right?"

"Right!"

Every day for the rest of the week, they suffered through the council meetings, drank the White Drink and threw up, smoked pipes of *kinnick-kinnick* until their tongues were raw, and listened to the high-pitched, formal orations of the Indian speakers as they wavered back and forth and all round the issue of whether to take up arms and help drive the Spanish out of Florida.

Some wanted no dealings with white men on any terms, and could not have cared less if all the colonists from Louisburg to St. Augustine got in their ships and sailed back where they came from. Some wanted to take the guns and stomp on the Cherokee and Chickasaws. There were questions about why the British didn't bring their troops and run out the Rebels up north, or take on the Spanish themselves.

It was maddening that any Indian of substance or reputation, no matter how lunatick his ideas, could get up and speak for hours, raising inane irrelevancies, which would have to be thrashed out completely before they got back to the main point. And, Cowell and his officers learned, chiefs and *mikkos* could not just decide and get on with business; they had to form a consensus of all parties involved, which took time to wear each other down until they were tired of arguing and gave in.

Alan's only consolation was to borrow a horse from McGilliveray's clan and go for a ride around the settlement during the afternoons, or ride Soft Rabbit in the corn-crib after supper. While he could not get his tongue to work around the guttural Muskogean words, he did have some success in teaching her some English, and showed her a few tricks he had picked up from whores he had known back in London. The days she spent doing the heavy chores for her owners were galling to him, and he had to own to a growing affection for her and her ways. She was sweet and modest in public demeanor, sweet and passionate in private, with an almost insatiable lust once the crib door was kicked shut for the night. Since he had so little part in the Creek council, he napped through most of the negotiations, or part of the afternoon before supper. It was the only chance for shut-eye that he got. How she ground corn, fetched and toted water and firewood, skinned and dressed hides and cooked during the day, and then rogered all night and awoke fresh and full of energy amazed him.

After a few more boresome days spent heaving for the amusement and edification of the Muskogee, Alan finally called a halt and went hunting with his men, who had been growing restless for some time. English lads from the country did well enough to fill the pot, and the ex-soldier Tom went along to teach them some woods-craft.

They returned with several deer, one of them Alan's that he had hit with his fusil at seventy yards. He was damned proud of his shot through thick brush, and was looking forward to eating the bugger.

"Alan!" Cashman called as they entered the yard of the *huti* with their kills. "We're out of here!"

"Everyone finally give up?" he asked. "I say, Kit, come take a look at this. One shot, just behind the shoulder and down he went like he was pole-axed." Alan stepped to the side of the horse that bore his kill to point out how well he had done.

"Damn the deer, man. They agreed," Cashman insisted.

"To what, actually?"

"If we give them the muskets and all the accoutrements, they go to war, on our side, soon's we land a regiment'r two."

"But we have to land the guns and munitions first, I take it."

"And show up with a fleet from Jamaica, and troops. But it's a start. And no matter how it turns out, we can get back to the coast and out of this place. Cowell's pleased as punch with himself."

"And I suppose McGilliveray is trumpeting the Apocalypse," Alan said, smirking. One blessing was that he had had much less to do with the man since he had started hunting by day and topping by night with Soft Rabbit. On a good day, he would only see him at the morning bath and breakfast, and didn't have to put up with his pontificating more than an hour.

"Well, he's mighty high in council now," Cashman told him. "Not that he wasn't already. I don't know if they're all that keen on all his ideas about a Creek alphabet and teachers and such, but they finally saw the light about their future security. We may leave tomorrow."

"Thank bloody Christ!" Alan exclaimed happily. "Another week of this, and my men would have gone native on me."

"It's been all I could do to keep my troops on their toes, too."

"Then let's eat this bloody deer of mine to celebrate."

"Gad, yes, he's a big'un, ain't he? Nice shot. For a sailor."

"We've bagged enough to feed the whole town, even the way they eat. He'll do for our mess, and we'll share out the rest. That ought to make the Muskogee turn back flips."

The supper was very cheery, and the smell of roast meat floated from every *huti* cook-fire. McGilliveray's Muskogee relations ate with the white party in the yard between the winter house and the summer, all smiles and laughter and singing, so different from the usual stoic silence that Alan had thought was normal for Indians. Everyone seemed hellishly pleased with their new-struck bargain of support.

It was towards the end of the supper that one of McGilliveray's uncles on his mother's side came forward to sit before him on the ground and offer a pipe. They smoked, blowing the smoke to the cardinal points, and talked back and forth in Muskogean for some time apart from the others.

"Ah, Mister Lewrie, this concerns you, I fear," McGilliveray said after the palaver was ended.

"Eh?" Alan asked, stuffed near to bursting and sleepy. "What the hell have I done now? I haven't offended them, have I?"

"Nothing serious." McGilliveray grinned, and if McGilliveray found it amusing, Alan was sure he wasn't going to enjoy it; their dislike for each other by that time was hotly mutual. "But it seems Rabbit, the Cherokee slave girl, no longer has need to go to the woman's house."

"The woman's house," Alan said with a dubious look, missing the drift completely.

"Surely I don't have to lecture you on what it means when a girl's courses cease, sir." McGilliveray beamed happily.

"What, you mean she's pregnant?"

"That is exactly what I mean, sir."

"Well, so what, then?" Alan asked, unable to believe it. "You're sure this isn't a jape? She's really ankled? I mean, do I have to marry her or something?"

"It would help if you did." McGilliveray chuckled.

"Well, I'm blowed, damme if I ain't," Alan gasped. "I mean, what's the difference, she's just a slave, right?"

"She's my uncle's property, you see, so that makes her part of his clan, and of this *huti*, this lodge," McGilliveray said, obviously enjoying every minute of it. "He would be insulted if you ran off and left your get. Marriage doesn't mean much in these circumstances, but it does preserve honor. If you don't, he can't sell her off, and he might come looking for you."

McGilliveray's uncle, a side of beef with a round moon-face, and a famous chief warrior, gave Alan a look as menacing as any he ever did see.

"He'll be stuck with a bastardly gullion, a bastard's bastard."

"But the boy'll be some kind of Wind Clan Muskogee, so he'll do alright. Or her," McGilliveray insisted.

"But we're leaving tomorrow, so . . ."

"Simple really. You shot that deer today? Go get a chunk of it."

"Now look here, McGilliveray, this . . ."

"Did I tell you my uncle's name is Man-Killer?" McGilliveray smiled sweetly.

"Oh, holy hell." Alan looked to Cashman, who was as amused as any of the others around their fire, laughing behind his hand. And damn their black souls, but Andrews, Cony, and the other seamen from *Shrike* were nudging each other and grinning at him openly! "It doesn't mean a damned thing, right? I mean, it doesn't really count, does it?"

"Even if she was properly Muskogee, it isn't official until the Green Corn Ceremony in late summer, and could be dissolved then. She'll gain status. Especially if you buy her from Man-Killer, and he adopts her as a daughter afterward. No more slavery for her then."

"Oh, alright, then," Alan sulked, burning with embarrassment at how funny everyone else seemed to think his predicament was. But he rose and fetched a large chunk of the deer from the roasting spits and brought it back to the fire-circle.

"This shows you're a man who can provide meat for her," McGilliveray said. "She'll present *sofkee* and corn to you to show she can provide grain from the fields, and cook it for her man. Now, before she can be married, you must buy her from Man-Killer."

There was much palavering, with a rant about how Man-Killer had gotten Rabbit in the first place, how he had slaughtered with the best of them and taken her from a traveling party of Cherokee hunting too far south of their mountain fastness, even if he was a little too far north of *his* usual haunts, poaching on Upper Creek lands.

Alan's bride cost him a dragoon pistol and saddle holster, with forty pre-made cartouches of round-shot and buck-shot, two of his deer hides Rabbit had already dressed, one of his shirts, and a leather cartouche pouch with George III's ornate brass seal on the flap. Alan suspected that buying the mort wasn't strictly necessary, since Man-Killer and McGilliveray/White Turtle both seemed to be enjoying it so much, but there wasn't much he could do about it, so he went along sullenly.

Once the purchase was done, Man-Killer got to his feet and went on another high-pitched, formal rant, which McGilliveray translated into short, pithy phrases now and again, the upshot being that he didn't know much about this young white man, but he would be considered "of Man-Killer's fire," which seemed a grudging sort of honor short of actually becoming Indian, more specifically of the Muskogee Wind Clan, since everyone Creek knew that they were the best people on the face of the earth, and they wouldn't adopt just *any* upstart as a Real Person until he had proved himself a superior sort of being, perhaps on par with a Seminolee or Apalachee, who at least could speak something like Muskogean. Man-Killer also grudgingly allowed that since this strange white man had bought the girl Rabbit from him at such a damned good knockdown price, he would allow her to remain in the Wind Clan and in his lodge as "daughter" instead of slave after the white man went back where he came from, so the offspring would be raised Muskogee, which Man-Killer thought would be the best for all concerned. He didn't like the way white men raised their children, anyway, with all that spanking and beating, which broke the spirit.

"At least the little bastard's going to be spared tutors and algebra," Alan sighed.

All through these preliminaries, the Indian women of the clan and the *huti* had gathered their sisters from the other *hutis* to witness the ceremony. Through it all they had yipped and whooped with delight, eager as harpies discovering a newly slain corpse to feed upon.

Finally, they brought Rabbit out. She had bathed and drawn her raven hair back into a single long braid, adorned with beads and a few feathers other than eagle. She wore a new, richly embroidered and beaded deerskin skirt, a little longer than her usual style, with a new upper garment much like a match-coat or bed-sitting coat, tied under the arms, which still left her right breast free.

"How much ritual does it take for her to get ready?" Alan asked as she was paraded before her new "sisters" of the Wind Clan. "I'd say this was arranged a long time before I heard about it. Well, damn their pleasures, I say!"

"More to the point, blessin's on yours, Alan," Cashman replied, sobered by how lovely the girl was, and by the solemnity of the moment, no matter how absurd it was. "If they were forcin' me to wed her, I'd think myself lucky. Damn shame you can't take her with you when you leave tomorrow."

"Oh, for God's sake," Alan groaned. Still, she was tricked out right handsome, even he had to admit that, and had been fawn-pretty before.

A way was cleared, and she knelt down before him on her knees, her eyes swimming with tears even as she beamed at him with happiness so open and adoring it silenced even the most cynical of his crew.

Man-Killer read the rites, which were simple to the extreme. He offered her the platter of venison, and she took a bite to accept him. She offered him a bowl of *sofkee* and an ear of corn still in the shuck, which he tasted. Then she was allowed to come sit beside him and link arms with him, pressing her young body to his side and gazing up at him in shuddering reverence.

"Now what?" Alan asked, putting an arm around her shoulders in spite of himself.

"That's it, you're married," McGilliveray said, and Man-Killer and the women said pretty much "amen" or "here, here," which raised whoops and shouts from all present. "Give you joy of this day, Lieutenant Lewrie. Go, take your bride to your new home yonder. It's only a summer *chickee*, but private enough. I helped built it yesterday."

"Damn your eyes, McGilliveray!" Alan said, unable to do anything other than smile as people crowded around to congratulate the "happy couple."

"Go forth, be fruitful, and multiply," Cashman called with an exaggerated bow. "Though you've a fair start on that, hey?"

It was expected that the newly-weds would retire immediately, and Rabbit was almost dragging him, so he finally allowed himself to be led off to a new and fresh-smelling *chickee* back towards those fatal corn-cribs, near the rear of the family *huti*. They climbed up onto the mat-covered floor and pulled the split-cane wall mats down for privacy. Almost before the last mat had fallen in place, Rabbit was on him like a ferret, dragging him to the floor. Taking heed of her lessons in passionate deportment from Alan's earlier teachings, she flung her arms about his neck and showered him with kisses, babbling away softly and rapidly in Cherokee/Creek/English, all the while tearing at his clothes.

"Ah-lan," she crooned, besotted with love and trembling with happiness at her freedom from slavery, and at her marriage. "You me!"

"You are mine," he corrected between kisses. She practically ripped his breeches open and rolled to sit astride of him. She took his left hand and rubbed it over her firm belly and purred like a very contented kitten, stirring her loins against him. "Baby," he said.

"Bebby, you me," she parroted. "You ... ahr ... mine."

"Ours," he said, tapping her stomach. "God help me."

"Ahrs, go'hemmy," she said, beaming, with tears of joy cascading down her smooth young cheeks and splashing on her upper garment and breast. Alan reached up and undid the knot that held the little match-coat together, and it fell away, revealing both of those delightfully springy young orbs. She slid further down his belly as his hands caressed her breasts and nipples, and in moments her vagina was slick and moist on his skin. She slid further down, reached and found his throbbing member. Press-ganged into marriage or not, she was still a damned attractive and nubile young piece, he decided. She steered him into her and rocked back to drive him deep inside, making them both gasp at the velvety pleasure of the first stroke of insertion, and it was as good as the first time they had coupled in the corn-crib, just as full of wonder and discovery. For her perhaps it was even better, for she was fulfilling her life's role as wife and mother-to-be, and her inspired exertions communicated inspiration to him.

There was no fire for her to tend that night, no more errands to run for others now she was a freedwoman, so they could exhaust themselves totally and fall asleep together. She cuddled to him in the crook of his arm, her head on his shoulder and one downy thigh flung across his belly, her breath stirring soft against his cheek and neck. Every movement he made was responded to with an unconscious hug, some little whimper of joy. She woke once briefly, sated beyond measure, and only kissed him, repeated his name and her few words of endearment in English, and sank back into sleep in his arms.

Alan woke just before dawn as it got a little chilly, and drew a red trade blanket over them. He looked down at her and snuggled to her cozy warmth, worn down to a nubbin and barely awake, savoring the last few minutes of closeness.

"Damme for a fool, but this marriage nonsense don't feel half-bad right now," he muttered. Long as it's over today, he thought. Being a daddy, though. That cuts a bit rough. Not that I'll be around to listen to the little bastard bawl, so that's not so bad. Feels good, this.

In his entire experience with women, he had rogered mop-squeezers and country girls, tumbling with them in the dark at the top of the stairs, across un-made beds, or rolling behind a hedge in the summers at the edge of a field, all quick and furious. He had lain at ease with whores between bouts of "the blanket horn-pipe," but for the life of him, as he lay there gradually coming awake, he could not actually remember *sleeping* with a girl. Usually his time was governed by being furtive, or the commercial nature of the transaction; on, off, and just where the hell's my hat?

This, though, this closeness and peacefulness of being in bed with a woman who wanted you as much as you wanted her, who smelled so good and intimate under the blanket, who snoozed away so trusting in his arms, and who would respond with affection to any sign of affection on his part—well, this was something else again.

Pity I *can't* take her with me, he decided silently, though it was a forlorn wish. She would not fit in anywhere he went, most especially aboard *Shrike*. It isn't that I really love her that much, he thought, but for now, she's a sweet thing, a girl with a good little heart.

As he came more awake, and listened to the sounds of the Creek town beginning to stir around their *chickee*, he was filled with an out-of-character sadness, not just because he had to leave her behind and probably never see her again. There was sadness regarding the whole Indian way of life, too. From all that McGilliveray and Cowell had said, there was little hope that the Creeks could retain their ancient traditions. The Rebels, who styled themselves Americans now, would press against the borders, the rum and whiskey and trade goods would contaminate the old ways. If there was unity of purpose for now between the Creeks and Seminolee and the fragments of other tribes, then it would not last long, and they would face their future uncoordinated, prey to any outside aggression. Even if Cowell and McGilliveray could convince the Shelburne government to commit troops and money to retake Florida with Indian help, the Indians would still wither away in the face of white civilization, nibbled to death instead of going out in one brave battle. There was no place for them to run, no lands further west that did not already have owners. They could survive by imitating white ways of living, but at what a price, and how much suffering and degradation?

And this dear little girl sleeping so soundly beside him would be doomed to be a part of it, one of the losing side, and, God help him, so would the child she carried—his child. Nobody had ever come back on him with a bastard and a belly-plea for support (so far, anyway), and he began to worry about what he might do, what he might be able to leave behind, some legacy or something of value to improve Rabbit's life, and the child's life, against the bad times to come.

God, what a bloody mess I've made of things, he thought, railing against his nature. If she wasn't pregnant, I could ride out of here without a backward glance, I think. Knowing our politicians, they'll not want to put out a penny more than needed, which means nothing Cowell dreamed up will ever be put into action. Rabbit'll be just another victim we've lied to. Oh shit, if this is growing up and acting like an adult, then I don't care for it, thank you very much.

He clasped his arms tighter about her and she nuzzled to him deep in sleep, her soft, satiny-smooth flesh warm against his, maddeningly sensuous and comforting. He breathed deep of her aromas of hair and flesh, clean woman-smell and hint of sweat, the faint scent of their love-making, her exotic muskiness of burned pine and loamy earth, of deer hide and cooking, native greases or oils with which she had been anointed for the marriage ceremony, and the foresty smell of the *chickee* and the green wood and mats around them.

"Ah-lan," she cooed, coming awake as he held her too tight.

"Dear little Soft Rabbit," he whispered back, brushing her cheek with his lips, feeling an almost fierce desire to protect her from all that would come.

"Ah-lan . . . mine," she said, drawing his face down to her hot round breasts inside the blanket, stroking his head and hair and making pleased noises as he sprang into sudden, overful arousal, willing as any bride for another proof of love before dawn. She rolled onto her back and stroked his back, drawing him between her open thighs.

"In for the penny, in for the bloody pound," he told her with a shaky laugh. "One for the road, old girl?"

"Ah-lan mine!" she giggled.

Chapter 7

There had been a lot more room in the boats on the journey back down-river. The man Tom/Red Coat had come along, just to see the coast region once more, and get a share of rum, most likely. While the Creeks and Seminolee went overland with pack-horses and mules, the men from *Shrike* were alone with their own kind for the first time in over two weeks, and it felt odd.

Not totally alone, even so. McGilliveray, still dressed Indian fashion, was with them, and Cowell in his new deerskin clothing, and three of McGilliveray/White Turtle's younger male kin and their traveling girls. And Rabbit.

At the last, Alan could not bear to leave her, and she could not bear to let him ride away on a spotted Seminolee horse and never be with her new husband again, and against his better judgement, he had let her accompany him. She rode as well as he did, it turned out, and she and the traveling girls did all the cooking for their party, delaying the day the soldiers and sailors had to fend for themselves again.

Not that he had minded the night on the trail, or the night in a Seminolee *chickee* at the lake where they had left their boats, for she had left him wheezing after their passion. She had never been in a real boat before, but adjusted quickly, and sat aft with him at the tiller of the twenty-five-foot launch, treating the whole trip like a honeymoon jaunt, and full of wonder at the life in the swamps, which she had never seen. And when Cony or Andrews fetched her an egret plume or some flamingo feathers she was as delighted as any miss just given a ruby bracelet. The hands treated her as deferentially as they would have a proper officer's wife, and she had begun to feel like a queen, or a chief's bride.

"You *talwa*!" she exclaimed, after McGilliveray had talked to her about what Alan did in the Royal Navy.

"Not a chief, dear," Alan laughed. "My captain is chief. I am his *mikko*. Tell her, McGilliveray."

With Soft Rabbit by his side, he felt charitable enough to accept the whole world, even McGilliveray and his ponderous lecturing.

"And an *imathla lubotskulgi*," McGilliveray informed her to her great delight. "A little warrior, too young to be an *imathla thlukulgi*, a big warrior chief. But he has killed many foes, haven't you, Lewrie? How many, do you think, so that I may praise you to the skies to her?"

"Well, I've fought two duels, cut one and killed the other. With swords, mind, not pistols at twenty paces," Alan bragged. "Damme, maybe a dozen more in boarding melees."

"Most impressive."

"And God knows how many with artillery," Alan concluded.

Soft Rabbit was thrilled that her man was such a bloody-handed warrior, and her awe of him, which was already considerable, went to new heights of reverence after McGilliveray translated that to her.

"She says she is honored to be the wife of such a brave young man, and is sure that your son shall be a man-slaughtering Hector as well, she'll make sure of it. Man-Killer will be his father and will teach him to be a warrior."

"Man-Killer? He'll be her husband when I'm gone?"

"No, you misunderstand. It's more important to Muskogee who your mother's relatives are," McGilliveray went on, happy to find an opportunity to preach. "The husband and father is not of the mother's clan, where she shall live. She's Wind Clan now, a very important clan in our way of life, and Man-Killer and all the males are her uncles, so to speak, and they fill the role of the father when it comes to rearing the child. You are only of their fire, *anhissi*, which means friend. What clan you are doesn't matter, as long as you weren't Wind Clan. Marrying into your own clan is a sin."

"She'll be well-treated, won't she?" Alan pressed.

"Do you really care, Lewrie?" McGilliveray asked, almost mocking him.

"Damme, yes I do care," he shot back, putting an arm around her, which she understood more than words, and she came up from her pad of blanket between the thwarts to sit at his side.

"Yes, she shall be well-treated," McGilliveray finally softened, after taking a long moment to consider Alan's fierceness on the subject. "She will have an honored place in my mother's *huti*, and in the clan. I suppose, technically speaking, she could never re-marry as long as you are alive and could come back to claim her. But since we both know that you shall never see her again, it would best if she used your absence at the next Green Corn Ceremony˙ as proof that the marriage didn't take. Love-matches can be repented then, if they aren't working out, even if children have already resulted. Being with child will make her more desirable as a wife, since it proves she is fecund and able to bear children. She could do right well."

"I'd like to leave something for her, something to help her in future. What do you suggest?" Alan asked in a soft voice, and some of his concern and sadness must have communicated to Rabbit, for she tucked her head onto his shoulder and hugged him back, eyes downcast.

"As a sop to your conscience?" McGilliveray snapped.

"Damn you to Hell, McGilliveray, I've had it with your bitterness at being born only half-white or half-Muskogee. What passes between us is no matter, though, as long as the girl prospers. And my child."

There, I've said it, he thought with sudden wonder. I've claimed the brat as mine, and her as my responsibility.

"And what do you want for your child?"

"I'd like him to grow up English, frankly, with proper schooling and all. There's no bloody future in growing up Indian."

"Hardly possible unless our mission is successful. And that after he's been raised Muskogee for his first few years. Best let him be what he'll be and let it go at that, Lewrie. I'll be staying on with the tribe, though, and I'll see that he knows who his father was, and what his legacy is. I am truly sorry for you about this."

"Then give me a little help here," Alan demanded.

"Blankets and such for the present. Make her a rich little girl when she goes back to the White Town. Her own skillets and pots and all the needles and thread you can, that sort of thing. Any spare shirts you have. Maybe some sailcloth you can spare. For the future, I can tell her the value of money, and you could leave her some. Small coins would be best, pence and shillings, so she can buy from the traders who will come. Could you come up with about twenty pounds in change?"

"Yes, I could."

"At five pence here and a shilling there, it will keep her and her babe in style for years," McGilliveray promised him.

"Good, then," Alan said, giving her another assuring hug.

The next noon found them at the mouth of the Ochlockonee River, in the long narrow inlet between the two arms of swamp and marsh that formed the hiding place for the Guarda Costa sloop *San Ildefonso*. It was too soon to expect the sloop to be there, but they were close enough to deep water to have a good view of the ocean beyond and could spot her arrival when she appeared.

They made camp on the east bank, though it was not much to look at, given a choice. Their new Muskogee and Seminolee allies would be coming down the east bank, so they had to suffer in silence. The ground was half-marshy, half-sand-spit, strewn with sea-oats and dune grasses, saw grass and palmettos, and cypress and pine inland to their rear. It teemed with biting flies, mosquitoes and gnats, and but for the sea breeze would have been uninhabitable for very long. They pitched lean-tos of cane and palmetto fronds for shelter and settled down to wait. Cashman sent some of his fusiliers out on picket, and the young Creek warriors went off to hunt silently with bows and arrows, and to scout the ground.

While Soft Rabbit and the other unmarried travel girls set up their pots and gathered firewood, Alan and Cashman went to the shore and found a place to spy out the sea.

"By my reckonin', this is the day you wanted the boat to come back for us," Cashman said. "If she makes it."

"Should have been safe as houses out there, out of sight of land," Alan said, extending his telescope and patiently scanning the horizon.

"Well, Red Coat ... Tom ... was tellin' me that when they took Fort St. George at Pensacola, Galvez fetched a fleet of sixty-four ships from Havana for the job."

"Sixty-four?" Alan scoffed. "They've not ten decent sail of the line in the entire West Indies. Damn few useful frigates, either. Most were merchantmen, I'll wager. You can depend on my captain to come back for us, you'll see."

"Two weeks, three weeks, is a long time to lay out there and kill time, though. Seriously, if he doesn't come, what could we do?" Cashman pressed.

"Sail off in the boats, I expect. I did it once before up in the Chesapeake, and that was with river barges never meant for the open sea. I could do it again, a lot better than before, with the launch and the gig."

"It's a devilish long way to Jamaica, though, ain't it," Cashman grunted, pulling off his moccasins and spreading his toes in the dry white sand. "What, two days' sail to Tampa Bay, another two to the Keys?"

"Let's not go borrowing sorrow so quickly," Alan replied. "If things go that badly, it might make more sense to borrow horses from the Creeks and go overland to Charleston. If traders can do it, then there's a chance we could, with some help from our new allies. Tonight's the night Svensen was due back with the sloop. If he doesn't make it, then we might have to change our plans, but I'd give him at least two days' grace before I started worrying for real."

" 'Nother thing that bothers me . . ." Cashman began.

"God, but you're a fountain of joy today, Kit."

"Notice we didn't come across any Apalachee on the way back?" Cashman droned on full of caution. "We gave 'em some muskets and truck, they got the drift of what we're doin' here with White Turtle and the Seminolee with us. I know they're a shattered lot, compared to the Muskogee, but you'd think they'd come out of the woodwork and give us a cheer or two, maybe try to cadge a free sip of rum'r somethin'."

"Hmm, have you asked McGilliveray about that?" Alan asked, now sharing a worry with the infantryman.

"Not yet, but I'm goin' to, right now," Cashman replied. "Never thought I'd be the one to say this, but I'll be tickled pink to see the sight of our Creeks and Seminolee show up with 'nough weapons and men."

"I'd like it, too," Alan agreed, putting down his telescope after deciding that not even an errant whitecap could be mistaken for a topsail on the horizon. "If the sloop comes inshore tonight and anchors here in the inlet, and our Indian friends are not here to take delivery of the guns, we'll be forced to wait for them with a target no patrol could miss."

"De sloop's heah, Mista Lewrie, sah!" Andrews hissed at the front of Alan's lean-to, where he had been sleeping with Soft Rabbit, after staying awake most of the night awaiting the arrival of *San Ildefonso*. He had barely lain his head down, it seemed, to sleep the morning away.

"I'll be right out," Alan said, groping for his shirt. It was the first night he had slept with her that they had not made love, or even removed their clothing. Soft Rabbit had gone to sleep without him hours before, after sensing that his duty took precedence over her.

"Ah-lan," she coaxed as he started to leave what little scrap of privacy they had in the lean-to with a blanket hung over the front.

"Got to go, Soft Rabbit, like it or not," Alan said. He gave her a quick hug and a kiss, then darted out into the dawn. It was not foggy on their sand-spit, though fog hung thick as the Spanish moss on the trees to their rear and inland. By the light of a few smoldering coals in the cook-fire from the night before, he could see that his watch read about half past four in the morning. It was false dawn, and the soft breezes coming off the sea were chilly. Waves rolled in and broke on the beach with a soft, continual hissing.

There was barely enough light to see where he was walking as he made his way down to the shore by the river.

"Where away?" he asked in a soft voice.

"Deyah, sah," Andrews said, pointing out to sea to the southwest. "Mustah missed de river in dah dahk un' come 'long de coast."

San Ildefonso ghosted out of the river fog, hardly a ripple of bow wave under her forefoot, and her sails hanging almost slack with the last gasp of the pre-dawn sea breeze. For a moment, Alan was worried she might have been a *real* Spanish Guarda Costa sloop, but he recognized several patches on her outer jib, and caught a lick of color aft on her mains'l gaff—the blue, white and red of a Royal Navy ensign.

"That's her, alright," Alan breathed with relief in his voice.

"If she's in the right hands," Cashman said at his elbow, which made Alan's full bladder jolt with alarm. "I'm keepin' my troops hidden 'til we know for sure."

"Good thinking," Alan replied, realizing that it was never good to see what you expected to see without making some preparations to be surprised by a clever foe. "Unfortunately, they'll expect to see some of our party. And me, or they'll turn about and sail out of here with the land breeze when it comes up. It's too late to be fooling about on a hostile shore with dawn in an hour."

"I'll leave you to it, then, Alan. Good luck."

Alan opened his breeches and stepped into the sea oats to drain his bladder while he had the chance. Then, gathering his nerves, he stepped out onto the river shore in plain sight and waved his arms at the sloop, hoping that Cashman's fear was not real.

There was no answering wave that he could see, so he lifted his telescope and eyed her as she came on without a sound on the still river, becoming more solid, with a bank of fog behind her on the western shore. It looked like Svensen at the tiller, but that did not guarantee that a Don officer might not be hidden, directing Svensen's movements.

"Damn you, Kit, now you've got me starting at shadows, too," he grumbled. He had to step out and call, softly "Ahoy the sloop!"

He hung the glass over his shoulder and waved both arms over his head. Someone at the bows waved back and the sloop altered her head slightly more bows-on to him in response.

"Ahoy derr!" Svensen boomed back at last, making every bird on the riverbank squawk in alarm and take wing. "Mister Lewrie, ja?"

"Svensen!" he rasped back in a harsh whisper. "Yes, it's me."

"Dat you, zir?" Svensen howled as though it was blowing a full gale. A bull gator began to roar somewhere off in the fog in response.

"Lieutenant Lewrie, yes!" he replied. "Svensen, not so loud!"

"Aye, zir, dis be Svensen! Und who be *mit* you, zir?"

"Oh, for Christ's sake," Alan muttered. "Captain Cashman of the 104th, Mister Cowell, Mister McGilliveray . . . Svensen, this is supposed to be *secret*, you know! Not so loud?"

"Vat, zir?" Svensen bellowed loud as the Last Trumpet. "Vat ship I from, zir?"

"*Shrike*, brig o' war, you noisy bastard!" Alan finally yelled back at full volume. "Now for God's sake, will you shut the hell up, and get your miserable arse ashore this instant!" The sloop swung about, let go her halyards and dropped anchor once she coasted to a stop.

"I'll have the damn fool's guts for garters," Alan promised himself as he motioned for the gig to be launched into the river. Within a minute, he was standing on a ship's deck once more, among his own kind, all of them beaming with relief that a hard and dangerous job was almost over.

"Zorry, L'tent," Svensen said. "But, by damn, ve been not a mile offshore all night, down t' coast here."

"Missed your land-fall in the dark, did you?"

"Aye, zir, 'bout five mile, I t'ink. Vas dark as a cow's arse, it vas, zir," Svensen said with evident relief. "Been vorkin' our vay off shoals und bars, und den der vind, 'bout vun hour ago, on us she die."

"You're here now, that's the important thing," Alan said, clapping him on the arm and forgetting his own promise to nail the ignorant bastard's hide to the main-mast. "Well done, altogether."

"T'ankee, zir!" Svensen expanded with pride. "Gott der cargo ready to hoist out, zir. Dem red-skins, dey gon' take it, zir?"

"Yes, they've agreed to aid us in getting Florida back. They haven't shown yet, but they're on their way, with pack-horses and mules," Alan explained. "I'll get the launch over here and we may begin stacking everything on the shore yonder. On the way down here they also may have picked up some canoes or dugouts from their friends the Seminolee."

"Vundered vat for we gif dem muskets, zir. *Ja*, ve start!"

The launch butted up alongside a few minutes later, and Alan was surprised that Soft Rabbit was in the boat. She scrambled up over the rail and came to his side, clad only in skirt and blanket. The sight of her beauty, with so much of it on view, made the hands stop their labors dead until Svensen gave the nearest man a kick and yelled at them to hop to it.

She gazed up at the mast, looking around the deck, and he realized that she had never seen such a powerful collection of civilized technology in her life, so far beyond her experience that it might as well be some shaman's magic.

"My ship," Alan said, tapping his chest and waving a hand about the deck possessively. "All mine."

She understood "mine," and looked at him as if he had suddenly stood revealed as a god from her perfect Upper World come down to earth.

"Cony?"

" 'Ere I be, sir."

"Thank you for bringing . . . ah, her, out to the ship."

"My pleasure, sir. Thought she'd like ta see her, sir."

"Please gather up some things for her in a pack. Needles and thread, twine and some scrap sailcloth. What blankets you can find, some cooking implements, too. She'll have to go back to her people."

"Aye, sir, I'll take care of it, sir."

He led her below and aft into the captain's quarters, which were now his again, even if only for a short time. As she gazed amazed and laughing at so much wealth in so small a space, he loaded her up with an embroidered and painted canvas coverlet from the bed-box, the sheets and the blankets, the small round mirror from above the wash-hand stand and the hand-basin, too, some towels, half a dozen pewter plates, cups and bowls, and all the silverware. They tied it up into small bundles that could be strapped across a horse's back for her return journey to the Muskogee White Town. There was his sea chest in the same place he had left it, and he opened it to lay out more treasure for her, including a suede purse containing his small change.

"Money," he told her, sorting out and counting the coins for her. "White Turtle will tell you what it's for. Traders, come. You give to traders. Oh, devil take it, you don't understand a word I'm saying."

"Ah-lan," she whispered, setting aside her new wealth. She took his hand and placed it on her stomach. "Mine bebby, you bebby . . ." She waved a hand at her bundles and gave him a smile that made him feel light-headed, indicating that she understood how much he was giving her and the child to come. She raised his hand to cup one of her breasts, shrugged off her blanket, and smiled impishly at him.

"There's not time for that now," he said, but to no avail, for she turned her head to see if the door was shut, lifted her skirt and stretched out on the bare straw-packed ticken mattress.

"Well, just this last once," he gave in as he looked down at how beautiful she was. "Never let it be said I refused a lady."

He came back on deck about half an hour later, just as true dawn was making itself apparent. Nearly a third of the cargo had been shifted, and was stacked ashore, covered with sailcloth to keep the damp out of the muskets and powder. And still no sign of the Creeks to take delivery of it. Soft Rabbit was still flushed with the last rogering he had given her, now dressed in a loose shirt that came down almost to her knees, cinched in with a kerchief for a sash over her deerskin skirt. Alan had changed back into uniform and had returned his precious hanger to his left hip. Even plain as a lieutenant's uniform was, to her it was cloth of gold, even though she thought that his cocked hat was sort of silly, and laughed at him every time he adjusted it.

" 'Bout anudder hour vor de cargo, zir," Svensen told him and knuckled his forehead in salute. "By damn, dat's vun pretty girl, she be, zir! Dey all vas like dat up de river?"

"Most of 'em, Svensen."

"Den by damn I'm zorry I not go mit you, zir. Been to der Cook Islands und to China vunst before de var. Sveetest little girls in der vorld, native girls ist," Svensen said in appreciation. "How long you t'ink ve have to vait on dese fellas?"

"No idea, Svensen. Once the cargo's been off-loaded, get a kedge anchor out, with springs on the kedge and bower," Alan said. "Load the cannon in both batteries."

"Loaded now, zir. Tompions in, vent's covered. Powder be dry, I reckon."

"Round-shot?"

"Round-shot und grape, zir. Didn't know vat to expect in de dark, zir."

"Very good. Light a coil of slow-match now, just in case, and tell off some hands for gunners. Andrews?"

"Yas, suh?"

"Send two men ashore and start dismantling our camp. Bring back everything the Admiralty'd miss. Oh, and see to helping Rabbit ... Mrs. Lewrie ... gather up my gifts to her and then put them ashore."

"Aye aye, sah."

They took the gig ashore with her gifts, and piled them all in one place for later packing out by horseback. Cashman wandered in from his picket line out at the edge of the trees and tipped his hat to them, which made Rabbit giggle and point to his cocked hat.

"She thinks they're hilarious, Kit." Alan shrugged. "Don't ask me why. Everything quiet so far?"

"So far so good," he agreed. "I've brought my pickets in from the marshes to a close perimeter 'bout fifty yards out. With this mist, that's 'bout as long a shot as we'll get. McGilliveray's warriors are further out, huntin' sign of their people, far's I know. You hear owls hootin' he tells me, that'll be them comin' back in. Well, damn my eyes if we didn't pull it off after all, me lad! 'Tis all over but the shoutin' at this point. Your crew see any Dagoes out to sea?"

"Not one sail in all that time. Almost uncannily easy."

"Knock on wood," Cashman said, grinning and rapping his knuckles on the butt of his fusil. He then strolled back towards the perimeter.

The cargo was finally off-loaded completely, the sloop swung about to direct its fire up-river, or overhead of the camp on the sand-spit to the marshes and swamps. The day dragged on until it was time for dinner, and the hands ceased their labors for "clear decks and up spirits" from a small puncheon of rum brought ashore for them. Rabbit and the other girls had a small fire going, and were almost ready to ladle out more bowls of the eternal *sofkee*, mixed with some dried venison they had been steeping in a pot of water. There was also some salt-meat from the sloop's galley, and biscuit.

The Indian girls looked up first, their ears more attuned to an odd sound than the whites. Owls were not known to hunt so close to the coast, or call anywhere in daylight.

"That'll be the Creek scouts coming back in," McGilliveray said. Cashman's troops were all back at the sand-spit by then, for the fogs had burned off or been blown away by a new day's sea breeze, and they were too exposed out by the edge of the marshes. Other than a few who stood guard from covert hides in the saw grass and palmettoes at the top of the beach, they were all queuing up for their rum and tucker.

"They're in a damned hurry if they are," Cashman said, going for his weapons. "Sarn't, stand to! Form, form open skirmish order!"

The Creek warriors came out of the woods at a dead run, first one who clutched his side where an arrow had pierced him, and then the last two, looking back over their shoulders as they ran as a rearguard for the wounded man.

Not a full minute after they stumbled into camp, a solid pack of painted and feathered warriors came loping out of the trees and across the shallow marsh.

"Apalachee!" McGilliveray shouted. "The bastards!"

"Take 'em under fire, sor?" the sergeant asked Cashman.

"Stand by . . ."

"No, Cashman!" Cowell pleaded. "We don't know why they chased these lads. They could have tried to raid the Apalachee just for the fun of it, they do that all the time. If we fire we might destroy whatever good will we've built here!"

"No, Mister Cowell, they're going to fight us," McGilliveray countered.

"Fire!" Cashman ordered, and the fusils cracked even as the first Apalachee arrows came arcing down among them with a sizzling rush.

There were some shrill screams as the leading warriors were hit and knocked down, and the rest checked their headlong rush and began to weave back and forth among the reeds in the marsh, leaping up as targets to draw fire, or dropping out of sight after they got off an arrow or a cane spear from one of their throwers. They seemed to dart forward and then fall back as if frightened of their own audacity, running in circles like the practice of a Spanish *tiercio* of pistoleers on horseback.

Alan ran to his fusil, which had been leaning on the cargo, and checked his priming. He took aim at a warrior in a bone-armor vest and let fly as the man paused to nock an arrow. The man whooped in pain as Alan's shot took him in the belly and the Indian dropped into the marsh out of sight with a great, muddy splash.

"Svensen!" Alan called over his shoulder to the sloop not sixty yards to his rear in the river. "Lay a gun on these bastards and shoot at the largest pack of them!"

An arrow whickered by him with a thrumming sound and he flinched as he pulled his weapon back to half-cock and began to load, rapping the butt on the nearest crate to settle the load after he had bitten off the cartouche and poured the powder in. Another arrow *zhooped* past his head, and his cocked hat went sailing off somewhere aft. Rabbit was kneeling near him behind the crates, and went to fetch it for him. She came back just as he stood up and shot another running man down in mid-stride, and as he sensibly knelt to load out of sight this time, she gave a blood-thirsty smile of encouragement, whooping in glee.

San Ildefonso's after-most larboard three-pounder barked, and the sound of round-shot and grape passing close overhead made them all go almost flat on the ground. The round-shot cut a warrior in half, leaving his legs and trunk standing, and his torso and head flying off into the trees, shattering against a cypress trunk when they finally hit something solid. The grape-shot frothed the water in the marsh and three more Indians screamed and erupted into bloody statues before they fell, which took the starch out of their courage. After a few more arrows were loosed at the encampment, and two more warriors had been clawed down by the fusiliers at over sixty yards, they made off back into the trees.

"Goddamn and rot the bastards!" Alan raged, snapping off his last shot at one Apalachee who stopped by the trees and presented his bare arse to them in derision. He laughed with delight to see that he had aimed a bit low and had hit the man on the inside of the thigh just a quim-hair from his genitals. "Try stuffin' what's left up your arse, you sorry shit-sack!"

"Nice shot," Cashman panted. "Nigh on ninety yards."

"Damn, but I like the fusil!" Alan shouted back with pleasure. "Now you give me my Ferguson, and I'd have taken his right nutmeg off!"

Rabbit brought him his cocked hat, now decorated with a long cane arrow with a flaked stone point and three raggled feathers at the other end. She pulled a metal knife from her waist and waved it in the air, making motions that he should go out there and lift some hair.

"God, it's just as well I can't take you with me," Alan told her, smiling so she would know he was pleased. "I'd love to turn you loose on some people I know with that thing."

"I should have known we couldn't trust the Apalachee, not with so much loot to be had," McGilliveray spat. "They once were a mighty people you could trust, but the Spanish have turned them into shabby dogs. They must have been watching all this time, waiting for us to get all the muskets landed, and for us to pull our pickets in."

"For all the good it did them," Cowell sniffed, clumsily trying to reload the musket he had snatched up and fired at least once.

Several shots boomed out from the marsh and the tree-line and they ducked down once more into cover. As Cashman crawled up to his furthest forward marksmen, the volume of fire increased.

"Damme, must be a platoon of 'em with muskets out there," Cashman shouted back. "Mark your targets and return fire, and keep your bloody heads down."

"Svensen!" Alan bawled. "Into the tree-line! Take your time and aim true, one gun at a time! Reload with grape and canister as you do so!"

"Aye, zir!" a thin voice called back from the sloop. Barely had the mate spoken than the first gun fired, and the trees rustled in shock as the deadly grape-shot thrashed at the hidden musketeers.

"We'll cut 'em to pieces if they try to rush us again," Cashman said as he rolled over onto his back to reload behind a palmetto and a mound of gritty sand.

"If they do try to rush us, it might be a near thing, even so," Alan told him. "I've not seven men aboard the sloop, and the crew for a three-pounder is three men, so that's not two guns able to fire more 'n once a minute. With a whole lot of luck, they'll try to rush us once more, get cut up between your fusiliers and the artillery, and go sulk or something until the Creeks finally stir up their bloody arses and *get here*, damn their lazy eyes!"

Rabbit was tugging at his sleeve urgently, and he turned to

her. She pointed up-river and growled something in her own language.

"Jesus Christ shit on a biscuit!" Alan cried.

The river was thick with dugout canoes, the canoes crowded gunwales deep with more Apalachee, and white men in dirty blue uniforms.

" 'Ware the river, Kit, we've been sold out to the Dons!" Alan warned. "Svensen, use the springs and heave her about!"

He had to stand to direct the mate's attention up-river, and a flurry of arrows and bullets flailed the air around him as he waved and pointed.

"Sarn't, six men this side of the cargo, use it as a breastwork," Cashman snarled. "Rest of you, stand fast along this dune line! Mister McGilliveray, you and your warriors up here, please. You, too, Mister Cowell. It's going to be warm work here in a few minutes."

Warm ain't the fuckin' word for it, Alan thought with a grim shudder of fear. Not two-score of us against at least a company of Dago troops and God knows how many Apalachee. Oh Christ, you could fit our little defense line into *Shrike*'s fo'c'sle. We're all going to get knackered and scalped. "Rabbit!"

"Rabbit, go to the ship. Understand me? Be safe there! Go ship! Swim?" he said, talking with his arms and hands in a flurry.

She shook her head and snatched the dragoon pistol from his belt.

"Let's have this crate opened, and that'un there!" Cashman was ordering. "You men, load as many muskets as you can and stack 'em ready for use. With enough volume of fire, we may blunt 'em yet."

San Ildefonso cut loose finally with her starboard battery of guns, which had yet to be fired. Round-shot and grape-shot tore the river into a forest of water fountains, and two of the leading canoes were shattered into scrap lumber, pitching their screaming paddlers and warriors into the river. Svensen had shot his bolt, though, with that broadside, for with only seven men it would take time to reload three guns.

"Swivels, Svensen!" Alan screamed. "Don't forget the swivels! Cony, fetch the two swivels from the boats. One here facing the river, one for the fusiliers to play with up on the dune line."

With no more cannon being fired at them from the sloop, the savages in the marsh whooped into motion. Alan stuck his head up and saw that there were at least thirty Spanish troops with them, probably the ones responsible for the musket fire. The boats were too far off to land close; it would be the pack coming from the marsh they had to deal with first.

"Feel like a gambling man, Lewrie?" Cashman asked.

"Aye, but the odds are bloody horrible."

"Bring your people up here to be my second line."

"Svensen, keep that lot off our backs!" Alan shouted out to his ship, which looked so *damned* safe and snug out there on the water, where he really much preferred to be. Damn the cargo, he thought with a sick, empty feeling inside. If we can fight these bastards off, we're out of here like a shot.

They met the charge with a shot from a swivel gun that had had its stand jammed down into the firm sand. Bayonets glinted evilly as the Spanish came on to the sound of a trumpet, and the Apalachee howled their death songs.

"First rank, pick your targets . . . fire!"

A dozen shots, perhaps eight men struck down.

"Lewrie, fire!" Cashman yelled.

"Take aim . . . fire!"

He shot one Apalachee down, tossed down his fusil and snatched up a Brown Bess from the cargo that had seen better days, but the lock came back with a firm snap, and when he pulled the trigger, it fired, and a Spaniard shrieked in shock as his chest was torn open by the .75 caliber ball.

"Yu!" One of the Creek warriors said from beside him, letting fly with an arrow from an osage-wood bow. Each time he aimed and fired he chanted some incantation under his breath for proper aiming and a good kill, then expelled "Yu!"—he was getting five arrows for every shot from Alan's guns, and his prayers were working wonderfully.

The charge faltered just short of the dune line, with the fusiliers rising from cover to let off their last shots and go in with the bayonet, for which the Apalachee were not prepared. Half a dozen of them died howling on the steel, and then they were fading away, taking the Spanish with them.

"Sarn't, one squad to cover the marsh! Rest of you, fall back to the breast-works! And reload that damned swivel!" Cashman shouted.

They were barely in time. Svensen had been banging away steadily at the approaching canoes full of warriors, but Alan doubted if some 5th Rate frigate in the same predicament could have made much of an impression on that flotilla of dugouts, even with a dozen carriage guns. The boats were within twenty yards of grounding on the muddy river bank when Andrews lit off the swivel on the breast-works and stopped the progress of one boat by killing everyone in it with a canister-load of musket balls.

An Apalachee came dashing through the shallows, eager to fight, and Alan shot him down with his fusil. The Brown Bess took down the second one ashore, and then there was no time to reload. Cashman's men got off a volley and stood ready to receive with the bayonet. Alan drew his hanger.

One Apalachee dashed for Alan, screaming loud enough to curdle Lewrie's blood, but he found the courage to step forward and meet him, tempered steel blade against a wooden war club, which he beat aside, and glided his point into the man's throat as he drew up for a second swing. He picked up the war club for his off-hand to use as a mobile shield, cutting the thong that bound it to the dead warrior's wrist by hacking the man's hand off with his superbly sharpened blade.

A second man with a cane spear died with one feet of steel in his belly, and a third got back-handed with the war club, which shattered his skull like a melon.

A Spaniard came against him next, a man with a small-sword, a smelly dog of a man with one of those infuriating mustaches and a smug look of eventual victory. Their blades rang in the first beat of their duel. The Spaniard was fast, but he had a weak wrist, and Alan threw a flying cutover at him, forcing his blade wide. To keep it there, he binded with the war-club and as the Spaniard leaped back to disengage and regain an equal advantage, Alan back-handed the slightly curved cutting edge of the hanger across the man's stomach, opening his belly and spilling his entrails. He would have finished him off with another slash across the throat, but there was another Spaniard there with a musket and bayonet.

Alan stepped forward to fight him, but the dying Spaniard on the ground groped at him and nailed him to the spot, and the musketman came forward. Alan deflected the bayonet down to his left, but the man got all fourteen inches of it through his thigh.

"Goddamn you!" he screamed in sudden pain and this time got a slash at the throat, which almost took the man's head off as they both fell. The bayonet twisted and turned as the gun behind it toppled from the dead man's grasp, ripping Alan's leg into agony. He saw stars and almost fainted from the indescribable pain of it. A shadow loomed over him, an Apalachee with a war-club ready to brain him, and then there was a shot and the man was toppling back into the ooze at the river's edge.

Rabbit was there by his side, a smoking dragoon pistol in her hands, crying and weeping as if he was indeed already dead. She got him under the arms, and he could not credit such a little girl being capable of it, but she seemed to *lift him* and bear him back behind the breast-works and shove a loaded musket into his hands.

"You silly bitch, I'm bleeding like a slaughtered pig! What the hell you want me to do with this, for Christ's sake?" he railed.

There was a shot next to his ear that almost deafened him and he turned to see Cony and Andrews flanking him, discharging muskets as fast as they could pick them up. Alan wobbled his weapon up over the crates and leveled it in the general direction and fired, not knowing where the ball went. He sank back, feeling very tired and sleepy, and looked down at his leg. The Spanish musket and bayonet had gone away, which he thought was nice of somebody, but there seemed to be an awful lot of blood, and he was frightfully sure it was all his.

"Christ," he muttered, feeling his skin pop out cold sweat. His ears were ringing like Westminster's chimes, and that was about all he could hear. Rabbit's face loomed up in his vision as she held him to her breasts.

Worse things to look at when you're dying, I s'pose, he thought.

IV

"*Oceanus ponto qua continet orbem,*
nulla tibi adversis regio sese offeret armis.
Te manet invictus Romano marte Britannus
teque interiecto mundi pars altera sole."

"*Wherever the Ocean's deep encompasses the*
   Earth,
no land will meet thee with opposing force.
The Briton whom Roman prowess has not van-
   quished
is reserved for thee, and the other portion of
   the world, with the Sun's path in between."
                    "Panegyricus Messallae"
                    —Tibullus

Chapter 1

Alan woke up in a lot of pain as someone tried to haul him up from his prone position, but damned if he wanted to move! He struck out at whoever it was, and several more hairy paws grabbed onto him to restrain him, and, still lost in a terrifying dream of being taken by savages intent on his scalping and mutilation, he let out a howl of fear and pain.

"Sorry, sir, almost done," Dr. Lewyss told him.

"Ah," Alan said, biting his lips trying to be stoic now that he recognized the good doctor, though his chest still heaved with panic. "Where am I?"

"Aboard *Shrike*, sir. In my sick-bay below the forepeak," the man said, between snatches of humming some song to himself as he fussed with a fresh dressing on Alan's leg wound. "Most amazing thing, really. Thought sure I'd have to take the leg, but God seems to favor you remaining a biped, sir. Even if there was the foulest poultice applied to it when you were brought aboard. Some pagan muck, egh!"

"When?" Alan groaned as Lewyss finally finished wrapping his thigh and allowed it to be lowered to the bunk, where it ceased screaming and settled down for some long-term throbbing.

"Yesterday, sir," Cony said from Alan's side, where he had been assisting in his restraint. "Got some brandy 'ere, sir, iffen ya feels up ta takin' some."

"God, *yes*, I'm ready!" Alan said with some heat.

"A drop or two of tincture of laudanum for that first," Lewyss suggested, reaching for his case.

"And then someone please tell me what happened at the river-bank," Alan ordered, now that he was up in a sitting position on the short cot.

"Them Apalachee an' Dons almost done fer us, sir, 'til them Muskogee an' Seminolee showed up," Cony related, offering him a squat pewter mug brimming with harsh *ratafia*, which Alan sipped from avidly. "Thought the ones in the swamp was acomin' fer us, but they was runnin' instead. God, they don't butcher half-fair, sir! Loppin' off 'eads an' arms an' legs and what-all fer the fun of it, aliftin' scalps an' laughin' like loonies, sir. 'Twas the scariest thing ever I did see, even worse'n the fightin'."

"What about the rest of our party?" Alan demanded.

"Well, Andrews got a cut'r two, sir, an' I got scratched up a piece," Cony went on. "We lost three of the 'ands dead, them sodjers got five killed an' ever'body else down with wounds. 'Nother minute'r two, an' there'd been nobody to save, sir. Near as damnit's a thing as ever I did see. An' we lost that nice Mister Cowell, sir. Apalachee nailed 'im all over with arrers, they did."

"I'm sorry to hear that, Cony," Alan sighed, feeling a wave of sadness. "He had no business getting mixed up in the fighting like us. What a mess. And Captain Cashman?"

"Fine, sir, 'ceptin' a scrape here and there."

"Thank God for that, at least. Wait! Rabbit?"

"Missus Lewrie got away fine, sir," Cony assured him. "Mister McGilliveray took 'er back to 'is people, with your gifts an' all."

"*Mrs.* Lewrie?" Doctor Lewyss muttered, rolling his eyes. "My, you *have* been a busy lad!"

" 'E said to tell ya, sir, that she'd be took good care of, 'e'd see to that."

"She was a sweet little thing at bottom." Alan nodded. He felt a pang of longing for her, but the idea of being a husband and father made him decide that as Anne Beauman told him, things work out for the best in the long run.

"You do get into the oddest scrapes, sir, if you'll pardon me for saying so," Dr. Lewyss chuckled. "I truly do believe you could turn up a willing tit amidst the agonies of Hell itself. It's not everyone has your success with the ladies, ha ha! Well, that should do you for now, sir. Tomorrow, should you feel up to it, and suppuration has not set in, I shall have you moved to the gun deck where you may get some fresh air and some sun. 'Tis my experience people heal the faster there."

"Thank you, Mister Lewyss, I'd appreciate that," Alan said, and took another deep draught of the brandy. The laudanum was taking effect and the pain was lessening to a manageable level now, and he felt the urge to yawn, perhaps close his eyes for a nap as long as he was flat on his back with no duties to attend to for the first time in years.

"Oh, Cony, did Rabbit receive all her presents when she left?"

"Yessir, she did." Cony nodded, looking as though something was on his mind, but reticent by class or position to mention it.

"Something else you want to tell me, Cony?" Alan prodded, knowing his man's moods by then.

"Well, sir, I didn't want ta mention it much, but . . ." Cony fumbled, turning red with embarrassment. "I know you was fond o' 'er, sir, but sometimes things work out best."

"Fond of her, yes, Cony, but not about to trot her back to London with me," Alan admitted. "She'd have been unhappy there. Probably been unhappy anywhere close to civilized."

"Well, that's it, sir," Cony said, summoning up his nerve. "When them Muskogee an' Seminolee was adone slaughterin', an' she'd finished puttin' some poultice on yer leg, she an' them other girls went out an' . . . Lord, sir . . . ever' man you killed, she took her knife to. Scalped 'em for ya, since you couldn't! Ears an' weddin' tackle an' all, and whoopin' fit ta bust, sir! Never seen the like, an' her a gentle little girl, too, sir, with a baby acomin'! Tried to give 'em ta me in a bag, an' I had ta take it'r shame ya, Mister McGilliveray said, but I put it over the side soon's we were a few mile offshore. Woulda took that poultice off, too, 'cept Mister McGilliveray said they was strong 'erbs in it, that'd draw the poison out, else you'd mortify an' die. Said 'e'd seen it work before, an' it was devilish good medicine."

"Must have worked," Alan agreed after another swig of brandy.

"Aye, sir, that wound wasn't half as angry t'day as it was when I saw ya bandaged there on the beach," Cony agreed heartily.

"Well, let that be a lesson to us, Cony," Alan finally said, smiling. "Never trust a woman with a knife, even the sweetest of 'em. They can be handsome as hell, but they've all got a mean streak when they're crossed. 'Specially after they become wives." He chuckled wearily.

"Yessir, I guess." Cony nodded.

"I think I'll sleep for a while, Cony," Alan said after draining the mug and licking his lips. "You're not harmed? Feeling alright?"

"Aye, sir, right as rain," Cony said, taking the mug from Alan's almost nerveless fingers as he closed his eyes. "You rest up, sir, an' you'll be back on yer feet an' runnin' this ship sooner'n you can say 'Jack-Sauce.' "

"Oh God, do I have to?" Alan murmured just before dropping off.

"Well, I'll say goodbye to you, Alan," Cashman grunted, picking up his weapons kit, now swollen with new items as souvenirs from their adventure. "Heal up and we'll hoist a few for old times soon, I hope."

"Somewhere quiet for a change, Kit," Alan agreed, hobbling to his feet and limping heavily to the rail by the entry-port with his crutch that Mr. Pebble the carpenter had made for him.

"You sound like you don't like excitement anymore. Once you've got two good legs to stand on, there's a world o' fun to be had out there." Cashman laughed.

"Give me a month or so, then I'll be ready for some amusements," Alan prophecied. "Though I'd like my excitement a little less neck-or-nothing than this last little bit. I'll suppose you'll be going back to Florida when we land troops there, since you know so much about the Indians now. Maybe *Shrike* will be involved in it. We'll see each other then."

"Bless me, Alan, there won't be any landing." Cashman frowned. "With Cowell dead, an' McGilliveray gone native, there's no one to say a good word for the idea, an' I doubt any officer in the West Indies'd spare a corporal's guard in a rowboat on the plan. Mind you, it *could* have worked, given half a chance."

"Damme, but I'm getting weary of seeing good men die for nothing, Kit," Alan spat, after a long moment to get over his sudden surprise. "Seems I've spent my whole time in the Navy taking part in ventures doomed from the start! Graves in The Chesapeake, Cornwallis at Yorktown, evacuating Wilmington . . . I could give you chapter and verse from now 'til supper and not repeat myself. Oh, we're good when it comes to the fighting, but witless when it comes to the planning for them."

"All the more reason for fellas like us to live long enough to be generals and admirals," Cashman barked, giving out with a short, bitter laugh. "We couldn't possibly be worse than the pack o' fools we have now. Too used to winnin' in the Seven Years' War, I guess, an' forgot all we learned from that one. McGilliveray was a hopeless stuffy bastard, but he had the right idea, I'll give him that. Least he's enough muskets to keep the Rebels from eatin' his people alive for a time, an' traders'll sell 'em anythin' they want, long's they come up with enough pelts an' hides to swap. Well, I'm off. Back to Lieutenant Colonel Peacock an' his shitten ways. All the best to you. Do write and let me know when you get 'married' again, and I'll be there to stand up for you one more time."

"Aye, I'll keep in touch, but I seriously doubt the marrying part." Alan smiled, taking Cashman's hand and feeling his sour depression lift for a while. He knew that half of it was being so incapacitated, that and the continuing pain of his wound. He truly liked Cashman, odd a bird as he was, and wished to give him a hearty send off. "Keep out of trouble. And should I get another girl in the family way, you'll *have* to stand up with me, else I'd run for the hills. Farewell, Kit."

"Hoist a Black Drink for me!" Cashman yelled from the boat after he had gotten himself and his dunnage settled, and then he was gone.

Alan waved once more and steeled himself to limp with the crutch aft to the steps to the quarterdeck, wincing with each pace. It would have been so easy to let the surgeons declare him unfit for duty, and he could be put ashore until he was fully healed. But *Shrike* was his world and he could not bear to leave her for another ship after settling in so comfortably. Better the devil he know than to be relegated to some new pack of strangers and begin the process of mixing in once more, probably in a larger ship where he would have less authority as a second or third lieutenant. After gaining mastery of his duties well enough to serve as a first officer, he would be damned if he would give it up unless made to do so. So he had risen from his cot the day they had anchored in Kingston harbor, and sweated and suffered to appear fit enough to stay.

The first step, balancing on the crutch with a death-grip on the man-rope, fancy-served with turk's heads, that served for a banister. A second step. And William Pitt, lashing his tail lazily at the top.

"Get out of my way, you mangy bastard," Alan whispered. "Oh for Christ's sake, don't do that!"

The ram-cat daintily hopped down to the step he was on and wound about his bad leg, making himself a moving obstacle to any further attempt to take a step. William Pitt was *purring*.

"Happy I'm crippled, are you?" Alan snarled. "Getting our

own back, are we, damn your eyes? Give way, you sorry shit-sack."

The cat leaped up to the next step, letting him advance, but repeated the performance, rubbing its chin and head on his good leg this time, and twining about him with tail and side like a snake.

"Need some help there, Mister Lewrie?" Lieutenant Lilycrop asked him.

"Somebody kill this filthy beast, sir, that'd suit," Alan said, sweating like a slavey for fear he'd go arse over tit any second.

"Stap me, but one'd almost think he's startin' to like you, sir," Lilycrop marveled. He came down the ladder and helped Alan up to the quarterdeck. "If you think you can manage it, I'd admire if you joined me in my cabins. You may lean on me, if you've a mind. No shame in acceptin' help now and again when ya need it, sir."

"Thankee, sir, I'd be much obliged."

Once ensconced in a padded chair, with a glass of rhenish in his hands, he felt much better, though the appraising way Lilycrop was looking at him was a bit disconcerting. Was he being sent ashore, try as he had to appear hale?

"I've given orders you're to shift your quarters for a while, Mister Lewrie," Lilycrop finally said. "You'll be comfortable enough in the chart-space yonder, and all the closer to the quarterdeck, with only the short ladder to manage 'til you're fully healed."

"I'm grateful for your concern, sir," Alan told him with a grin as his worries disappeared. "Doctor Lewyss says another couple of weeks more and I'll be fit enough for light duties. I thought you might be considering packing me off ashore, sir."

"Oh, not a bit of it," Lilycrop assured him with one of his round smiles. "We're used to each other's ways now, and I'd not like to break in another first officer. Not that one'd be forthcomin' from Sir Joshua Bloody Rowley for the likes of us."

"We didn't exactly fail, sir," Alan pointed out. "If he won't reinforce the overtures we made, it's his fault if he lets the chance slip away."

"He's nothin' to reinforce with," Lilycrop told him with a sour look. "Admiral Hood's off Cape Francois, blockadin' the rest of the French West Indies fleet, and Admiral Pigot . . ."

"Who the hell is he, sir?" Alan asked.

"Goddamn, but you still haven't learned to keep your ear to the ground, boy." Lilycrop frowned. "Pigot come out to take over from Rodney last year, just after The Saintes, an' after we got transferred. Anyway, one of de Grasse's junior admirals, de Vaudreuil or something, has most of his squadron penned up at Cape Francois, and at Porto Cavallo, on the Spanish Main. That's why there's to be no ships for any expedition to Florida. All the admirals want a last sea battle, a last crack at the Frogs."

"So everything we did was a waste," Alan spat.

"We weren't to know that, not at the time. Admirals change, plans change." Lilycrop shrugged. "Maybe after the war's over, we can run traders or agents in there, anyway, and still achieve somethin'."

"So we're just a little foot-note, sir," Alan went on, getting angry. "Maybe not even that."

"That's the way of it." Lilycrop nodded, reaching over to tap him on the shoulder. "Don't take it so hard, Mister Lewrie. You did all anyone could expect of you, and more, from what I heard. Sometimes all you can do is your duty, and your best just ain't good enough if they go and change the plan on you. Don't you think even admirals get their best efforts rejected now and again? 'Course, those never turn up in their memoirs, or the naval chronologies. Rest assured, Rowley give us a good report. And a nice pat on the arse on the way out."

"Out, sir?"

"Transfer back to Admiral Hood's flag, off Hispaniola. We're to be part of Commodore Affleck's group workin' close inshore to keep an eye on the Frogs at Cape Francois. Be good to get back to sea and have somethin' straight forward to do, for a change. Maybe get a crack at a merchantman tryin' to supply the damned place."

"I still think we'd have done better going back to Florida," Alan said, shaking his head. "The French will never come out, sir. We waste our efforts blockading them. And if they're blockaded, then we have a clear shot at landing the expedition."

"But if they learned we were doin' it, and took ships off-station, they would come out, and then where'd we be?" Lilycrop countered.

"Then we keep the fleet at sea, waiting for the second chance to defeat them, sir," Alan schemed. "What better lure to draw them out at all! Look here, sir, I'll wager you any odds that Admiral Hood had no idea this expedition was being considered. What if we could write him and let him know of it? He's senior to Rowley, is he not? If he could thin his blockade, provide enough ships to escort the expedition, the French would learn of it. We land our forces at Apalachee Bay, or closer to Pensacola. This de Vaudreuil comes out of Porto Cavallo and Cape Francois, maybe the Dons come out of Havana. Pigot could come west from Antigua or St. Lucie, and Rowley could sortie the Jamaica Squadron. We assemble off the Florida coast, threatening Havana, and meet them in that last glorious battle the admirals want so much!"

"Damme, you don't think small when you take the effort." Lilycrop laughed, then sobered. "But, one thing I've learned in this Navy in my time is, most people wouldn't stir their arses up if you set fire to 'em, Lewrie. They're happier layin' back, lettin' somebody else make the decisions. It's too much of a risk. It'd expose Jamaica again, an' this time, the Frogs an' the Dons might succeed in takin' it. The watchword is, 'when in doubt, don't.' Good for careers, but hell on the country. Been guilty of it meself at times, God help me. No, this time we'd best let our superiors make the decisions. They don't look kindly on lieutenants givin' em advice."

"Bad for the career, sir," Alan said evenly.

"There you are," Lilycrop agreed. "I'd forget about writin' any letters, if I were you. 'Sides, the war's so close to over, it wouldn't make much difference anyway. Now, why don't you see to as much as you feel up to, so we can sail tomorrow. Let Mister Caldwell help you. Him an' Midshipman Rossyngton can do your leg-work for you. Do the lad good to get a little authority. Park yourself in a comfortable chair on the quarterdeck, if you're of a mind."

"Aye, sir, I shall," Alan relented, half of a mind to write his letter anyway. He groped to his feet, got his crutch going, and went to the chart-space, where Cony had begun to lay out his kit and his chest. A small fixed bed-box had been cobbled together and fitted to the partition aft of the chart-table, much like a settee. Athwartship as it was, it would be more comfortable to sleep in, and it was high enough to allow him easy entry and exit, even with his game leg, if the seas got up once they were on-station.

"What career do I have to worry about preserving, anyway?" he muttered to himself once he was ensconced on the mattress, sitting so he could draw out a large-scale chart and study the Caribbean area. "Maybe I should write that letter after all. Not that it'd do much good, I suppose."

Alan thought that even if he did write it, and Hood was receptive, perhaps Pigot would turn out to be chary, or Rowley would be too cautious. It would take weeks to draw a consensus locally, and then they would most likely wish to send off to London for directions, and that would take months more. To act and fail on their own would hurt their careers. No one back home in the Shelburne government would care to strand a British army in the marshes where they would die like flies to alien fevers and agues, not this close to the end of the war, while they were negotiating a peace. It would risk Jamaica, or Antigua.

Yet what was war but a series of calculated risks? It was not an exact science, subject to mathematics, so that odds could be drawn from tables. It was an art, he had been told. How often had he seen success or failure balance on the fine-honed edge of a sword? And how many officers would see only hazard and fail to dare, while some other fire-brand would see slight advantage, and would go forth to sow confusion to England's foes.

What forces formed a Hawke, a Rodney, a general like Clive, he wondered? There was no chap-book like Clerk's little book of tactics to guide a run-of-the-mill officer, to turn him into the sort who could achieve a magnificent victory. Most came aboard as cabin-servants at eight years old, or at twelve as midshipmen, blessed with only rudiments of decent educations, and all they learned from school-masters and mates was how to curse, tie knots, drink, and be practical seamen. No one tried to teach them to *think*. And with material security tied up in first gaining one's lieutenancy, then gaining a commission aboard ship on active service, how much of one's very source of bread would someone be prepared to put at risk, it thinking too much led to half-pay idleness and penury?

He was free of that, thank God. Between his prize-money, his hoard of gold, his grandmother's bequest and his later inheritance, he did not have to depend on the Navy to put food on his table, if he was careful with his money. How much worse an officer would he make than most of the ones he had met, who could only stump about a deck screaming "Luff!" He was from a deeper well of knowledge, and he could think, when he was forced to. Did he really have more promise than most? And was the Navy a place to shine, because of that?

God help me, I think I shall, Alan decided. I'll write that letter, and the devil with the consequences. If the Navy won't have me after that, then that's their loss, isn't it? I'll have said my piece.

Fate, however, did not allow the letter to be delivered. *Shrike* sailed, and for days, it was as much like yachting, that watery sport of the aristocracy and the idle rich, as any cruise he had ever seen. The winds were bracing and fresh, quartering mostly from the nor'east to the sou'east. Once leaving Port Royal and Kingston, Lieutenant Lilycrop was in no hurry to rejoin Hood's squadron off Hispaniola, and the ship loafed along like every day was a "rope-yarn Sunday."

But, while they had good weather, a storm had blown Admiral Hood off-station at Cape Francois, and with a gust-front of wind and gloomy skies from the east, the fleet was blown down onto them the first week of February, on its way to Port Royal. All *Shrike* could do was to announce her presence, change flags to Hood's Blue Ensign once more, and beat her way east past the squadron of line-of-battle ships to make the best of her way to join the ships remaining on blockade. There was no contact close enough to allow Alan's epistle to be delivered.

Once past the fleet, *Shrike* took one last lingering look at the southern coast of Cuba, their old hunting grounds, and then a favorable slant of wind took them up the Windward Passage.

Alan finally discarded his crutch. Though the wound still pained him, he could make his way about the decks with more ease. He had to admit that the wood and canvas deck chair was comfortable, an admirable invention that should be standard equipment for the aspiring (but lazy) Sea Officer such as he. He was close to the wheel and the quartermasters, could see the work at the guns or the gangways, and could "stand" his watches in sublime ease for once. And noon sights could be performed just as well from a sitting position as they could be standing by the sunward rail and gritting his teeth with each pitch and heave of the deck.

When called to walk forward, or do his tours below decks, he could wince manfully, with Edgar or Rossyngton or Cony to aid him, and limp about, searching for a convenient handhold for which he could lunge the last few feet and utter a loud whoosh of relief from the titanic effort of performing his duties.

Secretly, the wound was no longer *that* troubling, but after a little over three years of hard service, he was not going to admit to any more agility than was absolutely necessary, certain he was due some ease. And it was fun to portray the wounded hero, stoically going about his rounds as though he were secretly suffering the agonies of the damned, and making a great show of shrugging off any offers of assistance or sympathy.

* * *

He had finished his morning watch and had turned the deck over to Caldwell and Rossyngton, but lingered in his deck chair with a mug of sweet tea, half-dozing with the "injured" limb stuck out stiffly in front of him. His chin rested on his breast and his cocked hat was far forward over his forehead to counter the early morning sun on this their third week of patrolling several leagues to seaward of Monte Cristi off the coast of Hispaniola. He took a sip of tea, then wrote up his lieutenant's journal. He had gotten past the usual bumf: "Fri., Mar 7th, 1783: Winds NW, Course NNE, Lat. 20.05N, bearing at dawn Isabella Pt. Monte Cristi SE by E off shore 5-6 leagues. Fresh breezes & Cloudy," and was wondering what else he should write down (and attempting to stifle a rather huge yawn) when the lookout interrupted him.

"Sail ho! Deck thar! Three sail, four points awrf t' starb'd bow!"

That brought him up with a start, almost making him spill his tea and the inkwell all over his journal. There was nothing to their suth'ard, or the east but French or Spanish vessels. Little *Shrike* would be no match for a squadron of foes that had escaped the blockade.

"Mister Rossyngton, go aft an' inform the captain," Caldwell directed. "You hear, Mister Lewrie, sir?"

"Aye, thankee, Mister Caldwell," Alan said, forgetting how "lame" he was supposed to act as he levered himself out of his chair and got to his feet to hobble (only slightly) to the bulwarks. "I have the deck now, Mister Caldwell."

"Deck thar!" the lookout called again. "Four . . . no, five sail to starb'd, now! 'Ard on t'wind onna starb'd tack!"

"On passage for the Bahamas, perhaps," Alan said as Caldwell joined him at the rail. With his telescope, Alan could just barely make out three tiny slivers of whitish-tan that could have been clouds on the horizon. The lookouts aloft would have a better view, at least one hundred feet higher above the decks.

"One sail's 'auled 'is wind, sir!"

"Falling down on us, sir," Caldwell said primly, sounding more annoyed than anything else. "To smoke us."

"I have the deck, sirs," Lilycrop said as he emerged from his quarters and strode to join them. "Hands to Quarters, put out the galley fires, an' stand ready to rig out stuns'ls an' haul our own wind to loo'ard."

"Bosun, beat to Quarters!" Alan shouted with the aid of his brass speaking trumpet.

"Mister Lewrie, sir, once Mister Cox's ready with his batteries, I'd admire we ease her a point free more northerly," Lilycrop ordered.

"Aye, sir."

"Midshipman aloft," Lilycrop snapped, turning to them once more before strolling to the abandoned chair and dropping into it heavily as though he had no real care in the world what was over the horizon.

Gangly Mr. Edgar swarmed his way to the mainmast crosstrees like a spastic spider.

"A flag, sir!" Edgar piped moments later. "Looks British, I think. Yes, sir, Blue Ensign, sir, and a private signal!"

"Might be a ruse," Alan speculated.

"'T' 'ands is at Quarters, sir," Fukes reported, with Mr. Cox.

"Private signal, sir!" Edgar added in a boyish yelp. "She's the *Drake* sloop, brig-rigged! Now she's flying 'Attend Me,' sir!"

"Presumptuous bastard." Lilycrop snorted at the audacity of another lieutenant master and commander much like himself, in command of a brig below the rate issuing pre-emptive orders without knowing whom he was addressing. "What're the others doin'?"

"Standing on north, sir!"

"Belay, Mister Lewrie," Lilycrop barked out, rubbing his white-stubbled jowls. "Bring her back to the original course. We can spy out this'n, if she's a Frog in disguise, if the others stay up to windward. Lay us close-hauled as may be and close her."

Within half an hour, the small squadron was hull-up over the horizon, and the *Drake* was within hailing distance. By the private code signals for the month, they could identify the other ships: the *Albemarle* frigate, a 6th Rate of twenty-eight guns, according to the List under the command of one Horatio Nelson; a 5th Rate frigate, the *Resistance*, of forty-four guns; another twenty-eight-gunned 6th Rate, the *Tartar*, under a Commander Fairfax; and *Drake*, under a man named Dixon. And bringing up the rear was a final 6th Rate twenty-eight-gunned frigate that flew French colors under a British flag, a recent prize.

"Ahoy there!" came a call from *Drake* as she surged close.

"Ahoy, *Drake*!" Lilycrop bellowed. "*Shrike*, twelve-gunned brig o' war! Lilycrop, Lieutenant, master and commander!"

"Captain Nelson in *Albemarle* is senior, sir!" Dixon shouted back. "His compliments to you, and he directs you to fall in astern of us! We are on passage for Turk's Island! The French have taken it!"

"When?" Lilycrop asked.

"Middle of last month, sir!" Dixon yelled. "Captain King in *Resistance*, with the *Dugay Trouin* frigate, were in Turk's Island Passage four days ago! They spotted two French royal ships at anchor off Turk's Island and gave chase. Took *La Coquette* here, and a sloop of war! Captain Nelson thinks we can overwhelm them if we act quickly!"

"Let's be at the bastards, then, Captain Dixon!" Lilycrop agreed loudly.

"Aye, aye, Captain Lilycrop!"

"Not the bloody Frogs again, sir," Caldwell groused. "Thought we had 'em bottled up proper once de Grasse was defeated. Don't they know to stay in their kennels when English bull-dogs are out on the prowl?"

"Been a year since The Saintes, almost, Mister Caldwell," the captain said. "Even curs get their courage back sooner'r later. Mr. Lewrie, stand the crew down from Quarters, if you please, and secure. Then proceed with the rum ration and the noon meal. Then I'd admire to have both of you in the chart-space with me."

"Dry as old bones, mostly," Lilycrop mused as they looked at the charts of Turk's Island, or more properly, Grand Turk. "Turk's, South Caicos, and Salt Cay, an' salt tells the story— 'bout the only export they got. With this slant o' wind, we'll fetch the Passage sure enough, if it holds."

"Miss the Mouchoir Bank, thank the Good Lord," Caldwell said. "Turn the corner north and east of the Northeast Breaker. There's said to be rocks and coral heads awash south and west of there. I'd prefer to see waves breaking before I'd turn."

"Or stand on as we are, into the Turk's Island Passage, staying clear of the Apollo Bank, sir," Alan said drawing on the chart with his finger. "Leave Sand Cay and Salt Cay to the starboard."

"Aye, be safer." Lilycrop nodded. "That's up to this feller Nelson. Hope he's a little caution in his bones."

"Know anything of him, sir?" Alan asked.

"Not much," Lilycrop informed him, marching a brass divider over the chart slowly. "Uncle's Sir Maurice Suckling, Comptroller of the whole damn Navy. Never hurts, ey? Funny. Thought Jemmy King in *Resistance* would serve as commodore to our little squadron. He's got a 5th Rate, Nelson only a 6th. James King was Captain Cook's second lieutenant out in the Pacific in

Resolution, you know. Maybe even with a 5th Rate to command, he's a couple names down the seniority list. No, don't go playin' with that, sweetlin'," Lilycrop admonished one of Henrietta's kittens, who had jumped up for attention, and had become entranced with the movement of the brass divider. She was pouncing on it, her short little stub of a tail wiggling in delight.

"Looks like a good anchorage here, sir," Alan said, shoving the kitten's rump out of the way long enough to indicate Hawk's Nest Anchorage sou'east of the southern end of the island. "Not much to look at from the chart, though."

"Been here before," Lilycrop said, now busy entertaining the cat. "Nothin' much but coral, salt and mud. Only drinkin' water is what they catch from a rain. More reefs around it than a duchess got necklaces, an' pretty steep-to, close under the shores. Hawk's Nest or Britain Bay up here seem best, 'less we just barge our way into this little harbor on the western side. But I expect the Frogs have a battery there. I would."

"What about fortifications, sir? Ours, I mean, that they've taken over."

"Nary a one, sir." Lilycrop shrugged. "Not much reason for 'em before, since it was only the salt trade that anybody'd come for, and that only in the summer months. God pity the poor French possession of the place, I say."

"If they landed back in the middle of February, they wouldn't have much time to build fortifications, sir," Caldwell pointed out. "Sand and log, rubble from the town perhaps. That sort of place would just soak up round-shot."

"Worth taking, though, sir," Alan said after studying the chart. "Look at all these passes. Turk's Island Passage, Silver Bank, Mouchoir Passage, and up north, the Caicos and the Mayaguana Passages. Put some privateers in here, and just about any ship using the Windward Passage from the west would have to run the gauntlet by here to get to the open sea for home."

"Nobody ever said the French were stupid, aye," Lilycrop said. "A little prospectin' for territory before the war ends. It'd be a year before the peace conference hears of it, and even begins to get the place sorted out in our favor. But, *Resistance* took two ships, and a sloop of war and one 6th Rate frigate can't carry many troops, or land much in the way of artillery. They're cut off on this island for now, without any ships to support 'em—what, not more'n one hundred fifty or two hundred troops? We can outshoot 'em with our three frigates, and muster more men from our Marines an' seamen. Best kick 'em up the arse now an' have done."

"I'll tell Lieutenant Walsham, sir," Alan said grinning. "God, he'll love it, after being stuck aboard during the Florida thing. Full 'bullock' kit and cross-belts for a proper show."

"How's the leg, Mister Lewrie?" the captain inquired.

"Still a mite tender, sir, but I'll cope," Alan offered. "It really is feeling much better."

"No, I've seen you wincin', try as you will to put a good face on it," Lilycrop replied, waving off Alan's enthusiasm for action. "If we land troops from *Shrike*, I may go myself. Can't let the young'uns have all the fun, now, can we, Mister Caldwell?"

Damnit, it was Alan's place to go as first officer, and he now regretted his earlier theatrics. But, to act too spry on the morrow would reveal what a fine job of malingering he had been doing; and, he considered, he'd done more than his share of desperate adventuring in the last few months—why take another chance of being chopped up like a fillet steak if there was no reason to?

"Well, if you really are intent on the venture, sir," he sighed, trying to give the impression that he was hellishly miffed.

Chapter 2

Their tiny flotilla arrived in Britain Bay off Turk's Island before sundown, just at the end of the first dog-watch. The holding ground was coral and rock, so getting a small bower and the best bower secure in four or five fathoms of crystal-clear water was a real chore. They had to row out a stream anchor as well. The *Tartar* frigate was driven off her anchorage, losing an anchor in the process, while Captain Dixon from *Drake* rowed ashore under a flag of truce to demand the French garrison surrender. The prize, *La Coquette*, stayed out at sea, standing on and off as the winds freshened.

Once they could pause from their labors and consider *Shrike* safely moored, Alan could see French troops ashore in their white uniforms, drawn up on a summit overlooking the ships, which were not over a cable to two cables' length from the shimmering white beaches. It looked to be, Alan decided after plying his glass upon them, not more than the one hundred fifty to two hundred men that Lieutenant Lilycrop had surmised.

Captain Dixon's boat came off the shore just at the end of the second dog, around eight in the evening, with news that the French had refused to surrender. That response was thought to be pretty much a formality for the sake of their honor, the prevailing view being that once a determined landing party went ashore in the morning and a few broadsides had been fired off, the French would shoot back a few times and then haul down their flag in the face of overwhelming force.

During the night, *Albemarle* and *Resistance* fired a few shots into the woods overlooking Britain Bay to keep the French awake and in a state of nerves for the morrow. *Shrike*'s people sharpened their swords and bayonets; the Marines went about hard-faced and grim, tending to their full uniforms (which were only worn for battle or formal duties in port) and seeing to their fire-locks, flints and powder. The rasp of files and stones on bayonets and hangers and cutlasses made a harsh, sibilant rhythm under the sounds of the fiddlers on the mess decks who went through their entire repertory of stirring airs before Lights Out.

At first light, just at 5 A.M., they stood to, ready to board their boats and set off for the shore expedition. Captain Dixon of the *Drake* brig would lead. Evidently, *Tartar* had not been able to keep good holding ground, for there had been no sign of her since she had lost a second anchor and been driven off shore in the night.

"Not much to the place by daylight, is there, Mister Cox?" Alan asked as their swarthy little master gunner strolled aft to the quarterdeck.

"Little dry on the windward end here, sir, true," Cox said in a rare moment of cheerfulness as he looked forward to some action for a change. "Same's most islands here'bouts. Might I borrow your glass, sir?"

Alan loaned him his personal telescope and let the man look his fill of the shadowy forests above the beach where the troops would land. There wasn't much to see, not in dawn-light. Sea-grape bushes, poison manchineel trees, sturdy but low pines and scrub trees that only gave an impression of green lushness rooted firmly in the sandy soil of a coral and limestone island.

"No sign of a battery this end, sir," Cox commented, handing the tube back. "And I'd not make those heights over forty-five feet above the level of the beach, even if there was. Good shooting for us."

Lieutenant Lilycrop came on deck in his best uniform coat, wearing his long straight sword at his hip, with a pair of pistols stuffed into the voluminous coat pockets. His face was red and raw from a celebratory shave, his first of the week.

"No stirrings from the French yet, Mister Lewrie?" he asked.

"Nothing to be seen, sir," Alan replied.

"Might be a white uniform in those trees, sir," Cox disagreed. "Sentries, most like so far. But no sign of a battery."

"They've had all night to prepare, even so." Lilycrop frowned. "Well, Lieutenant Walsham. Rarin' to have a crack at 'em, are ye, sir?"

"Aye aye, sir," Walsham answered, sounding a lot more somber than his usual wont. He was a recruiting flyer, the very picture of a Marine officer this morning, as if dirt and lint would never dare do harm to the resplendency of his red uniform. The gorget of rank at his throat flashed like the rising sun.

"Doubt we'll need springs on the cables," Lilycrop mused. "I 'spect the frigates'll cover the landin', and we won't be called for much firin', 'less they try to sweep 'round to flank us once we're ashore. If they do, they'll be in plain sight of our guns over there. And it ain't a full two cables to that low hill."

"Round-shot and grape should do it, sir," Alan commented.

"I'd worry more 'bout some Frog ship comin' in from seaward, if I were you, Mister Lewrie," the captain said, turning to look at the horizon from which the sun was threatening to rise. "Might've been more ships'n *La Coquette* and a sloop of war come here. Maybe a brace o' sloops already sweepin' the Caicos Passage up north to make some profit from this expedition of theirs. You keep a wary eye out for that."

"I shall, sir," Alan told him.

"An' you'll not muck about with my little ship while I'm gone, will you now, Mister Lewrie," Lilycrop said in a softer voice for him alone, not so much a question as an order.

"I'll not, sir, but I cannot speak for any French battery up in those woods." Alan grinned back, knowing by now that Lilycrop's blusterings were not as dire as he made them sound.

"Signal from *Albemarle*, sir!" Midshipman Edgar called.

"We're off, then," Lilycrop said with a grin. "Only wished we'd o' packed a heartier dinner. Ready, Mister Walsham?"

"Aye, sir," the Marine said moving towards the gangway entry port.

"Boats are alongside to starboard, sir, so the French did not see any preparations," Alan stuck in. "Side-party!"

The seamen and Marines gathered to render salute to their captain as he stepped to the lip of the entry-port for the first boat, doffing hats and raising swords or muskets in honor as Lilycrop swung out and faced inward to lower himself down the man-ropes and battens to the boat.

The entire squadron was issuing forth its landing force, most of it from the two remaining frigates, as they had more men to spare from much larger crews, while the little brigs below the Rate were perenially short of hands even on their best days. By counting heads in the boats nearest him, and then multiplying by the number of boats issuing forth, Alan could determine that they were fielding around one hundred eighty to two hundred men for the effort, minus those whose duty it would be to stay on the beach and safeguard the boats. They would at least equal the estimated French troops ashore. And the gunfire from well-drilled fighting ships would make the critical difference.

"Pendant's down, sir!" Edgar shouted.

"Cast off! Out oars! Give way together!" the captain's cox'n ordered as the signal for execution was given.

It took about half an hour for all boats to gather before the frigates, line themselves up in some sort of order, and then shove off for the silent, waiting beach.

"*Albemarle* signals 'Open Fire,' sir," Edgar said.

"Mister Cox, make it hot for them," Alan directed. The ships began to thunder out their broadsides over the heads of the rowing boats, thrashing the woods above the beach and the low hills behind with iron sleet.

"Slow but steady, boys," Cox shouted to his remaining gunnery crews, and *Shrike*'s little six-pounders began to bark, one at a time, aiming high with quoins full out, which made the deck rock and seem to sag down with each blast. Cox and his gunner's mate walked from one end of the waist to the other as the guns fired, counting out a pace which would allow the forward-most gun to be reloaded by the time the after-most piece had discharged, so a continual hail of round-shot and grape canister would keep the French down under cover, never allowing them to rise between broadsides for a musket volley.

"A little low, Mister Cox?" Alan asked as he saw the trees and bushes just above the beach tremble to a well-directed shot.

"Aim'll lift as the barrels get hotter, sir," Cox said, replying with a touch of petulant whine to his voice, unwilling to be questioned at his science, or his skill in the execution of it. But Alan did note that Cox then sent a gunner's mate to correct the elevation of Number 4 larboard gun, which had been shooting too low.

The boats were having a lively time of it, even inside the reefs that should have protected them from the worst of the off-shore rollers that swept in, driven by a fresh Sou'east Trade Wind. They rocked bow to stern, with the oarsmen slaving away to keep them moving.

Then the first stems were grounding on the sands, and Captain Dixon was ashore and waving back at the frigates. A signal went up from *Albemarle*, ordering "Cease Fire" so their broadsides would not hurt their own landing parties.

"Cease fire, Mister Cox!" Alan shouted down into the waist. "Mister Biggs, water butts for the gunners."

"Aye, sir," their weasely purser replied, sounding as if he even begrudged issuing "free" water.

"Looks like the landing is unopposed," Alan said. "Might be some French troops up in those woods, but they couldn't form for volleys under our fire."

"Marines are going in, sir," Caldwell pointed out.

Through the glass, he could see the thin red ranks form shoulder to shoulder, open out in skirmish order, lower their bayoneted muskets and start off for the interior, being swallowed up by the thick undergrowth almost at once, with the seemingly disordered packs of seamen in their mis-matched shirts following.

From then on, it was anyone's guess as to what was happening inland. There was no mast available for flag signals from the men ashore. Muskets popped, sometimes a whole squad fired by volley, and the rags of spent powder-smoke rose above the greenery, perhaps just above where they had been fired or perhaps blown through the trees before rising. It was impossible to know which side had fired, or where the true positions of whoever had done the shooting were. All in all, it didn't sound or look like much of a battle so far; just a little skirmishing and skulking, very desultorily conducted.

"Can't see a damned thing from the deck, sir," Caldwell growled.

"Aye," Alan agreed. "Nothing for it, then."

"Oh, send the lad, do, sir. Mind your leg," Caldwell replied, and, was it perhaps Alan's imagination, but he felt from Caldwell's tone that he was "on to him" about his earlier malingering.

"I told the captain I was spry enough, and I am, sir," Alan shot back, going to the main-mast shrouds. He ascended slowly, but he gained the fighting-top; though instead of trusting his leg's strength to go outboard on the futtock shrouds where he would have to dangle by fingers and toes like a fly, he took the easier path up through the lubber's-hole like a Marine or landsman.

Damme if I'm acting, he thought, massaging his thigh as it complained loudly at the demands made upon it. He sat down on the edge of the top facing inland, legs and arms threaded through the ratlines of the top-mast shrouds, and rested his telescope on one of the dead-eyes. Even from there, sixty or more feet above the deck and higher than the low hills of the island he could see nothing of note. The sun was up high enough to show him the small town on the western side, further down the coast. Was there a battery there, he asked himself, or was that a row of houses with their blank backsides to the offshore winds for comfort?

Mister Edgar came up soon after, scrambling and puffing at the exertion of ascending the shrouds (properly using the futtocks) and the concentration necessary to coordinate his body and mind to the task. He went on up past Alan to the cross-trees with the lookout, saying, "Mister Caldwell sent me, sir," on the way up.

As if his clumsy arrival had set events in motion, the lookout shouted not five minutes later. "Sail ho, to seaward!"

"Where, away?" Alan demanded, getting to his feet with a thrill of dread. Perhaps Lilycrop had been right, and a French ship had come back to check up on her new base. "Mister Cox, prepare the starboard battery to engage!"

"There, sir!" Mister Edgar called with excitement in his voice.

The ship headed for the anchorage was a brig, about five miles off, but she had the wind free and was making good progress. Perhaps a privateer or a French—what did they call them, *corvette*?

"Think you she's French, sir?" Edgar called down from his higher perch.

"If she is, we'll serve her like Hood did de Grasse at St. Kitts," Alan answered him. "Keep an eye on her, Mister Edgar."

"Oh, I shall . . ." Edgar replied as Alan glanced up at him, and Alan winced and sucked in his breath as Edgar, in swiveling back to gaze seaward, almost lost his seat on the slight support of the thin timbers of the cross-tree platform. Only the lookout's quick action in grabbing the lad by the collar had saved him from a deadly tumble to the deck. "Do have a *care*, Mister Edgar! Remember where you are!"

"Aye, sir," Edgar said, red with embarrassment and fright. He put his telescope back to his eye, then looked down once more. "One of ours, sir. Blue Ensign, and a private signal flag."

"Saying what?" Alan demanded.

"I, un . . ." Edgar stammered, searching his pockets for his sheaf of notes and almost over-balancing again. "Here it is, sir."

Alan shared a look with the lookout while Edgar thumbed through the papers, almost losing them to the fresh winds, until he found the month's private signals. The lookout raised his eyebrows and sighed heavily, making Alan grin back at him in a moment of secret amusement.

"*Admiral Barrington*, sir, hired Brig O' War," Edgar announced at last. "Lieutenant Charles Cunningham in command."

"Thank you, Mister Edgar. Why do you not go down to the deck and inform Mister Cox that he shall not have to engage her for now, but stand easy. I'd feel much easier with you there, sir."

"Aye, sir." Edgar nodded, and fumbled his way to a stay which he rode down to the quarterdeck bulwarks.

Admiral Barrington exchanged signals with *Albemarle*, then took course to Britain Bay, and anchored about an hour later. She was much like *Shrike*, a brig of only twelve guns, and from the looks of her decks, had only seventy or eighty men aboard total; not much reinforcement.

As she did so, there was more firing from inland, some volleys quite substantial, though they still couldn't see where they were coming from, or from which side. To Alan's ears, though, it sounded as if there might be more firing from higher up and inland, after a while. And more firing than about one hundred fifty French soldiers could make. There were, finally, some larger puffs of smoke and louder cracks of sound that could only come from field-pieces. So the French had artillery on the island, perhaps in some well-sited works, to deny the landing party any further progress towards the town.

Sure enough, around ten in the morning, a runner appeared on the beach and took a boat out to *Albemarle* to report. And a few minutes after that, small boats made their way from the flagship to the brigs. Alan slung his telescope and stepped out of the top. If his leg was quarrelsome this morning, there was nothing wrong with his arms. He rode a stay to the deck in proper seamanly fashion, making sure to land on his good leg. Even so, the shock made his game limb twinge.

"Ahoy the boat!" Fukes called.

"Passing!" the bowman shouted.

"Ahoy, *Shrike*!" an officer in the stern-sheets demanded. The hands eased their stroke to loiter near her side. "Have you an officer aboard?"

"Lieutenant Lewrie!" Alan replied, using a speaking trumpet.

"Lieutenant Bromwich, sir, second into *Albemarle*! Lieutenant Hinton and I are to take charge of the brigs and direct them to weigh. Captain Dixon is checked by a strong work, and requests we make a diversion with artillery opposite the town, sir. Do you need any assistance in so doing?"

Goddamn the man! Alan thought cynically. Do they think aboard *Albemarle* that we're cripples? "No, sir, we shall weigh directly. I think we *may* cope, sir," Alan drawled back.

"Very well, sir!"

"Mister Cox, secure from Quarters. Mister Fukes, hands to the capstans and prepare to weigh. Veer out on the stream anchor and heave in to short stays on the best and small bowers. I'll have the kedge served out for later use. Slip the stream cable once we've loosed tops'ls, and buoy it. We'll pick it up later."

"Aye aye, sir," Fukes replied, knuckling his thick brows.

Within half an hour, their evolutions were complete. They got up the bow anchors, and were held in check only by the smaller stream anchor off their stern. The fresh winds made the ship strain down from that anchor, and when they loosed tops'ls to put a way on her, and let slip the stream cable, they were underway and under complete helm control from the moment the cable was let go, as smoothly as anyone could ask for, which made Alan grin inside at the ease of it.

It was only a couple of miles to a new anchorage opposite the town, with the leadsman singing out four or five fathoms the whole way, even though the waters were so clear they could see sharp coral below them as if they were skating over glass.

"Bring to, Mister Svensen," Alan ordered at last. "Round up into the wind and back the fore tops'l. Ready forrard!"

Her progress checked against the wind, they let go the best bower and veered out half a cable. The cable thumped and shuddered a few times before they found good holding ground.

"Kedge anchor into the boat and row her out, there," Alan said, pointing aft and a little to larboard. "And once she's holding, place springs on the cables to adjust our fire."

"Aye, sir." Fukes nodded.

It felt good, Alan decided, to have complete charge of *Shrike*, with Lieutenant Lilycrop off ashore. There were none of the nerves he had suffered before, in being asked to shift their anchorage or commit her to battle against a shore battery, if battery there were. Some concern that he did not look ridiculous, but none of the nail-biting fear of taking any action at all he had once experienced. With a wry grin, he was forced to believe that the Navy had drummed enough competency in him at last, enough to make him aspire to more opportunities for independence from someone's leading strings.

"Springs is rigged, sir," Fukes reported.

"Very well. Mister Cox, stand by to open fire!"

Drake, as the flagship of their extemporized little subdivision, hoisted a signal, and all ships began a cannonade against the town.

"Seems a shame, sir," Caldwell said, after measuring any change from shore marks that would indicate *Shrike* was dragging her anchors or being blown out of position.

"What is, sir?" Alan asked off-handedly.

"Well, sir, looks as if the Frogs has already torn the town up for building material, and here we go, shooting the rest of it apart. It may not look like much to our lights, but it's their homes, sir."

"Umm, not for much longer, at this rate," Alan commented as the round-shot from the light guns tore holes in walls and roofs.

"Who was it, sir, one of those pagan Roman poets, said 'they make a desert and call it peace'?" Caldwell mused.

"Tacitus, perhaps," Alan answered. "Couldn't have been Virgil or Caesar. They were too proud of making deserts."

"Batt'ry, sir!" Cox shouted as a wall of gunpowder erupted from shore above the town. A round-shot, almost big enough to see in mid-flight, came howling over the bulwarks, and passed close enough to create a little back-eddy of wind.

"Damme, sir, that was a twenty-four-pounder, or I'm an

Arabee!" Caldwell groused with un-wonted vehemence, shaken from his Puritan demeanor for once enough to curse.

"Mark that, Mister Cox?" Alan asked, scanning through the smoke of the broadside for sign of the guns.

"I think so, sir. There, or close enough as makes no diff'rence."

The newly discovered French battery began to put shot around all the brigs. As Cox re-laid his guns to respond, Alan counted the shots, and tried to gauge what caliber they were.

"Mister Cox, let's concentrate our fire on one embrasure, if you will!" Alan shouted down to the waist. "That one, there!"

"Aye, sir!"

"Six-pounders, there," Alan said. "About four or five of them."

"Seems about right, sir," Caldwell replied, his voice still a little shaky.

"And at least four twenty-four-pounders," Alan added, feeling a little grim himself. "This is going to be warm work for three little thin-sided brigs. And works with field-pieces up towards Britain Bay to counter Captain Dixon's shore party. More Frogs on this island than a dog's got fleas, more than reported, at any rate."

They had to duck as one of those twenty-four-pounders placed a round-shot close aboard, close enough to raise a great waterspout that fell over the quarterdeck and wetted them down in a twinkling as it skipped overhead to fall into the sea on the disengaged side. *Shrike* was, at least, out of the main line of fire, a little more sheltered than the *Drake* or *Admiral Barrington*. As the day wore on towards noon, *Drake* took a ball aloft which brought down the gaff of her spanker, and the *Admiral Barrington* was hulled with solid *thonks* of iron smashing wood.

The artillery killed the wind; that was something Alan had heard mentioned before but had never witnessed for himself. Where before there had been fresh winds offshore that stirred up the waters of the deep passages and set the brigs to rocking like cradles, now the sea was flat as a mill-pond, and the wind had died to almost nothing. The ships were wreathed in their own palls of smoke, and the fort ashore could only be espied by looking for the base of the towering pillar of spent powder. It didn't do much for their aim, but at least it made the job of the French troops serving their larger pieces just as hard.

"Signal from *Drake*, sir," Edgar said at his side, coughing on the sour smell of burned niters. "Cease fire."

"Very well, Mister Edgar. Mister Cox, cease fire!" Alan said. "Mister Edgar, my compliments to the purser, and tell him it's past time for dinner. Have him issue some cold rations and small-beer for the hands."

"Aye aye, sir."

A rowing boat sped down from the frigates anchored in Britain Bay, and went aboard *Drake* while the men were eating and curing their battle-induced thirsts. After half an hour, the boat came back along the anchored brigs.

"Sir, Captain Nelson directs me bid you to weigh," the midshipman in the stern yelled, his voice cracking a little; he was awfully young. "You are to return to Britain Bay and re-embark your party."

"Very well," Alan replied. "Well, that's another fine mess we've made," he added, turning to his quarterdeck people. "It'll take the frigates down here tomorrow to shoot that battery silent."

"And make another landing, maybe on the other side of the island, now we know where the Frogs is concentrated, sir," Cox said, free of his gun deck. He and his gunners looked black as Moors from all the grime of powder smoke on their skins. Alan could see the closest gun being sponged out with a water-soaked wool rammer, and other hands hoisting up buckets of seawater to sluice off the muzzles and touch-holes. The guns were hissing as the water cooled them like sated dragons.

"Bowse 'em down to the port-sills and secure, Mister Cox," he said. "Mister Fukes, get your people ready to veer out on the bower and take up the kedge soon as the gun crews are available. Wind's coming about a little more westerly. Quick as you can, both of you, or we'll end up rowing her out with the sweeps if the wind goes foul and leaves us on a lee shore."

The wind had swung, not so noticeable during the cannonading that had deadened it; now more southerly, with a touch of westing. Sure sign of a change in the weather, and that was usually a sign of worsening weather, especially in the Caribbean.

They got the kedge up, heaved into short stays on the bower, but could not get it to release from the bottom. Damme, and this was going so well! Alan thought sadly.

"Flukes hung up on a coral head, feels like, sir," Fukes told him. "I can almos' see 'er down there."

"Belay what you have, Mister Fukes. Hands aloft! Let go the driver and jibs! With a little forward way, we might sail her off."

"Aye, sir." Fukes sounded dubious. And with good cause. The

anchor obstinately refused to let go her grip on the coral bottom, and no amount of straining at the capstans was going to shift her. The ship sailed up until she was almost standing directly over the anchor, with the cable bar-taut, and if anything, inclined slightly from the vertical, bent back under *Shrike*'s forefoot and cutwater.

"Least this'un ain't the best bower, sir," Fukes offered after coming aft from the beakhead. "An' them other brigs ain't havin' much more luck'un us'un. *Drake*'s arready cut, sir."

"The captain will have my hide if I lose an anchor, even the small bower, Mister Fukes," Alan groaned, thinking what a tongue-lashing he would receive when Lilycrop came back aboard.

With nowhere else to go forward, *Shrike* was now beginning to circle about her anchor, and the timbers around the hawse-holes were groaning alarmingly. The bow was slightly down and thumping.

"Well, shit," Alan sighed, giving in to the inevitable. "Cut the cable, Mister Fukes. Aloft there, loose tops'ls! Helm hard alee and hold her wind abeam if you can. Braces, shift the braces to the larboard tack!"

It was a sad trek back to Britain Bay, making slow progress until they could come to anchor again and clew up the sails to allow the boats to come alongside. Doctor Dorne and his lob-lolly boys from the surgery appeared, ready to receive any wounded men from the shore party, and Alan thought to have a bosun's sling rigged from aloft to help hoist injured men aboard.

Then their first boat was coming up to the starboard entry port, and Alan could look down into her. Rossyngton had the til-ler, and Alan was ready to rate him for preceding the captain's boat to the chains, but a quick look at the second boat showed no sign of their captain, either. Yet Lilycrop's old cox'n was in the first boat. Was he dead?

"Sir!" Rossyngton shouted up as the boat thumped into *Shrike*'s chainwales. He was filthy and sweaty, his hat gone somewhere. "It's the captain, sir!"

And there was Lieutenant Lilycrop, splayed out amidships be-tween the oarsmen where he could not have been seen, his cox'n supporting his head and shoulders, and another man helping hold his legs up out of the bilges. He was gritting his teeth in agony and rolling his head back and forth to keep silent before his men.

The bosun's chair was lowered immediately, and Lilycrop

helped into it and secured with a line about his waist. Gentle hands were there to ease his passage up the side, to keep him from bumping against the timbers. The stay-tackle hauled him up and over the gangway bulwarks and swung him over the waist. Lieutenant Lilycrop's right foot had been wrapped up in someone's shirt for a bandage, tied with small-stuff to keep it from falling off, with another length of twine about his leg above the knee to control the bleeding. Even so, his sodden wrap left a trail of blood droplets as he was lowered to the deck.

"Make haste here, damn your eyes, Mister Lewyss!" Alan called as he gained the waist and knelt over his stricken commander.

"Calm as does it, Mister Lewrie," Dr. Lewyss urged in a soft voice, patting Alan on the shoulder with a blood-grimed hand. "The captain already knows he's hurt, and we don't want him to take fright from all this yelling. Got to gentle the wounded, so ye do, like one would with a colt. Make 'em feel they have a chance, else they take fright and go all cold and grey. Seen it happen, and then you lose them, sure as Fate."

Lewyss shouldered on past him and knelt by the injured leg. As the loblolly boys were readying a carrying board, and Lilycrop was being freed of the bosun's sling, Lewyss unwrapped the bandage. Once he saw the wound, he could not help wincing and sucking air in through his clenched teeth at the sight.

The captain's right ankle was shattered. The shoe and stocking had been removed, though pieces of silk stocking still clung to the wound. The foot was a wine-dark horror, swollen beyond recognition, and hanging from the ankle by only a few remaining tendons at an obscene angle. Lewyss spanned his hand above the ankle, as though deciding just where he would start sawing to take it off, and found another wound, this one a bruise with a small blue-black hole in the center that oozed blood.

"Captain, sir," Lewyss said with as much false good cheer as he could summon. "We'll get you below to the surgery and fix you right up. Nothing for a man to worry about. 'Tis going to be a handsome thing as the ladies'll gush over in future. Take a few sips on this while my lads get you below, and there's more where that came from."

"Oh, shut up, you bloody Welsh fraud." Lilycrop grimaced. "I know you're to take my foot off. Gimme that bottle and get on with it, damn your eyes."

Lewyss offered him a small pocket flask of rum, which the

captain bit the stopper from and spat out. He drained it at one go.

"Hurry, Mister Lewyss, I beg you," Alan urged in a harsh whisper.

"Lewrie, that you?"

"Aye, Captain."

"Don't stand there lookin' like a specter, sir. Ship alright? No wounded aboard?" Lilycrop asked between waves of pain.

"All well, sir," Alan said, close to tears. "We lost the small bower, sir."

"Small enough price." Lilycrop groaned as he was rolled over onto the carrying board and lashed down. "Doctor, have you no more rum fer me, damn you? Let's get goin'! Get it over with, for the love of God!"

Lewyss nodded to his hands, and they lifted the captain up to carry him away, gripping onto the loops of rope in the carrying board to maneuver his form down the steep ladders of the main hatch to the surgery aft in the cockpit.

"It'll have to come off, of course, sir," Lewyss whispered sadly. "I could leave him most of the calf, but for that second wound. There's a musket ball about a hand-span above the ankle, and bones sure to be broken there. At least he'll have half his calf, and the knee, of course. Make things much better for him when it comes time to fit him for an appliance. He may walk almost naturally."

"Then you'd best be about it, Mister Lewyss," Alan snapped.

"Time enough, sir," Lewyss said, not to be hurried. "Let him have some more rum first, and let the numbness set in. If you will excuse me, sir."

"No one else wounded, Mister Rossyngton?" Alan asked, once the doctor had taken himself below to his sad duty.

"No, sir. Just the captain," the midshipman reported, shaken into somberness. "The landing was pretty much unopposed, sir, just some pickets to slow us down in the woods. But we came up against some heavy volleys once we were over the first hill. And we went to ground there, sir. We sent for a diversion against the town, as I expect you know, sir."

"Aye."

"The French fell back to a work above the town," Rossyngton went on, between sips of small-beer from a large wooden piggin. "And they had field guns there, maybe four of 'em, six-pounders. We could see seamen as well as soldiers, sir. Hundreds of 'em. Captain Dixon had just ordered us to retire—not much we could have done in the face of that work—and the captain gave a little grunt, sort of, sir. This cannon ball came rolling out of the bushes, spent almost, but it hit his foot and just flipped him arse over tit, sir, like an acrobat. How he got the second wound, I don't know, sir."

"Signal from flag, sir!" Edgar called. "It's . . . 'Captains Repair On Board,' sir."

"Damn that fool yonder!" Alan spat. "And just how does he think our captain can manage that, I wonder?" He was feeling a heavy wave of guilt. If he had not been malingering, acting as if he was incapable of fulfilling his duties as a whole man, Lieutenant Lilycrop would still have a foot. It was his fault that that good man, a man who had treated him more than fairly, was now undergoing the horror of Lewyss' knives, saws and probes. Then again, he rationalized, it could be him on the table, turning into a maimed figure of fun for the street urchins back home, who would taunt "Mr. Hop-kins" at any person with any sort of deformity.

"Um, think you'd better go in the captain's place, sir," Caldwell suggested, interrupting his furious musings. "To the flag, that is."

"Hmm. Me?"

"Yessir, with the captain down wounded, you're in charge for now, sir," Caldwell repeated.

"Damme, I suppose I am, ain't I?" Alan nodded, slowly comprehending it all.

Alan's boat ground against *Albemarle*'s side by the main-chains, with Cony holding fast with a painter and Andrews at the tiller as a temporary cox'un. It was with difficulty that he got up the man-ropes and battens to the deck. He was greeted with the shrill of bosun's pipes and the side-party due a captain, which made him shrivel up with guilt once more. He had not known where the other officers stood in seniority to him, so he was the last aboard, and once he had doffed his hat in return salute he limped over to join the others.

"I am Lieutenant Osborne, first into *Albemarle*, sir. And you are?"

"Alan Lewrie, first officer of *Shrike*, brig o' war," Alan replied.

"Sir, allow me to name you to the others. Lieutenant Lewrie of *Shrike*; Captain James King of *Resistance*, Lieutenant Charles Cunningham of *Admiral Barrington*, Captain Charles Dixon of

Drake. Our second, Lieutenant Martin Hinton, and our Lieutenant Joseph Bromwich. I believe you have already met earlier, have you not? Captain Nelson shall receive you in a few moments."

It was not exactly a pleasant social gathering. They all looked devilishly grim after being checked ashore and obliged to cut and run from the heavier French battery.

"Get that ashore, sir?" Captain King asked, noticing Alan's slight limp.

"No, sir. A few weeks ago on the Florida coast, when we were still part of Sir Joshua Rowley's Jamaica Squadron," Alan replied.

"Any casualties, Charles?" Dixon asked of Cunningham.

"Six wounded, sir," Cunningham replied. "Including the bosun."

"We suffered two, one of 'em our sailing master," Dixon told them all. "Damned fortunate, for all the damage we took. Gaff shattered, rigging cut up pretty well, and we have an eighteen-pounder ball in the timbers. Thank the good Lord they didn't run to heated shot. And how did *Shrike* fare, sir?"

"No one aboard is hurt," Alan said. "One wounded ashore with you—our captain, sir, Lieutenant Lilycrop."

"Hurt sore?" Dixon asked.

"He's losing his foot at this moment, sir," Alan stated.

"Ah, I'm damned sorry," Dixon sighed. "I tried to keep our casualties to a minimum ashore. No sense making a useless demonstration against their works and getting men killed for nothing."

"Trevenen says we should have reconnoitered last night, sent a boat ashore," King said. "Might have saved us the trouble."

"Oh, him," Lieutenant Cunningham sniffed. "I'm sure young Jemmy will put pen to paper about this."

"Excuse me, sirs, but Captain Nelson will see you now," Osborne told them, coming back on deck. He led them aft and below to the great cabins. Alan stuffed his hat under his arm and waited to see what their putative "commodore" looked like.

Well, stap me, he thought at his first sight. I do believe if they made me a post-captain tomorrow, I'd look older than this'un.

Captain Horatio Nelson was a skinny little hop o' my thumb, not much taller than some minnikin, slim and coltish as a young whippet, and a good breeze looked enough to blow him right away. His light hair was long, lank and unpowdered, tied back in a Hessian tail of such length that it rivaled Lieutenant

Lilycrop's seamanly queue. His captain's coat was the full-dress "iron-bound," stiff with gold lace, and of a fashion more suited to the last war, with over-sized pocket flaps. Altogether, he looked like an actor in some Drury Lane production portraying a Sea Officer, deliberately mis-cast in some parody.

"Gentlemen, well met," he began in a high, slightly nasal voice. "Though I fear we meet not in a victory worthy of British Sea Officers. Lieutenants Bromwich and Hinton inform me they were obliged to cut and abandon the cannonade on the town battery. How many guns?"

"At least four or five twenty-four-pounders, sir," Cunningham said. "And near on five or six six-pounders, by my count. A substantial work. And they were manned by seamen, I believe. Very accurate gunners."

"And Captain Dixon, you encountered at least four more guns, of at least six-pounds shot, at a work blocking your advance?" Nelson asked.

"Aye, sir."

"Quite a packet to be transported by *La Coquette* and that prize sloop now with the *Dugay Trouin* frigate," Nelson said, playing with the stock of his shirt. "And how many troops did you encounter ashore, sir?"

"I would estimate over two hundred men, sir," Dixon said evenly.

"I want to commend your sagacity, sir," Nelson told him with a small, shy smile on his long, narrow face. "Another commander would have tried to force the issue against that work, and would have been repulsed with heavy casualties. Obviously, there are a lot more men ashore than the captive French officers in *La Coquette* told us. Captain King, did you learn any more from them?"

"No, sir," King replied. "They said they'd escorted ships here, and *La Coquette* had given up five of her twenty-six guns to form a battery. I estimated that they could not have landed much more than one hundred fifty troops, plus seamen gunners."

"But to man that many guns, and provide a guard force for both works, and still leave at least two hundred troops free to operate against Captain Dixon, would make how many, do you think?" Nelson asked, trying not to give the impression that he might like to tear King's head off, even if he did. "If there were other ships escorted here, of which I *now* am informed."

This is damned interesting, Alan thought, watching the young man grill the older (and, surprisingly, senior) post-captain over the coals. So post-captains can act just as ill with each other as any pack of surly midshipmen fighting over shares of a pudding?

"It would make over five hundred men, sir," Alan guessed aloud. "My captain says there's nothing much on the other islands, so Grand Turk is the key, and they must have located all their force here."

"And you are, sir?" Nelson asked, turning to face him. He didn't look pleased to be addressed, and thrown off the topic.

"Lieutenant Lewrie, sir, of the *Shrike* brig. First officer. I stand in for my captain, Lieutenant Lilycrop, who's in surgery now."

"The officer wounded ashore with me, sir," Dixon added.

"Yes, Mister Lewrie, over five hundred men, with twenty-four pounders," Nelson said, turning to address all of them. "We put, what, about one hundred sixty-five men up against a French regiment, and a fortification with artillery heavier than any piece we have at our disposal. But, we may still seize the day. I propose to shift the frigates opposite the town to reduce the fortification. If we start now, we may pound upon it all night if need be. As for the brigs, make a demonstration above Britain Bay, at the far end of the island, to get the field troops marching that direction. Then, at first light, we land here, after taking anchor in Hawk's Nest Anchorage, on the other side of the island from the town and battery. They shall have to abandon the work up north, and we may now concentrate our forces against theirs properly."

"Would it not be better to blockade the place for now, sir?" Captain King advised, shaking his head. "Send one of the brigs off to summon Admiral Hood? He must be back on station by now, after watering at Port Royal. Heavy guns and Marines from the liners . . ."

"Weakening the blockade of Cape Francois, Captain King," the diminuitive "commodore" replied, rejecting the suggestion with an energetic wave of his hands. "Perhaps their expedition had that as a secondary goal. No, we have a chance to confound our King's enemies here and now. With enough energetic action, enough alacrity, we may still prevail."

"I'd like to point out, though, sir," Captain Dixon said with a heavy look, "that even if we stripped every vessel present, the French can still field more troops, and once ashore, we'll have no field guns to counter their battery. It was dirt, and they could dig guns in anywhere they wish, once they see where we land. They hold the upper hand when it comes to moving on interior lines, whilst we are forced to sail all around the island to find another beach."

While Nelson was digesting this view of things, there was a rap on the door, and Nelson bade whoever it was enter, with an exasperated tone to his voice.

The officer who entered was Lieutenant Osborne, first officer of *Albemarle*. "Excuse me for interrupting, sir, but the winds are come more westerly, and still quite fresh. Another hour and we'll be on a lee shore."

"Yes, thank you for telling me, Mister Osborne," Nelson answered, massaging his brow with long, slim fingers. He used his other hand to spin the map of the island about to stare at it. "There is no good holding ground on the eastern side. Shallow reefs and shoals, and then a steep drop off to truly unfathomable depths. Hawk's Nest Anchorage is possible, but under the guns of the battery, and too far for useful fire from our pieces." He gave a heavy sigh, a bitter realization that even the seas and the winds conspired against him, and Alan felt quite sorry for him. The man had rushed in hoping that he would gain a quick victory against light forces, and he had been misled by the intelligence he had received. The French ships taken by *Resistance* and the other frigate had not carried the expedition, they had escorted other merchantmen or transports, who had equipped the place for a long defense, with heavy guns. Now Nelson would have to admit defeat, and sail back to his admiral with news of his repulse. Better he had done what King suggested in the first place; keep an eye on the island and send word immediately to bring line-of-battle ships that could shoot the battery and works to flinders, land nearly a regiment of Marines and reduce the garrison.

"Even the sea and winds aid the damned French," Nelson mused, as if God had turned out to be a Hay-Market tout, and had given him a false report on some horse on which he had bet the family estate. "Gentlemen . . . let us weigh anchor at once and work off this shore before we start dragging anchors in bad holding ground. No sense losing a ship, or another man, on this miserable island."

"And the expedition, sir?" Captain King asked, as if he liked rubbing salt in wounds. Or had the tact of a mastiff.

"I fear I must concur with Captain Dixon's estimate of the situation at the last. No, weigh and head back for the squadron off Cape Francois." Nelson scowled, turning away to look out the transom windows, unable to face them in his moment of failure.

"How is the captain?" Alan asked, once he was back aboard his ship.

"Mister Lewyss thinks he'll live, sir," Caldwell told him in a soft voice. "Left him a good stump, sir. Didn't suffer much, nor make a sound."

"Thank God for small blessings, anyway. Mister Caldwell, I'd admire if you took over as first officer, acting lieutenant. Your mate to rise to sailing master."

"Aye, sir," Caldwell preened. "Though I hate to prosper at the captain's sorrow, sir. I must advise you, sir, the wind's come westerly and . . ."

"Yes, get us under way soon as you can. Lay out the sweeps if you think they might be necessary. Easier than being towed out by the boats. Mister Fukes, prepare to get under way!"

"Aye aye, sir!"

"We still going to try something else against these Frogs, sir?" Caldwell asked as the bosun's pipes shrilled for all hands on deck.

"No," Alan snapped. "They're too strong. The captain's going to lose his ship for nothing. Goddamnit, I'm getting tired of this."

"You and me too, sir," Caldwell agreed.

They veered out to take up their stream anchor, hauled back up to short stays on the bower, and got under way. The wind and waves were too much, and she paid off immediately, rolling her larboard rail almost under, even under bare poles. "Sweeps, Mister Fukes!"

Like an ancient oared galley, *Shrike* extended her sweeps, too few to Alan's eyes, but they needed strength to finish hauling up the anchor by the capstan, fish it in and ring it up on the catheads. More hands were already aloft, loosing the spanker and jibs, leaving only twenty or so hands to pull at the long oars. It was enough to hold her head up to the fresh breeze until the rudder could bite, and the fore and aft sails could give her forward motion.

Not trusting to square-sails until they were out beyond the reefs, they short-tacked away from the lee shore, employing the sweeps to get her head around on each tack and keep her driving forward no matter how slowly, until the sails could fill and impart drive. The leadsmen in the forechains swung their shorter sounding lines continually, until they reported no bottom. Then, when even the deep-sea lead could find no bottom, they hauled their wind to the south and loosed topsails and courses, now out over the abyssal depths of Turk's Island Passage.

Some of the other ships had had to use their row-boats to tow them out against the wind until they had room to pay off when loosing sails. *Shrike* had to stand off and on the coast until all vessels were safely at sea and in company together.

"Neatly done, sir," Caldwell told him once the off-duty watch had been allowed to go below and the ship was out in her proper element.

"Yes, we hadn't worked with sweeps before, but they did well," Alan replied. "We did a lot better than the others."

"Aye, sir. Um, I'll expect we should have someone strike for master's mate."

"How would Mister Rossyngton do, would you think?"

"Well, sir, he's a bit flighty for me." Caldwell frowned. "Long enough in the Navy, I expect, but my word, sir, he's a terror."

"It did me a world of good to get some little responsibility as acting master's mate. And it is only temporary. Let's give him a try."

"Aye, sir. Um, something else, sir. What about the captain?"

"Well, we can't sail for harbor for one wounded man, and I'm sure the captain would not let us, once he comes around," Alan replied. "We'll rejoin the squadron and see what they say. If Mister Lewyss thinks he will recover, he'd probably prefer to do it aboard his own ship. If we can be fitted with a false leg below the knee, he should do alright."

"No, sir," Caldwell said, throwing water on the tiny flickering embers of Alan's hopes. "They'll pack him off home, whether he heals or no. New commander for us, looks like."

"Poor old bastard," Alan muttered, feeling guilty all over once more about staying aboard during the landing. "Should be me in there less a foot."

"I think he would have gone, even if you'd been whole, sir," the sailing master told him, taking off his glasses and pulling out a large pocket kerchief to polish them clean of salt spray. "Something grand to do before the war ends, to make a name for himself. It was his last chance."

"Just like this Nelson fellow." Alan nodded. "Like my old captain in *Desperate*. To make amends for an earlier failure."

"Aye, sir. Like that thing up in Florida. Clear his name."

"But damnit, Mister Caldwell, we didn't fail in Florida!" Alan protested.

"Somebody thinks we did, sir, and that's the same thing." The older man shrugged. "Wonder what Captain Nelson failed at before, to make him so eager to tackle the French here?"

"Who knows?" Alan replied.

Chapter 3

The next morning, with Sand Cay, the last speck of land of the Turk's and Caicos Islands just under the horizon, *Albemarle* signaled *Shrike* to close her, and once close alongside, ordered her to back her tops'ls and heave to. As they wondered what the matter was, a boat set out from the flagship's side, bearing little Captain Nelson. He scrambled up the side and took the salute from the side-party, then advanced to where Lewrie and Caldwell were standing.

"Good morning, sir," Alan said. "What is the matter?"

"I have come to see your gallant captain Lilycrop, Mister Lewrie," Nelson told him. "I trust he is well enough to see visitors?"

"Aye, sir, he is," Alan replied. "If you will allow me to lead you to his quarters? Mister Caldwell, would you take the deck?"

"*Admiral Barrington* took the highest number of casualties," Nelson said as they walked aft. "It is my intention to go there later, to see to their needs. Your captain is recovering?"

"Still in much pain, sir, as I'm sure you'll understand," Alan replied, mystified that Nelson was making the effort. Was he salving a guilty conscience that people had been hurt at his orders in a doomed adventure? "I saw him this morning, and he was awake, mostly."

"Your surgeon holds hopes for his recovery, then, sir?" Nelson pressed.

"Aye, sir. He's very strong for his advanced age. Spent a lifetime at sea, you know," Alan told him, feeling the urge to put the needle in at Nelson's expense. "This was his first command. And now he'll likely lose it."

"I see." Nelson frowned, pulling at his long nose.

Lieutenant Lilycrop swung in his hanging bed-box to the gentle

348

motion of his ship. His usually dark-tanned face was pale, and he sweated a good deal, but the surgeon had said that it was good for him, to sweat out the poisons from the wound. The offending limb was propped up on a pile of pillows, wrapped in bast and gauze, looking no more harmful than a peer suffering a bout of the gout. There was a mug of rum near at hand, and every cat he had ever owned had gathered in some silent sense of commiseration, near the bed-box, or curled up in his lap or on the pillows.

The captain had his eyes closed, and they could hear him make soft groaning noises, wincing a bit as a wave of pain intruded on his senses. But he opened his eyes brightly when they were announced.

"Captain Nelson has come to pay his respects, sir," Alan said, and did the duty of introducing them.

"Are you in much pain, sir?" Nelson asked, taking a seat that Gooch offered him.

"Well, sir, you get your foot shot damn near off, then let a drunken Welsh sheep-coper saw the damn thing off, an' see how it makes you feel," Lilycrop said uncharitably.

"I *am* sorry, Captain Lilycrop," Nelson replied in a soft voice, totally abashed, and evidently wishing he were anywhere else in the wide world at that moment. "Since you suffer on my behalf, I was wondering if there was anything I could do for you, to make you more comfortable."

"Ah, don't mind me, Captain Nelson," Lilycrop said, laying his head back on the pillows. "Gooch, come prop me up a bit. That's it. I went for the fun of it. Can't let Lewrie have all the glory, and he's half laid up himself with a nasty leg wound. No one to blame but meself, see. One takes one's chances. Thankee for comin', though. 'Tis more'n I'd expect from most." Samson jumped up onto the bed, ruler of the cabins, and sniffed around for a place to lay close to his master, making a couple of more fearful others jump down. "Ah, we smell all medicinal, don't we, sweetlin'? Like some rum, Captain?"

"Thank you, no, Captain Lilycrop. I've never been much on rum, or spirits," Nelson answered.

Oh, God, please don't let Lilycrop call him a hedge-priest! Alan thought.

"If you're sure there is nothing I could do for you, sir?" Nelson said, beginning to rise.

"Oh, sit ye down, sir. We tried to do somethin' right, an' if I didn't get hit when I did, it'd a been later, tryin' to take the battery. Had a funny feelin' about the place, soon's I stepped ashore. Not your fault. No sense lookin' like a hanged spaniel on my account. I've had fifty years in the Fleet, man an' boy. Had to happen sometime. In the last war, with Pocock, thought I was a goner half a dozen times."

"In the East Indies?" Nelson brightened. "Where were you?"

There was a knock on the door, and midshipman Edgar relayed a message from Mr. Caldwell. "Excuse me, sir, I'm wanted on deck," Alan said and excused himself.

By the time he had discovered the reason for his summons, had tended to the matter of discipline, and placed a seaman on report for fighting, he fully expected Nelson to come out of the cabins, too, but Nelson did not. A full half-hour passed before he emerged.

"A gallant man, sir," Nelson said, his eyes a little moist as he came up to Lewrie. "He has served long and honorably, with little recognition or reward. And now this."

"Aye, sir," Alan agreed.

"If only we had been successful, I would not feel so badly at his loss," Nelson went on. "Though he would be losing the ship soon, in any event when the war ends. But there would have been a chance for further employment."

"The ship lacks a year till the end of her original commission, sir," Alan pointed out. "She's a prize, bought in out here."

"He has a family?" Nelson asked.

"None that I'm aware of, sir. Never married, either, to my knowledge. I get the impression that there was a lady once, but it didn't work out."

"There is always a young lady with whom things did not work out," Nelson said with such a wistfulness that Alan peered at him more closely. He didn't look like the sort of swaggering young buck to take love and pleasure wherever he would find it, and Alan got the idea that Nelson had been spurned rather recently, and still suffered.

"His only family is his cats, sir," Alan went on. "They're a great comfort to him."

"Yes. There are rather a lot of them, aren't there?"

"Would you like one, sir?" Alan grinned.

"Um, actually, no, thank you." Nelson essayed a shy grin of his own. "Well, I must be getting on to *Admiral Barrington* to see their wounded. Did you have any others hurt?"

"No, sir," Alan answered. "Um, one thing, sir, if I may be so bold as to ask. Is there any way you could do something for the captain? I'd heard sometimes that senior post-captains are promoted to rear admiral upon their retirement. And I was wondering if there was anything like that could be done for him, to promote a lieutenant to post-captain, even if it means the retired list."

"They call them admirals of the 'yellow squadron,' Mister Lewrie," Nelson said with another grin. "Usually because they're too stupid to trust with a command, and have too much 'interest' to just cashier, to make way for a more promising officer. He means a great deal to you, does he not, Mister Lewrie?"

"Yes, sir, he does. I had no business being made first officer of this ship, but he was patient with me, and taught me everything I know," Alan confessed. "Fifty years, from powder monkey to captain of his own ship, God knows how long a passed midshipman. He deserves a better retirement than a lieutenant's half-pay, or a cripple's pension."

"God bless you, sir, that was well said, and kindly meant," Nelson said, almost fierce with passion, and taking his hand to shake it firmly. "We do seem to treat our sailors in the shabbiest manner, and then depend on them to save the country, when anyone with good sense would run for the hills and tell us to get someone else to do the dirty work!"

"If you could make any sort of recommendation in his behalf, sir, I'd be forever in your debt," Alan offered.

"And I shall, sir," Nelson promised. "I shall speak for him to Admiral Hood once we rejoin the squadron. He has treated me with great kindness in past, though," Nelson added with a wry expression, "I do not know why he should continue to do so after this debacle."

"We didn't know how strong they were, sir."

"Still," Nelson said, leading him to the entry port where his boat waited, almost seeming to grow in size and importance as he began to enthuse, "I was always most pleasantly amazed over in Nicaragua how a smaller force could prevail over a greater one, if one went *right at them*. Conceive a bold plan, carry it out with audacity, bring all one's strength to bear upon one point, like Rodney did against de Grasse, and you give them pause. They seem to step back, to draw breath at your daring, and once checked, they are beatable!"

"I see, sir." Alan nodded, amazed at how energetic the slight little fellow could become.

"To pause, to question your own chances, is to surrender the initiative to the foe. Fire that challenge to loo'rd, and then go at them!" Nelson insisted. "Lay your ship yard-arm to yard-arm with the enemy, which is all that anyone can ask of a captain, and trust to the pluck of English seamen to win you a victory! Given decent odds, I'll put my money on our men every time, and then it's victory, or a place in Westminster Abbey! Either way, you've upheld your honor, or found glory."

Without a break, Nelson shook Lewrie's hand once more, and went to the entry port, doffed his hat to the crew in reply to the salute due him, and Alan was amazed that the hands were cheering, perhaps in recognition of his solicitousness in coming to see their captain as most officers would not bother to do. It was either heartfelt on Nelson's part, or it was the vainest piece of theatrics Alan had seen away from a stage. Yet there was something about the man, he had to admit.

"Uncanny sort, ain't he, sir?" Caldwell asked once they had the ship under way again. "That one'll go places, you mark my words. Wish he'd come aboard and got the hands fired up before we tried to take Turk's Island. With a little of his enthusiasm, we'd have had the bloody place."

"He is inspiriting, I'll grant you that, Mister Caldwell," Alan replied. But, he kept to himself, with an attitude like that, the little minnikin's going to get himself killed for certain if he keeps all that death-or-glory stuff up. And if Turk's Island is any example of his skills at war, I'd not want to be anywhere near him next time he feels inspired.

Epilogue

"You'll take care of my ship, now, Mister Lewrie," Lilycrop said as he was hoisted up to the bulwarks before being lowered into a rowing boat. It was hard on the man, to know that his career was over, to know that he was losing the only command he had ever been entrusted with. Still, in as much physical pain as

Lilycrop found himself, Alan knew that the mental pain was the greater at that moment. Lilycrop had insisted he would not go in his night-shirt and had Gooch and his cox'n dress him in his best lieutenant's uniform. Strapped to a carrying board or not, he would leave his ship with the proper dignity due a master and commander.

The Marines had turned out in their best, instead of purser's slops, and the crew had taken as much care with their own appearance as they would have for Sunday Divisions—faces shaved, clean slop trousers and shirts, shoes and stockings on their feet instead of the usual horny bare toes. Those that had decent tarred hats and short blue frock-coats had dug them out of their chests.

"I shall, sir, until they send a man over to take command," Alan promised somberly. "Though I don't know how they'll fill your shoes, sir. Uh . . ." He reddened.

"Well, that can't be too hard, Mister Lewrie, they only need to fill *one* these days, don't they?" Lilycrop asked, the sarcasm dripping.

"Sorry, sir," Alan murmured, knowing what a gaffe he had made even as he said it. "What I meant was . . . well, sir, there's no replacing you, sir, and even I'm capable of realizing it."

"Well, thankee, Mister Lewrie," Lilycrop relented. "Stand me up, there, men."

They stood his carrying board on end, so that Lilycrop could look about his decks once more. Tears leaked from his eyes, try as he did to control them manfully.

"Happens to the best of us!" Lilycrop barked in his old manner to his crew. "*Shrike*'s a good little ship, and you've been a good crew. You do your duty same's you done for me, an' no captain in the Fleet could ask for better."

He dug a kerchief from his pockets and wiped his nose. "Now, let's get it over with. No sense keepin' the flag waitin' fetched-to. Write me if you've a mind, Mister Lewrie. Same goes for the rest of ye. Let me know how you keep, now an' again."

"Aye, I shall, sir," Alan promised again.

"Enjoy the kitty. You'll find they're a comfort. Let's go, Gooch, damn your eyes."

The bosun's pipes squealed a long salute. The Marines and officers brought up their swords and muskets, and Lilycrop's carrying board was hoisted up with a yard-tackle. With his own sword strapped to his side, the captain doffed the cocked hat he could not wear to his men one last time, and Svensen started a cheer for him. The hands took off their hats and waved them over their heads, yelling their "hip-hip-hoorays," then roaring a cacophony of approval, which lasted until Lilycrop's gig had reached *Barfleur*'s side, and he was hoisted to the deck of the flagship. He waved his hat at them one last time, and then was lost to view among the side-party that paid him his due.

"Get a way on her, sir?" Caldwell asked once the hands had quieted and shuffled into small knots of sad mutters.

"No, we're about to be visited, it seems," Alan pointed out. An officer was coming down *Barfleur*'s battens to enter the gig, and a stay-tackle rigged to a main course yard was already hoisting out a sea chest. "Our new commander, looks like."

"Hope he likes cats, sir," Caldwell quipped.

Lilycrop had taken Henrietta, Samson, Hodge and a few others with him, along with his furnishings and chests, but the bulk of the kittens and yearlings had been parceled out among the warrants and senior hands. Even Edgar and Rossyngton now shared the midshipmen's mess with a brace of lean tabbies.

As a parting benison, Alan had been forced to accept a kitten, one of Henrietta's latest brood, a mostly black female of about four months age. To his chagrin, she was of pretty much the same disposition as her parent, a little pest who showed the same partiality for his stockings and lap and deposited her fur with the same liberality on every stitch of bedding and clothing he possessed. Since she was, like Henrietta, a starving whore for attention and petting, he had named her Belinda, after his hellishly licentious half-sister who had been instrumental in forcing him into the Navy. The captain had been touched that he had named her after blood-kin, and it was all that he could do not to strangle with secret, ironic humor, as he had tried to explain to Lilycrop just who Belinda was.

There was a possibility that *Shrike* might soon make her way back to Antigua. Perhaps Dolly Fenton would still be there. During that terrible last parting, she had said she'd wait for him, no matter how long he was away, and maybe she had meant it. Dolly had liked cats, would have been delighted to have one in their set of rooms while he was out at sea, but at the time, the last thing Alan had wanted was to put up with a cat on land, after being cooped up aboard a ship infested with platoons of them. She'd like Belinda, and would be delighted with such a reunion present. If she was still there, and still cared. He found it suddenly very important that she still be on Antigua, unattached.

"By God, I hate him already, whoever he is," Alan whispered, irked that Lilycrop would be losing out and going home a discarded cripple, while this new officer, from the admiral's wardroom, naturally, would take his place.

He had surprised himself that, when asking of Captain Nelson, or when later writing to Admiral Hood himself, he had not asked for the command of *Shrike*. He had only entertained that pleasing fantasy long after doing everything in his power for his former captain. For once he had done something for someone else whole-heartedly, with no thought of his own personal gain. Maybe it was his sense of guilt, he thought; maybe it was because Lilycrop had been so kind and fair with him, when anyone else would have chucked him for his incompetence. Whatever the reason, Lilycrop was the first captain in his experience that he would genuinely miss.

The side-party formed up once more as the gig attained the ship's side. "Ship's company, muster by the entry-port!" Alan ordered. "Off hats and salute!"

A cocked hat appeared over the lip of the entry-port. A stern face emerged as the bosun's pipes began to trill. The visage was not the old salt that Alan expected. This was a young man, perhaps only a few years older than he, a favorite blessed with membership in the flagship's officers roster. *La Coquette* needed officers, so officers with "interest" had gone into her. The prize sloop that *Resistance* and *Dugay Trouin* had taken needed officers. And now, like a gift from the gods, another command slot had opened up for Hood to fill with one of his protégés.

He did not look, though, like someone Alan would prefer to serve, even if he could have looked at him impartially. There was a set to the mouth, a squint to the eyes, that bespoke a "taut hand," a hard disciplinarian, one of those fellows with a harsh manner for all under him. Alan drew a heavy sigh, then drew his sword to give the man his salute. However, the cat William Pitt delivered his own version of salute first.

The cat, drawn by the commotion, had, in answer to the curiosity of his tribe, crossed the deck and wormed his way between the legs of the gathered Marines, pausing to "mark" a likely set of half-gaiters in passing. But at the sight of a stranger, he greeted him as Lewrie had been greeted when he had signed aboard.

There was a challenging yowl of displeasure, a slash of claws that caught the officer across the nose, and a startled squawk of alarm from their new commander. Then, losing his grip on the loose-hung man-ropes, and still vertical along the ship's side instead of leaning slightly into a larger ship's tumble-home (*Shrike* had none), the new captain dropped from sight as if he had never been there. A second later, there was a rather loud thud in the gig, and a chorus of shouts.

"Oh, shit, Pitt's killed him!" Alan groaned, sheathing his sword and dashing to the entry-port. "How is he?"

"Er, 'e's knocked 'isself h'out cold, sir," the temporary cox'n of the gig shouted back up. " 'E don' look sa good ta me, sir."

"Mister Lewyss to the gangway, on the double!" Alan shouted. Lewyss turned up a moment later with a small medical bag and descended to the gig.

"I'll kill that cat!" Caldwell vowed. "Who was the new captain, sir?"

"How the hell should I know, Mister Caldwell?" Alan complained. "He never got a chance to tell us. Somebody pass up his orders. They should be in his pockets. At least," he said in a softer voice to the temporary first lieutenant, "we can determine whom we've murdered."

"Nasty, sir," Mr. Lewyss informed them, regaining the deck with the documents requested. "Nasty cut on the back of his skull, and sure to be concussed. He's out like a light. And I don't like the look of his right arm, either, sir. I am certain he broke it. I'd be happier with him in *Barfleur*, sir. They have an excellent surgeon aboard, I'm told, d'ye see."

"Well, until he read himself in, he's not one of ours yet." Alan nodded in agreement. "And since he's in the boat and ready for transport, that'd be best. Mister Rossyngton?"

"Aye, sir?" the midshipman asked.

"Be so good as join the doctor in accompanying the captain back aboard *Barfleur*," Alan directed, handing Rossyngton the injured officer's orders. "My compliments to the flag-captain, and return these to him."

Alan felt his face tightening with a grin he fought to suppress. "Please extend our apologies to that worthy, and inform him we require another master and commander for *Shrike*. We . . . um . . . we seem to have broken this one."

"Um, ah . . ." Rossyngton replied crisply, trying to keep his own visage free of the humors that tickled him. "Aye aye, sir."

"Christ, I hope this . . . whoever he was, wasn't a *particular* favorite of the admiral's," Alan prayed aloud once the boat was under way. "I'd hoped to get out of the Navy with a whole skin. They'll probably hang me in tar and chains after this."

"Wasn't your fault, sir," Caldwell assured him. "Don't see as how they can go blaming you for his clumsiness. Or Pitt. It was probably for the best. Maybe *Shrike* didn't like the cut of his jib, or something. You know, sir, ships get souls after a while. Looked like a hard man, to me. Maybe the ship knew he wouldn't do right by her, or the people."

"Pitt surely didn't like the cut of his jib," Alan agreed.

"Might have done it for all the cats aboard, sir," Caldwell went on. "Some officers don't like pets of any kind, and would have 'em over the side to drown. Maybe things work out for the best, sir, after all."

"Signal, sir," Edgar called. "Get under way!"

"Thankee, Mister Edgar! Bosun, hands to the braces! Get the way back on her! Mister Caldwell, keep us on the larboard tack, near the flag, for now."

For the next hour, *Shrike* paced alongside the flagship as she caught up the squadron, like a calf will plod alongside her mother. And then came a signal for them to fetch-to once more, and the gig came back, the doctor and midshipman Rossyngton aboard, but no sign of a new officer to command the ship. Evidently, after the last wave of promotions, suitably senior lieutenants in favor were thin on the ground.

"This is for you, sir," Rossyngton said, presenting Alan with a canvas-bound sheaf of papers once he had gained the deck and come aft. "We are instructed to close with Commodore Affleck's flag, sir, the *Bedford*. Admiral Hood has deferred to him to choose another officer for us."

Alan took the bundle, a little irked at the smile that tugged at the corners of Rossyngton's mouth. "Mister Caldwell, alter course to close with *Bedford*," Alan directed, while turning away to break the still-warm wax seal on the packet.

"Sufferin' shit!" he muttered as he began to read.

My dear Lt. Lewrie;

The vagaries of Fate, and the fickleness of Dame Fortune conspire to alter my Intents, good sir. I had hoped to reward Lt. Ishaell Sharpe for his long and meritorious Service as my 4th officer, with Command, but it seems it is not to be.

In response to your generous, heart-felt, and commendable concerns anent your former captain, Lt. Lilycrop's, Future, and, having had converse with Capt. Nelson, a young man whom I hold in the highest Affection and Admiration, regard-

*ing both your cares and his view of the matter, allow me to
bid you allay your worries.*

*While my surgeons are not sanguine about his ability to
hold a further Sea Commission, they assure me he shall heal
well enough that future Service is not out of the question, perhaps as a Dockyard Superintendent, or officer of the Impress
Service, should he desire active Employment. I shall take Lt.
Lilycrop under my aegis, and make the strongest Advertment
in my power to Our Lords Commissioners of the Admiralty to
that effect.*

"Well, thank God for small favors," Alan smiled in relief. He
turned the letter over to read the rest of it.

Regarding the vacancy in command of Shrike, *basing my Decision upon the favorable notice you have elicited in past by
your gallant, resourceful and honourable past Service; having
myself formed an admiration of your Abilities during the affair in The Chesapeake, and your plucky conduct during your
escape; and, having had further converse with the gallant
Captain Nelson, and receiving from him an whole-hearted approbation of your Character; I did most recently consider taking you into* Barfleur *as 6th officer, from which post of favour
you might find an opening for Advancement. But, after greeting your Lt. Lilycrop, and soliciting his own recommendations
after Lt. Sharpe's recent Misfortune, I trust that command of
a small brig of war shall suffice. Be assured that in future you
should not be in any way hesitant in considering me your ad-
miring Patron, or in availing yourself of any kindness I may
be able to extend to you.*

Yrs;
Sir Saml Hood
R. Adml. of the Blue Squadron

"Jesus Christ," Alan breathed with a shudder partly of delight,
partly of dumb-struck consternation. "I'm going to have to start
taking all this nautical shit a lot more seriously!"

He had always thought Admiral Hood a poltroon, for his in-
explicable behavior in hanging back at the Battle of The Chesapeake. Even the empty defensive victory at St. Kitts had not
changed his opinion much—they lost the island anyway, hadn't
they? And now this!

The man must be more of an addle-pate than I thought, Alan told himself, his hands trembling as he scanned the second sheet of paper in the packet and saw what it represented. Anybody that'd give *me* command of a King's ship has to have his buttocks where his ears ought to be. Mind you, I ain't arguin' much.

He looked up at the people on the quarterdeck; Rossyngton with his slight smile because he knew the secret first; Caldwell on tenter-hooks to find out what it was all about, and sweating that it perhaps might represent a chance for him to keep his acting lieutenancy.

I'd better do this before they change their bloody minds, he thought, feeling an urgency to read himself in before that new officer from *Bedford* came aboard. They still had at least a mile to go before they were close enough to hail her, and a cutter from *Barfleur* had not even reached her yet.

"Mister Caldwell, assemble the ship's people if you would be so kind," he ordered.

"Aye aye, sir. Ship's company!" Caldwell boomed. "Muster aft and face the quarterdeck!"

Once they were gathered, wondering what this new summons was about, Alan folded out the sheet of vellum and scanned it so the words would not be unfamiliar and trip him up at this unbelievably fortunate moment.

"Issued aboard HMS *Barfleur*, flagship to the Leeward Islands Squadron, this 20th day of March, in the year of our Lord, 1783. From Sir Samuel Hood, Rear Admiral of the Blue. To Lieutenant Alan Lewrie, Royal Navy. Sir; it is my wish and direction that you take upon yourself the charge and command of his Majesty's 12-gunned brig of war, *Shrike* . . ."

He paused and looked up, feeling as if someone would shout over to them that they were "just *kidding*!" But there were no signs of laughter from the hands—no pulled faces or sidelong glances of alarm. They stared back at him, nodding as though his superseding to command in place of a real sailorman was his due.

So he savored every syllable, every nuance as he finished reading the document aloud. *Shrike* wasn't much, too small, and below the Rate, for a more senior officer, he realized. And she had been brought in as prize on a foreign station, so the dream could end the day after the war ended, and that blessed event could occur at any moment. Even if she stayed in service, there was only a year left of her original three years' commission. But for now, she was his.

What else should I say? he wondered, once he had rolled up

the precious document. "A new captain," he finally began slowly, "brings to his next command his own way of doing things. But since *Shrike* is my first command, and since I have learned the most in how to exercise command in her, from an officer we all revere as a real tarry-handed sailor, I can think of no finer way to begin than to continue as if Lieutenant Lilycrop was still with us in spirit. His order book, his discipline, his strictures stay in effect. They were sensible and fair, and I see no reason to depart from them, or any way to improve on them at present."

Not trusting himself to utter one more word, he turned to Mr. Caldwell and nodded, and Caldwell dismissed the hands to their duties.

There was no whole-hearted cheer such as Lilycrop had gotten. But no one was cursing and skulking, either, and no one was throwing loose objects at him, so Alan could be satisfied with his reception, if only slightly disappointed that he did not receive the same affection Lilycrop had evinced from them. Several hands were smiling broadly, and they went off to their work at least somewhat cheerful.

"Ah, Mister Caldwell," Alan said, noticing Caldwell's hang-dog expression at last. "I believe that Commodore Affleck is to be allowed to appoint a lieutenant into us, to take my place. Sorry you could not keep your acting status. I did mention you to the admiral when I wrote concerning the captain."

"That's alright, sir," Caldwell said, though it didn't look alright. It would have been his best, and perhaps last, opportunity to attain to a commission instead of a warrant, and he was already approaching fifty. "Who would you like for cabin-servant, sir? And your cox'n?"

"Cony," Alan said without a second's hesitation, and then gave the matter of cox'n some thought. A third of the hands were Island Blacks, and Andrews was at least listed as a free-born volunteer. He was deserving of some notice after Florida. "Andrews for my cox'n."

"Aye, I'll make it so, Captain," Caldwell replied.

That has a nice ring to it—*Captain*! Alan thought happily.

"I'll be aft for a moment," Alan said. "Summon me when we near *Bedford*."

He made his way aft of the wheel and the main-mast trunk, to the low poop and the coach-top built into it to allow standing headroom for entry to the hanging cabin. There was now a Marine sentry on duty, who banged his musket on the deck and brought it up to salute as Alan opened the door that offered the short flight of steps below.

His cabins! Though they seemed more spacious with all of Lieutenant Lilycrop's poor furniture gone, they didn't look all that grand. The black-and-white checkered canvas on the deck was frayed, and the wall paint had not improved with age. He could see that this unlooked-for promotion was going to cost him, to equip himself with dining space table and chairs, a sideboard, a wine cabinet, desk and chairs, and paint. Not to mention more lamps, and silver and plates. Still, he was now in receipt of five shillings per day instead of his earlier two shillings six pence; eighty-four pounds a year, for as long as it lasted, figured at the miserly twenty-eight days per lunar month of the parsimonious Admiralty.

"Thought I'd shift yer dunnage, sir," Cony said, entering the cabins with loose bedding and linen under his arms. Alan could hear a couple of seamen struggling with his heavy sea chest.

"Oh, there 'e be, sir. That damn cat," Cony snapped.

"Hmm?" Alan replied, coming out of his inventory of expenses. "Oh, him."

"Over the side with 'im, sir?" Cony asked.

William Pitt was stretched out on his side on the bare, straw-filled mattress of the hanging bed-box, tail curling lazily and supremely at ease, washing himself, as if he had won the space for himself with his claws. The kitten Belinda was huddled as far away as she could get on the sill of the transom windows, bottled up and sitting ready to pounce in flight. Between hisses, she licked her lips and chops nervously, for fear of what the bigger male cat would do.

"You mangy young bastard," Alan said, walking up to the bed. "Think you earned the right to stay aft just 'cause you did for that Lieutenant Sharpe, hey? Think I'm grateful to you or something?"

Pitt did not bristle up as he usually did when Alan got anywhere near him, but rolled to his stomach with his front paws stretched out, looking up with his yellow eyes. Alan put out a tentative hand, half expecting to get his fingers ripped off, but was surprised that William Pitt allowed him to actually touch the top of his wide, battle-scarred head and gently rub him between the ears.

"Well, I'm damned, sir," Cony whispered.

It didn't last long, of course; after a few too many rubs, Pitt had claws out and ready to swat, shaking his head vigorously.

Alan realized that it was probably not going to be one of those affectionate relationships between man and animal, such as the young cat Belinda offered; more like adopting a wild beast with whom one could maintain a wary but grudging regard.

"Well, maybe I should be grateful," Alan relented. "Sweetling."

William Pitt made his disgust plain by laying back his ears and assuming a most pained expression.

"Chuck 'im out an' over the side, sir?" Cony asked.

"No, let him be for now, Cony. There's room to spare."

CRASH! went the Marine's musket on the deck. "Sailin' master, SAH!" he bellowed.

"Enter."

"We're about two cables off *Bedford* now, sir, ready to fetch-to to receive her boat," Caldwell reported.

"Very good, Mister Caldwell, I shall be on deck directly."

He followed Caldwell out onto the quarterdeck—*his* quarterdeck, where the warrants and others allowed the use of the deck headed down to leeward to leave him the captain's prerogative of the windward side.

I suppose I can pull this off, Alan told himself. I had a good set of teachers—Railsford and Lilycrop. Even Kenyon, God rot the sodomite. If it's peace soon, how bad can it be? And then I can go home with honor. Who knows, they might even be daft enough to give me another commission, or another command? If I'm careful, this could be all cruising and claret!

But a second after boastful musing, he felt a tiny shiver of presentiment. Things had gone too well lately, and from hard experience he knew that every time he felt the slightest bit smug and satisfied, something always went disastrously wrong in his life. The ancient gods had always taken umbrage with satisfied mortals, had they not?

Afterword

*"Turne, quod optanti divum promittere nemo,
auderet, volvenda dies en attulit ultro."*

*"Turnus, what none of the gods would have
dared promise to your prayers, see what rolling
time has brought unasked."*

Aeneid IX 6–7
—Virgil

On April 6, 1783, Admiral Hood, whilst cruising off Cape Francois, received intelligence that a preliminary peace had been signed at Versailles in January. M. de Bellecombe, French governor of the Cape, sent a ship to his squadron, inviting Admiral Hood and His Royal Highness Prince William Henry, then serving as a midshipman aboard *Barfleur*, to enter the port and receive the honors due them.

Hood declined, though he did despatch the *Bloodhound* sloop into harbor to take the salute of the French. *Schomberg's Naval Chronology* does not tell us what thrilling deed, or, given the feeling against the French at the time, what egregious screw-up *Bloodhound* had committed to give her this dubious honor.

British agents were quite active among the Creek, or Muskogean, Indians, and their relatives the Seminoles, as well as with the Cherokee, trying to inflame all the Southeastern tribes to side with the Crown in the Rebellion to take pressure off Charleston, their last remaining port south of New York. What the members of the expedition feared would happen to the Indians did indeed occur; they became more "civilized" after the Revolution until they dressed, lived and acted much like white settlers, with wagons, farms, carriages, plantations and mansions for some, and even black slaves of their own. And they were still dispossessed, kicked off the land by armed bands, and resettled in the Oklahoma Territory by the Andrew Jackson administration in one of the great, un-mentioned shames of American history.

There was a real Muskogean/Scots student who left his studies in Charleston and went back to aid his people in 1779, one Alexander McGillivray, on whom I based my character. Unfortunately, he backed the Spanish under Governor Galvez and kept his people out of the Revolution, though he hoped for much

365

the same settlements and agreements as my fictional McGilliveray did. The problem was that no matter which horse they backed, the Indians would lose their bet, for no one was prepared to live in harmony with them.

Captain Horatio Nelson's encounter at Turk's Island took place pretty much as described. Nelson was repulsed and forced to sail away with his tail between his legs. This event has rarely, if ever, been mentioned by any of his biographers. Contemporary accounts such as *Schomberg's Naval Chronology* and *Beatson's Naval And Military Memoirs* give the impression that Captain King of *Resistance* was senior officer present and never mention Nelson at all! And Nelson must not have been very proud of it, for even his *Sketches of My Life*, published before he died at Trafalgar in 1805, failed to make note of it. Why Captain King deputed himself to a lower-ranking upstart has never been explained. Perhaps Nelson cowed him by dint of over-powering personality and the urge for action.

Nelson was indeed lucky he kept his commission. He rushed in rashly, throwing 167 sailors and Marines with no field artillery against 530–550 troops and talented naval gunners, with artillery, and antiship batteries heavier than anything his frigates mounted—the 18th Century equivalent of a reinforced battalion.

It was recorded by Midshipman Prince William Henry that Adml. Sir Samuel Hood tore a rather large strip of hide off Nelson's backside in private for not reporting to the fleet first, for assuming a position of "acting commodore" which he had no right to, and, finally, for failing to retake the island. Perhaps mollified by the fact that Nelson hadn't suffered any major casualties, and had known when to fold his tents and quit, Hood didn't break his career, as he had other officers' who hacked him off. The famous Nelson luck was acting overtime.

The Jemmy (James) Trevenen mentioned just before the conference aboard *Albemarle* was first officer of *Resistance*. He wrote his sister Betsy later that the whole affair was a "... ridiculous expedition, undertaken by a young man merely from the hope of seeing his name in the papers, ill-depicted at the first, carried on without a plan afterward, attempted to be carried into execution rashly ... and hastily abandoned for the ... reason that it ought not to have been undertaken at all."

Trevenen was another of Captain Cook's officers from the Voyages of Discovery. Like King, he was a real tarry-handed tarpaulin man of no mean skill as a seaman and navigator, but was forced to work his way up through the Royal Navy slowly, while people like Nelson (and Alan Lewrie) seem to lead charmed lives of "interest" and quick advancement. He was a bit miffed that *Resistance* had captured two French warships off Turk's Island (which started the whole thing) and no one, least of all himself, benefited from their capture in promotion or command. And since the war ended weeks later, their value in prize-money wasn't a tenth of what it would have been earlier, so one can understand his frustrations.

Captain, later Admiral Lord Nelson, never had a scintilla of luck on land. He came close in Nicaragua, but the expedition failed due to sickness among the troops and a lack of drive on the part of the Army. Nelson lost an eye and an arm on land, or so close to it as to make no difference. And he was always a little touchy when it came to criticism. According to Clenell Wilkinson's biography, Nelson was vain, open to flattery, and liable to over-react when his actions were questioned. No wonder he never mentioned the Turk's Island defeat in his putative autobiography.

So, there we are, then. Through no fault of his own, and by a series of fortunate flukes, our young hero is now master and commander into a small brig of war, but the war is over. What shall his future be? Shall he take heed of past warnings and behave himself for a change? Shall he stay up to windward of nubile young ladies with well-armed daddies; eschew the charms of "willing widows"; stay sober and industrious and make the most of his career opportunities in the Navy?

Perhaps *Shrike* will pay off and he will finally get a chance to go home and live the sort of life he's been looking forward to. Or will Soft Rabbit and a young master Lewrie pop up? And just where do William Pitt and Belinda figure into this?

I'm afraid you'll simply have to wait to find out, as do I when dealing with an impetuous fellow. Wherever Alan Lewrie shows up, though, we all know that nothing will ever be the same.

Dewey Lambdin
Elm Hill Marina
June 10, 1990

THE KING'S PRIVATEER

Back from the war in the Americas, young navy veteran Alan Lewrie finds London pure pleasure. Between the pungent shores of Calcutta and teeming Canton, Lewrie—reunited with his scoundrel father—discovers a young French captain on a plundering rampage. While treaties tie the navy's hands, a King's privateer is free to plunge into the fire and blood of a dirty little war on the high South China Sea.

**THE KING'S PRIVATEER
by Dewey Lambdin**

**Published by Fawcett Books.
Available in your local bookstore.**

The Naval Adventures of Alan Lewrie

THE GUN KETCH

A fighter, rogue, and ladies man. Alan Lewrie has done the unthinkable and gotten himself hitched—to a woman *and* a ship! The woman is the lovely Caroline Chiswick. The ship is the gun ketch *Alacrity*, bound for the Bahamas and a bloody game of cat and mouse with the pirates who ply the lunatic winds there. Sure that a powerful Bahamian merchant is behind a scourge of piracy, Lewrie runs afoul of the Royal Governor—who holds the most precious hostage of all. . . .

THE GUN KETCH
by Dewey Lambdin

Published by Fawcett Books
Available in your local bookstore.